RAINBOW

RAINBOW

A novel by

William Harry Harding

HOLT, RINEHART AND WINSTON • NEW YORK

Published by Holt, Rinehart and Winston,
383 Madison Avenue, New York, New York 10017.

Published simultaneously in Canada by Holt, Rinehart
and Winston of Canada, Limited.

Library of Congress Cataloging in Publication Data
Harding, William Harry.
  Rainbow.
  I. Title.
PZ4.H2639Rai   [PS3558.A62344]   813'.5'4   79-1245
ISBN 0-03-050396-5

First Edition

Designer: Amy Hill
Printed in the United States of America
10 9 8 7 6 5 4 3 2 1

for R. T. H. ————————————

Grateful Acknowledgment to
The Greater Saratoga Chamber of Commerce
Saratoga Springs, New York

"I won't say a thing to ruin your silly idea
of what con men are like. It'd scare you to
find out I'm no different from you. A little smarter
maybe. But I will say this: I never took
anybody. Just kept a rightful edge—like any
sane person."

—Titanic Thompson,
all-around proposition man
1892–1974

Prologue
SIGNPOSTS

Waiting.

It was the part he hated. Humid wind turned the brim of his panama. His shirt stuck to his skin. He clamped an elbow around his golf bag on the front seat and silenced the jangling clubheads. The headline of his *St. Louis Dispatch* told how Mr. William Jennings Bryan had died: in his sleep. There were pictures. Too many of them. Through the windscreen, cracking farmland stretched to the horizon. It would be every bit as hot down in Dayton, where schoolteacher Scopes was free after a measly hundred-dollar fine and Darrow, in those lavender suspenders, was already traveling north. The newspapers didn't care about it anymore. Gone were the photos of shirt-sleeved men and hand-held fans. Mr. Bryan, it said on the front page, was in a box on a special train headed east. The Monkey Trial didn't rate a single line of copy now. Rainbow missed that. He missed reading about East Tennessee.

White sun drove into the high cowl body of the Velie 48. The car was perfect—floor plates, not running boards, and a Victoria top with landau irons over the sloping rear deck. No one, not even Curtis Godfrey, could miss this oversized baby carriage. A stroke of luck.

The two men in the back seat argued with the driver about pennant races and politics, subjects they were unable to separate. They were petty gamblers who had been happy to give a fellow traveler a ride. They were pigeons.

"Coolidge should be good for baseball," the driver said. He sat on a big green pillow with gold fringe. "Harding didn't care much about sports. What do you think, Rainbow?"

Rainbow turned to the sports page. "Harding didn't care about nothing. None of them do."

Silence.

The men in the back said they didn't like that kind of talk about a President, especially a recently dead one.

Thin tires bounced through chuckholes, the engine began to unwind. Up ahead, a man in blue overalls waved a red flag near a section of highway under repair. A work party of blacks was raising a signpost: ST. LOUIS—27 MI.

The waiting ended. Rainbow fought a grin.

"Ain't they never gonna finish this road?" The driver shook his head and steered the car past the mammoth black who was supervising the workers. Stripped to the waist, sweat glistening on his muscles, the black glared into the car as if he hated the riders for being able to escape the sun. And for being white.

Curtis hadn't changed. Ugly as ever.

The driver mopped his neck. "Biggest damn nigger I ever seen."

"Pull over," Rainbow said.

"You got to take a leak or something?"

"Just pull over. Now."

The car stopped on the shoulder. Rainbow climbed out.

"We're losing time," the driver said. "Where you going?"

"Gonna set that nigger straight." The grin broke through and Rainbow walked toward the construction site.

"Can't park there," Curtis yelled. "Move that thing."

Rainbow kept walking, but slowly enough to let the men scramble out of the car and catch up to him. Then he pointed at the signpost. "That sign ain't right."

"What you talking about?" Arms folded across his chest, the black glanced over his shoulder. "Of course it's right."

"No more than twenty miles to Saint Lou from here . . . boy," Rainbow said.

Purple-dark shoulders twitched as if bitten by a fly. "Highway department says twenty-seven miles . . . mister."

A horn blared. The big white Packard that had just pulled up was threatening to ruin everything. Lashed to the roof: a curved-top trunk with decals and a yellow banner on it, the letters just a glare in bright sun. The driver, his white suit glistening, stepped onto the running board and said, "What's going on here?"

"No problem, sir," Curtis called. "Just drive right through. Sorry for the delay."

But the man didn't get back in his car. He pounded the big trunk.

4

"You have no business tying up traffic when you're working so far from the road."

Curtis didn't say anything, he searched Rainbow's face for a solution.

Rainbow stepped toward the Packard. "He said you could drive on through. Now why don't you just do that."

"Who do you think you're talking to?" the man said. "Do you have any idea of how much time you've cost me already? I have business in the city. Important business. I can't be stopping for every—"

Rainbow picked up a chunk of gravel, tossed it, caught it. "You have any idea of the scratch this rock'd make in that fancy paint job?"

The man muttered something and got back behind the wheel. Rainbow grinned and tossed the rock once more, just to show he meant what he said. And the white curtain over the Packard's back window opened. Inside, a woman. Dressed in green. To match her eyes. Eyes that held Rainbow, made him lose his grin, let the rock fall. She was beautiful. He reached to tip his hat, to apologize for his harsh words. Before he could do anything, she smiled. And he couldn't move. She was that beautiful. And she was leaving, her smile pulled along by the Packard, getting mixed with dust, the shimmer of heat off the road. Gone. Part of him went with her.

"Let's go, Roberts." The driver of the Velie 48 swigged whiskey and tucked the metal flask into a hip pocket. "No sense standing around in this heat."

Rainbow spat to the side. "I still got business with that nigger," he said and marched up the rocky knoll to Curtis.

"It's stupid," the driver said. "State don't make no mistakes like that."

Maybe he could still pull it off. He told Curtis, "That sign ain't only wrong, it ain't even close. Only twenty miles to the city limits. I know this road."

"I built this road." Veins on those big biceps looked ready to burst, huge fists got tight. "Twenty-seven miles. Exactly."

Rainbow smiled. "Fifty bucks says you can't count . . . nigger."

Curtis's stare went soft. He let out a sigh. "Ain't got that kind of money."

The driver chuckled and nudged an elbow into Rainbow. "Hell, if you want to throw it away, I'll take your fifty."

It was working. The Packard hadn't ruined it.

"Fifty to him." Rainbow spun around. "Five hundred to you. Of course, maybe you ain't got that kind of cash either."

The driver's face wrinkled. "I got it all right. More if you like."

5

He stuck out his hand. "We got us a bet or what?"

Both of the driver's friends wanted $500 each. Rainbow looked at the signpost, rubbed his chin: "Be inclined to let you fellows out of it if you like. No point in *taking* your money."

"You ain't worming out of it," the driver said.

Rainbow shook his head. These yokels didn't understand. None of them did. Ever. "You boys don't know how many times I come down this road," he said. "You're just yokels."

That did it: *Sale.*

"Listen, damn it." The driver's arm went stiff. "You take this bet or don't you? Long walk in from here." He winked at his friends. "At least *twenty* miles, ain't that right boys." He laughed and his friends laughed with him.

"If that's how you want it," Rainbow said. "Sometimes, you got to let people have their own way." With handshakes, he sealed the bets, then pointed at the signpost and grinned at Curtis. "Too bad you had to come out in this sun just for that, boy. Should of gone to church. And prayed for a brain." He flicked fingers against his hat brim and walked back to the car.

"We'll clock it." The driver beat his pillow until it got plump and read the mileage off the odometer. "Sure you don't want to boost the ante?"

The yokels enjoyed their laugh. One of the men in the back said, "You see that doll in the Packard?" The other said, "High-priced baggage. And probably worth every cent of it." The driver nodded and said, "We win us this bet from our friend here, and we'll have lookers like that drooling over us."

No amount of money would bring her back. The city would hide her. Forever. Rainbow picked up his newspaper: "Drive."

The engine cranked up, dust swirled, the clubheads started jangling again, and the car sped toward a low haze of heat.

And the church was empty. In an aisle pew, alone with the golden glow of the windows, Rainbow leafed through a hymnal. So far, he hadn't found a song he knew. Not one. The sturdy rectangle set off to the side of the altar looked like a giant soapbox on a stage. If he had to wait any longer, he was going to climb into that pulpit and see what it was like.

The big door to the street creaked open. Footsteps echoed up the aisle. He put down the book. The taped handle of the Colt .45 in his belt felt sticky. If those yokels were coming back for their money, he was ready.

The footsteps got louder, then stopped. A voice came hard, like stone against wood. "Finished with your prayers yet?"

Rainbow let go of his gun and smiled. From his jacket, he got out the envelope of money. There was no clock on the wall—there never was in these places, they didn't want anyone to know how long it was taking, they just kept everybody there until they were done singing and preaching—so he didn't know how late it was. He handed the envelope over his shoulder. "You're late."

Black fingers took the money. Muscles so brilliant in the sun lay hidden beneath a sky-blue suit. A blue hat shadowed a once-defiant stare that was soft now. That ugly face looked loose and there must have been some road dust still lodged in his throat because his voice came out lame. "Damn it's good to see you." And Curtis picked Rainbow out of the pew and hugged him.

"Good seeing you, Curtis." A pat on the back, a push to get free. "Ain't you the sharp one. New duds?"

Curtis waved the envelope. "Might even pay for them now."

"I split it same as always. Seventy-thirty."

"That don't matter now." Big arms reached out for another hug.

Rainbow turned, picked up his panama. "Ought to have a fancy handkerchief sticking out of your breast pocket. Blue, maybe. Or red. Let it spill out."

Curtis slapped Rainbow's shoulders, held them tight. "How long you staying this time? A week?" He glanced at the pew. "And where's your clubs? Didn't leave them at the Jefferson, did you? Be stole for sure."

"At the train station." The sun was moving in the windows, streaking the pulpit yellow. "Leave tonight."

"No, stick around a few days. I set you in a game already. Can't walk away from this one, sport."

"Big match in Chicago." The panama felt tight. "Just got the word my hog-grower finally came through. Lined me up a good one. My chance to break out of this penny-ante circuit."

"Now this fellah I set up for us is a pretty fair stud player. But you can handle him easy. Be like old times."

"You don't need me, Curtis. Take him yourself."

"Aw shucks, boss-suh." Curtis lowered his eyes. "Ain't no sure thin' less'n you's in the game."

"Knock it off." Rainbow threw a mock punch. When the black hands came up in a boxer's guard and the blue hat began to bob and weave, he peppered the air with jabs. "Christ, I leave you alone for a couple of years and you turn into Jack Johnson on me."

"Dempsey." Curtis imitated the champion's low crouch. "Watch out, sport. The Tennessee Mauler gonna rip your head off."

"East Tennessee, you moron."

"East Tennessee Mauler. Naw, that don't sound good."

"A decent boxer'd take you and Dempsey in the same night."

"All I got to do is hit you." Curtis kept moving side to side, up and down, leaning in and out, coiling like a spring. "Just one time."

"I ought to kick your nuts in."

The black deepened his crouch and winced. "Never did play fair, did you."

"Who does . . . ?"

Curtis's laugh came like a snort. He cocked his fists, bent his forearms in close. "C'mon, try and hit me. I been working on this. Thinking about touring as a prizefighter."

"Been wasting your time. Christ, your whole head's wide open."

"You two down there!" With that clerical collar and the scowl on his face, the old man in the choir loft had to be a preacher. "What on earth do you think you're doing?"

"Fighting," Curtis said. "Wanna referee?"

"You can't! Not in God's house!"

Rainbow shot a jab through Curtis's guard, into his nose. "See? Wide open."

"Again." Back in the crouch, Curtis resumed his snakelike weave. "Ready for you this time."

"He's not allowed in here!" the preacher yelled.

"Wait till I knock him out." Rainbow popped a jab to the nose. "Then come down and help me drag him into the street."

"The colored has to leave!"

The jab got through again. And again. Again-again. "You're pitiful, Curtis. Gonna bust my hand."

"It's the light in here, sport. Can't see nothing."

"It's the law! I'll call the police!" A sheaf of papers tumbled from the loft like great hunks of confetti. "Damn it. Now both of you, get out!"

Rainbow threw a soft punch, aimed high at nothing. He faced the loft, drew back his jacket flap, tucked it behind the pistol handle. And stroked the .45. "Gonna leave now, preach. That be all right with you?"

The sound of the preacher's swallow hit the walls. He nodded as though his neck were broken.

Rainbow started down the aisle. "C'mon, champ, this ain't no place for us." Sheet music littered the rear pews and part of the entryway. He didn't know any of those songs either.

Leaning out from the loft, the preacher spoke in a refined voice, the voice of relief. "It is the law, you know."

"Give 'em hell on Sunday, preach." Rainbow pushed out the door to sun-baked steps. *The law*. But he wouldn't want it changed so that every black could go everywhere and do everything. Just Curtis. That was fair, wasn't it? "Got anything on Old Cal?"

Curtis didn't answer.

Rainbow stopped walking. "You deaf or something?"

"Just grapevine stuff. Can't believe half of it." Curtis touched his nose. "How'd you do that? Never figured you'd get near me the way I was moving."

"Tell me."

Curtis stared at the grass as though he expected it to speak for him. Finally:

"This comes from the Bootblack King and, shit, you know he ain't never been right."

"Just tell me."

"I am telling you. But no matter how shaky this word is, you're gonna believe it and bust your ass to get wherever it is some fool says you can find Old Cal. Damn it, you been tracking that sucker long as I've known you. He ain't worth the trouble, sport."

"He owes me." Rainbow grabbed a handful of sky-blue suit. "Now tell me."

"Easy on that." Curtis brushed the hand away, smoothed out the material. "Just got this yesterday. Say, you really think a hand-kerchief'd do the trick?"

Long silence. Rainbow held his face tight. Curtis looked into the street, drew in some air, let it out. Then:

"They say Old Cal headed east. Five, maybe ten years back. Small-time pool shark, like you figured. Likes to follow the race crowd."

"That all?"

"Didn't have much time, sport. When you called about the signpost, I had to round up the boys and—"

"Is that *all?*"

More silence. Curtis sighed. "Guy I know, calls himself Dancer. Been making book the last few years all over New York. Didn't have time to check with him. If Old Cal's around, Dancer'll know about it."

Rainbow grinned. "Saratoga opens next week, don't it."

"There you go." Curtis flapped his arms. "East takes in a lot of places, sport. And this word's got nothing back of it. You can't go traipsing off like it was gospel."

The gospel according to Curtis Godfrey. Funny. Maybe that law was fine the way it was.

"Never been to Saratoga, have you," Rainbow said.

"For Chrissake neither have you. You can't go all that way on this word."

Going. First train.

"Give me Dancer's phone number."

"He's got a lot of them. Which one you want?"

"The one in Saratoga."

Curtis huffed and leaned against the sign on the church lawn that posted the hours and this week's sermon: HOW GOD CREATED THE WORLD. He copied a name and two phone numbers onto a page of his address book. "Giving you his city number, too. Call him there before you do anything." He tore out the page. "Be sure you call him before you go, understand? Last time you went on one of these treks you stranded yourself good."

"Last time ain't this time." Rainbow put the slip of paper in his jacket. Saratoga was far. But it didn't matter. Old Cal was going to pay. *A life for a life.* "Got a train to catch, Curtis."

"I ain't coming after you, sport. Don't care what you get into this time."

"You wanna walk me to the station?"

"I'm through pulling you out of tight spots. Got enough things to do around here. Can't be running off to save your ass no more."

"Look, you wanna walk me to the station or what?"

"Shit . . ." Curtis turned in a circle. "You're just gonna go, ain't you. All the way to Saratoga. You and that goddamn gun you ain't never even fired. No matter what I say, you're just gonna go."

It was true. About the gun. And going. Not wanting to leave, but forced to by time he didn't own, Rainbow held out his hand. "I'll be in touch."

"Yeah, you do that, sport. And don't make it three years again."

Three years? Impossible. Curtis always did exaggerate.

"Missed you, sport," Curtis said. "Sure wish you'd give up golf and come back to stud poker. But you're still trying to be champ, ain't you. The hard way." He grinned. And he said it again. "Really missed you, sport."

Rainbow made it a quick handshake and left the air filled with things unsaid. He walked off the lawn.

At the corner, Curtis caught up to him, hooked his arm, and pulled him across the street. "C'mon, I'll walk you to the goddamn station."

Book One ———————
JUNIOR

1

Cigarette smoke streamed over the top of his Aunt Ruth's newspaper, which was dated August 2, 1902 and had taken a week to come all the way from Knoxville. Her bathrobe sleeve dragged through a puddle of coffee on her table. "Says here they're building a casino next to that racing track up Saratoga Springs. Now if that ain't living." She put down her cup. "C'mon, Junior. See me or pack up."

Junior squirmed in the big chair and pushed a stack of silver dollars into the pot. "Raise you five."

She coughed and set her paper to one side. "Got you beat on the table, boy." Dark pouches under her eyes creased with suspicion. "You bluffing?"

He tried to hide the smile, but felt the corners of his mouth turn up.

"Damn you!" She slammed down her fist. Coffee splashed out of her cup. "Told you a hundred times—keep a straight face! Now I know you're bluffing." She grabbed his cards and threw them in his face. "Ain't you learnt nothing this summer?"

"Still got one coming." From the deck, Junior took the top card, looked at it, then slapped it down in disgust. She had beat him again.

"Even that no-account pa of yours could keep a poker face." She was staring at a spot a few inches above his head. "Guess you take after your mother, God rest her. She never could hold nothing in."

His eyes sank. "When's my pa coming home?"

"Never." Cigarette smoke hissed through her nostrils. "Not if he knows what's good for him. He sets one foot back here, I swear I'll blow the head clear off his shoulders."

He waited for the rest of it. She was going to tell him how his mother, Rosland— "Ain't that the prettiest name you ever heard, Junior?"—his Aunt Ruth's only sister—"And she loved you, boy, loved you more than anything in God's world."—how that wonderful woman had been killed by a drunk who ran off and left her during her sickness— "What they call pneumonia, boy, and she had it so bad she couldn't breathe without drowning."—and how that drunk, his pa, had never sent any money home and never would because he didn't care about anyone but himself—"And never will, boy."—and how she had taken Junior in and cared for him as if he were her own—"God give you to me and He must know you're better off with me than with your pa."—and how she'd see it through—"Don't mind it really. Rosland would of done for me if it'd been the other way around which, thank the Lord, it wasn't 'cause I'd of never let that bastard lay hands on me and then you'd of never been born, boy."

But she wasn't going to tell him any of it today. She was telling herself, though. It showed on her face.

Junior climbed off his chair and reached for the cards on the floor.

"Leave those be." She coughed twice. "And mind you, don't let me catch you giving away your hand again, unnerstand, boy? Now git outside and play some."

Head low, he walked out and shut the door. At the side of the cabin, he picked up his .22 rifle. Studying his reflection in the broken windowpane, he forced a sober face, held it for a moment, then shouldered his gun, slapped his thigh to wake up the old bloodhound that slept in the shade of rotting porch steps, and led his dog down the trail, past weeds, a fallen oak stump black with ants, and around the twin elms to the brush near the lake.

They were still out there.

For the last three days, those same two men in that yellow boat had fished the same spot close in to shore. They wore new clothes, cast with new rods and reels, and their skin was burned vacation red by mountain sun.

Junior held his dog's head. "Okay, Pearlie. Do just like I trained you." Wet eyes stared back, long ears drooped around jowls of age, a muffled whine rolled over a pink-brown tongue. And someone was giggling behind him. Junior spun, his rifle at the ready.

"Going to shoot me?" A dirty face, brown hair tied in pigtails, came through the weeds. Dee Flagg, the puny girl from down by the country store, ducked under the rifle and stroked Pearlie. "What's he got you doing this time?"

"Leave my hound be," he told Dee. "You're taking his mind off his work."

"Wish my pa'd let me have one. Got bit once and near died. He'd kill any dog I took home." She jumped up. "You want to kiss me?"

He shouldered his rifle, grabbed the dog by the neck skin: "Get out of here before you ruin everything." She didn't budge. She curled a braid around her finger. "I'm warning you," he said. "You as much as sneeze and I'll take a switch to your backside." She stuck out her tongue. Then giggled. He gnashed his teeth and led Pearlie to the water's edge. The small rock near the tree line would do just fine. He checked to make sure Dee hadn't followed, then shook the stone in front of Pearlie and tossed it into the lake. Water splashed near the boat.

"Hey, kid, quit that!" One of the men in the boat wore a store-bought cap with fishhooks stuck all around the sides. "You're scaring my fish."

His fish? Damn tourists thought they owned the lake. Junior petted his hound: "Just training my dog here to fetch rocks."

"Try a stick, sonny. Bloodhounds ain't retrievers. Now you and that mutt scram."

Junior swallowed carefully and walked into the lake. Cool water lapped against his waist. He stopped five feet from the boat. "Mister, she's the best damn retriever in this whole state of East Tennessee. If you threw a plain rock, she'd fetch it right up from the bottom."

"Sure, kid. How old are you, anyways?"

"Fourteen." A lie. He was eleven. He shot a glance at shore, praying that puny Dee wasn't standing there to say different. She wasn't. He told the men in the boat, "Almost fifteen."

"Then you ought to know by now no dog can do that," the man with the cap said.

"Mine can." Junior stroked his rifle. "Bet my gun against your fishing pole on it."

"Wouldn't be fair, sonny." The man with the cap shook his head: tiny fishhooks jingled. "Your pa'd be after me for taking advantage." He kept talking, but the words sailed over Junior's head. Finally, the mouth stopped moving.

Junior spat and started back to shore. "You city slickers is all the same."

"Somebody ought to teach that kid some manners," said the other man in the boat.

"Ah, let him go," the man in the cap said.

Junior stopped. They weren't going to bite. He whirled toward them: "I said you're all alike. Stupid."

"Don't you talk to those nice men like that." Dee's voice shot from farther along the shore.

Whatever chance he had once had was gone now. She had ruined it. "I told you to go home," he yelled.

"You treat her civil," said the man with the cap, "and try to learn something from her about how to talk to your elders."

"He's got this terrible problem," Dee said, bending to pet the dog on the bank. "It's a mean streak in him. Now Junior you come out of there and leave these gentlemen be. Can't you see they don't know nothing about wagers? And even if they did, they wouldn't bet with you." She flashed a grin. "They're scared of you."

The man in the cap laughed. "Don't know about betting. That's cute."

The other man in the boat thought the idea of being afraid of Junior was even funnier.

Dee said, "My momma says city folks only think they know what they're talking about, but deep down they're always scared. That's why you can't get them to do nothing. Now come on, Junior. Wanna play in the mudhole?"

Junior slapped the lake and started out. The whole thing was getting worse every second. He'd find a good length of branch and take down her britches and . . .

"Hold on," said the man with the cap. "Little girl, your momma don't know everything. Sonny, let's see what your hound can do." He wore a cagy smile. "You got yourself a bet."

The grin started, but Junior remembered in time. Dee was beaming, rocking on her heels. She was still ugly, but if she hadn't been so far away, he just might have kissed her. He held his rifle clear of water, reached down, and pulled up a rock from the bottom. Drying the stone against his overalls, he crayoned a blue X on the smooth face. "Marked it like this here," he said, "so's she'll know which one to fetch up."

"Bring it." The man in the cap took the rock, looked it over, nodded to his friend, and cocked his arm.

"Hold on!" Junior put out his hand. "She'll only do it if I'm the one what throws it." With a laugh, the man gave back the rock. Junior turned to shore, winked at Dee, pumped his arm: "All right, Pearlie." He tossed the rock in a gentle arc. Water splashed six feet from the boat, ripples spread. "Fetch, girl! Go fetch!"

For an instant it looked as though the hound would leap, but instead, heavy paws slid off the bank into the lake and out of sight. The long, lean body plopped onto the surface, the head craned up, ears left a double wake, and slowly Pearlie swam toward the boat. When the dog was over the right spot, Junior beat his palm on the water: "Now dive, Pearlie! *Dive!*"

With no grace at all, the brown head plunged under, the ears disappeared. More ripples, a few bubbles. Then the lake went still.

"Christ, she's ten feet from where the kid threw it." The man in the cap was grinning. "Looks like we got us a rifle."

Two seconds. Three. Six. No sign of Pearlie. Maybe she was drowning. Junior took a step—*Had it so bad she couldn't breathe without drowning*—and got set to dive. A black nose broke the surface, the long snout and trailing ears popped up. Pearlie swam.

"Good girl!" Junior stroked wet hair, took the rock from fleshy jaws, and gave his hound a shove back to Dee on shore. Without bothering to look, he held up the rock. The shock on both faces in the boat told him what he already knew: traced across the flat of the stone was a large blue X. He gave the rock to the man in the cap. "I'll take my fishing pole now, mister."

"Some trick, kid." The man in the cap dropped the stone into the lake. "Now you and that bitch get the hell out of here."

"Hold on, mister—"

"I said beat it, kid."

Each movement was a deliberate gesture: Junior raised his rifle, aimed it at the center of the man's cap, sighted down the barrel. "And I said, I'll take my fishing pole." The man's mouth wouldn't close. Junior had to squint to keep from laughing. "Now!"

"For Chrissake give him the damn thing." But the other man had to pry the pole from his friend's grip.

"Much obliged." Rifle poised, Junior took the new rod. He backed away and didn't lower his gun until he reached the bank and shook water from his overalls. Then his grin spread out. "You city slickers is all the same."

He slapped his thigh and led Pearlie up the trail.

Dee ran after them. "It's part mine."

He tightened his grip on the pole. "Run on home. You practically ruined it for me."

"I made them take that bet," she said, "and you know it. I get to use that pole anytime I want."

He stopped near the twin elms. "If I wasn't so kindhearted I might just tan you with this pole."

"Try it." She was rocking on her heels again: Miss Smug. "Oh, who wants a silly pole anyway." She batted her eyelashes. "You know what I want."

He swallowed hard and started walking.

She followed him past the tree stump. "You have to be nice to me in front of everybody. You have to call me Sweet Dee."

He stopped, squeezed the new pole.

"If you don't," she said, "I'll tell everybody you been kissing me every chance you get." And she was giggling and turning circles. "Sweet Dee Flagg. Say it."

He whispered it.

And ran.

His Aunt Ruth couldn't stop laughing. "You mean you put an X on all them rocks?"

"Nine wheelbarrows full." Junior fought the smile. "Damn near took me two whole days."

"Boy, you are the rascal."

"Ain't no reason to bet if you don't know for certain you can win," he said.

"That's right, boy." A tear ran down her cheek. It was the first time she had cried in front of him. "Taught you real good, ain't I." She held cigarette smoke deep in her lungs. "And you'll turn out fine. Not like that no-account trash of a—" Her cough didn't stop until she wheezed into her cards. She tossed two silver dollars into the pot. "What on God's earth would you of done if he hadn't give up that pole?"

Junior drew his mouth tight. "I'd of blowed his head clear off his shoulders." One by one, his silver dollars clanged on her table. "Your two and bump you five."

Eyes wide, fingers trembling, she gulped hot cigarette smoke. Her cough bounced off the hard stare on his face. She laid down her cards and folded her hand. "Pray to the Lord I ain't taught you too good."

2 ⸻⸻⸻⸻⸻⸻⸻⸻⸻⸻⸻⸻⸻

His Aunt Ruth was supposed to take him into town for his twelfth birthday, but she had a headache. Junior got fifty cents for the cake of his choice. On the way back, he balanced the box so that none of his frosting would rub against the cardboard sides. Around him, branches creaked, and under his feet a thin crust of ice traced a network of spiderwebs. Up the trail, past the lake, he homed on the smoke until his chimney appeared between the mated elms. From the old stump, he could make out the small glow of an oil lamp in the front window. It would be warm inside, even if some cold did seep through the planks.

He opened the door, grinning. The rank odor of urine blew out against him. Pearlie was cowering in the corner by the fire. "Damn you, hound." He put his box on the table, grabbed a handful of neck skin and dragged his dog across the floor. "Git on out!" He slammed the door. "Aunt Ruth! I got it! Real chocolate icing!" He looked for the spot where his dog had emptied its aging bladder. "Old Pearlie's pissed a river around here someplace!"

Behind him came a series of scratches at the door.

"No, you ain't getting back in. Damn worthless piece of trash."

The scratching grew more intense. His hound was whining.

"Ain't never coming back in, you hear?" He hurled a spoon against the door. "Gonna shoot you if you don't freeze first." He stormed down the hall to his room.

His feet stopped moving all by themselves.

The smell was stronger here. Her door stood ajar.

She sat in her rocker, the one she put out on the porch every spring, the one she counted fireflies in while she patched her quilt and talked about the time she went to Saint Louie and rode on the trolley and ate in a place where everything anybody could want was right there on the menu and all you had to do was ask for it and somebody'd bring it out on silver and set it down as though it were made of gold— and to eat it seemed a shame, it being so pretty and fancy and . . .

And her head was slumped on her shoulder. One arm dangled free, the other was folded in her lap.

"Oh, Lord, it did taste good, boy. Mostly 'cause somebody else cooked it and cleaned up, too. Now that was the real treat. But Lord, it did taste good."

It smelled awful in here. The bottom edge of her robe lay in the dark yellow puddle on the floor.

"Aunt Ruth . . . ?"

The foul odor answered for her. He turned away and went back to open the front door. Pearlie ran into his arms. Junior hugged cold fur for a long time, then stoked the fire, watched it grow. With a length of kindling, he lit one of her cigarettes. The smoke made him cough, but not the way she coughed. His was more like a burp. He tossed the butt into the flames.

By the time he carried the lamp into her room, a dark sky had buried the mountains from view. He kept staring at her and heard himself whispering her name over and over as if it were a curse. He made a fist and thought to punch her awake, but he couldn't bring himself to touch her. Finally, his hand slid under her chin. She was cold. Her stare went up over his shoulder. He closed her eyelids the way he had seen the preacher do to old Mr. Tandy when the whole town stood around that waterlogged body on the shore. The man hadn't looked like Mr. Tandy, but everyone had said that was who it was and how he could rest in peace once his eyes were shut by the preacher. And Junior had believed them.

Until now.

With her eyelashes matted against skin the color of a field left fallow, she looked neither peaceful nor asleep. She looked dead.

He ducked under her armpit, lifted her onto his shoulder, clutched her legs, felt the wetness of her robe. One step backward, a short turn, and he lowered her onto her quilt.

It took over an hour to scrub her floor and rocker. He left the small window open to air out her room. Her bathrobe didn't look so bad, but he had to undress her: the smell. He worked the robe off her shoulders and used it to dry her legs. She lay naked, her flesh rolling out flat, yet swelling up in bunches. He tried hard not to look. He looked at her a lot. Her long, narrow breasts ended in dark brown nipples that pointed toward her toes. Veins stood out everywhere, white lines creased her belly. Little circles of black swirled up her legs to blossom at her crotch in a coarse and ugly weave of hair. Her lips wrinkled in a snarl, as if her final breath had been sucked from poison. He tried to make her smile, but her mouth had set. The rest of her was freezing up fast.

In her closet, he found the only real dress she owned: the bright red cotton she wore on special occasions and God help the person who spilled anything on her then. She sparkled in red, it was her color. Now, her dress seemed shapeless and faded, as though it had wilted on the hanger. He forced her arms through the holes and when he had finished with all fifteen buttons on the back, he carried her soggy robe and quilt to the fire. Brown flannel and colored squares smoldered on the logs, a flame ate through and spread out in an ever-widening hole that snapped with fraying strands. Sparks popped, flakes of soot rode the thermals like hawks above their prey. With Pearlie at his feet, he studied the fire until the sun came up and a shaft of light crept across the floor. From a jar on the counter, he ate two handfuls of cereal grain, left his hound as a guard, and took the trail to town.

Sheriff Jackson said he knew just what to do and told Junior to wait in the office. The sheriff came back with his deputy and the doctor. They all got into the wagon, letting Junior sit in front, and rode out in silence through the morning cold.

The doctor spent an hour inside. When he came onto the porch, he rubbed his arms. "Was her heart. Surely went peaceful, though. Not a wet spot on her. Sign of a real lady."

Junior sat motionless on the steps. He wasn't going to tell. Not now.

"All decked out like she was going to the city, too," the doctor said. "She going somewheres, Junior?"

No answer, not even a headshake. The air was warming, brown earth caught the golden tinge of noon. Junior wasn't ever going to tell.

"Never knew she was ailing." The sheriff rubbed his stomach. "Must of been the chores what done it."

"I did the chores," Junior said.

"Sure you did, boy." The sheriff grinned, rubbed his stomach again. "Would of been a lot easier if he hadn't run off. Look at this place." He wiped his brow, walked to the wagon muttering, "Her own sister's husband. The sonofabitch."

Junior stood to face the doctor. "Can we bury her now?"

"Don't worry yourself none over that." The doctor put an arm on his shoulder. "Go along and get your things ready." With a soft smile, he went back into the cabin.

In the driver's seat of the wagon, Sheriff Jackson lit a cigarette—one of her cigarettes—and blew one smoke ring after another. Junior stepped inside his home. The deputy was sitting in her chair, licking brown icing from his fingers. The cake box lay open, crumbs littered her table. "Store-bought," he said. "Shame to let it go to waste." He nudged the box. "Have a slice?"

Muscles knotted, Junior started for his rifle by the fire, but stopped when the doctor came out of her room and put two stacks of silver dollars on her table. "Not much else I could find," the doctor said with that same soft smile. "She have anything hid away, Junior?"

Now?

Junior grabbed his rifle and spun toward the table. "Git!" His voice wavered, but he didn't care. Not anymore. The deputy jumped to his feet. "Git," Junior said, "you damn pack of thieves."

"It's for your own good." The doctor hid behind the deputy. "We're just putting her things in order, is all. Don't want nothing lying out for robbers."

"I ain't telling you again." He trained his rifle on the deputy's brass buckle. "Now clear off."

They didn't budge.

Squinting as hard as he could to make them believe his words and to stop his arms from shaking, Junior tensed his finger on the trigger.

Now. He pulled.

But a fat arm was already around his waist, his rifle was swinging up. *Blam-crack* shot to the roof, the bullet tore out a shingle. He squirmed, but his feet lifted off the floor and a burly hand was prying his rifle loose.

Sheriff Jackson held him and glared at the deputy. "You blame fool."

"He's just a kid," the deputy said. "How's I to know he'd pick up a gun?"

"Just take care of inventorying them effects." The sheriff took Junior by the shoulders. "Get your things, boy. You and me got to head into the city."

"I ain't going noplace." Junior pulled back. "This here is my house!"

"Do what you're told." The deputy had his mouth full of cake again. "And be thankful I don't take a belt to you."

"Martin, hush up or I swear I'll load that rifle for him myself." Sheriff Jackson straightened his shirt. "No kin to look after you, boy. I got to take you over Fairway House till—" His gaze ran across the floorboards. "It's what's best, son."

Junior backed up. Fingernails dug into his palm, his knuckles blanched. "I'll kill you if you touch anything around here." He worked the muscles of his face until his lips set tight. "I ain't going."

"We all feel your grief." The sheriff took a step. "But you got to come." Another step. "It's the law."

The deputy came out from behind the table.

Junior ran for the door. The sheriff caught him by the pants and dragged him down. "Don't make me put these on you," he said, patting handcuffs on his belt. "Martin, round up his stuff whilst I hold him."

The deputy went up the hall toward the bedrooms.

"I'll kill you!" Junior thrashed to get free. "I'll kill all of you!"

"Now I asked you." Sheriff Jackson bore down with all his weight. "Guess you want me to put them on you." He clamped a cuff on Junior's leg, threaded a piece of rope through the iron: *leashed*. He jerked the rope, made Junior stand, and pulled him outside, putting him in the back of the wagon, where he slapped the loose cuff on Junior's other leg, tied the end of the rope to a slat ring, and went back into the cabin.

Pearlie ambled over and sat silently by the rear wheel. Junior could hear them inside his house, touching everything. When he couldn't wriggle out of the shackles, he tried to untie the knot, but it was down low near the spokes, out of reach. He leaned back against the sideboards. And waited.

The deputy brought out a bundled sheet and the fishing pole. On the second trip, he carried the cake box and the rifle. "Ain't loaded, boy," he said. With a smile, he put everything in a corner of the wagon.

Junior took his .22, but he didn't touch the box or his pole. He just stared at them. They were contaminated.

Sweet Dee Flagg skipped up the trail, a green ribbon in her hair. She lost her grin near the tall brush and ran to the wagon, felt the handcuffs. "He came back, didn't he. And you shot him."

He let her cry. Then he told her. Her eyes got wide. She ran into the house. A scream leaked out the window. Sheriff Jackson carried her out. She thrashed, kicked, bit his leg. "I won't let them take you," she said, getting loose and trying to unknot the rope. The deputy grabbed her, threw her back against the steps. The sheriff climbed aboard and lashed reins about his fist, waving to both men on the porch. The deputy and the doctor nodded back; they wore smiles of relief.

"You can't!" Dee said. "He can stay with me. Ask my momma."

"No point to it," Sheriff Jackson told her. "The law's clear."

She tried to get to the wagon, but the deputy stopped her. Tears got in the way of her words: "Don't let them do this, Junior."

He drew a deep breath, ran a finger down the fishing rod. "Pole's yours now." He forced a grin. "You look real pretty with ribbon in your hair—Sweet Dee."

She took the pole, then sank into the deputy's arms. "I'll wait right here till you come back."

Junior wiped his nose, slapped his thigh. His hound surveyed the distance between ground and wagon, readied a leap, then shied back and whined. Junior glanced at the deputy. "Help her up to me, would you?"

There was a long silence. The doctor stared at the steps, the deputy wiped dried frosting from his mouth. The sheriff let out a long sigh: "She can't go, boy."

"But she'll starve up here!" Junior tried to climb down, but the rope held him. "Maybe freeze to death. She's old. And she won't eat unless I feed her."

"Won't starve and she won't freeze." The sheriff snapped the reins. The wagon lurched forward.

Junior fell back against the sideboards. His rifle slipped through his fingers, bounced onto dirt. He screamed toward the roof: "Pearlie!"

The deputy held the squirming hound. Sweet Dee ran after the wagon, the pole now clutched to her breasts: "I love you!"

The wagon turned the bend. The twin elms slid in front of the cabin, the chimney disappeared. Once past the old stump, there was nothing left to see.

"Won't be so bad." The sheriff tried a smile. "State'll put a notice in *The Journal* so's your pa can see he needs come get you. Then you and him can come back and live. Just like before."

It was the worst kind of lie.

Weeds bent in the wind. Waves rolled on the lake.

A single rifle blast echoed off the water, then froze along the still and stretched-out air.

Sheriff Jackson cleared his throat. "She was old. Needing looking after, you said so yourself. Couldn't of made it through winter. Not alone."

Junior picked up the cake box and hurled it up the trail. His trail, the one he knew by heart and always would. The white cardboard burst open, the cake skidded over frosty dirt and scraped a series of dark brown circles.

"Done her a favor, boy." The sheriff glanced back at the cake, shook his head, grunted at the horse. Reins cracked in his hands. Hooves clicked.

3

Whispers followed him down the long room to the bunk they said was his for as long as he stayed here. Junior rubbed the cold from his arms, untied his bundle, and spread his sheet out on that bed. The whispers stopped when Mr. Drumlin stepped into the doorway, arms folded, waiting for perfect silence to reach him. His black shoes shone like metal. He cleared his throat and must have liked how it sounded because he took a long time doing it:

"Our new friend likes to be called Junior. Now each of you remembers your first day at Fairway House. Let's greet Junior in that same spirit. Form the line, rear to front."

Feet shuffled, the makeshift line filed by. Junior shook twenty outstretched hands before he stopped counting. He didn't look at the faces. Mr. Drumlin put a little towhead with a broad, freckled face in charge of Junior, then glanced at a shiny gold pocket watch, turned on those shoes of his, and left. A murmur built all around.

"I'm Sammy," the little towhead said. "Where you from, Junior?"

"Cherokee Lake."

"But where? What town?"

Junior didn't answer. Until just now, he had never felt tall or big or thin, yet in comparison to the other boys here, he saw that he was. He allowed himself a small smile.

"I'm from Dayton," Sammy said. "How long you been an orphan?"

"I ain't no orphan." Junior kept sorting his things into piles. There was a box at the foot of the bunk. Everything had to go in there. He missed the three-drawer bureau in his room, even if the bottom drawer was busted. This room was cold. No fireplace, nowhere to get warm. He put his flannel jacket back on. Something hard tapped his shoulder. He faced bushy yellow hair standing a good foot above his own head, dark brown eyes, big arms.

"I run this place." The big boy stuck out his big hand. A tooth was missing from the upper part of his grin. "Jack Bender. How old're you, fourteen?"

Junior swallowed and shook hands. "Fifteen."

The big boy's grin drooped to a frown. He glared, then nodded. "Sammy, move his stuff down my end."

Sammy threw the piles into a bundle and hurried away.

"You got to give me something." That tooth wasn't missing after all, just discolored. "If you don't, I'll figure you and me ain't friends. Want to be my friend, don't you?"

Junior couldn't look at those big arms anymore. He studied the big boy's shiny new boots. "Got nothing."

"If you was younger, I'd just take it." Jack Bender folded his arms across his chest. The veins got bigger. "But you're almost as old as me, so I owe it to you to ask first. That's fair, ain't it?"

"They took my stuff. Got nothing but clothes."

"Pack of cigarettes, then."

"Don't smoke." Junior didn't know why, but saying that made him sad.

"Drumlin does." The big boy winked. "Keeps them in his desk. Third drawer." He turned and the others opened a passageway for him, then closed ranks after he had passed through.

"What's he want, cigarettes?" Sammy squeezed past the boys. "I can show you how to steal them."

"Don't steal." Junior walked to a high box-window. Small panes had been fitted in a crosshatch of wood. Trees blocked most of the view. The ground was patched yellow and brown and, in the distance, holes of sand encircled a green plateau.

"Golf course." Sammy tapped the glass. "You'll work there come spring. It's why they call this Fairway House. That's a fairway and—"

"What's he figure to do?" Junior said. "Beat me up?"

Sammy laughed. "He plans to smoke them cigarettes you're gonna steal for him." He looked away. "Seen him fight lots of times. He likes it. Guess that's 'cause he wins. You really fifteen?"

"Almost sixteen." The lie stretched, but these orphans would probably believe anything.

"That means you get to caddy," Sammy said. "We got to pick weeds till we get old enough. You'll be earning some money."

"How hard is it to get them cigarettes?"

"Mostly you got to watch when you try it. The Skeleton takes dinner where he sleeps and—"

"Who?"

"Drumlin," Sammy said. "He ain't around his office when we go to the dining hall. Means you have to not eat tonight."

Junior nodded. "Ain't got much choice, do I."

"I'll help you." Sammy was grinning. "And Jack ain't so bad. Just likes to scare you. You shave yet?"

"Got to." Junior rubbed his jaw: nothing, not even peach fuzz. And he didn't own a razor. "Say, does the Skeleton pack a razor? Lost mine coming over."

Sammy didn't get the chance to answer. A barrel-chested boy came to the window. Hair shot wildly from his scalp. He smelled. "Get me a pack, too."

Junior looked at him, then walked down the row between bunks. At the last bed by the door, he waited for Jack Bender to sit up on the blanket. "I ain't planning on getting them cigarettes. For you or anybody else."

"Thought we was gonna be friends," the big boy said.

"I don't steal."

Jack Bender stood. The others ringed the bunk; they got what they came for. The first punch hit Junior on the jaw and sent him down. A booted foot grazed his temple. He tried to get up, but a kick to the ribs flattened him. He held his breath, clutched his side. Whispers, like hisses, whirled around him. The big boy rubbed his nose and plopped on his bunk.

Staggering to his feet, Junior leaned on the next bunk where his bundle now lay. He drew three long breaths and dropped his clothes in the box at the foot of the bed. It hurt to move. He could feel the heat from their eyes, but didn't return their stares. He kept his face drawn tight.

A bell rang. Feet scuffled the dusty floor. A line formed at the door. "Dinner," Sammy said and he led Junior to a place at the end of the line. Heads kept turning, the boys kept sneaking looks as though they expected Junior to fall down again. The door opened. Everyone faced straight ahead. The line began to move.

When he reached the dining hall, Junior could breathe more easily. The sting in his side was almost gone. His lip wasn't bleeding. He took a tray and walked through the serving line, where a man ladled creamy brown over a piece of toast and put a small potato on the plate and another man with whiskey on his breath set a cup of milk on the tray. Junior followed Sammy to a table near the back. No one came to join them. The walls, chairs, even the floor, were all dark brown. A chill crept over the tops of Junior's shoes. The others were still staring at him, but when he met their gaze, they looked into their food. He picked up his knife. "How come they keep watching us?"

"They're watching to see when you cry," Sammy said.

Junior put down the knife. Sharp pains ran up under his ribs, his jaw hurt, but he couldn't stop the rhythm of soft laughter.

From far down the hall came a series of hard raps and a shout: "You there, stop that!" Junior covered his mouth, but kept laughing. The stern command belonged to a frail man who sat on the platform by the door. He looked more like a skeleton than Drumlin did. He rapped his hickory shaft on the base of the platform and went back to eyeing the boys.

Never, never. Junior started to eat. *They'll never see me cry.* He beamed at the boys, took them on one by one and threw them away, and when he had finished the potato, he sat back like a bloated pig. He saved a wink for Jack: dessert.

4

He talked himself out of it three times: the wall was too high, he had no money, spring was coming. He decided to wait.

No one was going to read the Fairway House ad in *The Journal*. His pa probably didn't know how to read and there was no one around he could ask about that—nobody down here had ever heard of him or his pa. Each time he asked about his Aunt Ruth, they told him she was resting in peace and he shouldn't worry himself sick about it. But they never said buried.

Maybe she wasn't.

Maybe they had tied rocks to her legs and thrown her into the lake. Pearlie they probably tossed into high weeds, where crawling things would pester her and eat her hide right down to the bone. Unless Sweet Dee Flagg had done something or got somebody to do something. And she must have, because she loved him. She would tell Junior just where to look for his aunt and his hound. It was the first thing he would do. Then he'd take time to find his rifle, or steal one—just borrow it actually—and go down and shoot Martin the deputy between the eyes. Then between the legs. Then in the ears, the mouth, up his nose. Before giving back the rifle, he'd run off and find his pa and blow his head clear off his shoulders. But first he would tend to his Aunt Ruth and his dog. No, *first* he had to escape from this place.

He thought about railroad yards and freight cars, how he would ride them north to the cities: alone. It wouldn't be right to take Dee along. No, Junior had to do that traveling part by himself. They'd probably use hounds to track him, but he knew how to throw them off a scent, he'd done it a thousand times with Pearlie. In the center of his thoughts lay an open meadow, warm with night and clear of rain, a place to dream in peace. He'd have to change his name, maybe dye his hair the way his Aunt Ruth said some women did. But he would be free. Of everything. *Someday soon.*

He made no mention of his plans. One day, he would come back to buy the orphanage a load of coal for winter. No one would bother him then because they could take one look and see he had turned out all right. Even the Skeleton would be proud. And grateful for the coal. Then Junior could leave and never come back. As soon as all the pieces fit together in his mind, he stopped remembering his dreams.

The other boys talked to him now, because Jack did. They played poker at night, but not for money, and Junior didn't deal stud for fun. "Only point to poker is winning," his Aunt Ruth had said. "Got to have something to lose before you can learn how to win."

So Junior kept to himself and, to his surprise, he read the history book they let him have. It wasn't much harder to read than her newspaper back home. Neither was the other book he got from the three-shelf library: *Robinson Crusoe.* Only this one meant more. Robinson was his own name. Junior liked the book because it proved that private kingdoms did exist, that good practical sense could win out over the cunning of city folk, that it is all right to own a slave. But he didn't understand why Robinson wanted to get off that island. Maybe the book wasn't finished. He hid it in the box by his bed. No one noticed.

Then it was April. The ground thawed. The younger boys—the ones who were his age—worked for the greenskeeper on the golf course, trimming grass, pulling weeds, rebuilding sand bunkers. Boys over fourteen became caddies. They were not allowed not to become caddies. For carrying a single bag over eighteen holes, a boy could earn ten cents, sometimes fifteen. It was a public course, which meant that anybody could play on it, except darkies, naturally, but not every golfer used a caddy, so days passed with Junior in and around the green and white caddy shack, waiting for his number to be called. He wore number 25. And hated it. It was a good number and it didn't matter that all the other boys had to wear cardboard tags too, each with a different number, or that the tags had to be worn on the front of their overalls, or that the caddies called each other by their numbers. What mattered was that this was the way the caddymaster said it would be. Had to be. That mattered.

"Hey, Twenty-five," Number Six said. "Wanna get in this hand?"

Junior sat on the grass behind the caddy shed. These boys played poker for money. Some pots ran up to a dollar. He waited three weeks before he had earned enough cash to enter the game. After that, he retired as a caddy. Whenever the caddymaster called out, "Twenty-five! Single! Eighteen!" Junior yelled back, "Sick today!" and went back to his cards.

Number Six laughed every time it happened. "Gonna use that trick myself when I don't need the money. Which I figure'll be never." Today he took Junior aside after the card game. "You really have that flush?"

Junior rattled a fist of nickels and dimes. "If you really wanted to know, you should of called me in the game."

Number Six bellowed. "Only time I'm playing from here on is when you is out hauling bags."

"You got a long wait," Junior said. "A *lonnnnng* wait."

"Bet a nickel you gets called tomorrow, boy."

"Dime says I won't carry no matter how many times I get called."

Number Six ran a hand over his chest. "No bet."

"Set you straight," Junior said. "One bag a day shoots five hours and only clears fifteen cents tops." His fingers dealt imaginary cards. "Now, I figure on making that much in one hour back here."

"You'll go bust in a week," Number Six told him. "Run yourself right out of suckers if you handle them like that." He used a cagy smile. "Best you and me work this out so's one of us always wins, but so's it don't look too tight."

"Don't need no partner." Junior started away, then stopped when he saw how it would be: exactly like in *Robinson Crusoe*. He turned, put out his hand. "Could use some help at that. Split eighty-twenty?"

"Sixty-forty."

"Ninety-ten." Junior made his face stiff with contempt.

It worked. Number Six furrowed a brow and stuck out his hand. "Seventy-thirty and we gives up the caddying business."

Junior made it a fast shake. "We start Friday."

"Why? What's wrong with tomorrow?"

"We start Friday for good luck."

"Well, all right." Number Six scratched his head. "Just so long's you don't try to press every deal. We can't win them all."

"Why not?" Junior grinned and headed up the path.

He didn't caddy the next day, but it was only a matter of time before the caddymaster got wise. "Twenty-five," the old man said, "you ain't worked in a month. How long you figuring on being sick again?"

Junior looked up from his cards. "Till my luck runs out, boss."

A wrinkled frown, gaunt lips set tight. "I got to put you to work, boy.

My policy's to see each of you gets a fair chance to earn some change."

Everyone knew how the caddymaster got an allowance from Fairway House: five cents a head each day, based on the number of orphans who had caddied that week. The money was supposed to be used to buy lunch for the boys. Lunch from the caddymaster was a penny apple.

Junior folded his hand, tossed in his cards. "Be feeling better tomorrow, boss."

"Twenty-five!" The yell blew out of the shack. "Single! Nine!"

Junior laid down his cards, picked up his money, nodded to Number Six, and walked to the front of the shed. "Like to have an eighteen, boss. A double if you got it."

"Feeling lots better today, ain't you." The caddymaster turned his grin into a scowl and pointed to the tan bag leaning against the wood rail. "Single nine's all you get—sick boy."

Junior lugged the bag to the first tee. The golfer teed off and marched up the fairway. On the second tee, Junior waved his arms above his head. Sammy ran out of the woods.

"Mister, I ain't feeling so good." Junior held his stomach. "Okay if my friend here carries your bag? He knows this here course real good. Better than me!"

The golfer said, "Sure, kid," and Sammy took the bag.

Junior ran through the trees, back to the rear of the shed, where Number Six was waiting for him. "Worked perfect. Pinned my number on him and made him a caddy." Leaning past branches, Junior eyed the caddymaster's stool, which stood beneath the overhang of the shed. "Bastard probably don't know one of us from the other if we don't wear them tags."

Number Six rubbed his chin. "Might not work for me."

"It'll work better for you."

"Six!" The caddymaster was up and shouting. "Single! Eighteen!"

Number Six crossed his fingers and headed toward the voice. He carried the golf bag down the first fairway and out of sight. Ten minutes later, he came out of the bushes behind the shed and waved Junior back to the tree line. "Boy, you a genius! Never seen a man so ready to switch caddies. How'd you figure it so good?"

Junior wiped away his smile. "I ain't never seen no darky get sick neither. Probably scare hell out of me, too." He led the way back to the poker game.

Sammy ran to the rear of the shed and opened his fist to show off the fifteen cents he had earned on his first day as a caddy.

Junior let him keep a nickel.

"Be millionaires," Number Six said, "if this here was a private club. They pay real good. Up to six bits on weekends."

Junior dipped his foot in the stream and cast his line out as far as it would go. Ripples beat the surface, the borrowed fishing pole gleamed in the sun. "How much you take last week?"

"Forty cent." Behind Number Six, the caddy shack loomed like a green-white blur on the knoll. "We what you call executives now?"

"Most likely."

"Wanna set up a game?"

"No sense to it no more. Them others won't play."

"Told you, boy. Should of listened to me. Might be I could get a few to sit in, though. But you got to promise to lose once in while."

Junior reeled in his line. "Can't hang around here all the time anyways. Too easy to get spotted back behind the shed."

"Sometimes I don't know why I bothers even talking at you." Number Six chewed on a cattail stem. "Ain't you heard what I said, boy?"

"I heard."

A handful of dirt plopped into the water. Number Six lay back on the grass. "Sure we ain't gonna get caught?"

"Nope."

"Maybe we ought to carry once in a while. Just to keep him straight."

"Not me." Junior jammed the end of the pole into the muddy bank. "Can't do nothing to me even if they was to find out."

"Won't let me come around no more, they catch me."

The foursome of golfers out on the fairway looked like they were having fun. Junior studied them: they were hitting and walking, hitting and walking, that was all there was to it. "Wonder what it'd be like."

"And I have to walk three miles every day just to get here," Number Six said. "They kick me out, boy, I got noplace to go all summer."

"You can come with me."

"Ain't no coloreds over Fairway House."

Junior pulled his feet out of the water. The men on the fairway weren't hitting or walking anymore, they were tapping. So that was another part of it: tapping. Probably the easiest part, too. He laced his boots. "Ain't staying there much longer. I'm gonna escape."

Number Six gave him a hard look and sat up slowly.

"What's a matter. Don't believe me?"

"Trouble is, boy, I does believe you." Number Six headed back toward the shed as though walking to the sheriff's to give himself up.

Junior picked up the pole and trudged after him.

Time.

To play.

Junior drew the niblick out of the golf bag. "He'll never miss this one. Look how many else is still in there."

Number Six watched from the doorway of the shed. "How you know that ain't the man's special club, boy?"

"I'll put it back. Ain't like I'm stealing it." Junior dug into the pouch on the side of the bag, took a handful of balls, picked one that was badly scuffed, and put the others back and went out the door.

Beyond the stream and past the practice field, a long, narrow clearing lay hidden between a border of trees. Junior dropped the ball and stood over it, imitating a golfer's stance.

"Snakes in them woods, boy." Number Six kept an eye out for the caddymaster. "Real big ones, too."

"I ain't aiming for the woods." Junior studied his grip. "Now quiet whilst I'm doing this, you ain't supposed to talk when a man's hitting. That's etiquette." He kept rearranging his fingers on the club. Nothing felt comfortable. "Hey, Six, does this look right?"

Number Six shrugged. "I hit after you."

"You know you can't play."

"Well you can't neither. Never hit golf before in your life, boy."

"I meant on the course." Junior glared at the ball. "You ain't allowed 'cept to caddy." He shook his head disgustedly, then raised the club over his shoulder and swung down hard: a lunge. The clubhead drove into the ground. A clump of dirt kicked up, flopped over, and covered the ball. He cleared his divot out of the way. The ball hadn't budged. He drew the club back for another swing. The sound of soft laughter stopped him. Number Six was covering his grin with his hand. Junior squeezed the grip, gritted his teeth, and swung with all his might. He didn't mean to make the same mistake twice.

He didn't. The iron whizzed through the air, the club whipped around his shoulders, pulling him off-balance. He staggered in a half-circle. The cuts in the cover of the ball weren't just gashes anymore, they were smiles. That ball was smiling back at him, daring him to hit it.

"How long you figure before you connect, boy?" Number Six dropped to his knees laughing.

Junior threw down the club. "I'm a natural lefty. Can't expect me to hit with no right-handed stick."

Number Six held his stomach. "Boy—are them snakes ever safe."

The darky was too big to swing at. Besides, it was next to impossible to hurt his kind. His Aunt Ruth had told him so: "Got to hit them right here," she had pointed to the side of her head, near the temple, "real hard, otherwise, they don't feel nothing. Got that extra bone all around." Her hand had waved across her skull. "And real thick skin, too. Why, I seen a man shoot a nigger oncet. Three times smack in the belly. And did that fool nigger go down? No sir. Not till the man hit him with his rifle. Right here." Her hand had pointed to that spot where the extra bone was. "That's what done it. The only way, Junior. You remember that now."

And Junior did. A grin cracked through his frown. He started to laugh. He laughed so hard, he even gave Number Six a chance to swing the club.

For the rest of that summer, Junior practiced with the borrowed niblick because the man who owned it never missed it or maybe he had given up golf. Or died. Number Six stood guard until it was his turn to hit. Together they made about two dollars a week from their substitute caddies. And from seven-card stud. Number Six said that he spent what was left of his $.60 after he gave most of it to his sister, whom he lived with in town. Junior saved every cent of his $1.40 a week. For a while, he hid his money in a handkerchief under his mattress. But worried that someone like Jack Bender might see him, he buried his cache at the edge of the clearing and marked the spot with a small pile of rocks. Even Number Six didn't know where the money was.

"Man can get to Saint Lou on twenty bucks," Number Six had said. He claimed he had been there once—for the fair. But Junior didn't believe that story. Number Six didn't know anything about restaurants or menus or silver trays or how the fancy food tasted: he had probably made the whole thing up. He was a terrible liar.

By the first turn of color in the leaves, Junior had $8.57 underground. He prayed for an early spring.

5

Large hands dwarfed the rusty niblick. Number Six took a powerful swing. The ball shot low along the ground and tailed off into the woods.

"Still trying to kill it." Junior snickered and scratched his cheek. "You ever catch it full, you'll bust it in half."

Number Six dropped the club. "Dumb game anyways."

Junior carried the iron to his ball. "See, you got to control all your power." He wriggled his hips, adjusted his feet. "The idea ain't to hit it hard. Just hit it good." He drew back the niblick in a long, smooth arc. Hips and shoulders turned, knees cranked forward. The downswing felt easy yet firm: fluid. He drove the clubhead through the ball: a solid *crack*, a patch of turf sailing out ahead, his ball floating seventy-five yards before falling in the center of the clearing as softly as if it had been placed there by hand. "See what I mean?"

"Had some real stuff on that'n." Number Six led the way up the meadow. "Feel like fishing some tomorrow?"

"Got to practice."

"For what?"

Junior walked several yards in silence. There was no point in telling the darky about his plans. What would a darky know about professional golfing?

"You ain't done nothing but play at this all summer." Number Six spat to one side. "Every summer."

"Nobody asked you to stick around down here." Junior stepped into the woods, poked the bushes with the club, and looked for Number Six's ball.

"Missed a fine game of stud yesterday." Number Six sat on the fallen log. "Made fifty cent. In two hours."

"Don't want to hear about it."

The black frown went sour. "Just when I get us the chance to make some real cash, all you can do is figure another way to waste our time."

Junior used the club as a scythe to cut down the weeds. "Won't gamble away what I saved."

"No gamble to it, boy. Not if you listen to me for once. Suckers'd never expect us to team on them. You being white and all. Make at least five times what we're taking now. These boys think they're good!"

"Need every cent I got." Junior found the ball, tossed it into the clearing.

"Yeah, I forgot. You was gonna escape." Number Six worked a troubled smile around his lips. "Got to have enough for that ticket by now. You waiting to buy the whole damn railroad?"

Junior didn't look at him. He started out of the woods.

"Know what I think, boy?" Number Six said. "You scared to leave."

Junior spun around. "I ain't taking that from you."

Number Six laughed and slapped his knee. "Real scared, ain't you."

With all his power, Junior drove his fist into the side of the black's face, just below the temple. Number Six fell back into the weeds. He jumped to his feet, rubbed that extra bone, then tensed his muscles and bent down, wrapping his arms around the log, lifting it to his chest. His grunt sounded like a wooden drumbeat. Junior stood fast. The log flew over his head and crashed into the bushes.

"Ain't never hit no white boy before." Breath hissed through clenched teeth. "But I ain't planning on being hit by one again. Ever."

Junior moved a sly grin across his mouth. "They'd hang your ass for sure."

After a fierce squint, Number Six lowered his eyes. His chin fell to his chest. All the strength ran out of his oversized body. He was pitiful.

"Won't have to escape anyways," Junior said. "They let me out next year when I turn eighteen."

"You ain't but fourteen and you knows it."

"They don't." His grin lingered, then vanished. "Besides, I got me things to do. Can't have nobody on my trail."

Number Six shook his head. He shoved Junior aside and walked into the clearing.

Squeezing the club grip, Junior came out and stood over his ball for a long time. He knocked a high floater down the meadow toward an imaginary target.

"Hit mine, too." Number Six refused to take the niblick. "You the one what's gonna be champ." His eyes shone hard. "Knock a good one now—champ."

Junior glared back. He stepped to the other ball, hurried his swing. The small white sphere skidded off the clubface. A low line drive screamed down the right side of the clearing and bounded toward the woods, stopping on the edge.

"Still trying to kill it—*champ*."

Junior nibbled at his lip and marched after the balls. Halfway there, the words came out all by themselves:

"Them people finally come for Sammy yesterday. Adopted him."

Number Six stopped walking. "Boy, you is plumb pitiful. Damn if you ain't the dumbest fucking smart-ass what is." Dark eyes narrowed. He measured his words. "Ain't nobody coming for you, sucker. No—body."

Junior cocked the niblick and swung out high, aiming for that extra bone. . . .

Number Six caught the blow on his forearm and grabbed Junior by the wrist. "You been here three years and he ain't come back." He squeezed until the niblick fell to the ground. "Your pa ain't never coming back for you, boy. Understand? Never!"

"I'll kill you!" Junior forced the pain from his face and replaced it with hate. "So help me, I'll kill your ass." These words tasted sweet: "You fucking nigger shit."

Number Six twitched, but flashed a small, easy grin. He let go.

"Could of broke my wrist for Chrissake." Junior picked up the club and stormed down the clearing, rubbing the sting from his skin. When he reached the ball at the edge of the woods, he listened to the rustle in the bushes. *Must be headed back up the caddy shack, that dumb black bastard.* He bent down to the ball.

A smothering blur shot out of the woods. He threw up his hands just as the thing—the big darky?—crashed into his side and rode him down. It grabbed, pinned him on his stomach, wrenched his arm up behind his back. The more he struggled, the worse his arm hurt. It felt ready to snap. "Goddamn it, Six. Let me up!"

"I got him!"

Sudden fear blocked out the pain. That voice didn't belong to Number Six, it belonged to Jack Bender. Junior strained to get free.

A bony fist slammed between his shoulder blades. It was no use, the bastard had him. Had him good.

Footsteps cracked over weeds. A pair of beat-up boots, the soles red with mud, stopped in front of his face, and a nasal twang made the breeze stand still: "Let him up."

Jack pressed a knee into Junior's back and stood. That rotten tooth centered his grin. "You heard Caddymaster Davis, boy. Get up."

Junior rolled over and got up slowly. The pain in his arm was sharp. He couldn't feel his fingers. How would it be, running with only one arm? There was no way to outrun Jack. *No escape.*

"You steal this, boy?" The caddymaster held the niblick. "Or was it the nigger?" His skinny hand rubbed up and down the shaft. "Be inclined to believe you if you was to say the nigger stole it."

Junior glanced over his shoulder, down the clearing: empty. "What nigger?"

Caddymaster Davis kept sliding his hand up and down the hickory. "Can't have no thieves around my shed, dark or white." He spat between his teeth. A tobacco-brown tongue licked saliva. "Tell your nigger to stay clear. Don't want to see neither of you by again. Unnerstand what I'm telling you, boy?"

Silence. Junior held his face rigid.

The hand stopped moving on the shaft, "Answer when spoke to," and the caddymaster slapped him behind the ear.

It took effort, but Junior didn't rub his head. "Nobody stole nothing. That club belongs to Mr. Frank and he said I could use it anytime I wanted. You can ask him." It was a lie, so he sweetened it. "He give me his street address and everything. I got it back at Fairway House and you can call on him and find out. Besides, don't you think I'm smart enough to keep away from niggers?"

The grin had disappeared from Jack's face, but the caddymaster wasn't believing any of it. He slapped Junior again. "I ain't hearing none of your piss, boy. You ought to git down on your knees and thank me for not reporting you to Drumlin like I should. But I got a good heart. Be enough if you was to tell me the nigger stole this iron." His hand started moving up and down the hickory again. "Jack here told me it was both your doing, and he ain't lied once in the two years he's been my right-hand man. Still, I ain't one to see nobody whupped till the proof's in. Now just tell me the nigger stole it and I'll even let you keep caddying."

Junior let out a fake sigh and nodded long enough to peer up and see the caddymaster begin to smile, to see a grin start on Jack's face, to see if maybe now . . .

Now. His overhand right caught the caddymaster by surprise. He smashed a quick left into the nose, planted a boot in the groin. Tired eyes bulged in agony, the caddymaster slumped to the grass.

Junior started a smile. But Jack's roundhouse right broke his grin in two. For an instant, the big boy seemed suspended in midair. Junior rolled away from the next punch and the bastard fell on empty ground. Scrambling back to the caddymaster, who lay on his side clutching his testicles, Junior snatched the niblick, hoping—praying—to find the perfect target: a dark brown tooth in the middle of a sneer. He spun and swung with everything he had. The clubhead slashed the air: nothing.

A few feet away, Jack Bender, the squealer who should be dead by now, was sprawled on his back, his neck limp, a smooth trickle of blood trailing down his chin. Number Six stood over him, fist cocked and begging for another chance.

Junior couldn't hold back the laugh. "I think you killed him."

From behind, a hand grabbed his leg. He whipped the iron down against the caddymaster's outstretched arm. The man let out a howl, pulled back his hand and stuck it between his legs:

"Little thieves! They'll whup you good for this! I'll see both of you to the rock pile!"

Junior wound the niblick back for one final swing at the old man's head.

"You crazy?" Number Six caught the shaft and hurled the club into the weeds. "Put us in jail for sure, you kill somebody." He rubbed bruised knuckles. "Probably shoot me."

"Ain't nobody gonna shoot you." Junior walked to the big boy's body. Jack Bender was still breathing. Not that it mattered. Not anymore. Running to the edge of the clearing, Junior kicked over the pile of rocks and clawed through a layer of soil to his tin box. Coins rattled. He tucked his box under his arm, waved, and at a run, led Number Six deep into the woods.

6

The streets ran slimy with kitchen water. Thin strands of brown-gray smoke curled above slanted roofs. People were living beneath, but these weren't houses, these were cardboard and crates of naked wood, sun-parched and rotting, stained by neglect.

"Jesus, we ain't staying here." Junior's lungs heaved, the odor of decay stung his nostrils. "Even jail's better'n this."

"For you maybe." Number Six stopped in front of a shack where a dingy sheet hung in the doorway. "Can't stay here anyways. First place they'd look." He pushed aside the sheet, "Wait out here," and went inside.

Voices leaked through thin walls: something about leaving. Withering stares came from blacks crouched low on doorsteps up and down the street. Junior felt the weight of his tin box, held it tightly under his arm as if to make it part of his body. Had these darkies seen it, heard the rattle of coins? He took long, smooth breaths to keep his money silent.

Number Six brought out a small bundle. A heavy woman came with him. She had three teeth. "Don't be 'way too long, now. Needs you here. Not too long?" She kissed him on the cheek and stepped back behind the curtain door.

Junior moved away from the shanty steps. "That your sister?"

Number Six was looking off toward thick, slow clouds. He nodded, cleared his throat, and started down the road.

Junior had to run to catch up. The coins in his tin box jangled. "Slow down some, we're making too much noise."

"Nobody gonna take it from you, boy. Leastways, not here."

"Ain't there some other way?" Junior sidestepped a stagnant puddle and scanned the crooked row of shanties. Dark and searching eyes haunted the street. "Why are they all staring at us?"

"Not us, boy." Number Six turned up an alley. "You."

"Ain't they never seen a white before?"

"Seen plenty. They plumb scared to death of you, is all. Must be that killer look you got."

Junior didn't laugh.

Up ahead stood a line of freight cars. At the tracks, he stopped, looked back at the shanties. "Don't know how you could stand it, Six."

"Couldn't." Number Six picked up a chunk of gravel and hurled it into dull gray sky. The rock got lost in flight, but Junior heard it land: a distant thud, soft on the edge of Dark Town.

"And it's Curtis," Number Six said, heading up the rails. "Curtis Godfrey."

"Sure you knows the way?"

Junior nodded. And hoped he was right. But what difference did it make? He'd find it. Eventually. And what could Curtis say—"This looks like the wrong turn, boy?"—or—"Hey, I recognizes that tree over there?" How was Curtis going to know?

"Don't want to get lost up in them woods, boy."

Junior smiled. "Can't get lost." *Can't get lost because you don't know where we'd be in the first place.* Traveling with Curtis would be easy.

The alley fed into a wide, straight street where a boy was using a long pole to light a gas lamp. "Hey, boy!" Junior called. "Which way's east?"

The boy took one look, dropped the pole, and ran.

Junior glared. "Should of known. You scared him off. They ain't used to seeing your kind around here."

Curtis pointed toward a row of houses set back on neatly manicured lawns.

It looked normal enough over there. Junior squinted. "Don't see it. What?"

Curtis sighed and crossed the street. "This way is *east.*"

Trees filled with the stir of night. Shadows darted between branches. Distant footsteps tracked over leaves. Something lay in wait.

Junior tried to look away. *If it's going to happen, let it just come right out of there and get me.* His muscles tensed. Curled around his tin box, he clutched the shirt to his neck. His mind sent out waves to the trees: *I'm right here waiting for you. Whatever you are.* Above, the winking lights of stars, like a city in the air. He shut his eyes and tried to memorize the pattern.

Leaves crunched, twigs cracked. Curtis came out of the tree line. He dropped an armful of branches next to the fire. "Thought you'd sleep a while longer."

Too cold to speak, Junior shook his head.

"Figured we can take our time, anyways." Curtis stoked the embers, then rattled a tiny cardboard box. "Only got four more matches. Ought to be enough, don't you think?"

Junior nodded. Who the hell gave a damn about matches? His mouth tasted of dried weeds. He held out his hand. "Knife."

Curtis gave him the jackknife. Wiping the blade on his overalls, Junior cut cheese for two breakfasts, then held his arms over the fire and shivered. "Dumb thing you done starting this bonfire. They could spot our smoke real easy."

"Get warm so we can start out of here." Putting the cheese back in his bundle, Curtis walked to the trees, dropped his overalls, and urinated.

Junior couldn't stop staring. Darkies would probably piss anywhere. He went into the bushes and dropped his overalls. A wispy cloud of steam rose from the leaves. Behind him, handfuls of dirt hissed on the fire. The smell of sweet green sap died in the air. He came out of the weeds. And stopped short. Curtis was holding *his* tin box, staring at *his* money. The big hands let the lid fall and held the metal square out at arm's length. Junior took his box and hurried up the bank. He walked along the south side of the road, with Curtis a few yards behind. *Probably gonna rob me. Better make him let me carry the knife.* Two miles of silence. Then the sound of hooves. He waved Curtis into the bushes. A farmer's wagon loaded with green vegetables rolled by and disappeared around the curve. Junior grinned. "Might be we'll get one of those headed our way."

Curtis stared at the ground and didn't say anything

Junior pulled up a dry weed and stuck it in his mouth. No one was going to pick him up. Not with Curtis along. He glanced up the road and, counting the thousands of steps he would have to take all because he was traveling with a darky, he walked out of the trees.

He had to stop. His arms ached: his tin box had grown heavy over the last five miles. Without a word, Curtis put it inside the bundle and started leading the way.

Junior fell in behind. He ate cheese when it was offered to him. And soon the questions ended. No longer did he hear, "This seem familiar yet, boy?" Twice they had to leave the road to hide from passing wagons, and whenever they approached signs of life from houses scattered in the hills, Junior found a route through trees to keep safe and out of sight.

It took three hours to circle the town of Blaine. He chose the north fork to his mountains. The afternoon sun began to drop over his shoulder, a wet breeze flickered down the path, ushered along by the push of night. He kept walking up the grade. A steady, silent trudge.

At the ditch, he pulled up so fast that he almost fell. The pain in his legs vanished. He breathed in the cool smell of water and yanked a fallen sign out of the bushes. Tearing off creepers and weeds, his fingers traced the lettering: MILL SPRING. *Home.*

He ran.

The path curved down to his lake. He found his side trail, now overgrown with heavy grass. He would have found it if they had built a whole city on top of it. His heart pumped. Twin elms arched toward the water, the roots of the oak stump swarmed with ants. The top of his chimney . . . smoke stretched long in the wind . . .

He pressed Curtis low to the ground and crept forward through the weeds. The top half of the cabin's east wall had fallen in. Splintered planks lay scattered in bushes that grew onto the porch. The roof sagged, loose shingles curled at the edges in warped defeat.

And the front door opened.

A man staggered out. Stubble spiked his angular chin. He had sky-blue eyes.

Junior pursed his lips: the sound almost escaped.

The man picked up a plank, turned to carry it back inside.

"Pa!" Junior raced into the clearing.

The man dropped the plank. For an instant, he stood perfectly still. Then he spun and ran into the house. The door slammed.

"Pa! It's me!" Junior jumped onto the porch. Boards creaked, his body groaned with excitement. He stopped just long enough to comb a hand through his hair and wipe his nose. A grin burst on his face. He pushed the door open.

A small fire. Broken furniture. Soft, dusty light. A mud-caked heap below the east wall. Wind.

He stepped inside. ". . . Pa . . . ?"

The back door banged. Footsteps pounded away, dry brush crackled.

Junior legged down the hall, past her room, his room, and dragged open the back door.

Leaves shimmered. Wind?

He tried to shout, but choked on his own breath. His legs wouldn't work. And night was crowding in. No way to track in the dark. Besides, Curtis was afraid of the dark, wasn't he? He slumped in the doorway. Why did the man run? Did he see the darky and get scared? *Why did you run, Pa?*

Heavy feet thumped down the hall. After a long silence, Curtis sat in the doorway. "Might of been just a bum. Lots of 'em must come through here by the looks of this place." He put a hand on Junior's shoulder. "You didn't get but one fast peek at him, boy. How you so quick to call out Pa like that?"

Those blue eyes. Like mine. Junior studied his trees, his mountains. The leaves kept shimmering, the wind was picking up. "Gets real cold up here. Being so close to water and all. Better lay some wood on that fire."

"We could track him a ways if you want," Curtis said.

Junior kept silent. He didn't want to find that man. There were probably a million men with sky-blue eyes. He slapped dirt from his clothes and moved up the hall to his room. His bunk lay in pieces, his mattress was gone. And his bureau. But the broken drawer sat in the corner. He stepped in, trying not to see. *Pack of thieves.* Out back, leaves flapped in wind, the sun was dying, the grass was getting dark. He would let Sweet Dee Flagg sleep cozy tonight. Tomorrow he would tell her the good news. Planks thudded on the floor in the front room, flames sputtered. He walked past his Aunt Ruth's room without looking in and helped Curtis with the fire.

"Moved off over two years back," the new man at the country store said. "Imagine they made it all the way to California by now, unless they stopped someplace to settle."

"California?"

"Relatives." The man had shiny skin. "Got this letter and the next thing you know they're packed up and leaving. Practically give away their house. Nice folks living there now."

California. As far as anybody could go.

Junior wiped sweat from the back of his neck. "She leave anything for me? Junior Robinson."

The name didn't mean a thing to the man behind the counter. "Boy, they didn't leave nothing but dust."

So far. How could she do it to him? After she said she loved him. Maybe they had to drag her off, kicking and biting. Maybe she forgot all about him. Maybe she never did care. "Love," he said, shaking his head.

"Love?" the man behind the counter asked. "What's got in you, boy? Now you want those licorice sticks or not? Five for a penny."

Junior took ten and flipped a nickel to the man, "Keep the change," and walked out. He took the long way home. There was no dog skeleton in the bushes, no grave for his Aunt Ruth. Maybe she had floated onto shore, swelled-up and gray, with ropes on her ankles and her red dress bleached to no color at all, the whole town gathered around for a look, not knowing who that could be. He wished he had been there to help her. And if the preacher had tried to close her eyes, Junior would have said he had already done that.

There was nobody on the lake shore. The water was still. A man fished from a small boat a little way out. Curtis was probably right, that man in the cabin was just a tramp. Whoever he was, he didn't plan to stay long: he had left only an empty whiskey bottle and a jar of beans with a colony of ants inside it. Junior lobbed a stone toward the boat. He turned before the water splashed and walked back to his house.

"No way you could be sure it was him." Curtis finished a piece of cheese. "Been a long time since you seen him anyways."

Junior didn't answer. He couldn't. He didn't have a face to remember. He put his feet up on her table and worked on the fishing line.

"Ain't much now, is it." Curtis stared at the hole high in the east wall. "Must of been fine once though."

"Probably fall in on top of itself with the first snow." Junior knotted the line, pulled it tight. "Got half a mind to burn it down when we leave."

"We leaving? It's real nice up here. 'Cept that lake of yours so cold it ain't fit for swimming." Thick arms stretched over a head of hair that looked like a black bramble bush. "How you coming with that?"

Junior cinched twine around hooked wire. "I'll finish her down at the bank." He swung his feet off her table. "Don't get too comfortable, 'cause we are leaving. Just don't know when, is all."

"Thought you said we could stay here awhile."

Junior stopped at the door. "Be looking for us. Might be someone remembers where I come from."

"Think it was 'cause he seen me in the bushes?" Curtis said, pushing his sigh over the wood planks. "That why your pa run off?"

"Just a tramp," Junior told him. "His kind run from most anything." He forced the words through his teeth like a bitter seed: "It weren't my pa. I'll know *him* when I see him."

He leapt off his porch and headed down to his lake.

7

A road, a train, a car . . . a broad-brimmed hat pulled down over his brow to make him look older, a half-filled satchel to shove under a seat—something to own, to claim . . . wind, blown around corners, across currents, like wire drawn through sinew—never straight . . . never anywhere for long . . .

His wad of gum rolled down the gutter on a river of rainwater and washed through the sewer grating. He cocked his hat, ran his fingers over the brim, tossed a solemn nod to Curtis across the street, and opened the door.

He stood inside the entrance long enough to scan each face. Two of the men had sky-blue eyes. He slapped a dollar on the edge of the billiard table, "Next game?," and sat on the bench by the window and waited.

Finally, the short man with brown eyes sank the eight ball and took a dollar from the man he was playing. "Okay, boy. Your table. Got a name?"

"Junior." He stalked their eyes for a reaction: nothing.

"Hop up and lag for break, Junior."

He took a lightweight cue from the bracket on the wall, bent low to the table, set himself, and tapped the cue ball. It rolled up the slate into the far rail, then started back in a slow reel of death, stopping less than a foot from the rear cushion. His moist thumbprint on green felt marked the spot.

The short man stroked the white ball too hard. He didn't wait for it to hit the back cushion on the rebound, he just walked away from the table. "Your break, boy."

Junior lined up the angle and drove the cue ball into the rack. A loud crack, a jump of colors: the red-striped ball slid into a corner pocket. He moved to the short side, chalked his cue. The blue-striped ball was a dead cinch in the side pocket. The only way to miss the shot was to hit too hard. He hit the ball three times harder than he knew he should have. It bounced out of the mouth of the pocket. He fought the grin, "Damn, missed an easy one," and walked in front of the window while the short man took his turn.

Outside, a trolley skirted down the rails, and for a passing moment, he couldn't see across the street. Wood plunked into leather behind him, but he kept staring into night. Under the lamp glow by the bench off the far curb, black hands rubbed the sides of a dusty yellow satchel. He smiled.

"Hey, boy. Your shot."

He raked the brim of his hat and faced the table. "Any of you fellahs seen Cal Robinson by here lately?"

None of the men around the table said that they had ever heard of Cal Robinson. The short man leaned on his cue. "Why you ask, boy?"

"I owe him." Junior took off his jacket. "Like to pay off my debt."

"Real honorable of you, boy," the short man said. "World could use a few more like you, ain't that right, boys." The other men agreed with him.

Junior smiled and called the six ball in the far corner pocket.

He had one dollar left. No one seemed anxious for him to leave. They bought him another beer. Then another. He suggested another game and the men fought for the honor of beating him. The short man won again.

Junior made it quick. He sank the eight ball before he had pocketed all of the solid-colored balls: the mark of an amateur.

The short man grinned and picked up Junior's last dollar. "Another one?"

Junior shook his head and started to put on his jacket.

"Aw, just one more, boy. Spot you three balls this time."

"Already took twelve bucks off me." Junior put his cue back into the wall bracket. He had already *invested* twelve dollars in these yokels. "I ain't no sucker. I know when I'm beat."

The men chuckled. Every one of them.

With a smile, Junior stepped toward the door. "But I do thank you boys kindly for the game." Seven pairs of shoes made the same sound at the same time: a shuffle. Every one of these men hated to see a pigeon leave so soon. Making each move a deliberate one, Junior stopped, frowned, bent from the waist, sighted down the edge of the table, straightened up, spread his arms out along the cushions, nodded. "Thought so. This here ain't no regulation table."

The short man laughed. "Right from the factory, boy."

Junior eyeballed the length of green felt. "Half-foot shorter than regulation, I'd say."

"You had too many beers," the short man said. "Done told you it's *di*rect from the factory. Only make one size."

"I know a short table when I see one." Junior stretched his arms over the tabletop until his chin touched the felt. His fingertips strained for the last bit of distance. "See here? On a regulation table, my hands'd never get so close to them pockets." He pulled back, shook his head. "Ain't fair. No wonder I been losing."

The short man scratched his neck. "Boy, you lost because you're pitiful. Ain't that right, men." The others agreed with him. "Besides, how is it you didn't see this *non*regulation table here right off?"

"Thought there was something queer about it." Junior brushed a few grains of chalk from the polished wood rail. "But you boys looked regular enough. Never figured you'd be running a short table on me. No sir, I seen you and I trusted you. Now I find out—"

"Wait just one damn minute, boy." The short man dropped his cue. "Ain't nothing queer about this here table." He turned to his friends. "Ain't that right, men?"

The men eyed the table with suspicion now. The thin man in the chair cleared his throat. "How long's it supposed to be?"

Junior let out a little sigh, but held his face together. For the last two hours, the thin man had sat in that chair, the only chair in the place, and had said nothing. The others called him Alben. It had taken only ten minutes to find him, and two hours to wake him up. But there was always an Alben. Junior dug into his jacket, pulled out a small pamphlet. "Let's just look it up, why don't we." He rippled the pages and read with his finger. "Says here, nine and a half foot's regulation length."

Alben waved him over and took the book. He read the cover aloud. *"Official Rule Book. Pocket Billiards."* He didn't bother to read the small print across the bottom: *revised edition, 1912.* Junior had revised it himself. This year: 1912.

He helped Alben find the section which detailed the size of the table and the balls. Alben read to the others where the book said a regulation table was nine and one-half feet long by four and one-half feet wide, and that was more than good enough for Alben. He squinted at the short man. "Why don't we get a tape and measure."

"It's *direct* from the factory, Alben. *Direct*."

Alben crossed his legs. "Like to see it measured out."

The short man slammed his fist on the slate. Balls jumped. "This here is a factory table. Cost me over eighty-five dollars. Alben, you was here when it come."

Alben nodded, but with indifference. "Never did like the feel of it, though. Victor's up Twelfth Street—now there's a true table." He gave the pamphlet back, got out of his chair, and sighted up the lawn of felt. "Could be the one over Victor's *is* a tad longer."

The other men inched closer, measuring the table with their stares.

"No young punk tells me I run a short table." The short man stormed into the back room and came out with a yardstick, laid it down on the table, flopped it over twice to reach the far end. And cursed.

"Only nine foot." Alben sucked his lip. "No sir, never did like this one much at all."

The short man hurled the yardstick against the wall. "But it's *di-rect!*" The look the others gave him sapped his voice of conviction: ". . . *direct.*"

"How'd you figure it?" Alben said.

Junior rolled the black ball into a pocket. "Tried jumping a regulation table once. Near broke my skull. After I played this one awhile, I said to myself, 'Now here's one you can clear easy.' It's that extra half-foot what gives me trouble."

Alben studied him. "You saying you can jump clean over it?"

"Just need a small running start." With his palm, Junior caressed the wooden edge of the table. "No problem with this here one."

"Like to see that." The short man kicked the yardstick toward the back room. "Sure damn well would like to see that."

Junior examined his fingernails. His lips began to curl into a smile, but he reacted in time. "Say it cost—how much?"

"Eighty-five dollars." Alben beat the short man to the punch. "I was here when they brung it in."

"Bet eighty-five dollars then." Junior let the grin through. "Buy you a new table if I don't make it. Regulation length and all."

The short man grew dark in the face. "You're gonna jump it, you is." Breath whistled through his teeth. "But you ain't gonna clear it, boy. Ain't nobody what can do that." His smile turned vicious. He went behind the counter, unlocked a small door, and came back with a fistful of paper money. "Eighty-five and that's a bet you ain't walking away from."

"Don't need to see your cash," Junior said. "I know you're good for it. Now just put it back in your pocket there. This here's a friendly wager." He turned to the others and patted his pants. "Anybody else want in? Got me an extra fifty to play with. All or part."

Two men wanted ten dollars' worth each. He accepted. He didn't have the extra fifty. He didn't have anything in his pocket except chewing gum and a .36-caliber bullet for his gun, which his partner had in the satchel across the street. "Ain't hardly worth the effort for twenty bucks. Sure you boys don't want in? How about you, Alben?"

"Might be you can make it, sonny." Alben shook his head. "But I ain't gonna bet to see you bust your brains up."

With a wide grin, Junior patted him on the shoulder. "I land short, you can help me down the hospital."

Snorts of laughter filled the room. Junior moved in front of the window. He took off his jacket and, finally, his hat. His partner saw the signal and waved.

"Got to clear it clean," the short man said. "Can't touch no part of it."

Junior marked off six paces from the front edge of the table, took three quick steps, and stopped short. "Could be I ain't up to it. No bet."

"Bet's a bet." A sour smile creased the short man's mouth. "Friend."

The other men chimed in with agreement. Even Alben. Especially Alben. He was counting his pocket money. "Take fifteen dollars' worth. No sense watching without making something on it."

Junior shrugged and sealed all bets: $120. He limbered up his legs. One deep breath, five fast driving steps, the loud slap of a leather sole planting on wood, a grunt, and he sprang—neck muscles stretching, his head shooting out and up, his arms straining for a clear patch of air, then tucking under with the final kick-up of his legs. His shoulders slammed down hard into a sprawl that should have been a somersault, but there wasn't enough room in this place. His feet whacked paint off the chalk-stained wall.

Made it. He got up as fast as he could and brushed off his pants. The floor felt unsteady, drifting. A deep, pulsing ache spread over his back. He leaned on the table, tried to find his breath. "My hat . . ."

The short man threw down his money. The others did the same. Alben's fingers said good-bye to his cash as if it were a dying friend.

Junior pointed to the window bench, but no one moved. "Get me my hat. Now!"

Alben brought him the hat. Junior put it on in a hurry, then staggered along the table to a spot in front of the window. He stood as straight as the pain would allow.

"You all right, boy?" Alben said.

Junior nodded to his partner, who was halfway across the street, pistol drawn and cocked. The dark form stopped and went back to the bench by the curb.

"You sure, boy?" Alben put a hand on his shoulder. "Look terrible to me."

"I'm fine." But he wasn't fine, he was broken: lame. He picked up his money, shoved the bills into his pocket. "Take that yardstick to Victor's."

"What for?" Alben said. "We know that's a regulation table."

"Just do it." Junior struggled into his jacket sleeves and walked out the door hunched over, arms heavy at his sides.

"What for?" Alben called.

Junior kept walking. He got most of the way across the street before he heard the door to the billiard parlor close. The bench by the curb looked too far away, but he managed the final steps and lowered his body onto wood slats. Glancing back at the face of the pool hall, he sighed and rolled over, each slat digging into his gut. "Clear."

Footsteps came out of night shadows. Curtis squatted beside the bench. "Made it again, didn't you. How much this time, sport?" He reached into Junior's pocket, pulled out the cash, dropped it into the satchel. "When you gonna stop trying to bust yourself in half?" he said, massaging Junior's back. "Why can't you just bet them yokels on the length? We got them dead to rights."

"Easy, damn it." Junior winced from the pain of strong fingers pulling at his bruised skin. "Let me handle the yokels."

"Just as glad you made it. Four-for-four now. We ought to quit."

Junior stifled a laugh. "They spend half their fool lives over them tables and don't even know how long one's supposed to be."

"That's why you ought to just bet them on the length!"

Curtis was right. He had city folk figured out the same way Dee Flagg had. And it worked. But it was never enough for Junior. Just winning didn't fill him up. Only revenge would.

"Listen to me now," Curtis was saying. "Show them where it

says *twenty* foot's regulation and they'd believe it, long as you got *official* wrote on the cover—hell, they'd believe anything. Why you got to take the hard way?"

There was a little silence, time to let the words die out along the street. Curtis breathed heavily through his nose. "Your pa wasn't in there, was he."

". . . Rub."

"Yeah, that's what I'm good for. Slave work." Curtis kneaded the aching flesh. "Well I ain't your slave, goddamn it. And you're through with this, sport. I ain't standing around waiting for them to cart you out dead."

"Not dead yet, am I?"

"And me with that damn gun." Curtis spat his words. In the open satchel, the money had scattered around Junior's long-barreled Confederate Colt .36. "You know what white folks do to me, they find me with a gun?"

Junior coughed. "Quit squeezing so hard, I told you." He draped his head over the end of the bench. "Up north, maybe we can work you into the setup. But down here, they'd just as soon shoot you as say hello." He closed the satchel. "I'm doing this for your own good."

"Got all the answers, ain't you. Especially about coloreds."

"That's 'cause I ain't one."

Curtis shook his head. "Last time, understand?"

Junior sat up and grinned. "Whatever you say, boss."

With a laugh, Curtis put an arm under Junior's shoulder and helped him to his feet. "Kind of gonna miss seeing you sail across that table, though," the big black said. "Sure did look pretty. Like you was sliding down a rainbow. . . ."

Book Two
IRIS

8

Rainbow hauled his golf bag and suitcase out of the cab and paid the driver. The Tam Lin clubhouse was bigger than he had expected. And newer: brown and gray stone. No fountain. He had expected a fountain. Maybe the place wasn't finished yet. He rubbed the ache in his neck—he hadn't moved from the coach seat once on the trip up from Saint Louis—and, yawning, dragged his bags to the railing.

Red hair flapping, a barefoot boy in denim overalls ran up from the caddy shack. "How come you didn't call?" the boy said. "I left word at the Jefferson Hotel you was supposed to call."

"Got tied up." Rainbow gave Murph the bags and a small envelope of money. "How you been, kid?"

"Lousy. You practice while you was on the road?"

"A little. Made enough to see us through September. I put an extra fifty in there to make up for not sending anything the last three months."

"That don't matter." Stuck in the top pocket of Murph's overalls, the envelope looked like a letter from home. "Why didn't you tell me you was coming in? I'd of drove you out."

"We come separate," Rainbow said. "You know that."

Murph nodded, shouldered the bag. "How far'd you get this time?"

"Louisville. Christ, Chicago's hot. How's the car running?"

"Went through two sets of transmission bands last month alone." Murph shook his head. "Didn't find him, did you?"

Rainbow fanned himself with his panama and didn't say anything.

"What I don't understand," Murph said, "is why you keep going over the same ground all the time. The same road. If Old Cal was there, you'd of found him already."

"You check all the pool halls?"

"Yeah and he ain't here neither." Murph studied the clubface of the niblick in the bag. "Damn, you ain't been practicing. Not a stain on any of these irons."

"Had them cleaned." It was a lie. "Tried to save you the bother."

Murph grew sheepish. "Well, you better hit a few on the shag field before we start."

"Take the clubs to the first tee, I'll warm up on the course."

"You crazy? I heard who we're playing. You know he holds the course record?"

"And put some dirt in your hair. You look too clean."

"Shit . . ." Murph drew his toes through the grass. "Why am I the one who has to do all this stuff?" He pulled the strap of his overalls. "Just look at me. It's stupid."

"I don't mean sand, either. Real dirt." Rainbow turned him around. "Where's your caddy tag?"

"They don't give them out up here. How come you always ask that? No matter where we play, you always ask that."

". . . Habit." Rainbow rubbed the back of his neck. "We're betting five grand a side today. Your game in shape?"

"Five grand each nine holes . . . ?"

"And five more on the eighteen. Told you this was the big one, didn't I?"

"But a five-grand Nassau? Where the hell we gonna get that kinda money?"

"Got us a sponsor. By the time I'm through with these yokels, we'll have the stakes pushed to the wall. Your game's in shape, right?"

"Yeah, but . . . five grand? A side? They'll kill us when they—"

"Put some dirt in your hair and start acting like a caddy." Rainbow went up the steps. Maybe they would kill him if they found out it was a setup. He stopped by the door. "Sure you been all right, kid?"

Murph shrugged. "Rather of been with you. Ain't nothing to do here."

"Next time. Promise." Rainbow's mouth was going soft, but he caught it in time. He had missed the kid. "And be careful with my bag. Got the .45 in the ball pouch." He pushed through the main door.

The lobby had the smell of money. He smoothed down his cowlick, walked past big leather chairs, down a wide corridor, following signs to the Men's Grill. One look from the doorway was all he needed. It had to be the table near the far windows. The stout old man wore a gray suit, gray tie. His hair was gray. So was his skin. The suntanned man seated with him was dressed all in white. His plus fours had been starched. He was muscular, bright-eyed, square-jawed. The all-American. A pushover.

"Mr. Taylor North?" Rainbow shook the old man's hand and sat in the middle chair. "I'm Rainbow Roberts. And you must be Jurgenson." He smiled at the golfer in white. "Your friends call you Jurgy, do they? Warm today, ain't it."

"Welcome to Chicago." North chuckled and set a glass of ice water in front of Rainbow. "Ever play Tam Lin before?"

"Never," Rainbow said. "Terrible disadvantage."

"It's an easy course," Jurgenson told him. "You could play it in your sleep."

The all-American pushover was an idiot.

"Not all that easy," North said. "I've never broken a hundred."

"In that case, Mr. North," Rainbow said, "I hope I'm playing against you." He waited for the old man to stop laughing. "Didn't know your man here was a pro."

The grin slid off North's lips. His fingers rapped the tablecloth. It must have taken years to perfect that impatient rhythm. "The understanding I have with your sponsor, Broder, is a five-thousand-dollar Nassau, automatic presses, championship tees."

Rainbow turned the glass in a circle. "If it's all the same, I'd like to make it thirty-six holes. So I can get a feel for the layout. Same stakes."

North's fingers went still. "That could run into quite a sum."

"It's only money," Rainbow said. "I know we're agreed to eighteen, but thirty-six is more interesting. And to make it fair, Jurgy can hit three balls every hole and take only his best score." He grinned. "I always like to give a duffer an even shake."

Jurgenson sat straight up. "Who are you calling a duffer?"

"Didn't mean to insult you, Jurgy. You're probably a real good golfer. Just not in my league."

"Your league . . ." Jurgenson snorted his amusement. "If you were in my league, I'd have heard of you. And I checked around. Nothing. Nobody's ever heard of you."

"Don't understand it myself," Rainbow said. "Good as I am. Bet it's 'cause I don't play tournaments. How do you stand it, Jurgy? All that pressure? No sir, give me a friendly round any day. Sportsmanship. That's what counts." Both men were staring as if he had just spat in their soup. He swallowed softly. "Thirty-six holes is a real fair test of golf. Might be I'll lose a little more, but Will Broder's good for it."

"No doubt he is." North put both hands together as though he meant to pray. "And Bob here hits *three* balls . . . ?"

"Every hole," Rainbow said. "Let's see if we got it straight. Thirty-six holes of golf. Match play: whoever takes less strokes on any hole wins that hole, total strokes don't count. A five-thousand-dollar Nassau: man who wins each set of nine holes wins five grand. With automatic presses, that's if a man gets two holes down at any time, the bets are doubled, right?" North and Jurgenson looked bored. Rainbow cleared his throat: "And we hit from the championship tees. Jurgy hits and holes out three balls every hole, then takes only his best score. Fair enough?"

North wasn't bored anymore, he was beaming. He offered his hand. It felt perfectly dry.

A long drink of ice water. Rainbow let out a satisfied sigh: "Tough bet."

"Nice to have you back with us, Miss Winslow." The desk clerk at the Palmer House turned the register. "How long will you be staying?"

"I'm not sure." Iris read the poster near the elevators. It was tall and painted with red letters: AMERICAN CONGRESS OF MEAT-PACKERS—JULY 27 THRU AUGUST 2, 1925. The men in the lobby were staring at her over their newspapers. Some wore cardboard hats with ACMP stamped in red on the ribbon band. Why couldn't any of them be as attractive as that man in the panama she had seen on the highway yesterday? Holding back her smile, she faced the desk and signed the register, dotting the *i* in her last name as though stabbing the page. She hated this name. Time for a new one?

While the clerk wrote a room number in the column next to her signature, something heavy thudded on the carpet near the doors. The last of her luggage had just arrived: a big iron-bound trunk, now rocking on its curved top. Decals of European resorts caught and lost the shine of lobby lights with each rocking motion. Across the front, a yellow banner: MAJESTIC FARMS—LOUISVILLE. At least it had survived being lashed to the Packard.

"Bet you're an actress, right?" The voice over her shoulder belonged to a man with big eyes that were brown and bloodshot. He wore one of those cardboard hats. He pointed to the name tag on his breast pocket. It said, WILL. He grinned and said, "My name's Will. What's yours?"

Iris blinked. "Won't."

The man swallowed most of his laugh. "I get it. *Won't*. That's a good one." He leaned on the desk. "I mean, with all those bags, and that trunk, you got to be an actress, am I right?"

"Excuse me." She walked toward the elevators.

The man with the name tag followed her. "Majestic Farms. Say, you don't grow hogs like the rest of us, do you?"

The other men in the lobby were smiling and staring hard. The newspapers were in their laps now. On the corner of that big poster, someone had penciled in "pig-fuckers" and someone else had tried to erase it. Iris tucked her purse under her arm. "Horses. My father raises thoroughbreds."

The bellman pushed a cart loaded with luggage and pulled the dolly with the trunk on it into the elevator, and Iris stepped in. The expanding mesh door slid across the threshold.

"We're having a little party later on," the man with the name tag said. "Be a lot of fun. Like to join us?"

The other men looked eager to find out what she would say. She didn't say anything. She blinked her eyes. The elevator operator pulled a lever in the corner, the outside doors began to close, wiping away the faces in the lobby. Iris breathed in deeply: safe. For now.

"You say thoroughbreds, ma'am?" the bellman said. "Know any of yours by name offhand? Might be I won a few dollars on them."

"Offhand . . . no."

The rest of the ride up to the eighth floor passed in silence. The bellman led her to a two-room suite. He turned on the light and the overhead fan in the sitting room and opened a window there. It had a view of the city. He put her luggage in the bedroom, turned on that light, and opened that window. Same view. He clunked the dolly onto the cart and waited.

"You'll be tipped when I leave," Iris said.

"Yes, ma'am. It's Ernie, ma'am."

Ernie.

He pointed to the name sewn on his jacket. "So you'll know who to ask for?"

Her fingers were trembling, she couldn't get the cigarette out of the pack. "Thank you . . . Ernie."

The door closed. She stripped a glove from her hand and yanked the cigarette free, fed it to her lips, lit a match. Drawing smoke deep into her lungs, she turned the key in the lock, bolted the door, and went into the bedroom. Her low pumps banged the wall. She untied her waistband, wriggled out of the green dress, rolled down flesh-colored silk stockings, threw them at the chair by the window. She missed. Two pins came out of her hair. She stuck them in the cloche hat and laid it on the dresser. Up over her head came the lace slip. She took her cigarette into the bathroom.

Harsh bands of light filled the mirror. Hands on her waist, she shook her head. Starvation diets to keep a twenty-inch waist. For what? Low waists had been in vogue for three years now. She straightened the wave in her hair. At least the bob traveled well. Just a few years ago, hair this short would have singled her out as a Communist, yet at the newsstand this morning, she had opened the last issue of *American Hairdresser* to a feature on the do-it-yourself bob.

Another long puff of smoke. She tossed the cigarette into the toilet. With hotel soap and hot water, she scrubbed her face. What a difference that little bit of rouge made, that trace of lipstick. Except for plucked and colored eyebrows, her face was naked. "So plain," she told her reflection. "Plain little Iris." How would she have fared in her mother's day when scarlet cheeks had meant shocked stares and lewd propositions? Dreadfully she was sure. And if the little-girl look ever lost popularity? She took off the brassiere, stood sideways at the mirror. But flat chests were in style now, weren't they?

She gave the loose-fitting teddies a casual glance: she had a fine ass. Fact. Her legs were a bit heavy, only the thighs, really. Nothing that minor exercise wouldn't take care of. If she ever found the time: 1:00 P.M. already. She took off her wristwatch. Barely enough time for a bath.

She found the valise on the bedroom dresser. The jar of facial cream felt cold. She worked white dabs into her skin. Music was coming from the sitting room. The bellman must have turned on the radio and now it had warmed up. *Ernie loved music. He loved to sing along with the radio.* She hated this song. How had it ever become a hit with such a stupid lyric: "Who's taking care of the caretaker's daughter when the caretaker's busy taking care?" She wiped her hands with a tissue. The radio was inside a cabinet near the window in the sitting room. She switched it off. On hotel stationery, she made a list: buy newspapers, send out laundry, call Grace at Tam Lin. And near the bottom, she wrote DADDY and underscored it three times. Starting with the *A*, she filled in the letters until DADDY disappeared and in its place an ink-black square stood out on the page.

"No use worrying over it," her father had told her. "You'll get married to a fine gentleman, the kind you deserve."

Poor Daddy. He was wrong so often.

Someone rapped on the door. "Miss? It's Will. From the lobby, remember? I forgot to tell you where the party was."

She marched into the bathroom, turned on the hot-water faucet over the tub, and shut the door.

The locker-room attendant was either reading the paper or sleeping behind it. Rainbow gambled. He swiped a towel from the shelf, left his suit jacket on the hat rack by the door, and walked out to the first tee. His stomach was growling. There might be a lunch stand at the ninth hole. His stomach could wait. He needed the sun's heat more than food.

Ringed by fellow club members, North and Jurgenson were standing on the tee. Rainbow went to his golf bag on the bench, pulled out his driver. Its hickory shaft was dull and in need of varnish. He took a practice swing: the rhythm felt wrong. With luck, he might get it back in five holes. He toweled down the leather grip. "You providing caddies, Mr. North, or do I have to carry my own bag?"

The club members laughed. North waved toward the caddy shack down the hill. In the distance, metal hinges squeaked, a wood door slapped shut, feet thumped on hardpan, bushes at the side of the tee began to rustle.

And like a rabbit, Murph popped through the weeds and up the bank. There was a smear of motor oil on his nose and cheek. His red hair was streaked with dirt, blades of grass jutted from his scalp as if rooted there. "A real honor carrying your bags, sir." He offered his hand to Jurgenson. "Seen you play lots of times and you're the best. Better than Hagen even."

The golfer in white didn't take Murph's hand. He nodded at the bench. "You'll carry his bag."

Murph glanced at Rainbow and frowned.

"Tell me," Rainbow said, "does a gentleman shake with a caddy or what?" He shook Murph's hand. "Glad to have you along, kid. Know this course?"

"Yes sir, I carry here three times a week and been playing on it every caddies' day since spring."

"Hear that, Jurgy? The kid not only hauls bags, he golfs, too. You don't stand a chance now."

It was the truth.

"Thirty-six?" Murph said in a whisper.

Rainbow nodded. "Your hair looks real nice. Got the charts?"

Out of a front pocket of the overalls came a scorecard. Each hole had been annotated in golfer's shorthand: penciled-in arrows showed on which side of the fairway the drive should be placed; distance to the flag stick after a drive or from landmarks on the course was given in yardage; an initial stood for which club should be used for shots to the greens. For the first hole, the card read D ↗ 165 MI: a good *drive* down the *right* side of the fairway would leave *165 yards* to the pin, calling for a shot with a *mashie iron*.

North tossed a coin. "Call it, sir."

"Tails," Rainbow said.

Stooped over like a rooster hunting for seed, North picked up the coin. "Tails it is. Your honor."

Rainbow pocketed the scorecard and stepped onto the tee. Where he tapped the sole of his driver, Murph built a moist mound of sand and placed a golf ball on it, then left the teeing area. The long narrow fairway bent to the right. Standing over the ball, Rainbow checked his stance. The grip felt sweaty all of a sudden. He swung. No rhythm at all. The *crack* from the wood clubface meeting the ball was louder than his grunt. His drive flew low over the edge of the rough, faded back to the fairway, and stopped in the left center 190 yards out. That fade meant trouble. His hands had lagged behind his body and had arrived late in the hitting area. Normally, his shots moved from right to left, the result of a natural draw. He gave Murph the driver, grip first. "Don't say it."

"Looked like your arms was falling off," Murph said. "It don't play from the left, can't you read what I put on the card? Bet you ain't even held a club in a month."

"Thanks," Rainbow said. But the kid was right.

Murph's mouth hung open. "Jesus Christ, look at that."

The steel shaft of Jurgenson's new driver gleamed in the sun like a sword. He stood over a new ball resting on a new wooden tee. With a relaxed, fluid swing, he boomed a tee shot that carried past Rainbow's ball on the fly. "I'll play that one. Can't hit it any better." He strode off the tee.

Rainbow sat on the bench. "Mr. North! Remind your man he's got two more to hit."

The men in the gallery stopped walking. Jurgenson turned back wearing a scowl. "I said I'll play that one."

Rainbow crossed his legs, stretched his arms out along the back of the bench. "Of course you're gonna play that one, Jurgy. Our bet is you play all *three* of them into the cup. Every hole." He tilted his head and got a faceful of sun. "Take your time hitting them other two."

Jurgenson muttered to himself, had a word with North, then slammed his club into the ground, walked back, and teed up another ball. His next two drives split the middle and seemed to roll forever on the sunbaked turf. Like a sheik, all in white, he led the caravan of club members down the fairway.

"Five grand a side." Murph was grinning. "Christ, are they gonna kill us."

"Not these boys." Rainbow draped the towel around his neck. "They're just gonna lay down and die." He started the long walk to his ball.

9

The fan in the Tam Lin dining room broke down for the third time in the last hour. Iris stirred her tea and set a photo of two horses against the salt and pepper shakers for the old woman to see. "They're just yearlings. But you're paying for more than their feed. Their training is included, too."

"Oh, I know, I shouldn't complain." Grace North turned her large diamond ring. "After all, they are thoroughbreds." She touched the diamond brooch at her collar, followed a gold chain to the rimless bifocals in her pocket, brought the glasses to the bridge of her nose.

And signed the check.

Iris smiled. Made out to Majestic Farms for $780, the draft was properly signed and dated. She put it in her purse.

"I wish you had been here to help me choose a wardrobe for my trip." Grace scooped up what was left of her second dish of ice cream and glanced at the simple tan dress Iris was wearing. "That's so chic. From Paris, of course."

"Callot Soeurs," Iris said. "One of the few things of theirs I could find without sequins. Everyone's trying to look so gaudy these days."

Grace smiled as though imagining herself in the dress, strolling down a Paris boulevard, lissome and stately—like a woman on a Renoir canvas. She blinked. "I can't wear the new styles. Those hemlines! Men have it so easy, don't they. Suit, tie, white shirt, the same tuxedo year after year. . . ."

"I have this theory," Iris said. "The way our fashions change is a form of cultural punishment. The top designers are all men."

". . . oh . . ."

"But I confess, I'd want to keep up with the styles even if we didn't have to. Even if no one had to."

In the little silence, Grace scratched her cheek. "I hate to go alone. Not that there's anything wrong with a woman traveling by herself. Not these days. They even smoke in public now, don't they. So unladylike."

"It is rather vulgar." The cigarette pack made a square bulge in Iris's purse. She put it in her lap. "Won't your husband be joining you?"

"After that silly convention, yes. What do meat-packers possibly have to talk about? They all live here, eat lunch together every day as it is. It must be horrible for you at the hotel, dear. All those men. Didn't you have the same problem last year?"

Iris tried the tea: still too hot. "Grain distributors. But they weren't as noisy as this group."

"Such a shame." Grace licked her spoon, then waggled it like a maestro's baton. "And the year before that—wasn't it those horrid stockbrokers?"

The old woman had a very good memory. Too good. Iris smiled. "I wish I could adjust my schedule and visit when it's quieter."

Grace took the last cookie off a plate that had once held four. "I could spend weeks listening to you talk about Paris. Did your father go with you this time?"

Iris sipped the tea. It burned her lips. "No, he didn't."

"Will he be coming out with you one day soon? We do so want to meet him."

"He rarely gets the chance for pleasure trips."

"Why couldn't I have married a man like that? Paris, Rome, Florence. You're such a lucky girl. And is that dear little man still training my thoroughbreds—what is his name? No, don't tell me, I have a wonderful memory for names." She stared at the ceiling for a long moment. "He's bald, isn't he?"

"Horace Wells," Iris said.

"You know, I've never even seen them, except in the lovely pictures your father sends me." Grace fingered the edge of the photo. "And when the wives ask me, 'Where did you learn so much about horses?' I tell them, confidentially of course, that I have this darling friend whose father owns a stable. In Kentucky. They're absolutely frantic to buy some. And I'm always dying to tell them I've already bought *two*. But I can't. Taylor is so careful with my money. He'd be furious with me."

Iris pinched the handle of the cup. "The wives weren't serious, of course."

"Oh, but yes. And when I mentioned you had this marvelous trainer, Mr. Wells—" Her eyes lit. "You see, dear, I did remember his name." She savored the moment. "If I'd only known you'd be in town. We could have had a party."

"It might be fun to meet one or two of the girls before I leave." Iris glanced at her watch. New customers were always welcome. "But I'm not sure we have any more yearlings for sale just now."

"I wouldn't want to bother you, dear."

"It's no bother. After all, with your leaving, what will I do in Chicago all by myself?"

"Dreadful, isn't it." Grace shook her head. "My leaving today and your just getting in. From *Paris*. Oh, it's so un*fair*. I could give you Adele's number, you'd like her. But no, you're being such a help already by taking the check back to your father for me. In all the excitement of my trip, I might have forgotten." She looked at the horses in the photo as if they were children. "And then these poor dears might have starved."

The tea had cooled. "Perhaps we could call Adele," Iris said.

"I'm wonderful with names, dear, but I never remember numbers. I'll have my secretary phone it to you." Grace flagged the waiter. Not another dish of ice cream! "The check," she said. "Now don't tell Adele about my horses. You might tell her I *used* to own some. That's not like lying, is it." She stared into her lap. "And she'll hear all about Paris before I do. I almost want to cancel my trip."

Iris patted the old hand: it was cold and full of bumps. How many more years before she had to wear gloves to hide age spots? "The trip will be wonderful for you," she said. The fan began to clink and rattle again. A gray-haired man in a gray suit led a large group of men past the tall windows and down the fairway. "Isn't that Taylor?"

Grace felt for her glasses. "Not with that convention on, dear. He doesn't even come home until the entire thing is over."

"I'm sure it is," Iris said, nodding toward the windows.

"Where? Which table? Is he with a woman? A young one?"

"No, out there. On the golf course."

The bifocals went limp on the chain. "He hasn't played golf in years. Too old, dear."

"He isn't playing. Just walking."

Grace laughed. "Too old for that, too. Honestly, he'd drive to the bathroom if he could." She signed the bill the waiter set before her.

"You gave me a start, dear. He hasn't lost his looks, you know. I thought . . ."

A man in a white panama followed the others down the fairway. *That* man. Here! Iris smiled. "I must have been mistaken." She turned to keep the broad-brimmed hat in sight. He had a wonderful way of walking, so loose and confident. "I've only seen him once or twice. Never really met him."

"And just think of all the times you've been to our house," Grace said. "It's an absolute crime. An insult! But what can I do? Taylor is never there. Even when there is no stupid convention." She dropped the napkin on the empty ice cream dish, got up, and put the photo in her purse. "I'll give you a lift back to your hotel, dear."

"No, it's so noisy there. I think I'll relax out here and take a cab back later."

"Fine, dear. Tell everyone you're my guest. And sign my name for whatever you need."

Iris followed her into the lobby. "You won't forget about Adele's number."

"First thing when I get home, dear." Grace stopped near the door. "Do you really think I'll like it? I hear it's such an evil place. All those gamblers."

"Saratoga is a wonderful place." Iris kissed her on both cheeks. She envied the old woman—all that money, freedom. "You'll have a marvelous time."

"I'd write you, dear, but I never know where you'll be. All that traveling you do. So exciting!" She hugged Iris and went out and down the steps. A long black car pulled up. Grace got in and kept waving, her hand like a gloved claw in the window, until the limousine pulled away.

Iris breathed in to silence the gurgle in her empty stomach. She hadn't eaten lunch for appearance' sake. Business before food. She walked through a dark hall out to the patio. At the railing, she moved a chair into the shade of an umbrella rising from the middle of a table. Bathed in greens and browns, the gentle yellow of drying grass, the golf course stretched like a soft blanket over the knolls. Only a fool would expect those idiot conventioneers to buy a thoroughbred. They'd probably slaughter it and serve the meat for dinner. Tam Lin was where she should try her luck. A few quick sales and the stable would be back in fine shape. Then she wouldn't have to carry her father anymore. And what if the horses she was selling didn't exist? People like Grace could afford it. They'd never miss the money. No crime in that.

She lit a cigarette, ordered a glass of lemonade and a dish of vanilla ice cream, and told the waiter that she was a guest of Mrs. Grace North.

Rainbow lost the front nine, two down with two holes to play. The automatic press was on, doubling the bet. Ten thousand dollars down the drain. Murph was growing anxious. Rainbow yawned. He was getting his rhythm back. And the sun was still his ally, a shimmering orange in the hazy sky.

"Do it now." Murph bit into a sweet roll at the lunch stand, a little white shed that smelled of sauerkraut. "Can't keep scrambling like this."

Rainbow ordered a hot dog and orange juice and walked the kid over to a bench. "You don't know what you're talking about and unless you watch how I do it, you'll never learn. Look at North, clowning with his friends there. Thinks he's on top of the world. Let him enjoy it awhile. Only makes it better for us. Now watch." He yanked the brassie out of the bag. It had a crack in the clubface, the result of banging around on cars, trains, trollies. "Goddamn you, been swinging at rocks, ain't you." He shoved Murph and cocked the club. "Broke my favorite club."

"Jesus . . ." Murph dropped the roll. "You crazy?"

"Leave the kid alone." Jurgenson stepped in like a referee. "Don't go blaming him just because you're losing."

"He broke it." Rainbow showed him the crack. "Ready to split in two. Wait a minute. You put him up to this, didn't you, Jurgy."

Jurgenson made a fist. "I've had about enough of you."

"Suckered me," Rainbow said. "You and North. Gave me one of your boys and told him to bust up my clubs. Now that ain't fair."

"I didn't do nothing, mister." Fighting a smile, Murph peeked around Jurgenson. "I swear, I never touched that club."

"Been swinging at rocks, you little twerp." Rainbow reached for him, but Jurgenson caught his arm and held on.

"The boy hasn't swung a club all day," North said. "And I resent the implications of your remarks. Look for yourself, the club's old. And warped." He escorted Murph to the lunch stand. "Another pastry, young man?"

"You expect me to play without my favorite club?" Rainbow said.

"That's your problem." North walked onto the tee. "Mr. Jurgenson, it's your honor."

The all-American let go of Rainbow's sleeve and went to his bag. Murph came back with another roll. "I didn't bust it, mister. Honest."

Rainbow sighed. "Sorry, been a bad day, kid."

". . . Now?" Murph said in a whisper.

"Not yet." Rainbow took the brassie onto the tee and waited for Jurgenson to hit his third shot, then dropped a ball on the grass. "Like to make up for how I talked to you, kid. Have a swing."

"You mean it, mister?"

"And don't worry about my club. After I *win* this match, I'll buy a whole new set. Might even get you a pair of shoes."

The men in the gallery chuckled. Murph took the brassie and swung. At impact, the clubface broke in three: the largest piece chased the ball for a short distance down the fairway. Varnished string which had once held the clubhead to the shaft now unraveled like a strand of curly hair. A small block of wood dangled from the twine. Murph dipped his head. "Sorry."

"Got a real nice swing, kid." Rainbow hurled the club into the weeds. "Might even be a golfer one of these days. Now tee me up."

Murph scurried to the sand and water buckets and made a tee. Rainbow set his stance, cranked up with his driver, and knocked the ball down the middle. "Yes sir, Jurgy. You better watch out for this kid. He'll have your job in a couple of years."

More laughter from the gallery. Jurgenson glared. "I got a six-year-old daughter who hits it better than that."

"Have much trouble beating her?" Rainbow grinned and strode toward his ball.

"What good did that do?" Murph said. "I see you got him riled, but—"

"Let's just say I'm taking advantage of a God-given opportunity," Rainbow told him. "And don't worry, we won't have to wait much longer."

It happened on the twelfth hole, a short par 3 with a pond in front of it. Rainbow hit a spade mashie, stopping his ball ten feet from the cup, sinking the putt for a birdie. The first hole he had won all day.

And the sun was still high.

Jurgenson's long drives—all three of them every hole—grew shorter. His irons—all three of them every hole—no longer floated onto the greens. Even his putts—all of them—lost their authority. He began pushing his drives into the rough, playing out from behind trees, hitting short of every green. He could hardly walk. Rainbow turned the match around with birdies and pars and put the automatic press on Jurgenson. The men in the gallery couldn't believe it. Their boy was done.

And the sun was still high.

Rainbow quickened his pace, reaching his ball long before his opponent, who, at North's urging, was taking his time. At the sixteenth hole, Jurgenson stretched out on the bench beside the tee, eyes closed, arms hanging to the ground.

Rainbow grinned. "The first eighteen holes are mine, four-and-two. I win the back Nassau five-and-three. You're pressed for the second eighteen, Mr. North. And it looks like your pro can't take this Chicago heat. Might get sunstroke. Think he better pack it in? Looks real bad to me."

"It's unfair and you know it!" North stomped out his cigar. He must have been waiting for Rainbow to bring up the subject. Typical: a sportsman to the end. *Stupid.* "He's arm-weary from hitting three balls every hole."

"Sure would hate to see him forfeit," Rainbow said, "just when I'm starting to enjoy myself."

"I'll concede the match." North raised a finger. "If you agree to end at eighteen. That was, after all, my original wager with your sponsor."

"*Our* bet was thirty-six holes," Rainbow said. "Concede now and you pay off on everything. Doubled."

The gallery's murmur only added dimension to North's anger. "I won't stand for this."

"A man shouldn't make wagers he don't plan to honor, Mr. North."

The old man glared. "I can have you arrested, you know."

Rainbow started to laugh. "Bet you could. All right, you win. If you say it's unfair, I'll let Jurgy hit just one ball a hole in from here."

"That's white of you." North offered his hand. "I knew you weren't—"

"But—" Rainbow gripped the old man's hand. "I'll have to insist we redouble the stakes. After all, I'm making a big concession here."

North's palm was sweaty. He bowed his head. ". . . Done."

"Feeling generous, Jurgy." Rainbow mopped his brow with the towel. "Still got twenty holes left. You can have the honor. Hit a good one now." He joined Murph at the side of the tee. ". . . Now."

Jurgenson got off the bench. "I'll take you apart hole by hole."

Rainbow patted Murph's shoulder. "Hell, you couldn't even beat my caddy."

"Sonofabitch!" Jurgenson threw down his club and started across the tee. It took two men to restrain him. There was a little silence. North walked over:

"I'd be willing to wager that your caddy could *not* beat him, sir."

"Mr. North," Jurgenson said, "I don't need—"

"Shut up!" North used a cagy smile. "Well, Rainbow?"

"Only a figure of speech," Rainbow said. "Can't see changing the bet again. But this kid probably could beat that duffer."

Murph dropped the bag. "Mister, I ain't allowed to gamble."

"You just play and have a good time, son," North said. "We'll do the gambling. I'll give you odds, Rainbow. Two-to-one."

"You think I'm crazy?" Rainbow shook his head. "Come on, Jurgy. Hit!"

North inched closer. "Five-to-two . . . ?"

"We're betting ten grand a side now," Rainbow said. "I can't risk that much on a kid's chances. But damn if I don't think he could beat Jurgy."

"Three-to-one then." North raised his eyebrows. "He has a fine swing, we all saw that. And I'll give him one stroke each nine holes."

Rainbow laughed. The God-given opportunity had worked. "Look at him, he can't be more than fifteen. So we saw him take a swing. But you want him to play a professional? Getting a handicap of only one stroke a side?"

"Just think of the odds, though." The heat of fast calculations shone behind North's eyes. "And Jurgy—er, Bob—here is tired. *Very* tired."

"Feeling fine, Mr. North," Jurgenson said.

"Shut *up!*" The old man coughed. "What do you shoot, son?"

"Had an eighty-five once," Murph said. "But not from these championship tees. And I ain't allowed to gamble, I tell you."

"An eighty-five?" North rocked on his heels. "That's remarkable for your age. I'll give him *three* strokes a side. Fair enough?"

"How do I know this ain't a setup?" Rainbow said. "I felt all along he was working for you."

"Never seen the boy before in my life," North told him.

"It's the truth, mister." Murph didn't look up. "Honest."

Rainbow rubbed his chin. "I'll need a guarantee."

North frowned as if stung by a wasp. ". . . Guarantee?"

"A big banker like you ought to know what I mean. I want the choice of hitting two shots each hole. And if I see the kid throwing the match, I can take over anytime I like."

"This is ridiculous," Jurgenson said. "I won't play a . . . a caddy."

"You'll play anyone I goddamn tell you to." North drew a slow breath. "All right, Rainbow. Are we agreed?"

"Ten grand a side at three-to-one's thirty grand." Rainbow fanned himself with his hat. "With a press on, that's sixty grand a nine-hole Nassau, and sixty for the match. Hell, that comes to a hundred-eighty grand!" He squinted into the sun. "Did I get that right?"

"Precisely." The old man put his hand out like a beggar.

"Helluva lot of money, Mr. North."

"But Rainbow," the smile was ruthless, "it's only money."

Biting off the grin, Rainbow glanced at Murph. "Want to play this duffer?"

"But he's a pro, sir!"

"That don't mean he's any good. I'm giving you a big lead. Hell, you could shoot straight triple bogies and still beat this hacker."

"Oh, I think I could make three over par each hole, sir." Murph scuffed his toes in the grass. "But see, I ain't allowed to gamble."

"You won't be, kid," Rainbow said. It was the truth. Even North agreed.

Murph shrugged and stared at Jurgenson's big white golf bag. "Could I maybe use them new steel-shafted clubs?"

"Of course," North said.

"Hold on!" Jurgenson put his hands on his hips. "These are custom-built!"

"I said he could *use* them!" North gnashed his teeth, a grunt escaped through his nose. "He'll be careful, won't you, son. Now, are we agreed, Rainbow?"

"Ten thousand a Nassau, the same for each eighteen," Rainbow said. "At three-to-one odds." He recounted all the special provisions, but stopped short of taking the old man's hand. "What about the tees? The kid's never played from the back markers."

North let out a lot of air. "He can hit from the regular tees."

"And you give him a three-stroke handicap each nine, right?"

"Yes, yes. Are we a*greed?*"

"Ordinarily," Rainbow said, "I never take this kind of bet. But if it suits you, I won't say no." He shook North's hand. Applause from the gallery.

Murph got a wood tee and walked to Jurgenson. "Could I have the driver, sir?" Jurgenson let the club fall and walked away. Murph took it to the white tees, 15 yards ahead of the blue championship markers, teed up, and took practice swings. "Feels real nice," he called back. He got ready and swung. The clubhead swept over the grass and into the ball— *swish-click*. The drive screamed down the center, bounding to a good lie 220 yards out. He leapt into the air, jogged back, and gave the club to Jurgenson. "Thanks, sir. Finest one I ever swung."

"Good shot," Rainbow said. "You can make *seven* from there."

This time the club members didn't laugh. They held their applause until Jurgenson's drive finished alongside Murph's. Rainbow grinned: "Big drive, Jurgy. Gonna give this little kid a run for his money, are you?"

Jurgenson stormed off, leading the gallery toward the distant white spots that lay on the fairway like aspirins on a billiard table. Too bad Curtis wasn't here to see this. Too bad there wasn't one person along to root for him, someone like that beauty in the white Packard: she'd lay down at his feet once she saw the truth of this. He lost his grin and grabbed Murph: "What's the idea of using his clubs?"

"Steel shafts," the kid said. "You see how good I hit that drive?"

"They weren't made for your swing. Haul my bag around, too, just to be safe." He got his .45 from the ball pouch, stuck it in his belt, then hoisted the bag onto Murph's shoulder and said, "Let's go, champ."

10

Like a gaggle of geese, strung out in a V, the golfers, their caddies, and the gallery of men came down the fairway of the home hole, number eighteen. Iris put her newspaper on the table, shaded her eyes. The golfer in white plus fours had a stately stride. Near a copse of trees, he hit his ball onto the front of the clubhouse green. The applause blowing over the grass sounded like whips cracking in the distance. The army of men started walking again.

She picked up the paper. At the baseball box score in the center of the page, she ran her finger down the Saint Louis lineup to the catcher who batted eighth: Wobers. *Ernie.* In the columns beside his name: a four and three zeros. Four times at bat, no hits, no runs scored, no runs batted in. He was still the hitless wonder. But she missed him, his laugh. His touch. His . . .

A ball landed nearby and bounded into the bunker next to the green. For a moment, it looked as though the caddy in overalls had hit it. The lanky golfer in the panama and the dull white suit seemed to be in a hurry, walking alone well ahead of the pack. The army closed ranks around Taylor North: the king and his court, following two knights and squires over a tournament field to the castle where, in the royal box, a princess sat, ready to bestow her scarf on the victor's lance. Only charging steeds festooned with armor and plumes were missing.

She let the waiter take the empty ice cream dish and the newspaper. The box score disappeared under his arm, and for an instant, Iris wanted it back. The golfer in the panama had just reached the bunker. His light brown hair needed a trim, his suit a pressing. His smile was thin, yet it threw a glint into his blue eyes. A fascinating smile. He kept looking from the ball in the sand to the flag stick on the green. He told the barefoot caddy in overalls, who arrived ahead of the gallery, "Carry it to the hole, kid. Leave yourself an uphill putt."

The red-haired boy got a club from the other caddy, dropped his own bag, and disappeared into the bunker now ringed with men. Everyone stood still. No one spoke. Something flashed above their heads—a golf club?—white sand shot up and showered the green, a ball floated down and ran a few feet past the flag stick. The men applauded.

For a caddy?

The golfer in plus fours looked like Douglas Fairbanks. With a graceful stroke, he nudged his putt down a little valley of green. The gallery's oohs and ahs grew loud, then died. So did the ball: on the lip of the cup.

"That's good, Jurgy." The man in the panama kicked the ball across the green to the other golfer. "Even you can make that one."

Iris covered her laugh. He was daring. Fascinating.

There was more applause when the barefoot boy sank his putt. Dirt caked his hair. No, those were weeds! In his hair? At the edge of the green, he shouldered the bag and followed the golfer in the panama down the trail. The rest of the men moved after North into the Men's Grill like mice after cheese. Wind sang over the empty fairways. Iris sipped lemonade, rapped her fingers on the railing. No one had noticed her.

"I'm telling you," the barefoot caddy was saying, "his clubs is fine. I don't need to haul these things around."

The golfer in the panama didn't say anything. He walked away from the practice green near the grill, down the path to the first tee. The red-haired boy left his bag at the low rail beside the green, grabbed a towel from the strap, and ran after him. The other men came out of the grill, but Taylor North was not among them. Some carried paper cups which halfway down the path they tossed away. Ice spilled onto the grass, wind turned the cups in circles. The handsome golfer had changed his shirt. He swaggered toward the tee and vanished behind bushes. The gallery stared in his direction until the *slap-crack* of his drive made their heads swivel. The men clapped. The barefoot boy hit next. More applause, but scattered like the laughs for an old joke in a vaudeville house. Before the ball landed, the golfer in the panama was on the march. The fairway filled with walkers. In no time, they moved out of sight and the sound of their voices got lost in the coils of the woods.

On the lunch bill, Iris signed "Mrs. Grace North." A narrow hall led to the Men's Grill: white tablecloths, climbing plants, flowers. She had expected wood and brass. At a table near the bar, Taylor North toyed with a telephone. Waiters in white coats with green epaulets made the rounds to other tables where men were eating, drinking, talking. Iris pushed through swing doors like those of a western saloon. The talking stopped, forks halted just short of open mouths, glasses froze in midlift as if to toast her. She smiled. No one smiled back.

A waiter hustled out from behind the bar. "You're not allowed in here, miss. Club rules."

"I only wanted a cup of tea," Iris said.

"I'll be happy to get it for you, but you can't drink it in here."

"Where's the Lady's Grill?"

"There is none, miss." The waiter took her by the elbow.

Iris yanked free. "I happen to be a guest of Mrs. Grace North!" It was said.

"Please wait outside." The waiter pulled one door flap open. "And how do you take your tea, miss?"

"Never touch it." Iris shoved through the other flap. It kept flapping until she reached the stairs to the lobby. Down the corridor, someone called, "Miss!" She didn't turn around. She went up the stairs wearing a smile.

"Miss, wait!" Footsteps beat the carpet. Taylor North hurried through shadows. "You said you were a guest of my wife? I'm—"

"Yes, I know." Iris turned at the landing and lost her smile. "We met once. At your home, Mr. North."

"We did?" He looked past her to the lobby. "She isn't here, is she?"

Iris folded her arms. "You don't remember me at all, do you. I'm sorry if I violated any club rules. Excuse me."

"No, wait." He climbed two steps. "Is my wife . . . here?"

"She left hours ago."

North grinned. Perfect teeth. Probably false. "Sorry I don't remember meeting you, but I meet so many people every day and . . . and I feel like an old fool not remembering a face as lovely as yours." He offered his hand. "Allow me to make amends, miss . . . ?"

She came down the stairs and took his hand. "Iris Winslow."

He squeezed her fingers. "Why, of course, Iris! Grace has mentioned you but I never paid any . . . er, you're not at all like the rest of her friends. Have you seen our patio yet? Splendid view." He led her down the hall, opened the door, and followed her into the sunshine. "I'm sure Grace would want me to show you some old-fashioned hospitality." He helped her into a chair near the railing, then snapped his fingers. The waiter left his newspaper on the bar and came running over. "Iced coffee for me," North said. "And what would you like, my dear?"

My dear? Maybe this was working too well. But worth it if he bought *two* horses. "Hot tea," Iris said, opening her purse. Matches and a small photo of two yearlings came out with her pack of cigarettes.

North grabbed the matches, lit one, cupped his hands around the flame, and held it out. "Thoroughbreds, aren't they?"

"Pardon me?" She took the light, glanced at the photo. It was a copy of the one she had given Grace. "Oh, these. Yes, they are."

"Beautiful at that age. Are they yours?"

"I'd like to say no, but I'm afraid they are."

"You don't want to own them?"

"Exactly. I'm doing a favor. For my father. He owns Majestic Farms in Louisville. These yearlings were to have been sold to a man here in Chicago, but he changed his mind. I was on my way home when I thought I'd drop in on Grace."

"Not to interest her in horses, I hope," North said. "I've tried for years to get her to the racetrack. She probably won't even go while we're in Saratoga. She thinks the only reason people go there is for the mineral baths." He sat back and laughed.

The waiter brought out a crowded tray, set everything on the table, and left in a rush as though afraid to linger in North's presence. But the old man's face was soft, like the wave in his silver hair. He didn't look like someone to be feared. That was probably his secret weapon.

Iris put the teacup to her lips, let the steam rise around her nose. "Are you a racing fan, Mr. North?"

"Who isn't?" He glanced at his watch. "I must make a few quick phone calls. When I get back, I may just let you talk me into buying those yearlings." He leaned forward and winked. "I expect to earn a little pocket money this afternoon. Out on the golf course. Now don't you go away, I'll only be a minute." Flashing his best smile, he walked into the clubhouse.

The photo stirred in the breeze. Yearlings were beautiful: so gangly and inept, yet full of energy and the hint of power which would fall upon them suddenly as if dropped into their sleep one night. After that, they would never be gangly again, never truly playful. They would lose all that—and gain mystery. And Iris would love them even more then.

Even if she didn't own them.

Wind pulled her cigarette smoke over the railing. The sun had a few feet to drop before it reached the treetops. That golfer in the panama was probably making a fool out of his opponent. Simply fascinating. She wanted to walk out there and find him, watch him. But she sat back and turned her cup. By the time North got back, the tea would be cool enough to drink. And that was worth waiting for.

Leaves rustled and behind the trees the sky was turning grapefruit pink.

And the ball rolled into the dead center of the cup.

No applause.

Murph picked the ball out of the hole, laid the putter on the white bag beside the green, and offered his hand to Jurgenson. Head low, the all-American marched off.

"Never seen anything like it," Rainbow told the men in the gallery. "Who'd of believed a young squirt could play so good."

One man was squinting and shaking his head. "I'd say the boy was a ringer."

"Then he'd be Mr. North's ringer," Rainbow said. "I didn't ask for this bet."

But the gallery was already on the move, heading across the rock bridge over the little creek that passed the fourteenth green and wound up the fairway. The men were going home: the match was over. Under the darkening sky, white shirts turned gray, the brown of tree trunks quickened black. Nothing looked alive.

"Maybe I should have held back a little." Murph rubbed dirt and weeds out of his hair. "Didn't have to close Jurgy out five-and-four. He never had a chance as tired as he was. And giving away three strokes a side."

Rainbow stared down at the bridge. "Don't you ever get cute on me. You play with your head, not your heart."

Murph stuck both hands into pockets already lumpy with golf balls. "Sometimes what we do just don't feel right, though."

"Feeling right's got nothing to do with it. C'mon, it's getting dark. And we got a paycheck to collect. After tomorrow's match, we'll be in the big time, riding *The Twentieth-Century Limited* to New York."

Murph stopped. "What the hell you mean, tomorrow?"

"Didn't I tell you? After our next match, we're going to Saratoga."

"What next match? They'll kill us for sure if we try to sucker them again."

Rainbow hardened his stare. "We never take anybody. Just beat them in a fair proposition. Keeping a rightful edge like any sane person."

"I ain't gonna help you do it again." Murph turned in a circle. "And I ain't wearing these fucking overalls no more." He took out a pack of cigarettes, lit one. "And I ain't putting no more dirt in my hair neither. Feel like a goddamn fool."

"That's the whole point." Rainbow said. "That's why it works. . . ."

"Yeah, well maybe I'll start hustling for myself then, instead of going around like this. I'm good enough to make my own living at it."

"You're good enough, kid. But you're not ready. They'd eat you alive."

"Says who?"

Putting a fist in his pocket, Rainbow walked toward the grove of trees. Murph took big strides to catch up. "And why're we going to Saratoga?"

"I want you to go down to Union Station and get two private drawing rooms."

"But we're rich now, we could buy a Packard. It'd be real nice driving, just the two of us. . . . I hate trains. . . ."

Rainbow pushed past the low branches of a pine. "Then get one drawing room. You can walk."

"Damn it, ain't I got nothing to say about it?"

"No." Rainbow walked into a clearing. But no footsteps followed him. He turned. No Murph. Cigarette smoke filtered through the branches at the edge of the grove. "C'mon out of there, kid. It's a long walk in."

Silence.

"I don't want to get caught out here once that sun sets," Rainbow said.

More silence.

"All right then." He raked the brim of his panama. "Camp out in the woods for all I care."

"You can't keep treating me like shit," Murph said, hidden by pine needles. "I ain't one of your pigeons. I'm supposed to be your partner."

Rainbow stripped leaves off a branch. "We're almost there, kid. After tomorrow, we'll be riding so high nobody'll be able to touch us."

"North'll have us locked up. He can do it, you know."

"He'll insist on a rematch, not me," Rainbow said. "Now c'mon out of there, it's getting chilly." And the woods were getting dark.

"Well, I'm the one with no shirt on," Murph told him.

Rainbow took off his jacket, handed it into the trees.

"Don't want it," Murph said.

"Jesus Christ, will you get the hell out of them trees!"

Murph came out rubbing his arms. "Gonna catch pneumonia."

"Quit that talk." Rainbow draped the jacket over the kid's shoulders. "I'll have to put this back on before we get to the clubhouse." He patted the .45 in his belt. "Can't let those yokels get nervous."

"Why do you tape the handle, anyways?"

"Better grip." Rainbow yanked the cigarette from Murph's lips, crushed it out, and started up the fairway. "Bad for your health. After dinner, while I'm seeing our sponsor, you see if they got a train leaving in the afternoon for New York."

"I'll be sick the whole way."

"You never been on a real train. Might be you'll like it."

"I'm sick just thinking about it."

"Then don't think about it."

"Why the hell are we going to Saratoga? And don't say for the races."

That was what Rainbow was going to say. He didn't answer. He kept walking.

"Aw, shit . . ." Murph stomped through the bunker at the crease in the dog leg. "And what if Old Cal ain't there?"

"Then we'll look someplace else."

"Know what one guy told me?" Murph said. "Told me we was looking for a dead man."

"He's not dead." Rainbow wasn't going to be cheated out of killing Old Cal. ". . . Not yet."

"Well nobody's seen him in years. And we looked everywhere." Murph clutched the jacket to his neck. "You aim to kill him, don't you."

Gonna blow his head clean off his shoulders. "Quit talking nonsense."

"That's why you carry that gun, ain't it. So you can kill him."

"I carry it for protection," Rainbow said. "Lot of dishonest people out there." He reached the crest of the knoll. Below, the clubhouse patio was noisy with waiters dressing tables for dinner. Chandeliers in the ballroom cast an uneven luster on the bushes lining the home hole. "Put my bag in the car and wait for me in the parking lot."

Murph sat next to a bush. "How come I never know the plan?"

"I just told you what we're gonna do."

"Yeah, that's what I mean. You just told me."

Pulling the towel from the strap in Murph's overalls, Rainbow spread it on the grass and sat. "In there is a guy with nothing better to do than give his money away. Now—the plan is—you and me are gonna take as much of that cash as the sonofabitch wants to hand out. Any more questions?"

"It ain't gonna work this time, Rainbow."

"Hell, they'll insist on it, all I'm gonna do is agree with them."

Murph sucked on a blade of grass. "You can't beat Jurgy."

"He's not Walter Hagen, kid."

"I ain't Hagen neither," Murph said, "and you can't beat me."

"Hell, I taught you the fine points of the game, didn't I?"

Murph was staring at the sky as if he wished he were someplace else. "You're gonna bet the whole thing, ain't you. Everything we got."

"That's what bankrolls are for, kid."

"You're not right in the head, you know that? Jurgy's gonna *beat* you."

"No chance," Rainbow said. "I got me too good a partner for that."

Murph rolled on his side. "They're holding the PGA Championship here, at Olympia Fields. I want to stay and see it."

"You're gonna give up Saratoga just to watch a golf tournament? And I'm the one who's not right in the head?"

"I wanna see if I can play with them guys," Murph said. "Or if hustling's all I'm good for."

Rainbow swallowed his laugh and stood. "You'd have to play twenty years on the tour to make the kind of money we did today. No point in it, kid."

"I just wanna see, that's all. If we was pros, Rainbow, might be they'd invite us back sometimes. The way it is now, we can't go back to noplace."

Rainbow cleared his throat. "I can't keep North waiting much longer."

Murph gave him the jacket and picked up the towel. "You better get at least two strokes a side for tomorrow. And don't set the match too early. I want to see you hit on the shag field first. You was lunging at the ball all day."

"Sure thing . . . partner." Rainbow reached out to put an arm on the kid's shoulder, but Murph jogged down the bank and hauled the golf bag from the practice green to the parking lot. Fast clouds swept over the sky to steal the remaining light and swirl it up to first stars. Rainbow buttoned his jacket, cocked his panama, and walked down the knoll to the Men's Grill.

The men were clustered in small groups about the room. Jurgenson was probably still in the showers, afraid to show his face. Alone at a table by the bar, Taylor North stared at the check lying in front of him. Word had traveled fast. The old man was ready to pay.

Rainbow sat in the chair across from him. "Seems only right to give you a chance to win some of it back, sir."

"I think not," North said. "Perhaps I should deliver the check myself. I'll be seeing Will Broder tonight after dinner."

"Part of my job to collect it for him." Rainbow slid the paper out from under North's stiff fingers. The check was neatly written, dated, and signed. Each zero had a diagonal line through it: they looked funny that way. All four of them—$180,000. "Pleasure to have met you, sir. You're a true sportsman." Rainbow made it a quick handshake. He pushed away from the table. "And I feel obliged to say something I felt since the fifth hole today. Find yourself another pro. Old Jurgy ain't got what we call the competitive edge. To be honest, Mr. North, I think I could beat your boy left-handed." He touched his hat brim and walked toward the saloon doors, grinning and counting each step.

"Rainbow . . . ?" North's voice came in the middle of step number eight.

Rainbow worked his grin into a squint and turned.

"You weren't serious." North was out of his chair. "About playing him—left-handed?"

Rainbow shrugged and walked back to the table.

Under the trees at the back of the parking lot, bare feet stuck out of the driver's window of the old Model T.

"Took you long enough," Murph said. "How many strokes you get?"

Rainbow opened the door. "Five over the whole match. We're on for seventy-five thousand. Start this thing, I'm hungry."

Murph set the ignition, got out, turned the crank. The engine wheezed and finally caught. What would it be like to own a real car? A fancy white Packard. With a beautiful woman in back. Rainbow watched the kid push the car out of the trees and race back behind the wheel.

"Damn reverse pedal went out three weeks ago," Murph said, feeding in gas. The car lurched forward with a sputter. Headlamps flickered on, the motor growled past the clubhouse and down the twisting road to stone pillars at the main gate. "Almost wish North hadn't of gone for it, though."

"Hell, the old goat couldn't resist." Rainbow nestled in the seat. Night wind smelled sweet. "Sometimes, kid, you got to let people have their own way."

11

Behind twin doors down at the end of the hall, hoots and hollers mixed with the sound of applause. The sign in the corner smelled of paint, the same blood red as on the big poster in the lobby: ACMP AWARDS BANQUET. Inside, someone far away began to speak. Rainbow opened the door. Men in red jackets and cardboard hats sat elbow to elbow at long tables. On a stage, the speaker stood under the glare of a spotlight, his eyes following the slow arc of a dinner roll as it sailed across the room. Forks banged on plates, another roll cut the air. Rainbow tapped a conventioneer on the shoulder:

"Know where Mr. Will Broder's sitting?"

The conventioneer hurled a roll into the far corner and yelled, "Hey, Will! You know this guy?"

At the head of the last table, Will Broder got up and lumbered down the lane between table and wall. He led Rainbow out the door into the hall. "What took you so long? I called the club around six and they said you were still out on the course?"

Rainbow unfolded the check, stretched it between his hands.

Will inched closer and squinted. "This a joke or what?"

"No joke. And we're on for another seventy-five grand tomorrow."

"A joke, right?" Will held the check up to the light. "Holy shit." He turned in a daze and punched his thigh. "North will ruin me for this."

"You got it wrong," Rainbow said. "He's not mad."

"This was supposed to be a little five-thousand Nassau." Will gulped and started talking to the ceiling. "Not . . . this."

"You told me this was the big one. I went after it."

"You don't understand. North can stop my business credit because of this."

"So get another banker."

"It doesn't work that way. Without North, I'd never get to the slaughterhouse."

"Maybe after tomorrow," Rainbow said, "you won't need him so bad."

"You idiot." Will paced the floor and talked to the ceiling again. "A goddamn yokel's going to wreck my business. Jesus, and I told North I'd see him tonight. You'll see him for me and call off tomorrow's match."

"I can't do that," Rainbow said. "I gave him my word. We shook on it."

"I'm your sponsor and what I say goes. It's off!"

Rainbow got out a pen. "Maybe you better sign this check over to me now. Had to work real hard just so you could get your seventy percent. Of my winnings."

"I got a lot of expenses," Will said. "Besides, without me and my contacts, you'd still be playing for nickels and dimes. Now you tell old man North it's off for tomorrow, understand?"

Inside the banquet room, there was a metallic crash, then a lot of applause and cheering. Rainbow held out the pen. "Sign. Then I'll tell him you want the match called off. You got my word on that."

A door to the banquet room opened. Someone inside called, "Hey, Will! They're announcing Man of the Year. Don't you want to hear?"

"Be right in." Will scribbled on the back of the check and waved the ink dry. "I'm not signing it over, just endorsing it. You hold it until we go to the bank in the morning. We'll split it then. And be there at eleven-thirty sharp."

Rainbow took back the check. The signature on it was barely legible, the mark of a man in a hurry: bank tellers always studied it as if deciphering a code. He put the check away. "How do I find North?"

"He eats dinner at the Steak House every night," Will said. "And no funny stuff. Just call off that match. And tell him I'm sick. That's why I can't see him tonight."

"You're sick," Rainbow said. "Got it."

Applause thundered within the banquet room. Someone called, "Hey Will! It's you! You won it!" Two conventioneers burst out, grabbed Will by the arm, slapped his back, and pulled him into the room. The door closed.

"A yokel, am I?" Rainbow told the burnished wood. "Well you and me is through, Broder. Man of the Year, my ass." He kicked the sign in the corner and walked up the hall to the lobby. He was in business for himself. At last.

It was the head of a longhorn steer, tan against a field of black, one of those clean drawings that drained the life out of the subject. The inside of the menu was the same: more dead steer, cut this way or that, cooked to order, with potatoes—without potatoes, there will be a five percent service charge added to your bill, please do not tip the waiters, thank you, the management. On the walls: branding irons and spurs now rusted and brittle. Hard benches faced oak tables, where the crumbs of the last customer had been trapped between the slats. This was Taylor North's kind of place: what wasn't dull was fake, what wasn't fake was silvered by hard light; and with so little difference between the entrées, there was no chance for a mistake.

Iris drank water to wash down the charcoal taste of her charred filet mignon. "It's always better to have more than one. As insurance against injuries. They have such delicate legs."

North splashed catsup on his porterhouse and cut close to the bone. "I'd have to see them, of course."

"Of course, Taylor." She laid the photo of the horses on the table.

"I meant in person. All things considered, my dear, this may not be the best time for me to buy. My expectations on the golf course fell a bit short today."

"You didn't lose, did you?"

"I lost," he said. "Warm in here, isn't it."

"These colts are from a line of champions." She scattered her food on the plate to make it look emptier. "And yearling prices are rising so fast."

"Yes, everything's going up," North said. "I don't know how some people get along these days. Even a man without a dollar is fifty cents better off than he was two years ago."

Iris smiled: he sounded just like her father. "I never thought you worried about money, Taylor."

"That, my dear, is all a banker ever does." He took out his watch. "I was supposed to see some friends at the Palmer House. But I don't feel up to that. A great pity." He curled his fingers around hers. "I'd be the envy of every man there with you on my arm. Still, I hate to end our evening so soon. You haven't seen my waterfall yet, have you?"

"Pardon me . . . ?"

"I put it in this winter," North said. "Not me, of course. Some little Oriental. Right in the middle of a snowstorm, he comes to the door and says he wants to build me a waterfall out by the creek. Says he'll do it for nothing, it would give him pleasure. Took him close to a week. God only knows where he found all those rocks. But he didn't steal a thing."

"And you let him build it?" Iris said. "For free?"

"I gave him five dollars. He didn't even say thank you." North leaned in close. "I have some very special brandy left over from before the Great War. That's the way to see it, my dear—under stars, with a warm feeling running through your body. If I were younger, I'd say it was romantic."

She found her smile. "I'd love to see it, Taylor."

He stroked her fingers, paid the check, and slid off the bench like a man of twenty-five. Past the wagon wheel outside, he took the night deep into his lungs and led the way to the pitch-black parking lot. His black limousine was not the same car he had used to drive Iris back from Tam Lin this afternoon and it was not the same car Grace had left in either. He must have a stable of them. He opened the rear door, waking the chauffeur. Iris got in and sat back against the cool leather.

"Mr. North!" The voice came from the edge of the lot. Someone was running over stones. "I need to talk to you." The footsteps got louder. Through the rear window, the outline of a broad-brimmed hat, flat and white, stood out against the trees. It was the golfer from Tam Lin.

"Not now," North said. "I'm in a hurry."

"But it's about tomorrow's match, sir. Broder wants to call it off."

"What?" North shut the door and stepped to the tree line. The voices got muffled. Iris rolled down her window, turned on the seat. Draped in shadows, the mane of silver hair and the white hat seemed to move independently of bodies.

"I won't stand for this," North was saying. "I have a right to in*sist*."

"Feel miserable about it myself, sir," said the golfer in the panama. "After all, I gave you my word."

"Tell Broder I won't let him out of it."

"Well, sir, they just made him Man of the Year and I guess he feels he don't have to do anything he don't want to now."

North laughed. "Broder? Man of the Year? If he doesn't let this match come off, I'll stop payment on my check."

"And I wouldn't blame you," the golfer said. "I told him, 'Broder, I'm through with your kind.' And I meant it. So if it's all the same with you, sir, I'll play Jurgy tomorrow like we agreed. And stake myself."

"Well," North said, "that's a bit irregular. You're not a member of Tam Lin and—"

"Yes, sir, I know it, it's irregular as hell. And to show good faith, I'll give you back your check if I lose. We can settle up any differences after that. Now it's all I got in this world, but I'll risk it, 'cause if I don't, that one hundred eighty thousand you lost today won't mean a thing to me. No sir, it'd just rot in my pocket and I'd be sick knowing you thought I ran off without giving you a fair chance to win it back."

The golfer in the panama spoke like a dynamo, never letting up, twisting his words around homespun charm and all that nonsense about *his word* and *honor*. He was perfect. Iris giggled. But $180,000? On a golf match?

"It'd be best if we didn't let Broder know," said the golfer. "Far as I'm concerned, he's got no part of this anymore."

"Done," North said. Stones crunched under his feet. "I'll see you tomorrow. Seven A.M."

"Say, you wouldn't be headed back to town, would you? I let my cab go soon as I got here."

"Sorry," North told him. "I'm going in the opposite direction." He got in the car, closed the door, rapped on the glass partition between the front and back seats, and said "Home" into a funnel attached to a tube. The engine started, headlights came on. The limousine rolled over pebbles, past the golfer in the panama who was walking back toward the restaurant. Without looking into the car, he held up a hand and let it drop to his side.

Perfect, Iris thought. She rolled up her window. "Who was that?"

"No one." North patted her hand as if it were a lapdog. "Just a little business, my dear."

"Do you think you'll win tomorrow, Taylor?"

"I always win."

He probably did. But not tonight.

The limousine pulled onto the highway. To one side, thin clouds held the city's glow, but ahead, the night had fashioned space for itself, black and quiet, without moon or stars.

"I always admire confidence," Iris said. And she let him squeeze her hand.

It might have been the heady aroma of night wind off the lake, or the warm brandy, or all that effort spent in playing the role of host-seducer. Whatever it was, it had worked fast. North was asleep. His hair bunched like a nimbus of silver on the purple velvet of the chaise longue. The gold watch chain looping across his vest seemed to be holding his stomach together. He looked dead.

Iris found the light switch: the veranda went dark. A floodlight at the edge of the roof continued to send a wide beam over the lawn toward a stand of oaks. It was quiet out there. The creek was dry with summer, only a trickle made it down the pile of rocks of the waterfall, which glistened with dew and stood like an agate of color— browns and grays, pale yellows, all blending as if the stones had become liquid and oozed into place. She went inside and closed the French doors behind her, leaving her brandy snifter on the bar. She tugged the thin length of tapestry against the wall. Far off in the bowels of mortared stone and timber, a tiny bell would be ringing, a single pair of eyes would watch it shake, and someone would jog up the service stairs, hustle through the halls, turning corners like a rat in a maze, knock at the big doors that sealed the room, step inside, put heels together like a soldier, and say, "Yessir!"

There was no knock. The door groaned open. The butler must have been sleeping, because the chauffeur walked in and said, "Yes ma'am?"

Iris hid her smile and got her purse. Poor Taylor had been so worried that, with all his other business pressures, he couldn't take on a new hobby like thoroughbreds. A hobby?

"Please take me home," she said.

The chauffeur led her through the main foyer and out to the car. The leather seats felt cold and stiff. The big car sped down Lake Shore Drive, past the imitation Rhine castles and French fortresses of the Gold Coast, into a tangle of lesser streets that snaked to the curb in front of the Palmer House. The hotel doorman looked like a sad pear with tired eyes, looked willing to let anyone beat him into the ground because he couldn't afford to lose the tips: he had that kind of face.

Like Daddy's.

Iris picked up her key and a note from Grace North at the front desk, then walked to the elevators. Whooping and cheering leaked out of the private room down the hall. And someone had scribbled on the lobby poster again: same message. No one had come to erase it yet.

In her suite, she opened all the windows, turned on the fan, and put Grace's message in her purse. The old woman had not forgotten: the promised phone number had arrived. Iris turned off the light. The glow outside got brighter, like an aurora, alive with twinkles and flashes. Down there, in the Levee, tuxedos and evening gowns would still be jammed into nightclubs. Dancing, drinking, and jazz would go on through the morning hours. A lady couldn't go down there alone, not to mix with the rest of the unescorted women—the prostitutes.

She buried her smile in the pillow. It might have been fun to keep Taylor North awake, to see if he had the courage, if he had enough life left in him to make a pass. A big sale to him would have put her closer to the end of all this nonsense, closer to freedom. One hundred and eighty thousand dollars on a golf match, but not a cent to spare on thoroughbreds. *The old fool.* And the golfer in the panama was probably going to win. Why couldn't she meet someone like that? Someone exciting who also had money. Why did all the best men have to be poor? Someday soon that might not matter. It meant everything now. Letting Taylor North touch her made about as much sense as going down to the Levee did. There was nothing there, not for her. Lights and glitter, nothing real, not even the people. They were frauds down there, fakes worse than the kind she was, because those people didn't know what they were. "At least you know exactly what you are," she whispered. But what was wrong with leading men on? Nothing ever happened, she made certain of that, she never lost her heart on rich old fools. Most women did a lot more and got a lot less in return. Some of them wasted their whole lives on men. Iris couldn't afford that luxury. Yet. How long would she have to wait to give herself to someone she could love? A man like Ernie. Like the man in the panama? No, that was silly, she didn't know anything about him. She smiled. She knew everything about him.

But she wasn't going to think about that now, she was going to keep her mind on business. Had it been a mistake to wear the blue dress tonight? Blue wasn't her lucky color. Tomorrow she would wear green.

12 ————————————————

Bad dream. This one had a bugle in it. Rainbow threw back the bed covers and rubbed his eyes. The bugle started playing again. He tossed the pillow at the lump in the blanket on the floor. "What the hell is that?"

A red mane lifted off the hardwood. Murph squinted as if he hoped to see by listening. "The trumpet player. He always starts now."

First light hit the window in blotches. Outside, tin roofs bounced rays into a cloudless sky. The wind was up. The air slipping under the sash was already warm and soaked with traffic noise. Something big and iron clattered in the distance: the el. Finishing one scale, the trumpet began another.

"Somebody ought to ram that thing down his throat," Rainbow said.

"Kind of nice if you ask me. Like he was serenading." Murph burrowed into the pillow, pulled the blanket over his head. "Besides, if you wasn't such a miser, we could of stayed in a good place. One with two beds."

"We're backing ourselves today," Rainbow said. "Got to cut corners till we're fixed right." The floor held a chill. He opened the door, called down the hall: "Knock it off for Chrissake!"

The trumpet stopped on a high note, then blared: an old, romantic melody, notes dripping out as though coaxed by regret.

Rainbow slammed the door. He got dressed and went down the hall to the bathroom. By the time he finished washing and shaving, the trumpet had stopped for good. Traffic made all the noise now. He walked back to his room, passing a thin man in a bathrobe who leaned on a cane and never took his eyes off the floor. This hotel was not only cheap, it was full of freaks.

Murph had moved from the floor to the bed. He didn't want breakfast, he wanted to sleep. And he was angry that Rainbow had set today's golf match so early.

"Bad enough us only getting a half-hour on the shag field as it is." His words sounded tinny, as if trapped inside a metal box. "And don't say you wasn't warned."

There were more words, but Rainbow had stopped listening. He stuck the .45 in his belt, made sure North's check was in his jacket pocket, and grabbed his panama. "Maybe I'll have wheat cakes with ice cream on them. Wonder what ice cream tastes like in the morning?"

"Quit it would you," Murph said. "I got to get my sleep."

"Plenty of time for that on the train tonight."

"Aw, Jesus." The ball under the sheets rocked back and forth. "Ain't it enough you sent me to the wrong station? Had me up half the night. Why'd you go and say it now for?"

". . . What?"

"Train."

"You got to get over that, kid. We'll be doing a lot of railroading from now on."

"They keep running into each other." Murph stuck his head out of the covers. "I seen pictures once. Everything splintered up and twisted. Know what they said? Said the bodies was MANGLED BEYOND RECOGNITION. Jesus . . ."

"Who besides me would even come out to look at you?" Rainbow said. "And I'd be mangled same as you, wouldn't I? You pick the stupidest things to worry over." He turned the doorknob, cleared his throat. "Sorry about mixing up the stations."

"Felt like a damn fool." Murph hid under the covers. " 'Everybody knows *The Century* leaves from La Salle Street, boy,' they told me. How'd you like it if some nigger porter made you feel dumber than he was?"

"Stop that talk." Rainbow stepped into the hall. "Wear your best duds today. I want them worrying you never was a caddy."

"And what was I gonna tell him?" Murph said. "We're on our way back to look for some dead man we been after for a long time and that's how come we ain't had a chance to know nothing about trains?"

"Knock it off, Murph."

"I wouldn't walk too far if I was you." The kid rolled over. "Way you know this city, we might never find you. Better take the car."

"I wouldn't be caught dead driving that heap." Rainbow closed the door hard.

Two blocks from the hotel in a diner called Biff's, his breakfast was cooked and served by a big man with blue tattoos: *True Love* scrawled on a heart, a coiled snake, its forked tongue twitching each time a muscle flexed. No one would ever hire a man like this. He had to own the place. Biff was a lousy cook. Rainbow left a full cup of coffee on the counter and no tip.

Around the corner lay a park overlooking a narrow beach by Lake Michigan. He followed the path to the trees at Lake Shore Drive. The water out there shone hard and clear, but it looked warm. The waves were bigger than the ones back home, and almost as loud as ocean surf. Stuck against the horizon like cardboard cutouts, boats made their way through early light. But the steel railing at the edge of the street spoiled the view. He cut through the oaks and walked fast. The sidewalk was warming up. This was going to be the biggest day of his life.

Murph stood beside the tin lizzie parked in front of the hotel. He was dressed all in white. He looked like a soft-drink ad. Perfect. "What took you so long?" he said. "We'll be lucky to hit a dozen practice balls by the time we get there now. And if this wreck breaks down we won't get there till noon." He spun the crank. "Damn piece of trash. So cheap it's only got one door. Stupid way to build a car." He opened the door. "Let's go, I'm starving."

The Model T rumbled to the corner, weaved through side streets, and headed north on State, past a bridge and out to sunlight on a road lined with vacant lots.

"You mad at me?" Murph said.

"No."

"Then how come you ain't said nothing?"

"Just thinking," Rainbow told him. "Whoever laid out this town must have been blind drunk. Everything's jumbled up."

"Yeah, but you get used to it after a while."

"Not me. This ain't a fit place to live."

A CITY LIMITS sign whizzed by. A few minutes later, the Model T was turning again. Dew slicked the gates at Tam Lin, mist hovered over the grass and curled around tree trunks. Murph parked by the oaks near the caddy shack and went inside to get some old balls. Rainbow put his gun in the pouch of the bag and hauled his clubs to the practice field, which ran straight up a little valley alongside the first fairway. There was no one out on the course. With his elbows, he held his left-handed mashie across his back, twisting his shoulders, stretching muscles that begged for more sleep.

"Rainbow!" Hands to mouth, Taylor North stood on the crest by the first tee. "We're ready to start!"

Rainbow waved with the club, then dropped it on the bag.

Murph tramped through the weeds with a paper sack full of balls. "Hit a few for Chrissake. He's got to give you time to warm up."

"It'll be all right," Rainbow said, but he wasn't sure himself.

"It ain't all right, it's crazy!" Murph poured the balls on the ground. "You're stone cold." He swatted a clump of grass with the mashie. "Look at these divots. Jurgy's spent at least an hour down here already. Tell North you need a half-hour more."

"Leave the balls and let's go," Rainbow said.

Shouldering the bag, Murph kicked the paper sack. Wind blew it toward the woods. "Probably take an eight on the first hole. Unless you warm up, you'll give away two holes to start. If I ever did that, you'd brain me."

"I might anyways. Now lay off."

"Oh, I'll shut up, all right." Murph slammed the mashie down on the other irons in the bag. "You just see how good I shut up."

"It's gonna be fine, kid, I feel it. No way this yokel can beat me today."

Murph didn't say anything.

"I'll stall them so you can grab a sweet roll from the clubhouse." Rainbow gave him a dollar. "Don't want you to starve to death on me. Buy a couple."

The kid didn't look at the money and he didn't speak.

Rainbow started walking. Clubheads jangled behind him like a tin drum counting cadence. At the rear of the old caddy shed, a bunch of boys were playing poker for matchsticks. He almost stopped to sit in on a hand. At the top of the knoll, an army of men, twice as many as yesterday, stood around North and Jurgenson.

"You have my check, I presume," North said. "On you . . . ?"

Rainbow patted his breast pocket. "Might not be a scorcher like yesterday," he said. But all the pink was running out of the blue in the sky. "Let's get started."

"The sooner the better." North went through the gallery and stopped between the championship tees. "Ready for the coin toss?"

"No need," Rainbow said. "I always let the loser have the honor. You're up, Jurgy."

The all-American sparkled in a white outfit which looked exactly like the one he had worn yesterday. He probably owned ten sets of the same stuff. But he had his eye on Murph's clothes: It was working. Taking words of encouragement from the gallery, he teed up his ball, then leaned on his driver. "Eighteen holes, match play, I give away five strokes total, right?"

"Which I can take anytime I want," Rainbow said. "That's our wager clear enough." He shook Jurgenson's hand. "Don't strain yourself, now."

"No presses, no special rules," North turned like a circus ringmaster announcing the next act, "winner takes all, seventy-five thousand dollars. *And*—Mr. Roberts will play the *entire* round left-*handed!*"

Applause from the gallery, a few snickers. Rainbow doffed his hat. "Lucky I was able to find a set of lefties on such short notice," he said, patting the special clubs. "Sure hope I don't bust none of them. Takes a long time to get them made up."

The snickering got louder until Jurgenson addressed his ball. A loud *thwack* sent the drive high down the fairway: a perfect tee shot. There was much applause.

"Don't try to drive with him," Murph said. "Play your own game." His hands were trembling. He built a sand tee where Rainbow wanted it and put down a ball. "And take it nice and slow on the backswing."

Rainbow nodded. The grip of his left-handed driver felt sticky. The ball looked all right, though. But the course looked different—it always did from the left side. He got set, blocking out stares from the gallery, concentrating until he lost track of the seconds and his muscles let go of the tension. He felt like a lump of putty, as though he were swinging in slow motion. His right knee slid ahead of the ball in a forward press. The clubhead drew back in a low arc. Hips coiled like a spring, a shoulder pointed down. At the top of the backswing, his wrists cocked, knees drove forward, his rear instep pushed against the ground, hips unwound. One arm led the way in a firm, straight line, the other hugged his side, elbow in and jammed with power. The ball seemed to squish against the clubface and float away. Specks of sand kicked up, both arms glided past his chin, the hickory shaft whipped around his body, his shoulders turned square to the fairway.

Then the feeling was gone.

His ball was rocketing down the right side, rising to a powerful height, as if it might never bend back to earth. He didn't bother to watch it land. No applause: the men in the gallery could not believe it. Not one of them. He gave the driver to Murph, flashed his best grin at

North and Jurgenson, and marched onto the links. The sun began to burn a yellow hole in the sky. It was going to be another scorcher.

The green dress wasn't working. And the morning was going fast. The phone number on the message Grace North sent over had been disconnected for the summer. And now this: conventioneers hurrying through the lobby, eyes bloodshot, mouths warped from lack of sleep, hardly bothering to glance at her. Iris had given up breakfast to sit here. She felt like a potted fern.

On the couch facing the elevators, a reporter with a notebook was interviewing a conventioneer who kept talking about the Armour Company and something called Vin Fiz. None of it made any sense. Iris walked to the phones against the wall. The second booth was empty. She called the New York Central Railroad at La Salle Street Station. The earpiece filled with static. It was almost as loud as the man's voice in the next booth:

"I only found out myself, just now," the voice was saying. "Know what he did to Gordon last winter? Told him he could drive a golf ball a quarter-mile with a putter. Not off a cliff, mind you, but on a flat surface. So old Gordy says, 'That's impossible,' and this Rainbow guy puts him on for five thousand, walks him out to the lake, sets a ball down on the ice, and knocks it halfway to Canada. That's the kind of cheater we're talking about. . . ."

Iris put a finger to her ear and told the railroad clerk that she was a secretary for Miss Winslow who wanted a lower berth on today's *Twentieth-Century Limited* to New York. The clerk told her to hang on. She lit a cigarette, opened the door a crack, and aimed her smoke into the lobby. *A golf ball on a frozen lake. Perfect.*

". . . And he keeps a kid caddy with him," said the voice in the next booth. "Ace golfer, that one is. Both real snakes. You can't miss him. Wears a big panama all the time. Cocky as hell. Ambidextrous, too—means he can play from either side. He's two strokes better as a lefty. . . ."

The railroad clerk confirmed Iris's reservation and thanked her for patronizing "The Greatest Train in the World." She hung up.

"I'm sorry as hell I got mixed up with him," the voice said. "If I were you, I wouldn't let him near your club. That's what I'll tell old man North, too, soon as I can reach him. When I discovered what sort of vermin this Rainbow was, I just had to let my friends know. . . ."

There was some mumbling in that booth, then the receiver slapped into the hook and the door squeaked open. A man stepped out.

Instead of his WILL name tag, he wore a large button with gold ribbons hanging from it: ACMP MAN OF THE YEAR—1925. He found a group of friends near the couches, shook a lot of hands, and led the way to the hall past the elevators, where a frail man was leaning heavily on a cane and hugging a paper sack under his arm: the bell of a trumpet was sticking out of it. The clientele of the Palmer House was going downhill. Fast.

At the front desk, Iris got her room key and a stack of messages from Taylor North's downtown office. She left them on the desk and told the clerk to send Ernie the bellman up to her suite. She was checking out.

Going home.

To Daddy.

13 ————————————————————————————

It was a bad lie.

Against the side of the only real hill on the Tam Lin course, Rainbow's ball nestled in the rough like an egg in a ratty nest. Just ahead, a group of young trees, branches beating in the wind, blocked his approach to the eighteenth green, 175 yards in the distance. The match was as good as over. Rainbow was stymied. He was going to lose.

Everything.

"Knock it left of them trees." Murph offered the pitching niblick, a highly lofted iron. "You can pitch close on your next shot and still make par."

Strung out in a thin line all the way to Jurgenson's ball in the middle of the fairway, the gallery was growing restless. North wore a big smile. The all-American paced back and forth, trying to stay loose. Rainbow peered around the trees:

"Can't waste a shot now, I need to go for it. Give me the mashie iron."

"You crazy?" Murph said. "No way to get home from here. Play it safe. He could duff one, you know."

"He ain't duffed one all day. Probably hole out his next one on me. Never played this good in his life. It just ain't fair."

"Quit talking that way," Murph said. "You been hitting the pants off the ball, best I ever seen you play. If you'd of practiced, you could beat him without them five strokes he give you."

"We're out of strokes." Rainbow didn't take the lofted club. It was head to head now: his rightful edge was gone. "If I'd of only made that three-foot putt on number twelve—"

"Don't be thinking about that," Murph said. "Only make you feel worse. If you both make par, we'll be all square and into extra holes. And I know you can birdie that first hole." He forced the lofted iron into Rainbow's hand. "C'mon. Use your head."

"What's taking so long up there?" called North.

Rainbow grinned down the hill. "I'm considering my options." Then, in a quiet voice: "Like to shoot that old goat right between the ears." He yanked the four-iron out of the bag.

"Don't," Murph said.

"Stand back, kid. And keep your eye on this."

"You're giving him the match, Rainbow. At least make him work for it."

"I'm giving him nothing." Rainbow tried to get set, but the slope forced him to stand with his feet well above the ball.

"It's gonna fly out of there," Murph said. "And fade. And you ain't never gonna stop it on the green even if you do get through them branches."

"I'm going under them."

". . . Jesus." Murph trudged to the top of the hill to watch the disaster.

Drawing a long breath, Rainbow cocked his hands far ahead of the ball to force a low trajectory. He swung. The clubhead tore through tall grass, the ball zoomed under the branches, then climbed, bending left to right—fading—toward the green.

"Jesus! What a shot!" Murph dropped the golf bag. "C'mon, get over that bunker, get over, *get* over . . ."

Landing in thick grass at the lip of the bunker, the ball kicked up soft and scooted toward the pin.

"Holy Jesus!" Murph yelled. "It's going *in!*"

A hollow *bonk* echoed down the fairway: the ball hit the flag stick and ricocheted a few feet away. Loud applause, a few cheers from the gallery.

"You see that?" Murph threw his arms around Rainbow. "If it wasn't for all that overspin, you'd of sunk it!"

"Quit strangling me." Rainbow pried loose, dropped the club. "Come on, Jurgy," he called, *"hit!"* He kept grinning until Jurgenson hit a towering iron shot to within twenty feet of the flag. More applause. All the men in the gallery started walking at the same time. "Told you he wouldn't duff it," Rainbow said.

"What a shot you hit." Murph forced the grin from his face. "I'm not saying it was the right one to try," his grin came back, "but damn if that don't put us where we can hold on for a tie."

"We ain't trying for a tie." Rainbow marched down the hill.

"If you'd of practiced regular," Murph said, "we'd be sitting pretty."

"I did practice." The smile came through all by itself. "But not regular."

Murph laughed with him. "I'm real proud of how you played. You could of beat me today." He silenced the clubheads with his hand. "It's real slick back by the pin 'cause everybody walks off the green that way. So figure it's a foot shorter than it looks."

Rainbow nodded, then doffed his hat to the applause from the gallery ringing the green. It was the first time anyone had clapped for his skill. It felt strange. But good. If only a special lady could be here to share it with him. The laugh tasted sour. No lady was ever going to be there. Not for long. He strode onto the green.

"Great shot." In a squat behind his putt, Jurgenson was taking the line. "Never thought you'd get it out of there and stop it on the green. Lucky you hit the pin, though."

"What I was aiming at, wasn't it?" Rainbow walked behind him. "Now, I didn't open my mouth once about the luck you been pulling all day, so quit trying to rile me."

The all-American straightened up. "I'm only saying you hit one great golf shot back there. I've been on that hill a few times myself. Never had the nerve to go for it."

"Yeah, that's just like you, Jurgy," Rainbow said. "Gutless."

Jurgenson shook his head, murmurs rippled through the gallery. Murph set the bag off the green and walked over, head low. "Why'd you have to do that for? He was only congratulating you, like I was."

"Big money at stake here, kid. No room for congratulations."

Murph peered over Rainbow's shoulder at the line of the putt. "Well, what about that time in Hot Springs when we seen Bobby Jones play out of the creek. Wasn't but a quarter of the ball showing. You even said you don't know how he got it out of there so good. And you walked right up to him and shook his hand."

"That was just some piddling *amateur* tournament," Rainbow said. But he remembered how he had felt watching Jones make that shot: thrilled. "You're away, Jurgy. Don't sink this one on me. I'm terrible under pressure."

The men in the gallery didn't laugh this time. Jurgenson's hands kept opening and closing on the grip, his head swung from ball to hole and back again. He made a smooth stroke, but left his ball a good three inches below the hole. Shaking his head, he tapped in for a par 4 and, amid vigorous applause, walked to the edge of the green.

Rainbow took practice strokes with his putter until the crowd quieted. "Looks straight, don't it?"

"Moves a little left." Murph was lying flat on his stomach behind the ball, squinting toward the hole. "Level as a pool table, though. Try the inside lip." He got up, put the heel of one shoe to the toe of the other and stepped off the distance from ball to cup. "Twelve and a half foot." Taking the flag stick from the other caddy, he leaned the shaft into the outside edge of the hole. "About here ought to do her."

Behind his ball, Rainbow bent low to the grass. He didn't see any break at all. He set his stance, wiggled his toes inside the heavy shoes, and squeezed his feel into the putter grip. But he couldn't get rid of the tingly feeling in his hands and feet. Except for the wind through the leaves, it was perfectly quiet. Sink this putt and you win, he told himself, you're off and running, in The Big Time. He swallowed the taste of salt, drew a slow breath and held it. He stroked the ball. *Too hard.* It jumped off the putter and shivered over bumps in the worn-out portion of the green, then banged into the back of the cup, leapt straight up like a kernel of bursting popcorn, and plopped back into the hole, out of sight. The gallery's applause sounded like hail on a slate roof. Some hats sailed into the wind. Rainbow punched the air, took three giant steps, grabbed his ball out of the cup, and hurled it into the woods.

Murph was running around the green, carrying the flag stick like a guidon. His face looked ready to pop. "Did you ever *ram* that one home." He reached out to hug Rainbow, but stopped and offered his hand. "Good thing that dropped or you'd of been twenty feet past the hole."

"But you got to admit," Rainbow said, "the line wasn't bad." He laughed and drew the kid close with a wrestler's headlock. "Goddamn, we did it!"

Jurgenson came toward him, his arm out stiff, hand open. "Great putt. After that iron you hit back there, I'm almost glad you sank it."

"Yeah, I'll just bet you are." Rainbow shook hands and went across the green, following North into the Men's Grill.

"Fast match," North said. The clock behind the bar showed 9:50 A.M. "Always is when the golf is good." He got out his checkbook. "That was a phenomenal shot you hit."

A phone rang twice before the bartender picked it up: "Call for you, Mr. North."

The old man stopped writing out the check, stepped to the bar, picked up the receiver, and listened with narrowed eyes to the voice crackling over the line. The rest of the men were pouring into the grill. Some stopped to pat Rainbow on the back, others led Jurgenson to the bar. Three dozen voices spoke at the same time.

"Vin Fiz if you got it," Murph told the waiter at the bar. Turning his head about the room, he pulled a chair to North's table. "Real plush, huh?"

"You're supposed to be minding my bag," Rainbow said. "Got my .45 in there."

Patting the bulge under his white shirt, Murph grinned and leaned close to the table. "I took care of everything."

"Give it to me under." Rainbow slid his hand beneath the table-cloth, waited for the feel of cold steel. He sneaked the big gun into his belt and buttoned his jacket. "Could have blown everything, kid. Now take your drink outside."

Frowning, Murph grabbed the glass of purple the waiter put in front of him, stood, and turned for the door.

North hung up the phone and walked back to his table. "Don't leave, son." He stared at Rainbow, tapped his pen on the unsigned check. "Interesting call. From your *ex*-sponsor, Will Broder." He aimed a cagy grin at Murph, who was half in, half out of the chair. "Yours, too, right—Murph?"

"I got to go outside, sir," Murph said. "Ain't allowed in no saloons."

"This hasn't been a saloon in years." North's grin was gone. "Sit down!"

Murph sat like a piece of crumbled paper. "Think I got to go to the bathroom."

"Later." North hardened his stare. "Broder is washing his hands of both of you. He's put the word out all over town. You'll even have trouble getting on a public course now. And he's willing to tear up yesterday's check."

"Be willing to tear up that one and the one you're about to sign." Rainbow got the check from his pocket. "Tell you what. I'll sell Broder's back to you for eighty grand. Just write me one for a hundred fifty-five thousand, and I'll start ripping."

"I'd have no difficulty stopping payment on any check." North pushed his checkbook to the side.

"Broder ever tell you about that guy from Hawthorne Race Track?"

Rainbow unbuttoned his jacket, tucked the flap behind his .45. "The one who tried to welch on me? Guess old Will wasn't up to that. But I ain't quite the gentleman he turns out to be." Sweet Dee Flagg didn't know everything about city folks: just talk wasn't enough. He stroked his gun. "Get my drift?"

North laughed. "Broder? A gentleman? He's an ass! He gives up the best hustler around because he's afraid I'll cut off his credit. I need his business as much as he needs my loans." He slapped the table so hard the glass in front of Murph tumbled over. Fizzing purple streamed onto the kid's clothes. North's laugh went away. "Sorry, son. I'll buy you a new set. Now cover that gun, Rainbow. This is a respectable club." Pen in hand, he opened his checkbook, tore out the old check and flicked it out of his way. "One fifty-five you said?"

Rainbow kept watching the pen move. How could it be this easy?

"Very generous of you to let me have one hundred thousand back," North said, blotting the new check. "And I can show my thanks by offering *my* sponsorship. Now, it won't be easy. Not after what that idiot Broder did already, but I have connections in the east. We'll start in New Jersey, then move into New York. All the top clubs. I'll pick up your expenses, of course. How does fifty-fifty sound to you? A true partnership."

Rainbow pushed back his panama and let out a long stream of air.

"Think of it this way," North said. "It will take us time to earn back what you've won from me. With interest, naturally. I'll be the one who has to wait, but you—and Murph here—you'll both be living high. I guarantee two matches a month, at say—fifty thousand each."

Rainbow took off his hat and stared at the tablecloth. "Mr. North, I think we should just settle up. See, I'm my own boss now, and, well—"

"We'll split sixty-forty then, in your favor." North's eyes were bloodshot; he must have been up half the night. "That's as high as I can go. I have expenses to think of."

Rainbow turned his hat like a top on the table. "I like being my own man."

"We'll have lunch and talk it over." North shook his head. "No, wait, I already have an engagement. Dinner, then. Best steaks you've ever had."

"I got to be on a train," Rainbow said. "Running late as it is." He read the new check over, put it in his jacket, tore up the other two checks, and pushed the pieces into a little mound. "Call yourself a cab, Murph. I'll dump the car. Meet you at the station."

The kid was watching the purple stains soak in. They looked like the outline of a country: a whole continent. He gave Rainbow the keys to the Model T and walked out.

"Fine boy." North watched Murph shoulder the golf bag and haul it across the practice green. "Has the makings of a great golfer."

Rainbow got out of the chair. "Ought to be on my way, sir."

"My car will drive us," North said. "We can ride together."

"Got my own transportation, thanks." Rainbow picked up the car keys. "One thing you could do, sir. Let them know down at your bank that I'm coming in. That might ease things a little for me. I'm on a tight schedule and—"

"I'll call right now. And you think about my offer. We could do great things together." He offered his business card. "Call me. Anytime. I'll be in Saratoga Springs in a day or so, but my office will know how to reach me."

Pocketing the card, Rainbow touched his hat brim, walked by the bar, nodded to Jurgenson and pushed through the swinging doors. The hall was cool. He went through the lobby, out the front door and down the steps. He tossed North's card in the bushes.

Murph was sitting on a bench at the corner of the clubhouse, hugging the golf bag. "A cab won't get here for at least fifteen minutes. Make better time if we was together."

Rainbow kept walking.

"It leaves at twelve-forty," Murph called. There was a brief silence, then irons jangled. Murph ran after him. "You ain't gonna let me be seen like this, are you? Feel like I been in an ink fight. And it smells terrible."

The parking lot sloped into the trees. Rainbow reached inside the tin lizzie, fiddled with the ignition. "Help me get it started."

Murph set the levers like the hands of a clock: ten minutes to three. He worked the crank. The Model T came to life. He stuck the bag behind the front seat and motioned Rainbow to get in.

"Thought you had to push it out of here," Rainbow said.

"Parked it on the incline, she'll roll back. C'mon, get in."

Rainbow got in. The car rolled out of the trees.

"Knew you wouldn't leave me here." Murph steered the black heap out of the lot and past the clubhouse. "Where we gonna dump her?"

Rainbow kept silent. The stone gate and pillars went by. The road was empty of cars.

"I been thinking," Murph said. "If I was unconscious the whole way to Saratoga, I couldn't worry about nothing. And I could get unconscious drunk before that thing ever leaves the station. See? It ain't gonna be so bad after all."

"You're a genius." Rainbow didn't say anything else for a long while. He let the kid ramble about how unconscious he was planning to get and what a great shot that mashie iron on the last hole was. Then the brick wall Rainbow was looking for came into view a half-mile down on the other side of the road and he said, "Pull over."

"What for? We're making good time."

Grabbing the wheel, Rainbow steered the car to the side of the road. Brakes squealed, the tin lizzie stopped on the shoulder. "Leave the engine running, and get out."

"We gonna push her down that gully?" Murph followed him out of the car and went to the drainage ditch paralleling the highway. "Don't look deep enough to me. We could find a real cliff somewheres . . ."

"There's a roadhouse a little ways down." Rainbow slid behind the wheel. "Call a cab and wait for me."

"Jesus, I can't go to no roadhouse like this." Murph tugged his shirt: the stains looked worse as they began to dry. "All them whores'd laugh at me."

Rainbow rested his forehead on the steering wheel. He knew exactly how the kid felt. "All right, wait here, then. Don't move an inch."

"Okay, but . . . where the hell you going? How come I can't come with you?"

"I ain't going nowhere and I won't be but a few minutes. Stand there till I get back." He put the car in gear. The tires spit gravel, the Model T hopped onto the road. He drove fast, then braked and turned across the highway, stopping short of the wooden gate in the brick wall. It was a high wall. The sign near the top read: LAMBERT OAKS HOME FOR BOYS. He left the motor on, dropped his clubs on the drive, and pounded the iron knocker on the gate. Back up the road, Murph was shading his eyes the way Indians did in the movies.

A short man with sawdust on his clothes opened the gate. Planks and part of a bookcase stood in back of him. He glanced at the car, then at Rainbow. "Are you from the farm?"

Rainbow patted the front fender. "It's a piece of trash, so don't bother to thank me. And it ain't for you. It's for the boys. To learn them how to drive. Now take it inside. You're wasting gas." He hauled his clubs to the edge of the road and waved his hat. Murph started running.

The short man clasped his hands together. "Thank you, sir. The boys will be thrilled!" He opened the gate wider and climbed into the car. "Won't you come in and—"

"No time." Rainbow walked across the road to the shade. The car engine raced, the horn started honking. The tin lizzie clattered up the drive to the big brick house. Young boys poured out and crowded around the coal-black wreck. A loud cheer rang out. They all tried to get into the car at the same time. The short man ran down the drive, waving his arms. Rainbow gave the golf bag to Murph and headed down the road.

"Hey, that's real nice what you done." The kid was looking back and waving to the man near the gate. "Drive it in good health!"

Rainbow grabbed him by the shirt and pulled him down the road. " 'Drive it in good health.' Stupid thing to say."

"Well, I ain't never give away a car before. Why'd you do it?"

"The roadhouse is right around this bend," Rainbow said.

"Yeah, but why'd you give that orphanage the car?"

Rainbow shoved him. "Walk downwind of me, you smell bad."

"Why ain't you answering? That's a real fine thing you done."

"Matter of fact, you ride on the cab's running boards," Rainbow told him. "That's how foul you smell. What is that stuff, Vin Fiz? Never heard of it."

"Grape juice. Real hard to get." Murph switched the bag to his other shoulder. "So tell me, how come you done it?"

"What time'd you say our train leaves?"

"Twelve-forty. You know I'm gonna keep asking till you tell me."

"And you know I'm gonna keep not telling you till you quit asking." Rainbow walked into the parking lot of the roadhouse and pointed to the bench near the doors. "Sit there. I'll be out in a second. Might even bring you a Vin Fiz." Inside, he used the phone beside the bar and called a cab. They said they would be right out. This time, he didn't mind the wait.

14

The flatlands were hiding in the dark. Through the windows on the other side of the dining car, moonlight ran like an oil slick on the black waters of Lake Erie. This speeding train was not just any train, it was "The Greatest Train in the World," and this was not just any night, but one of victory. There were plans to make, money to count— $155,000, stacked neatly in a new leather briefcase which cost $6.75, two dollars more than the other styles because this one had a lockable clasp. That was important to Rainbow: to have the only key. Especially now, with every second hurtling him closer to the time when all his waiting stopped, when his search was over and all debts were paid. It would be the last stop: the old bastard would be there, he had to be. Rainbow could sense it.

Taste it.

Seated across from him, Murph was pushing chunks of fish through a buttery ooze on his plate. He had wanted steak, not the "specialty of the house," whether all the high rollers ate it or not. He didn't find any difference in the escalloped tomatoes and he didn't know how people could eat consommé—cold soup that tasted like saltwater. Behind all his complaints was the speed of this train. He was scared. And fully conscious.

The black waiter hurrying down the aisle with a coffee urn didn't stop when Rainbow flagged him. "Be right with you, sir. Got to pour this for Mr. Karamonopolis while it's still piping hot."

Murph snickered into his hand. "Mr. what?"

"Stavros the Greek." Rainbow turned to watch the waiter.

"No kidding?" Murph leaned out into the aisle. "I hear he don't carry nothing in his pockets 'cause it spoils the lines of his suit."

At the rear lakeside table, the waiter poured steaming black into four cups. The two men seated facing the end of the train looked like a vaudeville team: a fat man in a pink jacket and a skinny cowboy whose ten-gallon hat was pegged to a chair post. Across from them, a man bigger than Curtis aimed a dull stare up the car; his face was lumpy and hard, as if carved from a tree trunk. The round-faced man in the corner wore a silk suit that must have cost $300: wavy black hair combed tight, a pencil-thin moustache stretching over smiling lips, jet-black eyes sparkling like the emerald stud in his tie—Stavros the Greek.

"Must be some action on this train," Rainbow said. "Lucky break for us."

A frail man hobbled through the green kitchen curtain and leaned on his cane by the Greek's table. He was the same little man Rainbow had seen in the hotel hallway this morning: the freak. Head low, a hand wringing the cook's apron about his waist, the frail man nodded like a slave while the Greek spoke to him. The men at the table started laughing. Even the waiter wore a grin as he came up the aisle and poured the dregs of the coffee into Rainbow's cup.

Rainbow snapped a crisp dollar bill between his fingers. "Make it a fresh pot. Piping hot."

"Fresh coffee coming right up." The cash disappeared beneath the long white apron which hung on the waiter like a dress. He took the cup away.

"The Greek looks like a king, don't he," Murph said.

Rainbow kicked him under the table. "Quit staring. Wonder why he's not in the first section with the rest of the big-timers."

"Station man said when they run more than one train, they try to keep everybody together according to what they do for a living." Murph stared over two yellow flowers in the vase. "I told him we was golf pros and he wrote it on his ledger, called it a sailing list. Dumb, ain't it? A sailing list on a train. Bet the Greek had them put down 'oddsmaker' next to his name." He opened the menu. "Think I ought to try this NYC baked apple?"

Turned sideways, Rainbow stretched his legs into the aisle, then bent to pick up the napkin that slid off his lap. Under the table behind him, slim ankles rubbed together as if to erase the sheen of cream-colored silk stockings. Nice legs. Young. She was alone, her face hidden by the sketch of a locomotive steaming past a castle on the menu cover. Young hands, too. Long, smooth fingers. White gloves lay on the small purse by her elbow.

111

"Not a lot of ways to ruin an apple, is there," Murph said. "Maybe I could ask how they make it and—"

And the menu lowered. *Her.* The lady in the white Packard. Opal-green eyes, soft brown hair tucked under a little tan hat. Her lips puckered, then flattened into a moist line: a smile so small and quick Rainbow couldn't be sure it had been there at all. Drawn by the intensity of his stare, she looked up. Her eyes widened with surprise, but her glance didn't last any longer than her smile had. She was even more beautiful up close. She looked sweet.

"Which is why I figure it's a better bet than this rice custard," Murph was saying, reading the menu with his finger. "Or this here steamed plum pudding. What's hard sauce, anyways?"

Rainbow gave him a twenty-dollar bill. "Buy that table there next to the Greek. Order yourself a steak."

"What for?"

"Time we started associating with the right people. Ought to know something about them before we play their game. Listen in on what they're saying."

"I eat a full dinner on top of this stuff, I'm liable to puke. Don't see how anybody can eat at this speed."

"Then don't eat it," Rainbow said, "just order it. And sit there till they leave. Then follow them. The Greek must have his own private car."

"I know we're gonna hit something," Murph said. "I can feel it." He stuffed the cash into his jacket. "Should of bought that whiskey, be unconscious by now."

"Be just about as stupid as them cigarettes you smoke."

"Only had two today. You gonna tell me folks die from smoking, too?"

Before Rainbow could stop them, his fingers curled into a fist. He ran his knuckles along the patterned waves in the tablecloth. "Do like I told you. I'll wait for you in my room."

Murph's chair scraped the floor, his feet thudded up the aisle. A moment later, he followed the black-coated steward back past the table.

"Piping hot!" The waiter set a new cup down, filled it with fresh coffee.

"Leave the pot," Rainbow said. "And clear these dishes." He winked. "That young lady? The one right behind me? Ask her to join me."

"Can't do that. Not on this train, no sir. Lose my job."

"There's another bill in it for you."

"Lose my job sure. No sir." The waiter left the urn and walked away.

Like mirrors in a fun house, the silvered pot threw back a wavy image. Rainbow smoothed his hair, picked up the urn, and turned. Her finger rubbed the edge of the menu, her eyes moved from side to side over the print. She was waiting, all right. No doubt about it. He cleared his throat. "Can't possibly drink all this by myself."

Her gaze swept across his face, lingered on the urn. She went back to reading the menu.

He set the pot on her table, raised his cup. "Nothing like a nice hot cup of coffee to help make up a person's mind. Try the Broiled Lake Superior Whitefish. Delicious."

"Please remove that," she said.

". . . What?"

Her stare drifted over the silver spout, found his face, and jumped back down to the urn. "That."

"What . . . this?" He touched the pot and grinned. "You take cream in yours?"

Something at the back of her eyes made them glint and glare at the same time. "If you don't remove that, I'll have the steward remove you."

"Be bad for business, don't you think?"

She raised an eyebrow and glanced out the window. The steward had finished seating Murph and was standing at the Greek's table, joining the laughter aimed at the frail man in the apron, who just leaned on his cane and took it. Rainbow snapped his fingers. The steward scurried up the car as if his thighs were bound together: "Yessir, a problem?"

"This young la—dy," Rainbow winked, "has been waiting a long time while you're back there amusing yourself. Bring her what you brought me and be—"

"I'd like the sole," she said in a firm voice. "Plain, no tartar sauce, no potatoes, a slice of lemon on the side."

"Very good, miss." The steward poured her a cup of coffee. "My apologies for the delay." He stared at the urn. "I thought you only took tea, miss. Tea with lemon, just slightly warmed."

She pushed the cup around the vase. "The coffee is his."

"I'll attend to it immediately." The steward set the pot on Rainbow's table. "Sir, kindly turn into your own table, your feet are a hazard to our waiters and guests. And I remind you this is *The Twentieth-Century Limited*. I trust I need say no more." He jerked his head at the waiter standing against the wall between tables. "Remove this and bring Miss Winslow a pot of tea."

Miss Winslow. Beautiful.

Shaking his head, the waiter took her cup and followed the steward down the aisle.

"They know your name and everything, don't they, Miss Winslow," Rainbow said. "You must travel this line a lot." She was keeping her stare in her lap and nibbling at what looked like a smile forming on her lips. He pulled out his wad of folding money, peeled off a fifty-dollar bill, and held it between his fingers. "What's the going rate on a train these days? Fifty?"

Her head snapped back. Her eyes narrowed. She swallowed hard, pushed away from the table, and stood. The purse popped open in her hand. A pack of cigarettes tumbled out, followed by matches, a compact that bounced three times before she caught it, and a small photo of two horses which floated down like a dry leaf. Letting out a little cry, she slapped the table with her gloves.

"Let me help you there." Rainbow picked up the pack of matches.

She swept the other items into her purse, then marched out of the car, slamming the back door. The steward hurried up the aisle, building his frown with every step: "Really, sir, I'm afraid I'll have to insist that you—"

"Get my change." Rainbow stuffed the fifty-dollar bill into the steward's hand. "I'm in a hurry." He turned back to his table and sipped coffee until the black coat went away. The yellow matchbook had a blue M inside a blue circle on the cover. She probably lifted it from a speakeasy or a hotel. The cigarettes she used looked English. Winslow sounded English, too. She was high-class baggage for sure. Rainbow picked up his briefcase and went to the head of the car.

"In my dining car, sir," the steward handed him his change, "I expect a gentleman to conduct himself as a gentleman."

"I'll work on it, smiley." Rainbow gave back five dollars. "Split this with my waiter. And don't try to stiff him either, I'll be checking on you." He walked to the rear of the car. Murph was too busy devouring a porterhouse to look up. At the Greek's table, that frail man with the cane was speaking broken English, accented by a hand that rolled in the air: Italian. The Greek and his friends were laughing so hard now they had tears in their eyes. The little guy wasn't trying to be funny.

Miss Winslow was not on either of the next two sleepers. Passing his drawing room, Rainbow went into the combination club-observation car. She might be outside by the open brass railing where, during daylight hours, a crowd of passengers had watched the tracks unwind around the lakeshore. Music filled the car. The jazz band that had sneaked on at Englewood, the first stop out of Chicago, where everyone had rooted for *The Century* to beat *The Broadway Limited* out of the station—that jazz band was still on board. They played a new tune, "Sweet Georgia Brown," as if they had written it. The cornet challenged the clarinet, the drummer beat his sticks on furniture, walls, anything handy. On a small table, a young boy dressed in top hat and tails danced to the beat. The passengers were clapping hands. Even the conductor with the pink in his buttonhole was tapping his foot. He was the same man who told the porters to put the "nigger band" off at Toledo because the society ladies who had ridden as far as Englewood just to hog the dining car and have their lunch in flouncy dresses didn't know what was becoming of "their train" if niggers were allowed to ride it. Those city ladies would piss down their garter belts now. The black musicians had conquered the crowd. The young dancer could have done it alone, the way he whirled and high-stepped, clicked his taps in triple time. If Curtis were here, he'd curse the little kid up and down for playing the white folks' fool— and for dancing so well. The big oaf had paid good money once to learn how to waltz and all it got him was a charley horse and a lot of jabber from the woman who taught him, saying he should never come back because she was tired of having her toes broken by an elephant who couldn't walk across a room without killing something. Rainbow covered his laugh and squeezed through the crowd near the door. As if swallowed up by the big club chair, Miss Winslow was seated at the divider on the lake side. Threading a hundred-dollar bill through the matchbook cover, Rainbow walked to her and put his briefcase on the arm of her chair. "You forget this, Miss Winslow?"

Her neck got red. Her eyes fired at the matchbook and the money he wiggled in front of her. Then she smiled and led the applause for the young dancer, who did a series of splits to a vamping flourish, bowed, and jumped off the table and began passing his hat.

Rainbow winked at Miss Winslow. "Am I talking your language now?"

"That's very generous of you." She snatched the yellow square out of his hand. Another fast smile and she was up and moving. She dropped the matches into the young dancer's hat.

The boy pulled the money out of the matchbook. His mouth hung open. He whirled to the cornet player. "Lookit, Pop!"

Miss Winslow patted the boy's head. And winked at Rainbow. The smile stayed on her lips this time. She strode past him up the car and out the door. He started to pivot after her, but something nudged the back of his knee. Down there, three feet high and all eyes, the young dancer was holding out his big black hat:

"Enjoy the show, mister?"

With a sigh, Rainbow dropped a ten-dollar bill into the silk hole. The boy danced his way to the other passengers. The cornet kicked off a reprise, the crowd started clapping to the beat. A woman with a blonde spit curl in the middle of her forehead took Miss Winslow's chair. Covered with spangles, her dress rose to midthigh when she sat:

"This is the most fun I've ever had on *The Century*. Usually, it's so, so staid." She blinked twice. "I like to have fun."

Her eyes were closer together than they should have been.

"Excuse me, ma'am," Rainbow said. "My wife's real sick and I got to look in on her now." He drew the conductor out between cars and flipped through his money until he found a five-dollar bill. "There's a woman on board, name of Miss Winslow. Now, what I want you to do is—"

"Sorry," the conductor said. "Not allowed to make introductions on *The Century*. Against rules."

"What the hell are you talking about? This is five bucks I got here. Whose rules?"

"The New York Central's, sir." The conductor touched the silver NYC badge on his lapel and went back into the last car.

"Staid," Rainbow yelled after him. "The whole lot of you." He yanked open the door to the sleeper and unlocked his drawing room. The light came on with a crinkling sound. The porter had made up the bed: there was no room to walk anymore. He dropped his briefcase on the mattress. Wind beat the fins on the window frame outside, thin sheets of metal designed to route fresh air inside, but the only thing they were good for was making noise. Standing in front of the full-length mirror on the door adjoining Murph's cabin, Rainbow got his panama off the wall hook, put it on, placed a hand on his hip, turned, put the hand in his pocket, turned again, folded his arms across his chest, slid them behind his back. "Couldn't be worth more than a hundred. I could buy a whole cathouse in Saint Lou for a hundred bucks."

The nerve of her to spoil his victory night like that. Who did she think she was, a princess? Spoiled rotten, that's what she was. Probably traveling with a millionaire who just had to snap his fingers and she'd give him whatever he wanted. It didn't matter. There was

116

important business ahead, in Saratoga. Old Cal was only hours away now. No time for courting a whore.

Missed your chance, princess.

But she was so beautiful.

And plucky.

He drove his fist into the pillow, then leaned back against the headboard. "Should of worn the hat, damn it."

"You want to see the manicurist first, miss?" The lady's maid wore a black dress with a frilly white apron down the front.

"The conductor, please." Iris cinched her robe and got into Lower 8. With the curtain drawn, murky light from the bulb above her head cast a sheen on the green-dotted weave of the Pullman blanket. Where her pencil was sandwiched between pages, she opened *The Crossword Puzzle Book*. A five-letter word for "small Spanish horse." In 17 Down, she wrote *genet*, coupled it with *feedbag* in 11 Across: "oat holder." She put down her pencil. This was last year's fad. Everyone was playing that Chinese game now, Mah-Jongg. Even the men. Especially the men. Sooner or later, she would have to learn what all those bamboo and ivory tiles were for and how loudly to call out "pung." But it couldn't be as much fun as crossword puzzles were. Could Mah-Jongg be played alone? She filled in *Greb*, "present middleweight champion," and mated it with *Lear*, "Cordelia's father." But she drew a blank on 26 Down: "in the near future"—two words, eleven letters. At the knock on the metal beam separating upper and lower berths, she opened the curtain far enough to peek out.

The Pullman conductor touched the brim of his cap, then averted his eyes. "You wanted to see me, miss?"

"One of your passengers insists on being rude to me," Iris said. "Please speak to him and straighten out this matter. I don't want to be disturbed during the night."

"The porter and I'll be walking your car all night, miss. No one'll disturb you. Could we let it go at that?"

Iris nibbled at the smile. "Certainly not."

"But miss, we, that is—do you know the man's name even?"

"A Rainbow something. I believe he's traveling with golf clubs."

"Oh . . . him . . . yes, miss."

"As long as you can assure me that he won't address me again, an apology will not be necessary."

The conductor tipped his hat and went down the aisle. The door at the back of the car shut as if sealing a tomb. Iris drew the curtain.

Her head rocked with silent laughter. It would serve this Rainbow right. No one talked to her like that. She covered her laugh and slipped out of her robe. Still, there was something daring about being mistaken for a prostitute, as repulsive and vulgar as it had first seemed. Even as a little girl, holding her father's hand at the races, Iris hadn't needed to be told what those women who wore furs in summer were. They didn't walk like the rest of the ladies. And they never seemed to look at anything. They were just there: waiting. One hundred dollars? For one night? Rainbow must have won again. Poor Taylor North.

She couldn't stop the laughter now. Something crinkled under her elbow—a flimsy piece of paper, the copy of the telegram she had given to the stenographer when he got off at Elkhart to transcribe the New York Stock Exchange closing quotations for the tycoons in the first section:

MR. HORACE WELLS, DAKOTA APTS, APT 14, 72ND & 8TH AVE, NY
ARRIVING NEXT 20TH CENTURY LTD STOP MEET
AT WALDORF 10 AM STOP BRING STABLE ACCOUNTS STOP
MISS WINSLOW

Horace should have it by now. With luck, he'd be sober enough to read it.

She slid the cable into her book. *In the near future—two words*. Not a clue. Bubbles churned and popped in her stomach. No dinner again tonight. But think of all those calories saved! The green curtain kept moving back and forth, steel wheels let out a high-pitched whine, the *click-clack* came in steady rhythm, unyielding, like a headache. Her face felt flushed. And the bathroom was so far away. And always occupied. *One should always travel with a bucket or a sack*. Under the covers, she took long, deep breaths, and turned off the light. It wasn't dark enough, but her sleeping mask was in her valise, all the way down there at her feet. She pressed her eyelids shut. Red dots moved by in flowing formations. The harder she pressed, the more dots she saw. What if Rainbow had followed her and was standing in shadows down at the end of her sleeper, waiting for his chance? To do what, rape her? Yes, he had the nerve. But not the disposition. And he looked so different without his big white hat. Like a little boy. How much had he won from Taylor North?

Another laugh. The red dots began to fade. Dreams that began with laughter were the best ones.

15

"Nothing." Murph walked in and sat on the bed. "No action. The Greek's just going to Saratoga like us. Only he's got a big poker game in New York first."

Rainbow closed the drawing-room door. "Who're those people with him?"

"The fat one in the loud suit's called Pete. Didn't hear what he does exactly, but he sure don't work for a living. He's traveling with Tom Edwards, the moving-picture star. You know, The Whip?"

"Don't go to movies," Rainbow said. "Waste of time."

"He sits up there on them rocks and waits till the last guy rides by." Murph used the briefcase as a footrest. "Then he knocks him off his horse with his whip and—"

"What about the giant?"

"Name's Asses, I think. The Greek's bodyguard." Murph leaned against the wall and laughed. "Heard your Browns got creamed today. The Greek says they got no chance without a catcher who can hit with power."

"I'd settle for one who could hit, period," Rainbow said. "Anybody'd be better than Worthless Wobers."

"And you was wrong about the private car, too." Murph was shaking his head. "Porter said if Mr. Vanderbilt himself rode this here train, he'd ride like everybody else. They don't allow no private cars on *The Century*."

"They don't allow nothing on this train," Rainbow said. But New York City was a different story. He picked up Murph's feet and put the briefcase on the floor. "Big poker game in the city, huh?"

"Glad we're getting off at Albany." Murph rubbed his stomach. "Damn relish they serve's going right through me. Heard the cook say it was watermelon pickle. That ain't possible, is it?"

"He the little guy with the cane the Greek was laughing at?"

"Yeah, that's him. I mean, there ain't no such thing as a watermelon pickle, right?" The kid belched, then sighed. "Should of figured he was joshing me. What's an illiterate little guinea know anyways."

"Illiterate?"

Murph nodded. "Talks terrible, too. The Greek calls him a wop right to his face and the poor guy just stands there and takes it like he was a nigger or something. At least this is the last time for him, he's retiring at the end of this run. Lives in Chicago, see, and they change dining cars in Buffalo—turn them around? The wop ain't turning around with them this time. He's going to Saratoga. As Efrem Roze's personal cook." The kid reached for the briefcase. "Let me have another look at our bankroll, will you?"

Rainbow glared at him and slapped his hand. "Efrem Roze's personal cook?" Roze was the king of the New York gambling underworld, one of the most influential figures in the country. Rainbow ran a hand through his hair and started pacing the floor. "Jesus Christ, how come you don't tell me this right off?"

"You said find out about the Greek, not some dumb cook," Murph told him. "Hey, if we stay in Saratoga mcre than a week, is it all right if I order me a set of new steel shafts? Factory ought to be able to make them up in a week, don't you figure?"

"Efrem Roze's personal cook," Rainbow said in a mutter. "Jesus. You sure the little guy's illiterate?"

"Told you what I heard." Murph stretched out on the bed. "None of them wops can read or write, that's what's wrong with them. All the signs on their stores? Wrote in Italian. They ain't never gonna learn English that way."

"Quiet, damn it, I'm trying to think."

"Well, it's true. I seen so myself when you had me downtown Chicago looking for old what's his name."

Rainbow grabbed his panama off the wall hook. "Got to find out more about that poker game. And that cook. Be back in a few minutes. Keep this door locked and your eye on that money."

"I'll come with you."

"Stay here like I told you. I'm just going to the dining car. It'd be best if we wasn't seen together right now."

"I thought we was done with that," Murph said. "We're in the big time. . . ."

"We'd be talking real money in E.R.'s crowd, kid."

"Jesus, ain't we got enough already?"

Rainbow unlocked the door and turned the knob. There was a knock outside. He flagged Murph and waited until the kid put the briefcase under the bed. He drew the .45 from his belt. "Who's there?"

"Conductor, sir. I'd like a word with you."

"You're having it," Rainbow said.

"Inside if I may, sir. It's . . . confidential."

Rainbow put his foot against the door. "I'm in conference right now. What's on your mind?"

"I'd prefer to be discreet, sir. This involves a complaint against you. By a young lady."

Rainbow opened the door a crack. There really was a conductor out there. He waved the man inside. "Murph, you'd best get some sleep. We got an early wake-up."

"I ain't tired." The kid sat up straight. "Besides, I already heard about you and that flapper from the dining-car steward."

The conductor closed the door and cleared his throat. "The young lady is a regular and valued passenger. We cannot tolerate—"

"She took my hundred bucks," Rainbow said. "Only I didn't get no satisfaction, know what I mean? Seems to me I'm the one who ought to be complaining about what I can or cannot tolerate on this wreck."

"Sir, she happens to be from one of the oldest and most respected families in Kentucky." Arms at his sides, the conductor kept opening and closing his fists. "Your conduct is unacceptable. Now, I don't like to put anyone off *The Century*, but if you try to speak to her again between here and New York—"

Rainbow's hand slid off the door. "You sure we're talking about the same woman?"

"I won't debate this with you, sir," the conductor said. "On my train, passengers respect each other's privacy."

"One of the best families in Kentucky?" Rainbow shook his head. "Who'd of believed there even was such a thing? All right, lead me to her. I'll offer up an apology, how's that?"

"Unacceptable, sir. Miss Winslow does not wish to be disturbed by you again. Ever."

"Well, I'll write out a note," Rainbow said, "and you take it to her and see if she'll join me for breakfast tomorrow."

The conductor opened the door. "You don't seem to understand at all. The lady does not want to speak with you. Period. If you try to approach her, I'll see that you *are* put off this train. Do I make myself clear?"

"You mean to tell me I don't even get a chance to apologize?"

"Yes, sir, I mean to tell you precisely that." The conductor touched the brim of his cap, "Good night—gentlemen," and walked out.

"How do you like that little—" Rainbow kicked the door shut. "Who the hell's she think she is?"

"Probably some rich dame who wants her men to speak French and screw her at the same time." Murph got off the bed and stepped to the door with the mirror on it. "They're all over this train, it's a goddamn circus." He turned the knob. "We'll be in Albany right after dawn. You still going to the dining car?"

Rainbow yanked the briefcase from under the bed and rubbed the smooth-grained leather. ". . . I'm every bit as good as she is now. . . ."

"What?"

"Nothing." He hung his hat on the hook. "Get some sleep, kid."

"This damn rumbling's probably gonna keep me up all night." Murph went into the adjoining room and closed the door.

Big-time poker. The Greek and Efrem Roze. One day more wouldn't hurt. The races in Saratoga didn't start until Monday. Old Cal would still be there. Rainbow jumped off the bed and opened the door to the kid's compartment. "We're not getting off at Albany."

"What?"

"Going straight through to New York," Rainbow told him. "Paid that special extra fare to ride this thing, didn't we? We'll catch another train up later."

"Another train? Jesus, you said we could *drive* from Albany. It's only thirty miles. I'll pay and everything. We're gonna need a car, ain't we?"

"No arguments. Call you for breakfast." Rainbow shut the door. Curses echoed in the next room, something hard banged against the wall, the door popped open, and Murph stuck his head inside:

"I should of stayed in Chicago for the PGA."

Rainbow unknotted his tie. "Take the next train back if you like."

Murph's moan turned into a grunt. "Damn extra fare's only nine-sixty. Ain't like it's gonna break us now. Jesus Christ, I never seen a miser like you." He slammed the door.

The mirror was still shaking when Rainbow smiled into it: "Mind if I join your *little* game, Greek?" He laughed, "Oh, hello, Efrem," shook hands with his reflection, "Meet my good luck charm here, Miss Winslow." Another laugh. "Not good enough to even talk to you, miss?" He cocked an eyebrow. "Bet? How about five grand? Fifty?" He held out a hand, shrugged. "How do I make my living? Oh, railroads. Inherited some stock. I only gamble to pass the time—what's that? Right, from my folks." His face got tight. What his Aunt Ruth had left him had been stolen. His mother's bequest wouldn't buy a cup of coffee, and his father's legacy . . . Rainbow jabbed the air with a stiff middle finger. "Up yours, sweet lady. You pay *me* this time."

Doors locked, window shade pulled down, he punched the light button and the small room got dark in a hurry. He undressed, slid under the covers, pistol at his side, briefcase cradled to his ribs, the pillow curled around his ears. The rumble of wheels over rails only got deeper, like a hoarse cough. One extra day wasn't going to matter. Not when it meant getting next to Stavros the Greek and Efrem Roze, and maybe a chance to shake Miss Old Kentucky Winslow out of her sweet-smelling panties at the same time. He closed his eyes and smiled. "Coming at you, boys," he said. "Straight at you."

Etched in mountain rock by the scars of time and weather, a thousand faces peered like sentries over clumps of pine, sycamore, white birch, and the flat river waters now golden gray with morning. Old Cal was back there someplace, maybe fifty miles away. Three feet ahead, the little cook sat on a wood slat chair, alone by the brass rail on the observation platform. His hat was squashed, as if someone had sat on it. Newly shaven cheeks hid behind the turned-up collar of his overcoat. There was a trumpet in his lap. Rainbow took his briefcase off the table beside the door, stepped back from the window, and gave the black cornet player a twenty-dollar bill. "Meet you at trackside, Larry."

With a nod, the musician pocketed the cash. "What if the porter wants in to make up your bed?"

"Keep the door locked," Rainbow said. "Tell him you're—I'm—still sleeping."

The cornet player grinned at the platform. "Beats camping out there for sure. Thanks, Rainbow. Be the best serenade you ever heard." He took the sleepy-eyed young dancer by the hand and led the other members of his jazz band up the car.

Rainbow went out into brisk air drenched with the smell of greening wood. Smoke from the locomotive curled like cotton above four sets of track along the Hudson. Wheels humming to the syncopated *ka-thwack-ka-thwack* of passing track joints, the train seemed to walk the rails on tiptoe. He pulled a chair up to the railing, set his briefcase on his lap, and offered his hand to the little cook. "Angelo Batori? The steward told me I'd find you back here."

Angelo Batori was shivering. Had they made him sleep out here, too? He stroked his horn and stared at the water. "Smooth, no? Like eh-skinny lake."

"Yeah, it's real nice. Listen. I'd like your help in a proposition I have going with our mutual friend, Stavros the Greek." From his jacket, Rainbow pulled out a note-sized piece of paper and a stack of bills with a red band around it. "How does a thousand bucks sound to you?"

Sad brown eyes that were glassy from the cold drifted past the cash to the briefcase. ". . . Lawyer?"

". . . Businessman."

The frail man's overcoat collar touched his hat brim when he shrugged. "What do I have to do for the money, Mr. Businessman?"

"Just spell." Rainbow gave him the piece of paper. "Learn these three words—and spell them right when I ask you—I'll pay you the grand." Each word was printed in capital letters: TENNESSEE, PNEUMONIA, PHARMACEUTICAL.

The note fluttered in Angelo's hand. "Maybe I no can do."

Rainbow slid the cash back into his jacket, put his arm on the frail man's shoulder, and grinned. "Don't worry, friend. I'm gonna teach you myself."

"My first chance to see New York!" Murph put both golf bags down on the trackside platform. "Don't see why I got to teach the guinea. It's your idea!"

"You spell better than me." Rainbow kept staring at the flood of passengers coming out of the green Pullmans and onto the red carpet. "You can still take in the sights. Just be sure he learns those words." Over his shoulder, the black cornet player told his band:

"Little 'Love-Sick Blues.' Up-tempo some. Real sweet now."

The kid shouldered both bags. "Making a fool out of yourself with this, hope you know that."

"Jack's Restaurant on West Forty-fourth Street," Rainbow said. "Meet you there in a few hours." He reached out to pat Murph's shoulder, but the young dancer was waving his stovepipe hat and shouting:

"Mr. Rainbow!"

Dressed all in brown, Miss Winslow stepped off the train onto the platform. The cornet took four beats of drumsticks on concrete, then aimed mellow tones at the steel girders overhead. The clarinet slurred notes in counterpoint. They smiled as they played. Passengers stopped to gape and listen. The brakeman leaned over the railing at the back of the train, porters peeked out windows. The marble cavern of Grand Central Station seemed to swell with music.

Rainbow stopped the lady in brown with an elaborate bow. "Had you figured all wrong, Miss Winslow. Forgiven?"

She blushed, lowered her eyes. The young dancer gave her a wink. Nibbling at a grin, she looked up. And slapped Rainbow across the face.

The horn stopped blowing, the clarinetist sucked spit out of his mouthpiece. The young dancer winced as though he had taken the blow. Passengers made gasping sounds, Murph started laughing. Rainbow forced himself not to touch the stinging cheek.

Miss Winslow flashed a dazzling smile. ". . . Forgiven." She walked toward the gates.

Rainbow matched her stride. "To make up for spoiling your dinner last night, let me take you to breakfast. Anyplace you say. We'll celebrate your—" He rubbed his cheek. "—Your forgiving me."

"Thank you, mister . . . ?"

"Roberts, ma'am. From East Tennessee."

She quickened her pace. ". . . But *no* thank you."

"A fine Kentucky lady like yourself wouldn't make light of a gentleman's duty to see her through these dangerous streets, would she? I hear they're just crawling with lowlife. Be a true honor to escort you." He offered his arm. She kept walking, but there was the trace of a smile on her lips. He was going to win: she was giving in. "Glad that's settled," he said. "Big load off my mind, knowing you'll be safe."

She stopped. There was nothing behind her eyes anymore, they didn't sparkle. Like water coming to a boil, a laugh bubbled out of her. She took his arm.

He led her through the black iron gate into the arrival station, a large square of polished marble crowded with people hugging and kissing, shaking hands, slapping one another on the back. The bulk of them gravitated toward the TO CONCOURSE sign above the glass doors in front of a wide corridor. He walked straight ahead toward the big room at the top of the marble staircase. But Miss Winslow tugged his sleeve and nodded at the door beside a tall blackboard that stood on the wall behind the arrival counter. A man with DOORMAN on his cap finished chalking *9:40* in the column next to TRAIN NO. 26: 20TH CENTURY LTD. ON TIME.

Rainbow put on his hat and followed her lead. But it looked dark outside that door. "What about your luggage?"

"It's all taken care of." She let go of his arm and went through the door. It was dark out there all right. A tunnel. The sidewalk sloped up to daylight, a row of cabs hugged the curb. He helped her into one at the head of the line. She slid to the far side of the seat. "Thank you for the escort. I'm sure I'll be safe now." That smile again. "The Waldorf-Astoria, driver."

Rainbow climbed into the cab, put his briefcase on the floor, and shut the door. "Stroke of luck, isn't it, us going to the same hotel? Must be fate." He tapped the front seat, "You heard the lady," and leaned back grinning.

As the cab pulled up the ramp to Forty-third Street and tall buildings caught the shine of day, he wasn't so sure this was worth the effort. Old Cal might go broke today and leave Saratoga, the chance would be lost. Miss Winslow wasn't worth that, no princess was, not even a real one. But whoever heard of anyone going broke *before* the races started? A small-timer like Old Cal wasn't going to get there until opening day, and what good would it do to wait around some hotel with nothing but time to kill when New York was a city full of action, with connections to be made in all the poker games around and . . . And wasn't she sitting right there, wasn't she talking to him now? Who knew what this might lead to? Rainbow didn't have to force the grin anymore. This was the right thing to do. It was going to work out fine. It might even be fate.

16

Due north, a square finger of cement dominated the skyline. There was a lot of scaffolding near the top where little spires on the corners of the slanted roof and a big spire in the center jabbed the clouds. They were still building it. Rainbow leaned away from the rear window of the cab and shook his head.

"The new Ritz Tower." Miss Winslow was looking, too. She had been silent since leaving Grand Central Station. Her voice sounded foggy. "Forty-two stories. Marvelous, isn't it."

He stopped staring at her and glanced back at the tower. ". . . yeah."

"That's nothing compared to the Woolworth Building." The cab driver had turned sideways at the wheel. "Tallest in the world. I could drive you by, it's just over the West Side."

"Thank you, no." She exhaled through her nose. All the haziness had run out of her voice. "And please watch the road."

The driver shrugged. "Going up like crazy now. All over town. Hear they're gonna tear down the Waldorf. Put up something really big—maybe a hundred stories. Nothing like that in Chicago, am I right?"

"I really miss the old cabs." She raised an eyebrow, glanced out the window. "Where one sat behind the driver in a private compartment."

Facing front, the driver tapped his fingers on the wheel and drove faster. Three blocks south, he turned down a cross street onto Fifth Avenue and parked at the curb in front of a bunch of awnings near the corner of Thirty-fourth Street: "Waldorf."

"Again, thank you for the escort." Miss Winslow nodded at Rainbow, took the doorman's hand, stepped onto the sidewalk, and walked toward the awnings. The instant she stopped by the entrance and looked back, Rainbow felt that he had known she would all along. He smiled and handed a dollar over the front seat. The plaque on the dashboard read CITY FARE 50¢, but the driver put the bill in a cigar box and tapped an impatient rhythm on the wheel.

Rainbow slid his briefcase over the seat and put a hand in the front window. "Your tip's a dime."

The finger-tapping stopped. No longer in a hurry, the driver made a lot of little noises and handed over the change. The hotel doorway stood empty now. And a man in a bowler hat had already jumped in the back of the taxi. The cab sped away. Nothing in this city ever stopped to take a breath.

Rainbow took a long breath. He went inside the hotel. Miss Winslow wasn't near the front desk, which wasn't a desk but a curving marble slab framed by a brass trellis. She wasn't standing by any of the big marble pillars either. The lights hanging by ropes from the beamed ceiling were just fancy bowls with nipples on the ends and strange cuplike things shooting up from the rims. He rapped the dark wood paneling: solid. If they did try to tear this place down, they'd have their work cut out. He walked past the low couch facing the desk. Miss Winslow was standing at the far side of the lobby, talking to a balding man who was at least sixty and practically a midget. They seemed to have a lot to say to each other. She took the little man's arm and went down the corridor, disappearing through the first open doorway on the right. At the end of the lobby, Rainbow left his hat on the rack in the corner. He counted to twenty-five. Then he went down the corridor and turned into the first open doorway on the right.

It was a dining room. And a different world, a world of wide striped ties, of silk and glass beads, cut crystal, pressed white linen. There was nothing heavy in there, the whole room could have floated away in the wind. Even the overhead fans, their big propellers buzzing quietly, seemed delicate. At a table near the lace-covered windows, Miss Winslow was deep in conversation, leaning close to the hairless dwarf. Rainbow cleared his throat to get the maître d's attention, then pointed at the empty table behind Miss Old Kentucky. "I want that one," he said. Snapping the big menu under his arm, the maître d' led the way.

Less than two feet away now, the short bald man was studying the tablecloth. His round face was full of creases. It was hard to tell if he owned a smile. He looked tired, as if his body had got up hours ago, but his gray eyes were still asleep under the covers. Nice suit, though: pure silk. Miss Winslow's stare inched sideways over her menu.

Rainbow leaned toward her and nodded at the gold braid that kept the crinkly paper from slipping out of the menu. "I was a little hungry myself. What do you recommend?"

Her lips parted in a small smile. "Eggs Benedict is rather good here." The bald man looked confused. She put a hand on his arm. "We met on the train. Mr. Horace Wells, this is—"

"Rainbow Roberts." He got up quickly, offered his hand to the little man, who had a surprisingly strong grip. "Seems we both like jazz."

Her eyes were someplace else now, hiding.

Rainbow glanced at the table behind him. "Look, I'm so close over there, we might as well be having lunch together anyways. Mind if I join you? My treat."

Her smile widened. "Fate again?"

"Must be." He sat in the chair beside her and grinned at the bald man. *Horace Wells, Horace Wells:* the name was as familiar as an old friend, yet lost, misplaced. "You in vaudeville or something?"

"I train for Majestic Farms," Wells said.

Rainbow rested his shoe on top of his briefcase. "Train the crops, do you? Always wondered how they did that. Must be easy for you, though, built so close to the ground like you are."

The bald man owned a fierce squint. "It's a racing stable."

"Love to watch them run," Rainbow said. "Maybe you could give me a tip. Headed for Saratoga later today."

The old man started nodding. "Could have guessed that much. Good luck."

Horace Wells . . . "Not Horace Wells?" Rainbow said. "Ancient Ruler's jock?"

"You see?" Miss Winslow patted the little man's hand. "Not everyone has forgotten." The look she gave Rainbow was soft; it said thank you.

"How about that!" Rainbow leaned back in his chair. "Great horse."

"The best," Horace said. "Never another like him."

"You two will have something to talk about while I excuse myself." Miss Winslow pushed back from the table and carried her purse to the doorway.

"You from Chicago?" Horace said.

"East Tennessee. Saw you ride once. Louisville, about ten years back."

The old jockey made a face like an unhappy clown. "Then you ain't never seen *me* ride." He stared at the napkin in his hands. "None of my business really, but I seen lots of flashy guys run after Iris because of her old man's money. Truth is, things ain't so good with him no more. So if that's a factor to you—"

"It's not." *Iris. Iris Winslow.* Beautiful.

Somewhere in the expressionless face he studied, Horace must have found a glimmer of satisfaction. He watched his hand rub the edge of the table as if he knew he had said too much. "What line you say you're in?"

"Leather." Rainbow held up the briefcase. "Make these and ship them all over the world. Suitcases, too. And golf bags." He stowed the case back under his foot. "This Majestic Farms—big stable?"

"Used to be." Horace leaned forward. "Ever thought about owning horses? Man in your position ought to. The yearling sales at the Springs is a good place to start, but I got two beauties you should see first. Sired by Clarionmate, the Ruler's grandson, you know. Train for you myself."

"Sounds a little rich for my blood."

"See, but I can give you a deal on both of them. You'd save a bundle, and have enough left over to take on this four-year-old I'm thinking of running up north. Old Smoke. Class all the way. Likes that Saratoga track, too."

Rainbow put an elbow on the table. "You seem awful anxious to sell."

"I ain't." The bald man tugged his ear. "If it was up to me, they'd never go on the block. Like I told you, things ain't so good with the stable no more."

"How much, Horace?"

"Don't want to lose these yearlings. If I trained them, see, that's what I'm getting at. Give you a fair price and we sign a contract with me as trainer. I do all the work for next to nothing. Just a piece of their winnings. All you do is pay the feed."

"How much?"

"It ain't the price so much as it's the principle of the thing."

"How much if you train them, Horace?"

"See, I couldn't work this if I put them up for bid at Keenland or the Springs. Somebody'd steal them from me. Now I know what you're thinking—Clarionmate didn't do much on the track. But he's the Ruler's grandson! These yearlings is champions."

Rainbow sat back. Around the room, people were nibbling at their food, drinking with their little fingers sticking out from the cups. He shook his head and stood to greet Miss Winslow, who made her way between tables.

"Why are powder rooms always so crowded?" Iris let him help her into the chair. "Haven't they brought my tea yet?"

"Show him the picture," Horace said.

Fingers tight around her purse, she turned to Rainbow. "Perhaps you might be able to get it for me."

Rainbow signaled the waiter. "Some tea for the lady. Right now!" He leaned on the table. "Got a glimpse of that photo on the train. Like to see it again. Horace is a good talker. Has me real interested."

She put the purse in her lap and patted the bald man's head. "You'll have to excuse Horace. Horses have been his whole life. He doesn't know that I've promised these yearlings to friends whom I'll be seeing this afternoon."

Little specks of red in those gray eyes fired at Rainbow. "They're yours for ten thousand apiece," Horace said. "And six for Old Smoke." He lowered his gaze. "We got to think of the stable first, Iris. I already told him. Now show him the picture."

Her eyes lost their luster. She seemed on the brink of tears. She squeezed lemon into the tea the waiter brought her and stirred it as though hypnotized by the swirl. "You don't want these yearlings, Mr. Roberts. The Sales at Saratoga would be much better for you. Horace might enter one of our horses there. Perhaps he could help you bid."

In the long silence, Horace rubbed his hands. He looked cold. "Might be Old Smoke could do something up there. He's ready to run right now. You sure that's the way you want it, Iris?" He answered her nod with one of his own. "All right. Sorry, Rainbow. Can't sell you them horses. Shame, though. Any purse Old Smoke might win would only keep us in feed for a couple of months. And his winning ain't no sure thing."

Another silence, darker than the first. Iris looked so fragile that the flick of a finger might have shattered her. Rainbow scraped his shoe over the briefcase. Why not mix business with business? "We could make it a sure thing."

The bald man's face wrinkled with surprise, then suspicion. "Takes a lot of money."

"You're on the inside," Rainbow said. "No risk. Won't matter how much it costs." His grin felt easy. "I've made boat races before."

"Not in Saratoga you ain't." Horace sucked on his lip. "Can't fix no race up there."

Iris stopped stirring her tea. Her eyes got hard. "Horace, I think we should leave."

"Now hear him out," the bald man said. "He may just have something."

"It's dishonest." She glared at Rainbow. "So are you."

Something in him wanted to hurt her. He held the heat of her stare and threw it back until a twinge of pain darted across her face and she lowered her gaze. She was trembling, her eyes were welling up again. "Just trying to help out," he said. "None of my concern what you do." He grinned at Horace. "But we can do it. At Saratoga."

The little man nodded as if he didn't mean to. "Thirty years riding and fifteen teaching them how. Never a dishonest race. I won't start now."

Iris managed a smile.

"Sorry, bad idea." Rainbow got his briefcase, offered his hand across the table, and started to stand. "Nice meeting you, Horace. Good luck."

Iris put a hand on Rainbow's arm, then quickly withdrew it. "Don't leave, please. We—" She wasn't able to look at him. "I'd better fix my face. Would you order for me?" She stood and walked up the aisle.

Horace waited for her to get through the doorway, then he came around the table and sat in her chair. "Could you really do it? I mean, you got that kind of money?"

Rainbow put the briefcase down. "How much are we talking about?"

"Lightest field we'd be safe in is seven horses. Three grand per jock makes what, twenty-one grand? Five more to ease the overnight line . . . And fifty for me."

"Sounds like training doesn't pay so good."

"Nothing legal pays good." Horace ran a hand over his scalp. "Christ, if I was riding today, I'd make more in a year than I made in fifteen back when I was up. And I was bringing them home. Ain't fair somehow."

"Never is, Horace." Rainbow toyed with his napkin. "Your fifty thousand sounds a little steep to me."

"Look, I'm taking a big risk here. If Efrem Roze's boys find out, I won't get near no New York track."

"You leave E.R. to me."

"You know him?"

Rainbow grinned. "Let's say we got a mutual friend. I'll handle the Greek, too. Nothing to worry about."

"Leather, huh?" Horace was nodding again. He did own a smile. A big one. "Okay, you bet my fifty for me. Should get at least four-to-one. Hell, nobody's seen Old Smoke since the winter. I'll only take three-to-one on the payoff. You keep the extra point as vigorish. Whatever else you lay down is yours, I won't claim a cent."

Rainbow sealed the deal with a handshake.

"Now Iris can't know nothing about this," Horace said, his hard fingers turning a fork in circles on the tablecloth. "The fix is between you and me. I been in a fair amount of boat races in my time, so here's how we'll do it . . ."

"You'll do exactly what I tell you," Rainbow said, *"when* I tell you. First time you get out of line, I pull the plug."

Horace let out a lot of air. "Your money. You got the right to call it."

The waiter collected the menus. "Gentlemen, our soup today is—"

"Eggs Benedict all around," Rainbow said. "And bring me the check."

The waiter walked away. Horace scratched the back of his hand. "Our horse is a four-year-old, golden chestnut. Be moving him up to the Springs tonight. Had him out three times this year."

"Any wins?"

The old jockey winked. "Not yet."

Rainbow sat back laughing.

"T-E-N-N . . ." Angelo Batori leaned forward on the park bench, shaking his head at the small piece of paper in his hands. "How come we do this?"

"You're doing it to earn the money." Murph didn't look at him. A yellow box kite was dancing in the breeze above the scaffolds on the big tower just south of the park. "Start over. And quit stopping in the middle. Go straight through all three words till you get the hang of it. Just read them off the paper. You can read, can't you?"

The little man's hand fluttered from side to side. "Mezz-a-mezz. My nephew, Tag, good spell. Pass the test, first-eh time." His cheeks swelled with a grin. "Becomes the citizen five year already."

"Yeah, well maybe we ought to get him to learn for you. Jesus, how'd you ever land a job with E.R. anyways?"

"Scuzeh?"

"E.R. Jesus Christ, the guy you're working for. Efrem Roze."

Angelo shrugged. "Mia—my-eh sister's boy, Tag. Big man. Run the casino, eh-Saratoga." He slapped his upper arm. "Strong to this Roze."

Murph frowned. It was even worse than he knew it was going to be. The dumb guinea was hopeless. *No wonder Rainbow wanted to dump him on me.*

"I no understand." Angelo tapped the paper with his cane. "One thousand dollar? For this?"

"It ain't that hard," Murph said. "Now keep going through all the letters till I tell you to stop. You understand? Go through each of them—"

"Sure, each one, no stop." Angelo began reading the letters. In that stiff monotone, he sounded like a baritone parrot.

For a while, it was easy to take, but soon the buzz of traffic from nearby streets and the summer yells of boys playing baseball farther down the path made it hard for Murph to concentrate on what the little cook was saying. And what if someone should walk by and see him sitting next to a crippled wop? Murph stood. "Let's go."

"I do no so good?"

"You're doing great." Murph pointed down the path. "We're just gonna find us some trees so you can practice without being stared at."

Angelo turned in a half-circle. "Nobody noplace by here."

"Yeah, well it gets crowded in a few minutes. C'mon, it'll be like a picnic. You know what a picnic is?"

"Sure, all the time backyard on the grass, no?"

"Jesus . . ." Murph let out a long stream of air and led the frail man deeper into Central Park.

The dress Iris was wearing was the same brown as the stones in the bridge that spanned the path sloping down into Central Park. Rainbow switched his briefcase to the other hand. "And you went all that way just to go to school?"

"Louisville wasn't a fit place for a lady. My father wanted something better for me."

"Never seen Paris, but I can't see how anybody could think *this* was better than Kentucky."

Her smile came back. "You're right." A few silent steps, then: "You must travel the trains a great deal in your line of work."

"You get used to it after a while."

"Not me. All that rumbling."

"Yeah, keeps you awake, don't it." He cleared his throat. And cursed himself. "Some people it does, I mean. About what I said in the dining car. See, most women on trains, traveling alone, that is—"

134

She didn't say anything. He cursed himself again.

Lined with trees and tall grass, the trail snaked around a meadow where some boys were playing baseball. They used flat rocks as bases, an old board as the pitcher's rubber. The boy on the board wasn't throwing hard, but from the look on his face, he was pitching the last game of the World Series.

"What do you do," Iris said. "I mean—really?"

The shapes in motion on the ball field lost their edges. Did it matter what he said? After this walk, which was such a *marvelous* idea according to her, a woman who had been around the world ten times and yet had never spent any time in Central Park, after this little stroll she would go back to the Waldorf. Or Europe. Or Paris. Thank God she wasn't talking about that place anymore. All through that ten-dollar breakfast she had made him feel like a child. Compared to her travels, he had never been anywhere, never even gone out the door. She had been up in an airplane once, too, but that was probably a fib: who'd be stupid enough to go flying with a woman?

"It's none of my business," she said. "You don't have to tell me."

He drew in a short breath, held it. "I play golf. Some poker, a little pool, horseshoes, things like that."

She stopped walking. "I meant, how do you earn your living?"

"I just told you."

There, it was said. But she wasn't frowning or laughing. Her face got tight, yet her eyes held a sadness, as though she were almost sorry the game was over. If he had sold leather goods or owned a railroad or a bank . . . But even then, the game would have ended at some point. It always did, didn't it?

A ball cracked off a bat, high-pitched yells laced the breeze, a boy ran the bases of that make-believe diamond.

Rainbow raked his hat brim. "I know you got some friends to meet. If you want to head back to the hotel, I'll get you a cab."

She was staring at the grass. "I keep forgetting you have business here. I don't want to ruin your schedule."

"No, it's just, I thought . . . Maybe we could have lunch first. Before I leave."

"I'd like that." Her eyes rose slowly and she found her smile. "I think it's exciting that you're a gambler. Really. Are you very good at it?"

He grinned. "Truth is, I never gamble." Her eyes narrowed, but she didn't stop smiling. The sun on the back of his neck made him shiver. He nodded toward the meadow where the boy slid into third.

"I'm a little stiff after the train. Gonna try to loosen up over there. Only be a minute."

"Can't I come, too?"

He took the narrow path through the grass. Between pitches, he guided her past the boy standing behind the batter and left her on a spot in foul territory, halfway to first base, then walked toward home.

The young pitcher stopped his windup. "Watch it, mister, or you'll get beaned good."

Rainbow held his hand out to the dark-haired batter. "Just want one swing."

"Can't, I got two strikes on me." The boy tapped the end of his bat on the piece of slate which served as home plate, then swung and missed a high fast ball. He threw down his bat, pointed at Rainbow. "I get one more. This jerk made me miss."

"You're out." The pitcher dropped his glove and walked in the rest of his team. "We're up."

". . . Jerk." The dark-haired boy kicked the bat at Rainbow's feet, ran to the pitcher's board, and put on the glove.

Picking up the bat, Rainbow laid his case on home plate and stepped into the left-hand batter's box. "One swing's all I'm asking."

"It's a private game," the dark-haired boy said. "Who made last out?"

"Bet you can't get *me* out." Rainbow pulled out a dollar, waved it at the pitcher, then tucked the bill under the corner of his case, straightened up in a hitter's stance, and swung the bat in a lazy rhythm out to the pitcher's mound and back again. "One swing. You get me out, you get the buck."

The dark-haired boy flicked the ball into his glove and called toward first base. "Hey, lady! Get this jerk out of here, would you?"

Iris was laughing. Rainbow tapped the bat on the briefcase. "C'mon, throw one in. Buy you a new ball if you get me out."

The boys on the field and around home sounded like a tone-deaf chorus: "Go ahead, Danny." "Yeah, throw him your curve."

Muttering under his breath, the dark-haired boy pointed to the small kid in right and waved him across the field. "Little Roger, you take left. Buzz, move over." As the outfielders scurried to new positions, the boy wet his fingers and gripped the ball. "Okay, jerk. Let's see you hit *this*." More shouts of encouragement. It was a long windup, double-pumped, as though the boy were trying to take off in flight. His arms flapped, his leg kicked high.

He threw the curve.

It hung over the outside corner of the plate. Rainbow went with the pitch, blasting it to left field. With the solid *crack* of horsehide against wood, he dropped the bat, grabbed his briefcase and the dollar, and started running. The ball soared higher than the tops of the buildings in the distance. The little kid in left ran like a whirlwind. His cap flew off. He looked back over his shoulder, flung his hands up, and jumped. Something went *smack*, and he tumbled, got to his knees. And held up the ball.

"Way to go, Little Rog!" The dark-haired pitcher leapt high off the board and walked toward Rainbow, who stopped between first and second. "Okay, mister. Let's have that buck."

Iris had both hands over her mouth. Her body was shaking with laughter. Rainbow marched into left field. Shouts chased him: "Hey, you welcher, pay off." He stopped in front of the small boy who was putting on his cap. "Robbed me of a home run, kid." But he chuckled and gave the boy the dollar. "Great catch."

"Let's get sodas!" The little boy scampered toward the trees. His friends ran after him. There was a lot of laughter. The meadow emptied in a hurry. It was just grass now, dotted with a few rocks and a warped piece of board.

Still laughing, Iris walked onto the field. "I never thought he'd catch it. He was so small. And *you*. You looked so funny running with *that*." She pointed at the briefcase. "It was wonderful."

"Yeah, well . . ." Rainbow tucked the .45 deeper into his belt, buttoned his jacket. "I didn't hit it full."

She looped her arm through his. "Are you—loosened up—now?"

He laughed with her. Dry grass crunched underfoot. Beyond the trees, the path stretched south toward a big statue. He stamped the dust off his shoes. "I don't get you, Iris, you know that?"

"I don't either."

Her arm felt warm and light. He swallowed softly. "Too bad you're not going to Saratoga for the season. I hear it's pretty good up there."

"It's not what it used to be."

"Yeah, but with Horace entering your horse, you ought to be there to represent the stable, don't you think?"

She glanced at the bronze figures standing and kneeling on top of the monument at the entrance to the park. "I suppose so."

Trolley cars circled the pedestal of the tall statue in the middle of the street. Rainbow put his briefcase on the stone bench near the curb. "Got some people expecting me up there,"—*I have to kill a man there*—"or else I'd maybe stay a day or so and . . . It's just that I have to go."

"I don't." It was a whisper, but she said it like a curse. "I—can't."

"Look, if it's a question of money, I could help. Like an investment. In your stable."

The breeze ruffled the hair sticking out of her little hat. She faced the street.

"Not as charity," Rainbow said. "Why, if Horace Wells can train one-tenth as good as he could ride, that makes it a sound venture in my book. They say he was the best."

"He was."

He put his hands on her shoulders, felt her stiffen, turned her. "Iris . . ."

She stared at the pavement. "Don't look at me."

He raised her chin. "I want to."

She didn't try to turn away. The sunlight bouncing off the buildings made her eyes look glassy. "Maybe I could go. But just for the race. I'll see. . . ."

Maybe was good enough for now. There was always a chance with a maybe. And after he had taken care of Old Cal Robinson, after he had helped Iris's stable earn some big money from the fix, who could tell what that maybe would turn into? She wasn't so snotty after all, she was just fragile. And fine. And probably fed up with all the men who must have tried to get next to her, as beautiful as she was. What would it be like to run a real racing stable? He could do it. But he wasn't going to run wild with this notion, he was going to take his time. Time was on his side now. That changed everything. There was nothing he couldn't do.

Traffic snarled, people hurried by, but he saw only her. He put one hand on the briefcase and laced the other through her fingers.

"Jesus Christ." Murph stopped short of the statue guarding the edge of the traffic circle and grabbed Angelo by the coattail.

"No, this way." The frail man used his cane to point to the tall monument in the center of the street. "Colombo. . . ."

"That bastard." Eyes burning, fists clenched, Murph turned away from Rainbow and that woman at the curb and steered the little cook back into the park.

17

The murmur from a hundred voices talking at once rumbled off the walls, harsh laughs stabbed the air like intermittent thunder. The extra chairs around the tables had been dragged away to suit the needs of cliques that kept changing as newcomers walked in. Gamblers from all points came to Jack's Restaurant, a meeting place with its own geography: the Boys from Trenton in the far corner, the Pride of Philadelphia near the windows, North Jersey High Rollers at the alcove by the bar. The smells of spicy colognes, hair tonics, smoldering tobaccos, fought the aroma of steak and onions, rashers of bacon. At the table between Atlantic City and Long Island, Rainbow drank ginger ale from the bottle: "It's an opportunity, kid."

Murph filled his glass and set the bottle next to one he had already emptied. "I don't like it."

"You don't have to. I won't use your share of the bankroll on it. Besides, if I don't like how it's going, there'll be plenty of time to pull out."

"You sure it's business? Nothing else?"

Rainbow hardened his stare. "If it was something else, I wouldn't of told you."

"But you ain't never fixed no horse race before. How you know you can do it? And we don't know squat about these people."

"Horace Wells is like a legend for Chrissake," Rainbow said. "We're inside all the way, stand to make a killing. We'll take it step by step. No way to get hurt."

Murph ran his thumb over the rim of his glass. "You tell her you was a gambler?"

"She knows."

The kid grinned and raised his glass. "Well, I guess that's that."

Shaking his head, Rainbow glanced at his panama on the rack near the windows. The light coming through the drapes was speckled, as though filtered through sand. With his leg, he pressed his briefcase against his chair. "Got our stuff moved into the Shelton Hotel?"

"When we leaving?"

"They got a special train. Tomorrow. All these guys'll be on it. Lakeside Monroe right over there. And the tall guy with the moustache? That's the Stork—plays golf on one leg. The cream of the crop you're looking at, kid. And we're right there with them now."

"But we could be in Saratoga for dinner instead of—"

"We're staying," Rainbow said. "The Greek's game is too important. Now, the Stork says all we have to do is feed the manager of the Shelton." He peeled a hundred-dollar bill off the wad in his pocket. "Give him this. Tell him it's for my in."

Murph pushed the money away. "A hundred's too much. I'll handle it."

Rainbow stuffed the bill into the kid's jacket. "Do exactly like I tell you. A hundred's nothing for an intro to the Greek. Puts us close to the well. And the word is, Efrem Roze himself might drop by. In which case, we are *in* the well, lapping up sweet water." He grinned and rapped the table. "While you're down the station, get us on that special train, too. Now what the hell took you so long in getting here?"

Murph stared at the bubbles in the glass. "Wanted me to learn that wop, didn't you? Dumb as he is, it might take me a year."

"I need him ready by tomorrow."

"Then you learn him."

"You saying you can't handle it?"

"Not me—*him!* Jesus, he don't even know what them words mean."

"Just make sure he can spell them," Rainbow said. "Stay up with him all night if you have to."

Pouting, Murph folded his arms across his chest. "I ain't going to no guinea party."

"What are you talking about?"

"He's staying with relatives he ain't seen in years. They're having a party for him. Bad enough trying to talk to him. Jesus, think of what it'd be like with a whole gang of them jabbering away like they do."

"Better keep him at the hotel. In your room. All night."

Murph turned sideways. "No."

"Look, we need him on that train tomorrow. No time to do it any other way."

"We never got time for nothing except hustling."

"Got to make a living, now don't we?"

"We got a hundred and fifty grand *on* us for Chrissake!"

"Keep your voice down."

"Well, don't we?" Murph whispered. "Wouldn't hurt to take a week off and relax. It ain't like they're closing down Saratoga tomorrow. Old Cal'll still be there. *If* he's there. Hell, he might even be in here. Right now!"

Rainbow's leg stiffened against the briefcase. "They wouldn't let him in the door of this place." He rubbed the edge of the table. "When we get through with the fix, maybe we can go back down to Hot Springs and play a little golf just for the fun of it."

"You mean it? I ain't been home in years! You really mean it?"

Rainbow nodded. "What do you think we're doing all this for? So we can stop doing it, that's why. I don't plan to spend the rest of my life running after money."

Murph's smile went away. "You ain't gonna stop and you know it."

". . . Bet?"

The kid didn't laugh at the joke. "Probably gonna run after her till she snags you."

"Is that what's got you?"

"Got you, you mean. Sweet on her, ain't you."

"You're talking nonsense again."

"I seen you." Murph nudged his glass into the bottles. "Holding hands like you was engaged already. . . ."

The kid would have found out anyway. It had been just two hours since Rainbow left Iris at the Waldorf. He missed her. He wasn't going to play this one as though he didn't mean it. "You don't understand, kid."

"What do you take me for, a two-year-old?" Beneath the red bangs, dark eyes narrowed with contempt, then softened and drifted over scratches in the tabletop. "Besides, no real lady'd ever pay us no nevermind. Said so yourself."

"This is different."

Murph stared into his lap. ". . . Is it?"

The room noise seemed louder now, the laughter was exploding like blown-up paper bags. A waiter with a towel draped over his arm and

JACK'S sewn onto his pocket stopped at the table: "What'll it be, gents?"

Rainbow grabbed his briefcase and stood. "Some fresh air."

The top floors of the Shelton Hotel were set back from each other, creating the jagged outline of steps against the early evening sky. It was the tallest building on East Forty-ninth Street. Everything inside looked new, felt new, smelled new. Murph crushed out his cigarette in the circle of heavy glass that was either an ashtray or a coaster and walked across the lobby to the little alcove off the main entrance. He knocked on the door marked PRIVATE. Footsteps inside the office grew louder, the door opened. The manager wore thick glasses. The five or six hairs on top of his head were plastered down— glued there. Maybe he just didn't want to chance losing any more of them.

Murph pulled out a five-dollar bill and tried to make his voice sound like a casual yawn. "Heard you could get a man into a poker game."

"Possible," the manager said.

"The Greek's got a game on tonight, right?"

"Sorry. Private."

Murph put another five-dollar bill next to the first one. "You sure?"

"Sonny, that wouldn't get you in the elevator."

"Make it twenty-five, then. I'm a guest here, you know."

"Well, that makes it different, doesn't it." The manager was smiling. He looked like a bug squinting. "Nice little game on the fourth floor. Interested?"

Cursing to himself and shoving the money into his pants, Murph got out the hundred-dollar bill. "It ain't for me, it's for Rainbow Roberts. He's a friend of the Stork."

The money disappeared into the manager's vest pocket. "Have him call me so I can look him over before I take him up. I'll provide the introduction, but make sure he knows it's up to Mr. Karamonopolis from that point on." Another grin: sly, mocking. "And, of course, even if he's not allowed to play, there can be no refunds."

"Yeah, yeah." Murph faced halfway into the lobby. "What time?"

". . . Anytime, sonny." The manager's high-pitched chuckle sounded like a water turbine winding down. The door closed *snap- click*.

Murph marched out to the curb. It took three stick matches before the flame beat the wind to the end of his cigarette. Coming around the corner through the deepening waver of dusk being blown along the street, a tall man in a ten-gallon hat and a fat man in an orange suit walked side by side: Tom "The Whip" Edwards and Pete. They were sharing a laugh. And holding hands. At the tree by the lobby entrance, The Whip stopped to straighten the scarf about Pete's neck. Then the two men went inside the hotel, a pair of bowlegs leading the straight-armed swagger of a dock worker.

"Jesus Christ Almighty. Nothing but assholes and queers in New York." Murph flicked the butt into Lexington Avenue and started walking south.

Rainbow couldn't move his hands. Body stiff, yet melting inside from the taste of her lips, the warmth of her breath on his cheek, he swallowed all his eagerness and sat on the edge of the bed kissing Iris as though she were made of wood. He couldn't believe she was actually there—with him. She deserved better.

Turning her head, she smoothed out the wrinkles in her dress and cleared her throat. "We'll be late for dinner. . . ."

He stepped around the bed to the bathroom door, keeping his back to her to hide the tightness in his pants. It hurt down there, like a welt. But at least she wasn't running out the door. Yet. "Give me a second to wash up," he said, "and we'll get some dinner."

"You're angry, aren't you."

"Let's just get some dinner, okay?"

"I'm not hungry." She pinched one of the tiny balls of thread which pimpled the bedspread. A silence hugged the room. Then she hiccuped. "I should have waited for you in the lobby."

More silence, trapping all the little sounds he made while standing still: the crinkle of shirt against jacket when he breathed, the creak of shoe leather as he tried not to rock from heel to toe, the soft gasp of flesh against flesh when he opened his fist. "Look, I don't want you to think I planned this. . . ."

"It's not that," she said. "It's just"—another hiccup—"just you."

"Terrific. Just me."

Like a car backfiring, two hiccups scrambled the purr of her nervous giggle. "I meant, it was a mistake to—" She hiccuped again.

"Try holding your breath."

". . . Maybe a glass of water."

He filled the glass from the bathroom tap. The tightness in his groin was gone, his erection was curling back on itself like the head of a snail drawn into its shell. He knelt beside her. "Drink from the opposite side. And hold your nose."

With her lips on the far rim, she held her nostrils and leaned forward, but a loud hiccup shook the glass and water spilled onto her dress. Her gaze wandered across his chest. ". . . I can't."

"Well, just drink some, maybe that'll help." He walked to the chair, listened to her sip water and squeak with air. He could still taste her lips. *I can't*, spoken so softly that he had barely heard it, now echoed like a solitary marble in a tin box. Hadn't she really meant: "I won't. Not with you." He picked up his hat and briefcase. "Some air might help. Walk around the block?"

"I think they're gone." She put the glass on the night table and sat there watching her hand caress the wet spot on her dress, material so fine that it shimmered, so pale a brown that it looked like flesh. And he was wearing the same suit, same shirt, same everything as when he had met her, because it was everything—all he had except an extra shirt which didn't fit too well and had one frayed cuff. And if the valet service at the Shelton had taken any longer this afternoon, he would be standing here in his underwear, and for all he knew that might have worked out better.

Her hiccups were gone. For a moment, he wanted them back. At least they had given him something to do.

"Rainbow, you in there?" Three knocks rattled the door, the knob turned, and Murph ambled in. "Saw the goddamn mana—" His mouth stopped moving, his stare followed Iris from bed to window.

"Should of called first," Rainbow said.

Murph kept looking at the rumpled bedspread as though someone were buried there. "The manager said he'd take you up, but he don't guarantee the Greek'll let you play."

"What time's the game start?"

"Already has. You can go up anytime." The kid leaned in close. His whisper sounded like a threat: "Ain't you even gonna introduce me?"

"Wait outside," Rainbow told him.

"You must be Dave." Framed by a window of quiet sky, Iris's smile could have hung in an art gallery. "I've heard a lot about you all day."

"Been wondering when you two'd get the chance to meet," Rainbow said. "Miss Winslow, my partner, Murph." He squeezed the kid's shoulder to prompt a reply.

"Nice meeting you, Miss Winslow."

"Iris," she said. "Nice to have met *you*, Dave."

Sheepishly, Murph studied the floor, then his shoes, then the bottom of the chair. "I better change and get ready to go to that thing with the—with Angelo."

"I'll only be a minute, kid. Wait for me." Rainbow ushered him into the hall, closed the door, and put on his hat. "Just as well you're not hungry, Iris. This poker game'll probably last all night. Want me to call you a cab?"

She was looking out the window. "I can manage."

"I could have Murph take you to dinner if you like." From the suitcase by the dresser, he got his .45 and sneaked it into his belt. "Or he could ride with you back to your hotel. Like an escort."

"I'll be fine. Why don't you just go ahead. I'd like to freshen up before I leave."

He kept changing his grip on the briefcase handle. "I thought sure this game would start late enough to give us a chance to relax and—"

"Please. Don't explain."

"Seems like I can't buy you dinner even when you let me, don't it."

She wasn't looking at his grin, she was moving to her purse. She got out her cigarettes and lit one before he could think to do it for her. Her smoke drifted toward him like a wall. "I hope you win."

"Sorry about the timing." He dug into his pocket, came out with a five-dollar bill. "At least let me pay for the cab."

She eyed the money as though a bunch of snakes had slithered into the room. A quick drag off the cigarette, another stream of gray from her mouth and nose, and she snapped the purse together and walked back to the window.

He stuffed the cash into his pants. *Did it again, you ass. Just leave!* His fingers stuck to the doorknob. "I don't want to leave like this."

"It's as good as any other way, isn't it?" Her cigarette smoke bounced off the window. She turned, lowered her eyes. "I'm sorry. I keep getting in your way, don't I. All the things you have to do—"

"Yeah, you're a regular pest." He took her smile down deep to the bitterness festering in his gut. "I don't call these games or say when they're over. Wish I did. Tired of running everywhere just to make ends meet. Wouldn't expect a true lady to understand the half of it much less put up with it." He couldn't look at her anymore: she was there, but he might as well have been in an empty room, any room, staring at the remains of a dinner he had just ordered, remembering he had ordered the same thing night after night for years, and time hadn't made it taste any different. "It'd be the same tomorrow, Iris. Or the day after. So I won't tell you it'll get any better. Time's what's in my way, not you. Time and all the things I got no choice to fill it with."

There was no use in continuing. She hadn't raised her head or tried to say anything. And she probably hadn't heard a single word. A woman like her would have already made plans to be someplace else.

But at least she wasn't laughing. He was going to remember that about her.

"Like to see you tomorrow before I leave," he said. "Could I call you?"

"It might be easier if I called you."

He chuckled to himself: *What did you expect, you ass!* "Sure, that might be a whole lot easier." He opened the door. "Nothing here worth worrying over, but I'd appreciate it if you'd lock up when you go."

She nodded, her neck curved down like the ash on her cigarette. "Good luck, Rainbow."

Not words, but little puffs of air, never even alive.

He went into the hall and gently shut the door.

Murph was leaning against the wall, legs crossed, shoulders in. "Don't blame you. Beautiful, ain't she. Looks rich, too. You tell her to call me Dave?"

Rainbow punched the elevator button. "Bring Angelo around to my room early tomorrow."

"I can't promise he'll be ready, then. Besides, that special train don't leave till the afternoon. That's what my mom called me."

". . . What?"

"Dave. Only sometimes—when I done something wrong?—then it was David."

Rainbow drew a short breath. "I'll be up by ten. If Angelo needs more coaching, I'll help you out. You'll be busy anyways."

"Aw, Jesus, doing what?"

"Buying us both new wardrobes. Don't think we're going to Saratoga like this, do you?" He let out a laugh and ruffled the kid's hair.

But she was gone.

From the start he had known it would be only a matter of time before she left him. She had to, it didn't make sense any other way. And he didn't want her. Not really. He just didn't like losing her. He hated losing. Anything. He slapped the elevator button again. And again and again.

The tears never came.

I'll be fine, Iris told herself. Freshen up. Leave. She was only getting in his way, he in hers. They were both tired of running and for both of them it would be the same tomorrow and the day after. It wouldn't get any better. It had been a mistake.

And he was so tender. . . .

She switched off the bathroom light. Leave? There was noplace to go. The streets were dark and hostile. Horace was already on the road, the apartment would be filled with luggage and piles of week-old dishes. But what choice did she have? She turned off the light in the bedroom, lit a cigarette, and sat in the chair by the door. The pointed glow of burning tobacco breathed when she did. The blindness of night crept through the window, the fire of city lights went someplace else: straight up to blank out stars, low along the avenue in horizontal bands to guide the walkers, riders, hiders—all those with time they would never own. Prisoners of time. Like her.

Tender and innocent, like a little boy.

No voice in the back of her head, no secret sound or feeling. Just the whisper from her own lips surprising her in the darkness:

"Stay."

18

The face in the painting on the wall wore the sneer-smile of a New York founding father and the bug-eyed stare of a moron. It dominated the small room which stood off to the side of the suite like a walk-in closet. In the corner, the Greek's bodyguard watched night air suck cigar smoke out the window; he was a half-foot taller and fifty pounds heavier than Curtis. Rainbow loosened his tie. It was quiet now, that brief pause after all bets had been made and the pot was "right": the hesitation before new cards came out. Getting into this game had been easy: these people were glad to have him, he belonged here, not with Iris. And he was winning—stacks of money, IOUs. He could have left his briefcase behind and played with the $10,000 he had put in his jacket. It was their own money these high rollers were trying to win back. He was happy to give them that chance. But it didn't feel full. Something was missing. She was gone.

Cards shot faceup around the table. The dealer called them as they landed in front of the players: "King to the Jack"—Tom "The Whip" Edwards pushed back the brim of his hat. "Possible straight still working"—Rainbow let the four of clubs slide over his other cards. "No help for the nines"—the mountain of flesh in the orange suit cursed in Russian. "Pair of fives now"—Stavros the Greek checked his hole cards against those lying faceup before him. "And a big bullet"— the dealer put the deck to the side. He had cod eyes set in a pasty face. Moles speckled his neck and one cheek. He was immaculately dressed in black and white. And he smiled too much. He was Efrem

Roze. After a quick look over the table, he flicked a finger at the fat man. "Your nines are still talking, Pete."

"Three hundred." The fat man dropped three hundred-dollar bills into the pot.

Stavros saw the bet, but Roze gathered his cards into a precise pile. Tom The Whip tossed in his money. With no possible straight working, but with the chance for a bluff if the Greek dropped out, Rainbow pushed $500 into the pot. The fat man in orange stared at him like a little boy who had just been slapped, then his thick fingers moved more money into the center of the table. Stavros folded his hand. Tom The Whip fed the raise.

"Pot's right. Down and dirty." Roze dealt the three remaining players one card facedown, allowed a breath for consideration, then coaxed the play: "Nines bet."

The Russian must not have wanted to be raised again. His $500 landed in the pot like a rock. Carelessly, Tom The Whip bowed out and flipped his cards over. He had a nine in the hole. No wonder the fat man wasn't betting as if he had three of a kind: the other nine was tucked away among Rainbow's facedown cards. Fighting a smile, and without bothering to look at the last card dealt him, Rainbow played as though he had already made the straight and put $500 in the pot, then floated a thousand-dollar bill on top of it. "Your five, Pete. And one dime."

The fat man studied the four, seven, Jack, three lying faceup in front of Rainbow, then fingered two stacks of money which couldn't have totaled more than $10,000—one-third of what he had come in with. He dropped one stack into the pot. "And five thousand."

"Good thing it's a friendly game." Rainbow tapped his foot on the briefcase under his chair and pushed out all his cash. "Your five. And thirty more."

The air seeping through The Whip's teeth sounded like a dying whistle. Only the shadow of a glance passed between Roze and the Greek. Drawn inward as if by a magnet, the fat man studied the bet, checked his money, his cards, the meager mound of bills in front of his friend The Whip, and scoured Rainbow's deadpan face. He must not have liked what he saw. Maybe it was what he didn't see that bothered him. He didn't have enough cash to meet the raise.

Roze tapped the deck. "Is his IOU okay with you, Rainbow?"

"If you say it's good, E.R." Rainbow leaned on the worn felt. They said the Greek took this table with him everywhere he went. Had he ever been to Paris? As many times as Iris had?

"Thirty grand to you, Pete," Roze said impatiently.

The nervous weave of the fat man's stare hugged the tabletop. Finally, he put down his money, pushed himself up, and turned his back to the game. Nothing moved in the shallow silence until Roze nodded at the money. With no sign of enjoying his victory, no private surge of excitement inside him, Rainbow raked in his winnings and began stacking the cash.

Stavros lit another tapered cigar. "How'd you get the name Rainbow?"

"Something to do with a pot of gold, Greek." His pat answer, and it worked tonight as always. But these results meant more than all the others put together, for this wasn't a bunch of yokels, this was Efrem Roze and Stavros the Greek laughing with the full-bodied gusto of men who respect only what they admire. It felt good. Better than Iris could ever make him feel. Better than she knew how. It had taken over five hours, but he was finally rid of her, her sullen stare, fragile beauty. He felt sorry for her. And he joined the laughter.

Roze picked up his cash. All night he had paid out in IOUs when he lost and collected hard cash when he won. No one had even raised an eyebrow. "Maybe we'll see you down at my club a little later, Rainbow. Next to Delmonico's. The Greek can show you. Otherwise, drop in The Park up at the Springs. I'll show you around myself. You are going to Saratoga, right?"

"Wouldn't miss it, E.R." Rainbow took the silver dollar off the stack of IOUs totaling more than $5,000. "You ready to settle up on these?"

Roze lost his smile for a moment and folded his cash as if he meant to pocket it. "You can always trade those markers for chips at either of my clubs. Be like playing with house money that way."

Rainbow pushed the notes toward the smile on that pale, thin face. "Like to settle up now if it's just the same to you."

The Greek snapped his fingers. The giant by the window got out of his chair and lumbered toward the table. Rainbow slid a hand to the .45 in his belt.

"No problem." Roze spread the IOUs, peeled off bills from his wad, and laid his money down in neat piles. He picked up his markers, ripped them in half, then in half again, and tossed the pieces on the floor. Not once did he lose that leaky-eyed grin. "Wouldn't want to disappoint a customer." He offered his hand to Rainbow. "My clubs can always use the excitement of a winner."

That hand felt cold and dry. Rainbow gathered the money while

Roze said his good-byes and walked out to the hall, where four men in dark suits and gray hats formed a square around him and led him to the elevator.

Tom The Whip pointed a wiry finger at Rainbow. "Watch him, Greek, he's hot. Glad I work steady." He laughed and helped the fat man into the orange jacket. "Come on, Peter. It's late." Cramming what was left of his cash into his pocket, the fat man marched out with The Whip at his heels.

The door closed. Stavros blew a smoke ring, shattered it with a laugh. "First time I ever saw E.R. pay up like that. You're either lucky or stupid. Maybe both."

Rainbow tried a smile. "Can't figure how you let him play with your cash and pay with his credit. Nice enough fellah, though."

"Salt of the earth." Another smoke ring, this one left free to float toward the ceiling. "Two glasses, Aziz." Stavros waved his giant to the bar, then fingered the emerald stud in his tie. "Big thing with E.R., them markers. Wants everybody to trust him."

"I didn't mean it to look like I wouldn't take his word," Rainbow said.

The Greek held up an open palm. "Like he said, no problem. Besides, he likes you." Those jet-black eyes sparkled with both warning and the delight of a dare. "Wouldn't try it again, though."

Rainbow jammed his money into his pockets. In the glass the big man set before him was the outline of a lovely face, carved in sweating ice by the heat and weight of alcohol—a face in an empty hotel room, melting away to nothing. *"I hope you win."* She was back again. Rainbow blinked, but the face in the ice was still there. "Say, that Russian's not really the world's expert on tunnels, is he?"

"That's Pete." Stavros laid his cigar down. "A fucking ditchdigger." He bellowed and swirled ice and whisky in the tumbler. "If we double-teamed him tonight, we could have cleaned his ass. Worth plenty, too."

"I'm not greedy," Rainbow said.

"I am." Stavros smiled, then raised his glass. "To Prohibition. The dumb bastards."

The whisky was Scotch, smoky with the flavor of charcoal, smooth from years of gentle aging. And the face in the ice had swung to the other side of the glass. Rainbow studied the dark portrait on the wall, wondering why he didn't feel like drinking. Or laughing. He felt like leaving.

"A bluff, wasn't it?" Stavros said. "You didn't have that straight."

No smile, no hint of one. "Cheers, Greek." Rainbow drained his glass. He chomped on the ice, cold splinters with no taste at all. A bluff? A bluff all the way: his Jack-high nothing against a solid pair of nines, maybe two pair, but with a fool for a master. Not so much to be proud of, less to feel good about.

And she was gone. No way to get her back.

"Gone is gone." Rainbow thumped the empty glass on the table and let the Greek give him another drink.

Wrapped in twists of brightly colored foil, the dozen pieces of saltwater taffy that made up the poker pot caught the muted light leaking out the living-room window onto the porch of this two-story house on Arthur Avenue in the Bronx—a guinea house, filled with loud people who laughed at anything, anytime, a house crowded with kids in Sunday clothes who walked around as if in a daze, afraid to speak. The *rupp-fff* of riffled cards came like a hurried breath. Murph's voice rose a half-tone, irritated by the break in play, fueled by whatever they called the licorice-tasting white stuff in the bottle by his hip. "How many you want for Chrissake?"

One of the dark-haired brothers, the quiet one who was about eleven years old, put down three of his cards. Picking up the discard, Murph dealt him three new ones facedown and aimed the deck at the smaller boy seated nearest the taffy box. This kid was lucky to be alive at age nine. He might never see ten. He had shifty eyes, brown circles that glistened hot or cold depending on what he was after. His name was either Freddie or Mascalzone, maybe Freddie Mascalzone, except that he was a Tagliafera like his brother, so why would these wops call him Mascalzone? The boy was still rubbing his chin, stalling again.

"Jesus Christ." Murph reached for the kid's cards. "Let's see what you got."

The boy jerked his hand back. "Like hell."

"Freddie, stop that." The girl stood in the front doorway wrapped in a brown shawl, arms folded across a full bosom. She was at least twenty. It might have been the way the night air stuck to her face, but she looked even prettier than that Iris: large dark eyes, long dark hair, dark lips, wet and glossy. She was the only one here who spoke decent English. A little too good really. Maybe they had adopted her. "We don't use that language in this house, young man," she said.

The small boy winked at her. "I ain't in the house, Sis. This is the porch."

Her voice rang like a cast-iron bell: "Freddie!"

"All right, all right." The boy threw down a card, squinted coldly. "And from the top this time."

"Why you little—" But Murph couldn't hold back the laugh. "You saying I'm dealing you seconds?"

"You're winning, ain't you?" the small boy said.

"Aren't you," corrected the girl in the doorway.

"Well, he is." The boy pointed to the taffy piled in front of Murph. "And he won't let us deal, neither."   *

"Ah-*ha!*" Fat Mrs. Tagliafera stuck her long, wart-dotted nose past the girl in the doorway. "So this is how *mascalzoni* spend the time with Zi'Angelo, eh? So quiet inside with them outside, no, Gina?"

Gina? Hadn't they called her something else a while ago? Maybe she had two names. The girl shivered away from the old crone's hand. "They're having fun, Mama. Let them be."

"Children of your own you boss." The fat woman waved her wrist as if she meant to slice the air like bread. "You two, *in*. Kiss your mother and your zio who comes so far to see you. Then straight to bed."

The small boy took three candies from the pot, gave one to his brother, and stood. "You're lucky, Murph. I would of cleaned you this time. Full house." He snatched another taffy and ran inside.

"Be sure this one he puts them back," the old crone said in a whisper to the girl. "Your papa brings the candy special, from Atlantic City. No for put on the floor, eh?" She cast a look of suspicion at the girl and Murph—"You help with the table, Gina. Five minutes,"—and walked back into the living room.

The girl knelt to the taffy, dusted the foil with her hands, and began putting the pieces in the box. "You don't like our party, Mr. Murphy?"

Murph reached out to help her, but grabbed the small boy's cards instead: Jack, nine, a pair of sixes, three. *Full house my ass.* Where did a little twerp like that learn to bluff? Murph took a swig from the bottle. "It's nice, but, well, I can't understand anybody in there."

"They have a little trouble with your English, too."

A frown, another swig of white stuff, much longer than the first. "Why's she call you Gina? That ain't your name is it?"

"It's Ellen."

"Yeah, that's it." Almost all the candies were in the box: she'd be gone in a second. He swallowed air. "Don't sound Italian to me."

"I'm American, Mr. Murphy. Like you. My mother calls me Gina because she thinks I look like my grandmother. She's the one in the picture over the fireplace."

These people had pictures all over the house, some in crusty standing frames, others on the walls—all sober faces staring as though they hated the man who photographed or painted them. It was like a museum in there. "Never seen so many pictures in one house before," Murph said.

"It's a European custom. We like to be surrounded by those we love."

"You mean to tell me you actually love *all* them people?"

Her smile was a quiet one. "I didn't know all of them." She set the box on the swing couch, pulled her shawl back into place, and stepped to the corner of the porch rail. "My Uncle Angelo says you're quite religious."

"Who, me? Jesus Christ, where'd he get that idea?"

Another quiet smile. "I didn't think so."

Uncrossing his legs, Murph got up, brushed off his pants. There was a lot of black scrollwork on the label of the liquor bottle he held. He wiped the rim with his jacket flap. "Want some of this, Ellen?"

"I don't care for anisette, Mr. Murphy." She wasn't even looking at him. "Why did you come here with my uncle?"

The white stuff—anisette—wasn't bitter like that wine inside. This tasted exactly like licorice but it didn't say licorice on the bottle anywhere. Murph took another taste. "Well, it's a long, complicated thing. But don't worry none, I like the old guy." He sat on the rail, not believing he had just said that about a guinea, but it was true, he did like little Angelo. The old cook wasn't really stupid, only a slow learner. And he hadn't practiced his spelling once all evening. Rainbow was going to be mad. But it was a stupid con. The Greek wouldn't be dumb enough to take the bet, he'd know the guinea had been prepped just for this. And then it wouldn't matter what anyone said or did, they'd probably have to cart Rainbow out on a stretcher. It would serve him right. On the other side of the window, a crowd of people stood around the dining-room table, hugging one another, lifting glasses filled with dark red, laughing arm in arm. "All those folks related, are they?"

She was looking at him now. Glaring, like a princess learning how to growl. "He said you were teaching him so that he could be paid."

"Right. Long, complicated. You know the Greek? Me and my partner, we got this proposition, and Angelo, well, him being with E.R. and all, we just couldn't pass it up. A real opportunity."

She smiled and shook her head. He smiled back: "Tell me, what're them little honey things all stuck together?"

"Strufoli." Her smile got broader. "You have a sweet tooth."

"Yes ma'am, I know it." Those little round balls of fried dough no bigger than marbles and coated with honey and shredded orange peel were delicious. The ravioli took first place, though. Each one was as big as a pack of cigarettes and served steaming under a lava of red sauce. It was impossible to eat more than ten of them, yet a big man with a hook nose had shoveled down twenty-five at dinner tonight and still had room for dessert. Murph patted his stomach and glanced through the window. "They all live here?"

"Of course not, only the family." The sharpness of her tone surprised him. But now she was covering a grin. "Careful you don't fall into the bushes."

"No problem here, no problem." Murph braced against the crossbeam. The light was hazy, his head felt light, and the bottle was growing heavy in his hand. And now Angelo's trumpet was leading voices soaked with wine around the slow rhythm of "Santa Lucia." "Must have a picture show around here, am I right? Want to take one in tomorrow?" Murph didn't know where those words had come from. Was she laughing at him yet? "Of course, I got to be on a train to Saratoga, so it'd have to be early. Saturday, ain't it? Matinee! Solves the problem." He couldn't shut up. The bottle was too heavy to hold. He put it on the rail. "Pretty girl like you's probably booked up a month ahead, ain't that right?" He tried to look at her, but his eyelids were sagging, his tongue felt too big for his mouth. "Love the movies myself. Seen them all. Personal friend of Tom The Whip's, too. You know The Whip? I could tell you stories about him make your head spin."

"The children are big fans of his," Ellen said, staring at the floor. Had she meant to call him a baby? She was only two years older than him at the most. "I'm sorry," she said. "I didn't mean it to sound that way." Somehow, she had made her voice different: soothing.

"Gina, we clear the table now." The old crone was back, eyes haunted by the night, arms awake with quivering flesh which hung like dead meat on her bones.

"In a minute, Mama." Ellen—Gina?—waited until the fat woman left the doorway. "Do you know my brother Frank in Saratoga?"

"Who?" Murph said.

"Frank. Uncle Angelo goes to work for him tomorrow."

Murph scratched his head. "Thought he was working for E.R."

A *tap-tap-tap-tap* on the window, the wart nose looming in the pane, the girl Ellen/Gina walking to the door, saying, "I hope you're enjoying yourself here, Mr. Murphy." She was going.

"Hey, wait a second." Murph tried to make it sound like a joke: "What about our date?" It sounded like a threat.

She studied his face, the bottle on the rail, her dark eyes swelling with the air that lifted her breasts. "Perhaps my uncle will bring you to the house again. Someday soon." She swung her gaze through the doorway and followed it inside.

There was no response to the elevator call button. The operator must have been asleep or out for coffee. Following the banister down the steps, Rainbow felt a bulge in his jacket. He had forgotten to put his original table stake back into the briefcase after the game. He savored the grin. Forgetting about $10,000 was something only a true high roller would do. At the next landing, he unlocked his briefcase and put the cash in beside the money he had won tonight: $32,000, a thick layer of bills lying on top of the rest of his bankroll. He had made a three hundred and twenty percent profit. Against heavyweights, too. And last week he was hustling for loose change. His grin got so wide that it threatened to rip his face apart. He swallowed the shout building in his gut, relocked his case, and hurried down to the fifth floor.

But there was no reason to hurry. His room was going to be dark and empty. This entire city, the largest in the world: empty. Besides Murph, and he was probably asleep by now, the only people Rainbow knew in New York were those he had just left, and he couldn't do anything with them except gamble and drink, and he was tired of that. It was The Big Time, but it was still work.

And Iris wasn't coming back. Ever. What would it be like to have her fill his empty room, if only for tonight? He got the room key out and knocked on Murph's door. No answer. He knocked again:

"Wake up, kid. Got something to show you." Still no answer. He tried the knob, but when it didn't turn, he knocked harder. "C'mon. Angelo, you in there?" Nothing. The kid was probably lost. Letting him go all the way to the Bronx alone had been a mistake. He might be drunk in the gutter. Or run over by a truck. Rainbow cursed himself. Then laughed. He had something more important to do now, something to fill the minutes before sleep. He patted his breast pocket where he had stashed the phone numbers Curtis had given him. Tonight might be a good time to call the Dancer and draw a bead on Old Cal—get a jump on things. It wasn't going to be so lonely in that room anymore.

He stepped to his door, unlocked it. Without bothering to turn on the light, he closed the door, locked and bolted it. The noise behind him made him shiver with fear. Someone was here. *Thieves, a pack of them.* The rustle of fabric cut through the dark. He dropped the briefcase, jerked the .45 from his belt, spun toward the sound, his finger tense on the trigger, his arm straightening into a firing position.

She was lying on the bed—Iris—her dress bunched around her knees, her shoes beside the night table which held her purse and tiny hat. *Iris?* She was raising her head off the pillow, squinting, rubbing her eyes. He hid his gun on the chair, under his panama, and slid the briefcase away from the door. His heart was pumping fast, he couldn't hold on to enough air to get a word out. The window was letting in the warm colors of a night city: fine beams of gold and smoky gray, each the thickness of wire, dying in the shadows a foot short of the bed. His mind felt scrubbed down, yet thoughts kept dripping off the walls in there. *Scared hell out of me, lady, I almost blew your head off.* He couldn't talk, couldn't move his feet.

She was sitting up now, smoothing out her skirt and hair. "Did you win?"

He drew in a long breath. "Always."

"I knew you would." The darkness was doing something to her voice, making it sound lower than it usually was. "I didn't want to wait until breakfast to see you again."

. . . see you again . . . Six short steps and he was sitting beside her, feeling the tingle of those little pimples of thread on the bedspread, hearing his whisper: "Iris." She silenced his lips with a finger. Her touch told him she was real. Her mouth didn't taste the same as before and her waist felt smaller. She was warm from sleep. He ended the kiss and stared at her: such a delicate face, but like a mask, without expression, not even around the eyes.

"Is it all right?" she said. "Can I . . . stay?"

He had never felt his body stretch like this, like taffy being pulled, yet he was getting heavier at the same time, as though waterlogged and sinking into the mattress. The kind of squawk that was ready to work its way out of a throat as dry as his would only scare her off. Unwilling to pull away and let her go, he answered with another kiss. Of course it was all right. She could stay as long as she wanted to. Longer. Her arms slid around him, her knees drew up to his. Then air gurgled in back of her teeth and she put her head against his chest and held on. She was crying.

Crying?

What had he done to make her cry? If she kept this up, she was going to ruin his good shirt and he would have to wear the one with the frayed cuff. He hugged her and smiled. She could cry all she wanted. He wasn't going to do anything except sit there all night and hold her—if that was what she wanted. He wouldn't try to get in her pants while she slept. Not even a peek. He wanted to tell her that and make her believe it, make her see that he had a strong will and always kept his word. She could ask anyone. She was safe here. With him.

Something hit the door. Then: "Hey, you in there yet?" Murph sounded drunk. The knob clicked back and forth against the lock. "I got him with me. Say something to him, Angelo. Say, Hello Rainbow, loud so he'll wake up."

In the little silence, Rainbow stroked her hair, kissed the top of her head.

"All right then," Murph said. "At least tell him how good I taught you them words."

"He's no inside, eh? We talk to no-body."

"Jesus Christ, two A.M. ain't it? Of course he's in there." More pounding on the door. "Hey, you in there? Got some real good stuff. Anisette. Made from licorice. White, though. Hey, how they do that, Angelo?"

"We sleep now, no?"

"Yeah, he probably got himself tied up by now if I know them queers he's playing with. Well I ain't gonna rescue him. And I ain't going to see no more of his movies, neither, the goddamn fairy. Hey, you ain't one, are you? Aw, Jesus, you sleep in the bathtub, understand? With the door locked." Murph's voice got farther and farther away, then the door banged shut.

Iris was trembling. Rainbow held her tightly. "Sorry," he said. "Guess I'll have to straighten that kid out one of these days."

But she wasn't frightened and she wasn't crying anymore. She was laughing. "He's wonderful."

"Yeah? Well, see—I taught him. Everything."

She giggled and gave him a little peck. Her cheeks were wet. He guided her down to the pillows. Not gone. *Found.*

19

With the door closed and the light over the medicine chest bouncing off the mirror, the bathroom would have looked the same at any hour of day or night, but the lather Rainbow was working into his beard felt sticky and his head ached: this had to be morning. He liked being alone with it.

She was still asleep, lying under the covers like a soft bundle. If he went in to kiss her, she might wake up and start crying again, the same way she had after letting him make love to her last night, or earlier this morning—whatever time it had really been. But she had started it, she had practically undressed him, hadn't she? Being held wasn't enough, she had to be touched, fondled, stroked, she wanted to sweat, to make deep, hollow sounds. And when it was over, she had needed to cry. "No," it wasn't anything he had done, and "No," she wasn't sad. Before he had found out what her tears meant, she had fallen asleep in his arms. On his arm. He had not moved that arm all night for fear of waking her, and now it felt as though it had been run over by a beer truck. Soon she would be up, see where she was, remember what she had done, and want to kill him. Wisely, his .45 and his briefcase of money were hidden in the suitcase standing between the washbasin and toilet. If she found the gun, she might shoot him, and if she found out that she couldn't shoot him, she would probably settle for robbing him. But making love had been her idea. He wouldn't have touched her if she hadn't begged him to. She hadn't. She had simply allowed it to happen, but he wasn't going to let her accuse him of anything. He shaved a long path across his cheek and flicked lather off the razor, aware of his movements, trying to be quiet. In five more minutes, he would be done, dressed, and ready to deal with her. She was going to accuse him—of everything. He had it all planned: ignore her. No matter what she said or how loud her screams got, he was going to pretend she wasn't even there.

The doorknob turned. She came in like a sleepwalker, robed in his suit jacket, which didn't quite cover the dark patch between her legs. Maybe that was just a shadow. He tried not to look. Without saying "Good morning," or "Excuse me, I didn't know you were in here," without looking at him, she went straight to the sink. Is this how it was? They walked in and took over as if no one else existed? He stepped back, grateful that she hadn't noticed his gray undershorts, the pale skin below the line of sunburn which ringed his neck like the collar on a duck. She hadn't noticed him at all. She pulled out the stopper. Sudsy water ran down the drain, slurping greedily the way kids sucked the last bit of milk shake through a straw. She turned on the tap, splashed water on her face. He managed one swipe with his razor before she opened the cabinet, swinging the mirror toward the door. He stepped sideways to find his reflection, cocked the razor to his cheek. She took a glass from the bottom shelf, a tube of toothpaste from his toiletry case, and closed the mirror door. Cursing silently, he moved back behind her and recocked the blade. But now she was making noises—rubbing toothpaste on her teeth, gargling water, spitting it out—noises which claimed possession of the ground on which she was standing. The sounds of a conquering invader. He squeezed the razor handle: "Thought you society girls slept all day."

Lips coated with white foam, eyes half closed, she tossed a grumpy stare into the mirror, then lowered her head and finished rinsing out her mouth.

"Probably cut myself wide open." He started a long, upward scrape with the razor. Her head popped up, she ran a brush through her hair, almost hitting him in the face. He stopped shaving and moved to the side. Her arms were in the way, he couldn't get a clear view of himself in the mirror. As small as she was, she took up the whole thing. He grabbed the suitcase. That wasn't a shadow between her legs, it was her. She was flopping around inside his jacket like a baggy-pants comedian. It wasn't funny. He took a towel from the rack and walked out. His jacket landed on the bureau, the bathroom door closed, the lock inside clicked. She was completely naked in there. He tried to remember what she had looked like in bed last night. He couldn't. The room had been too dark. He could only remember her smoothness.

She had warmed his jacket with her body: the coat didn't feel like his anymore. He tossed it on the bed, laid his razor on the bureau, and stepped into his pants.

The lather was beginning to dry. He rubbed his face with the towel while he hunted for his shoes among the clothes on the floor. Her lingerie was light to look at, but not to hold. No wonder women felt so heavy. Held up loose and empty, the bra looked like the kind of binding that would make a prison warden grin: straps this way and that, big iron clasps all over. Maybe it came with instructions on how to get into it without wrenching a shoulder. Did she have to wear it so tight? It had left ridges in her back and along her sides—welts he had not needed to see, he had felt how hard and hot they had left her skin. How did she stand it? How did she breathe? He bundled her clothes, dropped them on the bed, and sat to put on his socks and shoes.

Three knocks shook the door to the hall: "You up yet? Time for breakfast."

Guess who. Rainbow flipped the bedcovers over her clothes and opened the door.

"He's ready." Murph led Angelo into the room and sat on the end of the bed. "How'd it go last night?"

There was a stain near the pocket of the good shirt: she had ruined it. Maybe the jacket would hide it.

"How come you ain't dressed yet?" Murph said. "Ain't even shaved. Jesus. Probably got a little drunk, didn't you?"

Rainbow found his tie under the night table. "I ain't in the mood for your crazy talk. Go down the lobby and wait for me."

"No, listen." Beaming, Murph snapped his fingers. "Do it, Angelo. Just like I taught you."

The little cook closed his eyes and drew a deep breath. "T-E-N-N-E-S-S-E-E, P-N-E-U-M-O-N-I-A, P-H-A-R-M-A-C-E-U-T-I-C-A-L." His eyes opened slowly as though afraid of the light.

"Perfecto!" Murph made a circle with his thumb and index finger. "Well? Ain't you gonna say, 'Good work, Murph,' or 'Nice going, Angelo?' What the hell's the matter with you?"

The kid must not have seen the purse or the hat on the night table yet. Rainbow grinned and steered Murph to the door. "Great work. Better than I expected." Patting the little cook's shoulder, he got out a ten-dollar bill. "Angelo, you're a scholar. Order steak and eggs. On me."

"Look at this." Murph pocketed the cash and brought out a small heart-shaped locket. It was gold-plated and not very shiny. The clasp for the neck chain was broken. "She give it to me," he said. "For good luck. Ellen. Angelo's niece, but she's American, like us. You should of seen her. Prettier than that Iris. I think I am in *love!*" He let out a little yelp, the kind a dog might make in its sleep. "Tell him how beautiful she is."

"*Bellissima.*" Angelo was grinning, but his eyes were starting to tear. "Like her nonna Gina. Mama mia, gone fifteen years." He made the sign of the cross and muttered under his breath.

"Yeah, that's great." Rainbow started to close the door. "You can tell me all about her when I get down to breakfa—"

The toilet flushed. The smile on Murph's face turned into a questioning stare. Angelo cocked his head. Rainbow cleared his throat: "And I want to hear all about it, you can bet on that. I'll hurry and—"

And the bathroom door opened. Iris stepped out wrapped in a towel which left her shoulders and most of her thighs bare. She stopped so abruptly that she teetered on tiptoes, frozen like a statue long enough for Angelo to blurt out an apology and grab Murph by the arm. Then she scurried back behind the door and slammed it shut.

Murph's fist closed around the locket. "Why didn't you say something so I'd know she was in here. Probably heard everything I said and take me for a fool. Damn you!" He jammed his hand into his pocket and went down the hall.

In three big steps Rainbow caught up to him and pulled him to a stop. "She didn't hear nothing. Now quit this. We got business to think of."

"All you ever think of, ain't it." Murph yanked his arm free. "Well I spent all night on your business while you was joyriding with some, some—"

"E.R. was in that game last night." Rainbow gave the kid a little shove. "You call that a joyride? Made thirty-two grand, you think I wasn't working?" Another shove. "Got in tight with the Greek, too." He pushed Murph up against the elevator. "All the time you're partying in the goddamn Bronx, cozying up to some girl and—"

"I didn't plan on meeting her," Murph said. "She lives there for Chrissake. You're the one who told me to go."

"Don't see me shouting at you because of it, do you? I think it's fine. And it's real nice of her giving you that locket for good luck, too. How come you can't treat my luck the same way?"

In the brief silence, Murph stared at his shoes as though lacing them with his eyes. "At least I told you right off."

"How am I supposed to tell you anything when you're talking all the time?"

Murph's face got tight, then softened. "You sure she didn't hear me say I was—you know—in love?"

Rainbow slapped the elevator button. "Hell, she didn't even know anybody was there, you saw that."

"Yeah. Jesus, she looked ready to die, didn't she." The kid gulped down a nervous laugh. "You won't tell her. I mean, about me and Ellen."

"Of course not."

Nodding and grinning broadly, Murph waved Angelo to his side. "We'll wait in the lobby. Unless you and her want to have breakfast in bed or something, which is understandable, I mean, you ain't gonna see her for a while and, well, me and Angelo'll be fine together. Meet you in a couple of hours in case you two want to, you know, say good-bye real slow. I ain't in no hurry about the new wardrobe. We can do that just as easy in Saratoga as here, right?" The elevator door opened. He ushered Angelo inside. "Take your time now." That red mane popped back out of the dark hole in the wall. "And apologize for us, will you? Say: 'Dave's real sorry about interrupting.' " He winked and disappeared behind the sliding door. At last, the hallway was quiet.

Rainbow shook his head to clear the muddle and walked back to his room, locked the door. "They're gone now."

The bathroom door opened a crack. Checking the tuck of the towel, Iris came out as though nothing had happened and went to the far side of the bed. She turned in a circle, searching the floor.

"I put them under the covers," he said. "Sorry about the . . . interruption."

"No, it was my fault." She pulled back the bedspread and began sorting her clothes. "I was trying to hurry so you'd be able to—" Her hands stopped moving. "I'm not used to sharing."

Probably never had to share nothing being born with a silver spoon up your ass. He cursed himself for wanting to be so tough with her. She looked hurt. From behind, he put his arms around her waist. The towel was dry and rough, her skin smooth and warm. He kissed her neck. She made that noise, almost a groan. His pants were getting tight in the groin again. That towel wasn't going to stop anything. What would she do if he ripped it off and dumped her on the bed? Probably scream. He let go and strode to the bathroom, stopping in the open door. "Won't run off on me, now will you?"

She was standing perfectly still over her clothes. "No."

"In that case," he tried to make his voice sound sexy, "and since I won't get to see you for a while—does a departing man get any last requests?"

Her gaze rose slowly, a smile cracked her lips. "No."

He laughed. "Could be in a train wreck. Mangled beyond recognition. Be too late then." She was giggling, but it wasn't going to work. She was going to get dressed and by the time he had fought through all those underthings she wore, his train would be ready to leave. She would be gone again. He cursed Old Cal Robinson. The bastard was still running his life. He couldn't stop staring at her: she was perfect, no need for lipstick or the stuff she put on her eyes and cheeks, no need for fancy clothes, that towel was all she ever had to wear. And this was the last time he might ever see her. "Just think how terrible you'd feel."

"I'd feel mangled, too." She sat on the bed. The towel parted high on her thigh. She pushed a hand through the clothes. What did they put on first, the panties? She didn't pick out anything to put on first, she just kept moving her hand through the pile. "Because I'd be in that wreck with you."

That sounded like love. She was saying that a part of her would always go with him wherever he went, that she would feel what he felt, the pain, the joy—all of it. He scratched his neck. "Well, I'll be careful. Trains are safe and it's just a short ride up. I could call you when I get there. Or send a wire. It was just a figure of speech about being mangled and I don't even know why I said it. Stupid of me, I know, but . . ."

Shaking with laughter, she made the bed creak. Had those springs made that noise last night when he was moving inside her? How could anyone not remember hearing a noise like that? But he could hear her laugh. It was all he could hear. This wasn't love, then. This was a joke. He gripped the knob, wanting to rip it off and bounce it off her skull: "I'll hurry and shave. Only take a minute."

"I meant I'd be on that train, too." She had both hands up to the wrists in the clothes as though trying to steady herself. "I'm going with you."

The chill running up his back got warm when it reached his neck. He glanced around the jamb. She was wearing her smile, the one that could melt and freeze at the same time. Maybe that was what he had felt shooting up his spine. He braced against the bureau. "You mean it?"

Part of him wasn't sure that he believed her or wanted to take her along, the same part that didn't want to be invaded anymore. But he grinned like a little boy because he felt like one. "Guess I better make another reservation."

"I'll do it, you shave." She picked up the phone and jiggled the receiver hook. *"The Cavanagh Special,* isn't it? What hotel?"

"Figured we'd check in once we got there."

"No, there'll be a crowd. But we can still get a suite, I think." More slaps at the hook. "If they'd ever answer. You do want a suite, don't you? The Clarendon will be filled, but we might get a cottage at the United States or—" She hung up as though she had just heard bad news from home. "You'd probably want to make the arrangements yourself, wouldn't you."

"Who, me? You know all the places up there. I'd never get it straight like you. Makes no sense for me to do it. Unless you want me to. Is that it?"

That smile again, only this time, she really looked happy. While he tried to remember what he had said to make her feel that way, she kept slapping the phone hook and shooting pieces of her smile at him until a voice on the line caught her attention and she started talking into the mouthpiece, knowing everything to say and just how to say it. She was amazing. The poor clerk at the other end couldn't possibly have enough brains or hands to keep up with her.

Rainbow carried his suitcase into the bathroom. She was really going. With him! He grinned at the half-shaven face in the mirror: "Hah! Yes sir, with me!" And humming the tune the jazz band had played at trackside, he worked up a new batch of lather.

The kitchen was too small to hold all the debris. Greasy dishes and pots encrusted with burnt food had crept out to the dining and living rooms to mingle with dust, old newspapers, the empty tin cans scattered about tables, chairs, the sofa, the floor. A chafing dish, used once as a cereal bowl, thereafter as an ashtray, was lying on top of the toilet tank. A trail of spoons and forks, most of them caked with the residue of forgotten meals, wandered toward the bedroom. Did he eat with his fingers now? And the fan was still broken. Iris had known it was going to be bad, but this was a disaster. In less than a month, Horace had managed to turn a stylish apartment into a slum. There was no safe place to sit. What had it looked like two days ago before her cable had arrived? No, it couldn't have been any worse. He hadn't even tried to straighten up. She wasn't about to lift a finger in this place again. *Thank God I didn't come back here last night.* Sitting on the iron-bound trunk amid the rest of her luggage in the center of the living room, she got the crossword puzzle book from her valise, leafed to Puzzle 31, the one she had started on *The Century,* and put the pencil to the page: "in the near future"—two words, eleven letters. Bleats from sheep grazing in a nearby meadow of Central Park floated in over the hum of street traffic. Two hours to kill before the train left. Going to Saratoga with Rainbow was just an impulse, wasn't it? The Congressional Hotel, the only one with a suite available so close onto the season's opening, was no doubt a dreadful place: new, big, unrefined, no history to it whatsoever. And Grace North was staying there, too. The old bat would want to know everything, then she would thumb her nose to a gambler—so unladylike. Grace could go to hell. Rainbow was marvelous. Except that he would never care enough or let himself. He might never stop trying to prove how clever he was. Iris lost her smile. *Maybe I can't stop either.* What was the point in going to Saratoga, then? It would only be a mistake. Like last night.

She put down the book. Somewhere in this mess there had to be a whiskey bottle. Or had her telegram tipped Horace off? She always tipped him off, didn't she, to protect him, to give him the chance to hide the evidence so that she wouldn't have cause to be angry. He had straightened up, all right. He had thrown out his flasks and bottles. All of them? She rummaged through the papers and cans near the sofa: no bottles. She marched into the bedroom, turned on the light.

And there he was. Out cold. A small, rumpled mass, strewn over sheets that hadn't been washed in weeks. Lying in his underwear, his bald head shiny, a strand of saliva dribbling out the corner of his mouth.

Daddy.

Choked by stale air, she went past the dresser, where her telegram was stuck between perfume bottles. She drew the curtains, opened the window.

Horace raised his head off the mattress and coughed. "Where the hell you been? I was worried sick."

"You said you were driving to Saratoga." She kicked the pillow on the floor. "Another lie?"

"Now don't start in on me." He sat up, ran a hand over his scalp. "I couldn't get Belmont to give me a van. Wanted twenty bucks and I didn't have it on me. Waited up all night for you. Why didn't you call?"

"It's past noon, Horace." She picked her telegram from between the bottles. So businesslike, so cold. The whole thing was a ridiculous

166

game. The wire should have read: Dear Daddy, I love you, I'm worried about you, I'm tired of feeling nothing but pity for you, for God's sake let me see something in you I can love again. She dropped the note. "All right, where is it?"

". . . What?"

She lifted the sheet. "The bottle."

"Now stop that." Near the door, he found his pants and put them on. "I ain't touched a drop. Look all you like. If you'd of come back like you was supposed to, I'd be gone by now. With him, weren't you. All night."

"It's none of your business."

"Noooo." He always made it sound like a growl. "None of my business what you do. Bullshit. Damn, you're worse than your mother. What am I supposed to do, close my eyes?" She brushed past him to the living room, but he followed her out. "Well? Am I?"

"Your eyes *are* closed." She kicked the stack of newspapers blocking her path. "Look at this place."

"I ain't talking about this here, I'm talking about you, what you're doing to yourself. Sleeping around like you do with—"

"Stop it."

"—with every sport that comes along. You think I don't see? What do you know about this Rainbow? Tell me. Smart-ass ploughboy if you want to know what I think. Probably get you pregnant, too. Damn, you're a disgrace to me."

"A disgrace? To *you*? Do you want to hear about disgrace, Horace?"

He held up a hand and tried to lose his frown. "You know I just got up. Ain't fit to be with till I get a . . . something to eat."

She hurled a tin can over his head into the hall door. "Eat!"

"Now c'mon, Iris." Booting the can aside, he put on the blue-striped shirt he found under a chair in the dining room. "Told you I would of been on the road if it weren't for them punks at Belmont. Imagine the nerve of them bastards, not trusting Horace Wells with a lousy van up to the Springs. Why, I knew that track when it was nothing but a—"

"Please, I don't want to hear this." From her purse, she got a twenty-dollar bill and held it out to him. "Pay them."

He took the cash. "Yeah, well, it's a matter of Old Smoke's feed, too." She dug into the purse again. He dragged a bare foot over the rug. "And gas for the car. Always use more pulling a van. Hate to get stuck halfway up."

She snapped her purse shut. "I gave you two hundred dollars yesterday."

"I know it. It's in the bank and they ain't open today. It's safe, though. You can look at the savings book." Hunched over, he searched a small piece of floor. "Around here someplace. You'll see I'm telling you square."

She took out a hundred-dollar bill, tossed it at his feet, and walked back to the curved-top trunk and sat, opening her book, trying to concentrate on the puzzle: two words—"in the near future."

"Think I drunk it already, don't you." He stuffed her money into his pocket. "Well I didn't."

"In the near future"—eleven letters.

"You eat yet, Iris? Let me get dressed, I'll treat." He disappeared into the bedroom and shut the door.

The apartment felt like a prison. Only her past was alive here. There should be a sign over the doorway: THIS IS ALL THERE IS FOR IRIS WELLS, ALL SHE WILL EVER KNOW—THIS IS REAL. No present, no future. Horace had stolen them, saddled her with more weight than she could carry, breaking her down with every stride she tried to take. She couldn't get free. And she couldn't be like her mother and leave him. The old fool would drink himself dead in a week. Leaving him would be the same as killing him.

Two words, eleven letters: "in the near future." Nothing to crosshatch the letters, no clue. The page was getting fuzzy. Hadn't she earned a vacation? Didn't she deserve one after all the things she had done for Horace and the stable? Some stable: one horse, probably half starved by now, and a dozen yearlings which existed only in the minds of people like Grace North in cities all over the East and Midwest. A joke.

Her life.

Horace came out looking chipper. His smile was too broad. He had a bottle stashed in there somewhere. "Now don't worry about this mess, I'll have somebody in to clean up, you won't have to touch nothing. Comes out of my pocket, too." He kissed her on the forehead. No trace of whiskey on his breath. He was drinking vodka again. "What say we get us some breakfast. I'll shave if you want me to. Want to come out to the track and see me off?"

"I've already eaten." Coffee and a piece of toast. She couldn't keep the checkerboard of squares on the page in focus. "And I have to get ready. I'm going to Saratoga."

"No way I can foot that kind of bill." His eyes hardened. "Oh, I get it. Paying for everything, ain't he. Real swell you latched onto this time, huh?"

"Don't, Horace."

"Nooo." His growl again. "Won't say another word. At least this Rainbow don't look like no twelve-time loser like—"

"Horace!" She jabbed the pencil on the page. The bastard was going to throw Ernie in her face now.

"Only saying he don't look like the basket case Ernie Wobers was."

She slammed the book against the trunk. "Damn you."

"Don't be cursing at me."

"Damn-damn-*damn!*"

He let out a long sigh. "What'd I ever do to deserve this."

"Oooh, you bastard!" She threw the book at his shin: direct hit. "I should have left you long ago. Who'd pay your bills then?"

Hobbling on one leg, his pained grimace had part of a smile in it: he was faking for sure. "Tell me how lucky I am, go ahead. I brung you up to be a lady. Could of married some real gentleman, but no, you got to throw your life away on jerks. Well, I got a right to speak my mind. Wobers was—*is*—a first-class, absolute punkhead." He let go of his leg and looked at her as though fearful of being hit with something else. "Can't hit. And he's a slob. And he plays for—"

"For the worst team in the league." She squinted, gritted her teeth. "That's what really bothers you about him, isn't it."

"Well, it don't help none, does it. He's a loser."

"I still love him."

"Bullshit. You never did. Don't even know what love is. Probably think you love this Rainbow, too. What the hell kind of name is that for a man, anyways? Goddamn faggot's name." He wagged his finger. "Now you watch it. He's a sharper if ever I seen one. Trusting him'd be like going to the movies with Jack the Ripper. Full of shit, too, but I got him right where we want him. You leave this jerk to me, understand?"

"What are you talking about?"

"Nothing."

"Bullshit."

"Quit cursing, I tell you. It ain't ladylike." He shoved a mound of litter off the sofa and sat on the armrest. "Has his eye on horseflesh, is all. I'm taking yur suggestion and helping him pick out a few at the Sales. He'll pay for my savvy. Pay me good when he sees what he's getting."

"Bullshit." She stood, put her hands on her hips. "Now tell me."

"Ain't no more to it than that." He managed a hopeful smile. "Ready to go? My treat remember."

"I'm not going anywhere with you." She yanked the front door open. "Get out."

"Hey, goddamn it, I live here. Don't go bossing me around or I'll—"

"Get *out!*"

Glaring and shaking his head, he got off the sofa and stormed back into the bedroom, slamming the door. He made a lot of noise in there, bouncing things around, muttering to himself. But this temper tantrum was a mild one.

Iris gripped the doorknob. How different it would be to live with someone who cared about her. Someone like Rainbow. He was exciting, too. He had made her forget about Ernie. A rough laugh crawled out between her lips. Ernie the glutton was never satisfied holding her or talking to her; he had to be tied down most of the time, always anxious to have sex, but only when he felt like it, and then he thought only of himself—she became the object he used, a toy. But Rainbow was different. So far. Timid, yet tender and thoughtful. So far. Was it foolish to expect that kind of attention from a man? To demand it? Perhaps she was kidding herself. There was no future with Rainbow, with any man. There was only Horace: more of the past every day.

"I'm leaving." Horace stood in the hall doorway, suitcase in hand. "Fifty speakeasies on the way, but I ain't going in a one of them. And do you care? Noooo. I won't touch a drop. Ought to, though. Just for spite. But, see, I got a horse to run. And I ain't doing that on account of you, neither. Time I showed them what Horace Wells can do. Done all right for myself long before you was even born." He set the suitcase down gently: there had to be a bottle inside. "Sent you to all them fancy schools. Who paid for that? You're looking at him, that's who. What kind of thanks do I get? 'Get out,' she says. Curses at me, too. Get out? That's what I hear from my own flesh and blood?"

This was his little act. After he had said, "Ain't fair, my luck to be so good-hearted all the time," he would bow his head, peek out of the corner of his eye, and test whether she was ready to give in and love him again. She stood there, waiting, hating herself for allowing him to set the trap.

"Ain't fair," he said, nudging the suitcase with his shoe. "My luck I got to be so damned good-hearted all the time." He glanced out of the corner of his eye, his voice got soft. "Be nice if you could come give your old man a kiss. For good luck if nothing else."

How had she ever been fooled by this charade before? Not this time. She let go of the knob, turned toward the windows.

"I'm doing what you want, Iris. Going back to training, ain't I?"

Another lie? "We'll see, Horace."

"Damn right you will. Old Smoke's ready, you wait. Guarantee he'll win his first time out. Just got to find him a proper field, don't want him in there with no Man o' War, now do we. But I got a good feeling about it this time."

She pawed at the drapes. "I don't want you to try anything with him, do you understand?"

"Who, Rainbow? Noooo. Wouldn't waste my time. You take my advice and stay clear of that one."

"I can't."

"Aw, shit. I should of known it." He picked up his case. "All right, then, go with him, love it up. Leave your old man to do the hard work. Horace Wells don't mind. Never turned his back on work a day in his life." He stepped over clumps of paper and tin cans to the open doorway. "Look, I, well, I don't feel right leaving this way. Ease up on your old man. You'll see I'm doing good."

Her sigh washed against the windowpane. If she turned, the sadness in his eyes would lure her to him, make her kiss him and wish him good luck. She was determined to wait him out. He would leave if she didn't turn around. But the silence was hurting too much. He was just standing there. Was he on the wagon? Really? Should she have come back here last night? She turned. His eyes were dead. She went to him, kissed the top of his head. "Good luck, Daddy."

"That's my girl." He gave her a little hug. "Now if you do go north with him, you be careful, understand?"

"Yes, Daddy." It was awful. The trap was squeezing the life out of her.

"Seems like a nice enough fellah, so long as you know it's a passing fancy. No harm in that, but . . ." He tried to clear his throat. "The rent come due on this place and, well, since I banked that money you give me, maybe you could, you know, pay it this time. I'll see you get it back."

"I'll take care of it." Her stomach growled, her legs felt weak. Breakfast in bed had been a mistake. Why was sex so tiring? "You'd better go now. It's a long drive."

"Naah, be there in two shakes. Nice day for it, too." He grinned, winked, and headed down the stairs. "Come by the stables if you get up there. Otherwise let me know where you're at so I don't worry." His wave vanished around the bend in the stairwell, but his "See you, Iris" echoed after him.

Iris shut the door: a hollow *thud*. The pictures on the walls looked every bit as lifeless as the clutter all around her. It would take days to clean up this mess. In the bedroom, she found her work clothes on a hook in the closet, then carried them back to the living room and sat on the trunk, kicking off her shoes, rubbing her stockinged feet together. In less than two hours, Rainbow would board *The Cavanagh Special* for Saratoga. By dark, he would be miles away. The distance would help to block him out of her mind. *No future*. Let him call the Waldorf and find out that she had never registered. Let him leave without giving her a second thought. It would be better that way—safer.

She picked up the crossword puzzle book, found the pencil nearby. "In the near future"—two words, eleven letters. She took a chance and penciled in *someday soon*. And didn't have the strength to fight the tears.

20

The concourse of Grand Central Station was a cool refuge from the afternoon heat. Around the four faces of the golden clock, which from up close looked more like polished brass than gold, appointment-keepers stood in a makeshift circle while passengers rushed by mute, unseeing, shoes scuffing the cream-colored marble floor, clothes rustling like wind, hands and arms flapping, their every gesture giving rise to a common voice, a throaty whisper that sounded like sea foaming against rocks: the language of motion. Rainbow wondered how much volume he was adding to it by standing there, waiting. For her. Iris was a good half an hour late. She'd said the golden clock, hadn't she? Was she tied up in traffic? In an accident? *Mangled beyond recognition.* His tongue was dry. He put his briefcase in his other hand and walked around the clock, hunting for a water fountain. She wasn't near the baggage counter, either. She would be easy to spot in this crowd. Maybe she wasn't coming. But women were always late, she'd get here before the train left. Only fifteen minutes to go. He cursed her for making him go through this.

Overhead, the December-blue ceiling curved like sky. Most of the stars up there were golden, but some were lighted to help outline strange figures: a giant with a club, a bull, someone with a spear. A few comets, too. Or was that just the plaster cracking and peeling off?

"They're backwards." Murph held up a pamphlet marked *General Information: Grand Central Terminal.* His new blue sweater was unbuttoned again. "Says here it was on purpose." He read with a finger on the page. "The winter zodiac de-picted by Paul Helleu is—"

Rainbow grabbed the pamphlet. "You're supposed to be by the train, not sight-seeing. And button that like I told you."

"It's too tight." Murph shifted the big book and the magazine under his arm and buttoned the sweater. "Should of got the one I wanted, with them stripes on the arm. Would of done just as good as this."

Rainbow yanked the magazine from him and pointed to the young man in a sweater pictured on the cover below the title, *College Humor*. "They wear them buttoned, see? Now keep it that way." He handed back the magazine. "Where's Angelo?"

"In the men's room. Practicing."

"Well go get him and put him on that train. And don't let the Greek see you together. And don't even come near me till I take my hat off, understand?"

"Yeah, yeah." Murph glanced at the stone balcony over the ticket windows. "Maybe she ain't coming."

"Will you get lost?" Rainbow dropped the pamphlet and kicked it toward the wall of arches behind him. "What if the Greek comes by now? You'll blow everything."

"Okay, I'm going. But we still got time to cash in her ticket. No sense spending the money if she ain't coming." Murph took three steps and stopped. "And don't miss the train on account of her, all right? I don't want to be stuck up there by myself."

Rainbow scowled and leaned toward him. The kid hustled away. Just in time. With his giant, Aziz, beside him, Stavros the Greek came down the ramp from the waiting room off Forty-second Street, followed by Tom The Whip and the fat Russian, in yellow.

Rainbow took cover behind two ladies in brightly colored summer dresses. No luck. The women weren't fat enough. Stavros waved and walked over, shook Rainbow's hand. "Called your room this morning," he said. "No answer. Thought you might like to see a private screening of The Whip's new movie."

"Real shame," Rainbow told him. "Must of been out shopping." A lie. He had been there the whole time. That phone never did stop ringing. It had almost ruined everything: "It might be important," she had said, trying to get him to answer it when all he had wanted to do was keep her under the sheets and make her groan some more. He grinned at the cowboy. "Good action, I'll bet."

"My best yet." The Whip was beaming. "Don't you think so, Peter?"

The fat man adjusted the sleeves of his bright suit, nodded at the clock, and grunted at the wall of arches.

"Yeah, better go." Stavros hooked Rainbow's arm. "They're holding part of a Pullman for me. You're my guest."

Rainbow wriggled free. "Ah, you go ahead and I'll join you, okay?"

The Greek blew cigar smoke at the stars on the ceiling. "You waiting for somebody or what?"

"No, nothing like that. There's a guy who owes me, said he'd pay before the train pulls out. I'm supposed to meet him here."

"Yeah, that's what I just said." Jet-black eyes narrowed. "You're waiting for him."

"Oh, yeah, right. I'm waiting for him."

Stavros glanced at the clock. "Only got a few minutes. It's the Pullman behind the first diner. Save you a seat." He led the foursome toward the arches.

"Appreciate it, Greek." Rainbow held his smile together until the men were out of sight. *Darn that bitch.* He walked toward the bank of telephones near the baggage counter. If she was still at the Waldorf-Astoria, she'd never get up here in time, but at least he could tell her off. That would be easier over the phone anyway. But what was the point? Why admit that he had waited so long, that she had disappointed him? He pivoted on a heel and strode toward the boxed herald, CAVANAGH SPECIAL, above the arch in the center of the wall. A slotted sign listed six Pullman-car numbers, two diners, two day coaches. Bronze letters followed the smooth curve of the arch: ALL PASSENGERS WILL BE REQUIRED TO SHOW THEIR TICKETS AT THE GATES. He patted the tickets in his pocket and went through to the black iron gates at trackside.

The tall gate board posted CAVANAGH SPECIAL and only one stop, SARATOGA SPRINGS. The mob of men by the train didn't look anything like *The Century* riders. The few in conservative suits were probably horse owners and trainers. The rest of them were gamblers and bookmakers. Dancer would be in that crowd. Rainbow cursed himself for not having Curtis describe the bookie: a lot of time could be saved now by getting a line on Old Cal Robinson. But Cal wouldn't be within twenty miles of Grand Central Station, he'd be in a boxcar, sleeping on fruit-stained floors and jumping off before the freight train reached the station. It didn't matter. As might have happened any number of times over the last fifteen years, in towns along the highway out of Saint Louis, the old bastard could have walked by right now and Rainbow wouldn't have recognized him. He couldn't. He didn't have a face to remember. Did he keep seeing Old Cal without realizing it? All the years spent combing billiard halls and the alleys behind them, and all the miles logged in the company of brass-headed yokels—for what? To get here? Still searching for something that might never be found. Still alone. It didn't seem worth the trouble. He pressed his arm against his .45. Old Cal had to be in Saratoga. Pulling the trigger would make everything right. At last.

Down there, in the middle of the crowd, Stavros was getting into a Pullman. The sharpers and bookies treated him like royalty. Aziz had to push the men away. But Rainbow had been invited. As a guest. It felt good. At the far edge of the platform, Murph was standing by himself and, near the train, the dark immobile figure of Angelo Batori was surrounded by swirling colors of flashy suits, the clamor of voices. The bags would all be loaded by now. Everything was set to go.

And she wasn't coming.

What if she had just arrived? What if she had reached the golden clock the second he had left it? Rainbow turned toward the concourse. *The hell with it. With her.* He checked the clasp on his briefcase and walked up to the gate where a guard with DOORMAN on his cap nodded at the long pieces of printed cardboard in Rainbow's hand and waved him through. Rainbow didn't walk through. He separated the tickets: how was he going to get his money back on hers? Was there time to check the golden clock again? And make a fool of himself? *Get on the train, tend to business.* He raked the brim of his panama and went through the gates, keeping close to the iron grillwork to avoid being run over by a porter's handtruck which rolled by laden with suitcases stacked around a big trunk. The wobble of unsteady wheels made the banner across the front of the truck shimmer under the bright lights: MAJESTIC FARMS—LOUISVILLE. *But that was*—his throat felt scratchy—*she was*—and he spun around—

Here.

Like a jewel, her green dress stood out against the gates and buff-colored walls. She was smiling, but her eyes lowered as though she were ashamed to look straight ahead. Rainbow pursed his lips and worked the big grin from his face. She was even more beautiful than before. And she was here.

"Lady says she's with you." The doorman rushed his words. "I need to know because without a ticket, I can't let her through."

Rainbow stepped to her and took her hand. "She's with me."

She still couldn't look at him. The doorman ushered them onto the platform and threw a switch at the siding. The gates swung shut.

"Sorry I'm so late." Iris squeezed his fingers. "You didn't call the hotel, did you?"

Rainbow led her to the edge of the crowd. "There wasn't time."

"Good, I was worried that—" Another finger-squeeze. She looked at him. Her eyes were a deeper green than her dress. She glanced away. "Oh, doesn't he look cute." She hurried to Murph and rubbed the arm of his sweater. "Dave, you look so handsome in this."

The kid smiled but he couldn't hold his head up anymore. His whole body sagged. And he was speechless. How did she do that?

"Didn't you get anything for yourself?" She looped her arm through Rainbow's. "The prices in Saratoga will be outrageous."

Rainbow swallowed. He'd had no time to shop in New York, he'd have to suffer those high Saratoga prices. Still, his veteran suit only needed a press, and the stain on his shirt, which was her fault to begin with, was hidden under his jacket. He didn't look that bad. "The Pullman in back of the first diner," he told Murph, then he steered Iris toward the train. "Sure, I got a lot of new stuff, but it's all packed. No sense dirtying it up traveling. That a new dress?"

She flicked her bodice with the purse. "I've had it for years."

"Real nice. Listen, you got to pretend like you don't know Murph. Just for a little while, okay? It's important."

She hugged his arms. "If it's important, I suppose I can pretend. For a little while."

"Just business, is all." He guided her through the crowd to the Pullman near the front of the train. She would understand when she saw him pull this one off against the King of the Oddsmakers. She was going to find out just how smart Rainbow Roberts was. "Some people I want you to meet," he said. "One of them's a movie star. You like the movies? If we'd had more time this morning, we could of gone to a private screening of his new picture." His neck got warm. Was she thinking the same thing: we had all the time in the world and we just stayed in bed? "Slipped my mind. With all the fuss about reservations . . ."

"Who is it?" She tugged his arm like a little girl after candy. "I love the movies. Did you see *The Sheik?*"

"Oh, sure." He helped her up the steps. "The Whip was great in that."

". . . who?"

"The Whip. Tom Edwards? The cowboy . . . ?"

"Oh, the cowboy." She sighed and the excitement drained out of her. "I don't think I've ever seen one of his pictures."

"Makes two of us." With a smile, he led her down the aisle.

"There he is now." Stavros the Greek aimed a coarse laugh between Tom The Whip and the fat man. At the rear of the Pullman, Angelo Batori was returning to his seat behind Murph. "And if a lady wasn't present," Stavros said, his fired black eyes sweeping across the aisle to the padded bench on which Rainbow and Iris sat opposite the dull stare of Aziz, "I could tell you another one about the little guinea."

"Remember when I was doing *Tombstone Dust?*" Tom The Whip said. "One of my best. Anyways, we got Angelo to drink saltwater. Carried it all the way from Atlantic City, ain't that right, Greek?" His laugh got in the way of his words. "And the stupid wop thought it was mineral juice."

The steel walls magnified the laughter, making it sound harder than it really was. It was getting difficult to listen to. These high rollers had been grinning since the engine change at Harmon, a spot about an hour north of the city, where Rainbow had dropped Angelo's name into the conversation to get the ball rolling and to ease the tension that Iris had caused. She didn't belong here, on his arm or otherwise. She was an intruder and the Greek hadn't tried to hide his displeasure: "Bad luck traveling with women." But he and the others had been nice enough to her, watching their language and gestures, trying to censor their stories before they got to the punch lines. And she looked happy. Every now and then she made her eyes smile or squeezed Rainbow's arm and told him, "Yes, I'd rather be here with you," meaning that she didn't want to join the handful of other women on board who rode the last car, a coach reserved for whatever luggage wouldn't fit in the baggage car up front and for the one or two blacks who had the cash to buy a ticket on this special. Being here was probably better than that.

Feet flat on his briefcase, Rainbow leaned away from her, into the laughter which was still going strong. "I say the little guy's got to be smarter than you think. Reads all those dinner orders and menus, don't he? And would E.R. hire him if Angelo didn't have brains?"

"Brains?" The laugh came out of Stavros like a snarl. "I'll tell you what he's got for brains—meatballs!"

"Yeah, all wops got meatballs." The fat man's stomach quivered. "Get it, Tommy?" He elbowed The Whip and burst into a roar.

Rainbow nudged Iris and when she looked at him, he winked, then turned a blank stare on the King of the Oddsmakers. "Be willing to bet he can spell better than you, Greek."

The laughter stopped. The Greek's pencil-thin moustache slanted over a mouthful of cigar, his eyes narrowed into black specks. He tossed off the insult with a smirk. "That guinea spells his name with an X for Chrissake." A nod to Iris—"You should excuse the French"—and he started to chuckle.

Rainbow didn't let his grin get through. "Fifteen grand says I'm right."

Tom The Whip spat out the remains of his laugh, the fat man held his stomach. Stavros chomped on his cigar as if it were raw meat, but an instant later his eyes brightened and he held out his hand. In the same motion that Rainbow shook the pudgy hand, he took off his hat.

Iris grasped his arm. "Fifteen thousand?"

"Shhh, business." He stuck a hand into the aisle to stop Murph, who was buttoning his sweater and walking toward the front of the car. "Excuse me. My friends and me have a little proposition going. Mind helping us out?"

The kid adjusted the book and the copy of *College Humor* under his arm. "I'm not sure I understand, sir."

"Looks like a smart young fellah, don't he, Greek?" Rainbow leaned on the armrest. "Why don't we get him to write down a few words. You pick any one of them you like and we'll see if Angelo can spell it."

Stavros eyed Murph with suspicion. "You know any long words, kid? They got to be tough. Longest ones you can think of."

Murph scratched his neck. The book and magazine slipped from under his armpit. Aziz caught them and started to hand them back, but Stavros snapped his fingers and the big man gave him both items. Glancing from the cover of the magazine to Murph and back again, the Greek let out a small grunt, as though he distrusted what he saw. As though he remembered seeing a red-haired spy on *The Century* diner. But his eyes took on a glint as he ran his finger over the gold letters on the heavy book: *The Complete Works of William Shakespeare*. He sniggered and tossed the book into The Whip's lap.

"Ah, the great bard." The Whip rubbed the brown leather binding. "Always wanted to—" His hand went dead, his face stiffened. He cleared his throat and grinned. "What line you in, pardner?"

"Line?" Murph tucked the magazine under his arm. "Oh, I go to college right now, sir. Harvard University. Plan on teaching English. Ain't—aren't you Tom The Whip? I go to all your pictures. Every one."

The Whip beamed and shook the kid's hand. "Got us an Ivy Leaguer, Greek."

But Stavros wasn't smiling. He was studying the blue sweater. "Harvard's colors is red."

Murph caught Rainbow's squinting frown and swallowed hard. "Ah, right, only, well, I'm just a freshman and . . . they don't let us wear red till after our first year, it's a rule, tradition, the law. Up there, I mean."

It served the little dunce right. He had been told not to say which college. Rainbow crossed his legs. "Sort of like having to earn a badge, is it?"

"Yes sir, that's it exactly." Murph put a hand into his bangs. "Could I have my book back now, Mr. Edwards? I got to study."

Stavros patted the empty seat beside him. "Sit here, kid, next to the Greek. Write us some college words."

Murph sat and took a pencil and a piece of notepaper from his pocket. "I'm not sure I should. Are you gambling? My mother lives in Saratoga and she hates gamblers. She'd tan me good if she knew I was—"

"No, no, no, nothing like that." Stavros waved his cigar smoke away. "Trust the Greek. This is no gamble. You just come up with some tough words."

"Long ones?" Murph said.

"Yeah, like . . . like—" Stavros flicked his eyebrow. "You know. What's your name, kid?"

Out of the corner of his eye, Murph glanced at Iris. "Dave. David Murphy."

Stavros grabbed his hand and shook it. "Stavros the Greek. You know The Whip, this here is Pete, and Rainbow, and that's . . . Miss Winslow there with him. Okay, you know everybody. Now write."

"Yes sir." Murph used his knee to brace the notepaper. "Let's see, long words."

"Like to have a little of this myself, Rainbow," The Whip said.

"Me, too." The fat man leaned around the cowboy. "Another fifteen."

Rainbow threw up a hand. "I'm strung out with the Greek as it is, boys. Can't handle another fifteen grand."

"Fifteen!" The fat man put an arm in the aisle. "Bet."

The Whip leaned on the yellow sleeve and lowered it. "Peter and me'll take fifteen between us, won't we, Peter." He nodded at the kid. "Be a sport, Rainbow. Won't let me disappoint one of my biggest fans, now will you?"

"Fifteen . . . between you?" Rainbow rubbed his chin, then shook the cowboy's hand.

"What on earth?" Iris gripped his arm. "That's . . . that's—"

"No problem." He stroked her fingers: the blood had run out of them, the skin was cold. They didn't throw money around like this in Louisville. She was getting her first big taste of The Big Time. Rainbow grinned. "What you got so far, kid?"

"Let's see. *Pneumonia.*" Murph tapped the page. "Always gives me trouble. And . . . *spaghetti*—"

"No, no, no." Stavros waved his hand. "No wop words. Scratch it."

Murph brushed the bangs out of his eyes. "And . . . *Tennessee.* And *pharmaceutical.* If you give me more time, I could—"

"Let's see that last one." Stavros grabbed the paper. His face bunched up, then drew out long. "No more time. Aziz, get the guinea. Back there by the window." As the giant lumbered away, Stavros slapped the paper with his fingertips. "*Pharmaceutical.* Let's see him get this. Okay with you, Whip? Pete?"

The Whip and the fat man nodded.

"Hold on," Rainbow said, "that word don't even sound English. It's too tough. That pneumonia one was okay, but—*pharmaceutical?* What's it mean?"

Stavros blew cigar smoke at him. "You said I could pick it. A bet's a bet." He put an arm around Murph. "You did good, kid. Want a cigar?"

"At least give me odds, then." Rainbow tossed his hat on the vacant seat across from him. "Two-to-one, okay, Greek? After all, how was I to know the kid was in college? Looks young enough to be in high school yet."

Murph frowned and stuffed a thin cigar into his shirt pocket.

Stavros held up an open palm. "Did I twist your arm? You stopped him, you go with his words. Our bet's even money. You want out? Buy out. Ten grand and the bet's off. Save yourself five big ones." He smiled around the cigar between his teeth. "The Greek's got a big heart."

Rainbow let out a long sigh. He had wanted the two-to-one odds: that would have been the topper, something he could have talked about forever. "I won't argue it. Rainbow Roberts never goes back on his word."

"That's good." Those jet-black eyes watched a cigar ash hit the floor. "I knew I had you figured right. You'll go a long way."

Rainbow slumped in his seat, but he felt tall with praise. "Yeah, on these kind of bets I'll go straight to the poorhouse."

Iris didn't join the men's laughter. She didn't even smile. She pulled away and stared out the window as if hypnotized by the streaks of reddening sun on the Hudson. "Maybe I am bad luck for you," she whispered.

Rainbow laid a hand on hers: still cold. "This won't even put a dent in me. And who knows? I might even win."

She kept looking out the window. But couldn't she see what was happening, didn't she know that this was Murph—Dave—over there? What did she need, a road map to figure this out? She would cheer up once she saw the truth of it. And she didn't have long to wait. The giant was steering Angelo to the edge of the seats. The frail man looked frightened. He took off his hat, leaned on his cane, and bowed to the Greek.

"Okay, meatball." Stavros read from the notepaper. "Spell *pharmaceutical.*"

"Ease up on him, Greek." Rainbow dipped his eyelids at the little cook. "Just a friendly wager, Angelo. I say you're pretty smart. So do your best. And take your time. The word we want you to spell is— *pharmaceutical.*"

Angelo's hands moved nervously around his cane grip. He closed his eyes, drew a deep breath: "T-E-N-N-E-S—"

Holy shit.

". . . S-E-E, P-N-E-U—"

Aw Jesus Christ, NO!

". . . M-O-N-I-A, P-H-A-R-M-A-C-E-U-T-I-C-A-L."

Stavros was studying the words on the paper. The Whip and the fat man were exchanging puzzled frowns. Murph broke the pencil and cursed under his breath. Angelo gulped and opened his eyes. Iris started to giggle.

Rainbow clapped. Maybe it could be salvaged. "Exactly right!"

"No, no, no." Stavros drew his arm off the kid's shoulder and took back his cigar. "You think I'm falling for this setup?" He handed the notepaper to the cowboy. "See there? He spells all the words. They trained him like a parrot. College kid, my ass." A nod to Iris: "Excuse the French."

"I do no so good?" The frail man's face was a mass of wrinkles.

Rainbow forced a stack of bills into Angelo's hand and glared at Murph, who looked ready to cry, his knuckles blanching around the splintered pencil. "You did fine, Angelo. It's not your fault."

"Hey, I get it." The Whip traced a finger over the words. "A setup."

"Nobody said that's the only word he had to spell." Rainbow reached for his panama before the giant sat on it. "Why, he could of run through the whole dictionary if he wanted. Long as he spelled the word we gave him. Which he did. Pay up, boys. You been had."

"Had, my goddamn—" Stavros made a fist beside his leg. "Excuse the French. Now listen. Nobody sets up the Greek. You pay *me*, understand?"

"And me." The fat man held out his hand.

Rainbow turned the hat in his lap. "Of course I set it up. I'm not dumb enough to go head to head with somebody as sharp as you, Greek, and not keep a rightful edge. So he spells another word first. No crime in that. It don't spoil the fact that he did spell the word we was after, am I right? Anybody not hear him spell it? Angelo, spell *pharmaceutical* again."

The frail man glanced at the money in his hand and took another deep breath and closed his eyes.

"No, no, no." Stavros said. "Sure, we heard him. But it wasn't our bet, see? He was supposed to spell just one word. Nothing else."

"You never said that," Rainbow told him. "You said: 'Angelo, spell *pharmaceutical*.' So he warmed up a little first. But he spelled it. What we got here, I think, is a dead heat." There was a hard silence. It was time to run right at them. "You can see I'm right, Greek, you got that look in your eyes." There was nothing in Stavros's eyes except contempt. Rainbow shrugged. "And me, well, I got a big heart, too. If you're not satisfied I won fair—I'll pay off." He got out his key, unlocked his briefcase, and, shielding his bankroll from the others, counted out $30,000. The gasp over his shoulder belonged to Iris, whose eyes were struggling to take in all the money: she had probably never seen so much in one place before. He remembered how that felt. He closed the lid, slapped his cash down on the leather. "Thirty grand. Now you boys are sure you want me to pay off, right?" The fat man grunted, The Whip nodded, but Stavros took a careful drag off his cigar. There was something in his eyes now: distrust. Rainbow rippled the edges of the bills. "The Greek don't look so sure to me. Maybe he figures the next time we wager and there's a difference of opinion, he might have to give in to my way of thinking. And maybe he figures I'm just smart enough to make sure the stakes then are a lot higher than they were this time." He brandished the cash. "And he'd be right. You boys claim you won and I claim you didn't. But I'm reasonable-minded. I'm paying off, because when the time comes, I know you'll do the same for me." He draped his arm along the seat, drawing his jacket flap away from the .45 on his hip. Like a magnet, the big gun drew the men's stares and held them.

"Might have to persuade you a little then. But I don't mind that."

Stavros nodded as though he liked what he had seen and heard. He blew smoke across Murph into the aisle. "Dead heat, boys."

Rainbow buttoned his jacket and sighed silently.

The Whip pushed back his big white hat. "You said he lost, Greek."

"The guinea spelled the word, didn't he?" Stavros brushed an ash off his pantleg. "But we see it's a setup, so we don't lose. Nobody wins here. Lousy bet. An exercise." That something in his eyes had turned into a smile. "You boys can do what you like. In my book, it's a dead heat."

The little silence was spoiled by short exhales that left angry words unspoken. Rainbow blinked his thanks to Stavros, put the cash away, locked his case, and put it on the floor, resting his foot on it. He smiled at Iris, but her face was blank. Was she disappointed that he hadn't won? But he had: the stalemate was a victory. He threw a salute into the aisle. "My thanks, Angelo. Give my best to E.R."

The little cook squinted, then tapped Murph on the shoulder. "You come?"

The kid shook his head and kept turning the broken pencil in his hands.

"He's going." Rainbow took the book from the cowboy and dropped it into Murph's lap. "Go read or something. I got no more use for you here."

"Oh don't," Iris said, leaning into his arm.

Rainbow ignored her and signaled the kid to leave by jerking his stare toward the rear of the car. Murph bit his lip and stormed down the aisle with Angelo hobbling after him.

"Nice kid." Stavros rolled the cigar in his fingers. "Your partner?"

Rainbow crossed his legs and fought the urge to shout his rage. "He helps me out now and then."

"Yeah, I can see that." Stavros broke out in a laugh. "Mostly then, ain't it."

The Whip slapped his knee. Even the fat man thought it was funny. But Iris wasn't laughing. She was gazing out the window as if she wanted to get lost in the darkening water out there. It was probably a mistake to have brought her along. Bad luck. She didn't understand the way it was in The Big Time. The odds were that she never would. Rainbow shifted his body away from her and joined the laughter.

21

The trees along the track no longer zipped by, they passed in groups of threes, then twos, then one at a time, rising like sooty fingers into the night. Air brakes squealed, steam hissed toward the soft orange glow inside the buildings and houses that lined the right-of-way. And with the slowdown in speed, a hush fell over the Pullman car: Saratoga.

Rainbow nudged Iris and she opened her eyes, raised her head from his shoulder, and sat up. "What time is it?" she said.

"About ten thirty." It was exactly 10:30 P.M. according to her wristwatch, which she could have looked at herself if she wanted to know the time, so her question had to be her way of saying "Hello" or "How are you?" or "Where am I?" It was a game she played and it was going to take some getting used to. He put on his hat. It felt small. Five years of sweat had taken its toll: the inside leather band was cracked and flaking. With luck, there might be a decent men's store up here, one that carried standard clothes instead of the fancy stuff they stocked in Chicago or New York. No wonder it was always so easy to spot city slickers—they all dressed the same. Like sissies. Or queers. He leaned away from Tom The Whip and the fat Russian across the aisle. They didn't look like queers, just close friends. Besides, whoever heard of a queer cowboy? Rainbow gnashed his teeth. He should have known better than to trust anything Murph said. Back where the kid was sitting, men stretched their limbs to shake off the stiffness of a seven-hour ride on straight-back seats.

Some of the more eager passengers inched toward the doors, but slowly, as if drawn by gravity. They were feigning indifference to mask their haste to get a jump on everyone else. Would they let a lady go first? Not this crowd. They'd pretend she wasn't even there. Rainbow put his briefcase in his lap. "No point in hurrying. You did make reservations, right?"

"I told you that this morning." She sounded grumpy, as though she needed more time to get over being drugged with sleep. "Why do you keep on asking?"

Talking to her now would be as stupid as trying to get the giant, Aziz, to focus his stare: it couldn't be done. This was going to take a *lot* of getting used to.

Harsh light flooded the window on the Greek's side of the car. Strung below the steeples of the stationhouse roof, a banner swelled with the roll of heavy black air: WELCOME TO SARATOGA SPRINGS. The trackside platform was jammed. A throng of villagers, their faces hot with smiles, stood behind dusky porters whose eyes were as empty as the baggage carts they tended. A group of men with billboards slung front and back over their shoulders milled about as walking advertisements for casinos, hotels, nightclubs. And a makeshift band—tuba, saxophone, bass drum, two trumpets, and a glockenspiel—was assembling to one side, waiting for the leader's baton to drop. With a final blast of steam shot long and low across the cinders, *The Cavanagh Special* stopped, its doors slid open. Passengers rushed out into cheers, a shower of confetti, and a chorus of "Hail, Hail, the Gang's All Here" from the band, which got some of the notes right, though their music didn't have a chance against all the shouting:

"Follow me to the Grand Union!"—"The Chicago Club is now open!"—"Ford's on Broadway, best food in town!"—"Honest chuckaluck at The Park, E.R.'s casino for the elite!"

The shills in the billboard sandwiches kept yelling as they led the way into town with the band in close pursuit and the crowd congealing into a fluid mass until it wasn't possible to distinguish tourist from resident, schoolteacher from sharper.

"I'm at the United States." Stavros the Greek gave Rainbow a small card: STAVROS KARAMONOPOLIS, ESQUIRE, MEMBER, NEW YORK TURF EXCHANGE. "Flash this if you got problems." He glanced at Iris and struggled to hold back a wry grin. "And stop by tonight. If you get the time, that is." He led his giant up the aisle ahead of The Whip and the fat man.

Now even the train staff had debarked. The Pullman was empty.

Rainbow walked to the door. "Heard about this place since I was a kid." He swallowed a memory: *"Saratoga, now if that ain't living."* And helping Iris down iron steps to a roadbed coated with shredded paper, he found the courage to say: "Glad I'm seeing it the first time with you."

She squeezed his hand. Her eyes were soft, but her smile was only half there. "It's a marvelous place . . . but dangerous, too. I didn't want you to come alone."

Cute. As if all 105 pounds of her was going to protect him. She had to be in love. Or else her brain was warped. She nodded toward the head of the siding where Murph was stacking golf bags and luggage. "I'd better give him a hand with mine." At the edge of the circle of light, she touched the kid's shoulder and stepped to the dark mouth in the center of the baggage car.

Murph pawed at the clubs and watched her point her suitcases out to a porter. "About what happened with the spelling, Rainbow. I never figured Angelo didn't know to do the words separate and—"

"Not now." Rainbow studied the sky: a nice moon and enough blinking stars to prove that this village was a long haul from the glare of city lights which always stole a lot of stars. Too many. Every night. "I'm in a bad enough mood after that ride."

"Not me. Jesus, it was all right, trains ain't so bad, I didn't get sick or nothing. Both times." Murph straightened the row of cardboard suitcases stenciled with a New York clothier's logo. "I tried to teach him."

"Should of done it myself. Now drop it."

"You can take the grand we paid Angelo out of my share of the bankroll," Murph said. "Say, that was real smart how you got a dead heat."

Rainbow yanked his hat down to stretch it some more. "We let the Greek and everybody on that train know we're partners. You got any idea how much that's gonna cost us?" He spat his sigh. "Now drop it or I may just pole you right here. Go put her stuff with ours."

Murph went to the pile of luggage next to Iris. Her big trunk was coming out of the train. He said something that made her smile and walk back to Rainbow.

"That's all of it." She didn't sound grumpy anymore. "They should have it loaded on a cart in no time."

He put his arm around her. "See they get all this stuff over the Congressional Hotel, kid! Meet you in the lobby!" He turned his back on whatever Murph was muttering and on the porter's lament: "Can't stack them, gots to do one at a time, damn Saratoga trunks." Beyond the stationhouse, he followed the street with twin banners draped across it less than fifteen feet apart: THE PILGRIMAGE PLAY, THE LIFE OF THE CHRIST and SPECIAL ADVANCE SCREENING: POLA NEGRI IN A WOMAN OF THE WORLD.

Iris stared at the bright lights in the near distance. "Why do you have to be so hard on Dave?"

Now she was going to tell him how to run his business. He fought the urge to shout and tried a vacant tone of voice, one that would make his words sound final. "Because being easy don't work."

She got the message. She didn't open her mouth until they reached the corner where all the lights were: Broadway. She looked into the crowd around the big hotel two blocks down; it loomed like a white castle with slender pillars supporting a massive porch.

"That the one we want?" he said.

She shook her head. "That's the United States. The Congressional is past that grove, near The Park. We should cross here."

"You're leading." He let her take him across the street and into the swarm of light-colored jackets, the din of two thousand voices. It didn't seem to bother her. She sidestepped everything and everybody and when she turned up a road that could have passed for a country lane, she didn't even stop to check her bearings. How many times had she come here? Five? A dozen? With how many other men? *At least a dozen.* But she didn't walk the way fast women did, her body was too tight. He kept watching her ass to be sure. To the north, buried deep in the park, a three-story building sent filmy light into tall trees and over a quiet pond. Whatever it was, it was drawing a big crowd. He tugged her elbow. "Sure that's not it over there?"

"That's The Park," she said.

What did she call this, the forest? "Yeah, but that could be our hotel, right?"

"That's The Park. A casino!" Her grumpy voice was back. She pointed up the road. *"This* is the Congressional."

The brick building around the curve was five stories high, with columns going all the way to the doghouse dormers on the peaked roof. Amber light poured out the high church-style windows at ground level and the box windows above. The undulating lawn was planted with giant elms; birches lined the widening lane. As if taken in tow by some magical power, Rainbow couldn't turn away or take a backward step. And if she was talking to him, he couldn't hear her or any sound except his feet crunching gravel. Then even that was gone, replaced by the slap of shoe leather on a concrete porch, and finally, the deadened thud of footsteps on plush carpet. A red and gray carpet. To one side, a line of sleek walnut chairs. Maroon couches in the center of a big room where white pillars rose like sculptured granite to what must have been a thirty-foot ceiling. The noise came back all at once. Men were crowing for service by the registration desk. The jazz band that had played the serenade at trackside in New York was playing that same song in the far corner. People clapped rhythm for the young dancer, who did his tap dance on a coffee table. Small wheels of baggage carts moaned for oil, bellboys picked up bags and scampered toward the elevators, one hundred separate conversations were being held on the wide staircase opposite the main doors, a desk bell kept going *ping!*

"The reservation is in your name," Iris said. "And I asked for Dave's room to be on the same floor as ours."

Rainbow escorted her to the empty couch in the near corner. A beautiful woman sitting alone in this place would attract a crowd. And trouble. "Sure you don't want to use the powder room and freshen up after the ride?"

"I'll do that in the suite."

He hurried to the edge of the mob around the front desk. Fists of money waved in the hope of getting the clerk's attention. If she hadn't made sure of those reservations, tonight would be spent outdoors on the grass. At least it wasn't raining.

The clerk's shout was no match for the clamor he faced, but he kept trying. "Anyone with reservations?"

"Right here!" Rainbow held up a hand, clutched his briefcase flat to his chest, and squirmed past dark stares and muttered curses, through four rows of men. "Roberts. A suite."

"I was here first!" A gray-haired lady in a beaded dress tapped her jewel-encrusted hand on the counter. "Where are they?"

"On their way from the vault right now." The clerk smiled and glared at the same time, as though he dreamed of using a pile driver on her. He stopped looking for Rainbow's reservation card to take a narrow iron box from the young man who came out from behind the wall of mail slots. "Here you are, Mrs. North."

With a key, Mrs. North opened the box. Everything in it sparkled: rubies, diamonds, emeralds, jade, gold filigree. Oblivious of the sharpers and thieves all around her, she reached in, letting bracelets, rings, loose gems roll off her hand into the box as if she were pouring sand into an hourglass. She couldn't be Taylor North's wife. Much too old. And she handled those gems like precious memories: she had to be a widow. Maybe not. But there was something pitiful about her.

"Has to see them every day," the clerk whispered. "We get all kinds up here." He laid down a card and turned the register. "Will you be registering for Mr. Murphy as well, sir? Or has he canceled on us?"

Rainbow scrawled his name across the unlined page. "He'll be along with the luggage. Can I get a boy to stand by?"

"Certainly, sir." The clerk slapped his bell—*ping!*—and started to shout, but waved as if to erase his thoughts. "It's impossible with all these people. Could I ask you, sir, to instruct the bellman yourself?" He handed Rainbow two keys: 325 and 319.

Stealing a glance at the multicolored fire that arced from the jewels in the iron box into Mrs. North's face, Rainbow worked through the crowd and wrapped the keys in a ten-dollar bill. He gave the bundle to the bellboy who was leaning against the wall as if on vacation. "Want you to take me up to three twenty-five and come back here and wait for my—a red-haired kid. He'll be carrying golf bags and a big trunk."

The bellboy slid the money into the pocket of his gold uniform. "And the name, sir?"

"Roberts." Rainbow waved his hat at Iris, who was still alone on the couch. "We'll wait for my—for her and then go up."

"Yessir," the bellboy said. "Will Mr. Roberts be able to tell me which bags belong to you and your wife and which are his?"

"What? Oh, yeah. He's Murphy."

The bellboy squinted, then smiled. "Follow me, sir."

Rainbow gave Iris a little hug. "We got the same floor. You did great."

Instead of the smile he expected, she frowned and got into the elevator ahead of him. "I know you don't want me to say anything about this, but . . . but he feels badly enough about the little man on the train—the spelling bet. You don't have to persecute him, do you?"

"Who, Murph?"

"Oh, I see," the bellboy said. "Murphy Roberts. I've got it straight now."

Rainbow choked the briefcase handle and leaned close to Iris. "Let's leave it that it was my idea, okay?"

"I told him the same thing at trackside." Her eyes hardened. "And he told me it was always your idea."

Rainbow didn't say anything. He couldn't. She had shut him up.

The elevator stopped, the door opened, and Iris followed the bellboy past a wooden bench against the wall. "I only wish you didn't have to be so tough on him," she said. "Don't you see how sensitive he is?"

Sensitive? For ruining the bet, the kid deserved to have his neck wrung like a rag. "I'll square it with him," Rainbow said. " . . . Somehow."

She touched his arm and flashed her smile. "It was a marvelous setup. I wish you had told me beforehand. It was so, so—ingenious!"

He tried to shrug it off, but his grin wouldn't stay back.

"Do I have time to light your rooms, sir?" The bellboy unlocked the door to 325. "Or should I go down right now and wait for Mr. Roberts?"

"Yeah, go wait for him," Rainbow said. "Remember—red hair."

"And golf clubs." The bellboy went up the hall to the stairs.

Iris was standing in the doorway, arms folded, foot tapping impatiently on the rug. " . . . Well?"

"Oh, sure." He squeezed past her, set down his briefcase, and patted the wall for the light switch. "I'll find it in a second."

Her arms fell to her sides. "Aren't you going to carry me inside?"

He held down his laugh. "What's the matter, sprain your ankle?"

Wearing a smirk of playful anger, she cocked her purse as if to hit him, then winced, raised a foot, and rubbed her ankle. She gave a fair imitation of a limp before leaning against the doorjamb. "It really hurts. I may never walk again."

"Right." He snatched her off the floor. "And after the third week in bed, remind me to call you an ambulance." He whisked her across the threshold and kicked the door shut.

Rainbow walked into 319 and closed the door. "This is all right, huh, kid? Mine's the same, just a little bigger because it's a suite." His suite was three rooms and each of them was larger than this one. Out the window, lights from Broadway silhouetted massive elms, spindly birches. "Got the same view, too. I don't know why I treat you so good, dumb as you are."

Head low, Murph leaned the golf bags against the wall, put the cardboard suitcases on the bed, and began unpacking his new clothes.

Rainbow opened his briefcase. Each of the seventeen stacks of bills he tossed on the bed was wrapped in a red band: $1,000. "There's your bankroll."

The kid looked at the money, but didn't touch it. "That ain't fair."

"The hell it's not. I didn't even take out for your clothes! Only for half the thirty grand you cost us today."

"We didn't lose it. I can see you taking out for Angelo's grand, but—"

Rainbow slammed the case lid shut. "Had that cash as good as in our pocket, and now we're out the whole bundle because you couldn't deliver your end. It *is* a loss. And like any partner, I'm splitting it with you. Even if it's not my fault, I got to bear half the blame."

"But you ain't out nothing," Murph said. "My share's supposed to be thirty-two grand. You still got fifteen of it right in that case. I'm the only one taking a loss here."

Rainbow grinned. "You're getting real good at figures. Makes me feel like you're learning something after all."

"I'm learning all right, don't you worry none about that."

"I don't think I like that tone of voice, kid."

"Well . . . shit." Murph made a fist and sat on the bed, tucking his legs under him. "Still say it ain't fair. Told you I tried."

"Trying's not good enough." Rainbow pulled the chair up next to the phone. "Now first thing tomorrow, take the clubs over and feel out the golf course. We got a match with the Greek. Claims he's an athlete."

"Any good at golf?"

"Wants four strokes." Rainbow yawned. "Think I could beat him left-handed."

But the kid didn't laugh. He dug into the clothes and dumped them out.

"Look, you got to learn to get things right the first time you try," Rainbow said. "Making you pay for your mistakes is the only way I can be sure you understand that." He sailed the Greek's business card onto the bed. "Carry that and use it if you get into trouble. I'll get another from the Greek tonight. And don't get suckered by the tables up here, they're all rigged. And don't trust the cops either. They get paid to keep their eyes closed during the racing season."

"Jesus, engraved!" Murph fondled the card. "Can I come with you tonight?"

"You better walk around and think about what happened today, where you went wrong. I don't ever want to see this kind of thing again, understand?"

The kid nodded. "But if they already know we're partners, how come I can't go with you?"

"You won't miss a thing," Rainbow said. "Besides, you can help me out by checking on Iris while I'm gone. She likes you."

"She does?"

"Yeah, and she's responsible for me being so easy on you, too. But don't think I'm not wise to it. Next time I won't slack up a bit. No matter what she says."

Murph shoveled the stacks of money into one of the suitcases. "How do you know she likes me? She say that?"

"You ain't exactly the main topic of our conversation, kid." From his jacket, Rainbow got out the piece of paper Curtis had given him. "Hide that cash and carry only what you need. No way these streets can be safe."

"Think the hotel vault's a good idea?"

If the hotel safe was good enough for Mrs. North and her crown jewels, it would probably be fine for cash. Rainbow nodded. "Get a box. One with a key. And check on it every day we're here." He took the phone receiver off the hook and read the last entry on the page to the operator.

"I could ask her if she wants to come with me." Murph stuffed a stack of bills into his jacket. "To see the sights. That be okay with you?"

The phone on the other end of the line stopped ringing and a lifeless female voice said: "Grand Union, Saratoga's finest, may I help you, please?"

"Like to speak to the Dancer." Rainbow put the page back in his pocket and covered the mouthpiece with a hand. "Just check on her. You're on your own."

Murph shrugged. "Who's this Dancer?"

"Just a bookie."

The static filtering through the earpiece ended with a pop. "Dancer."

Rainbow sat up straight. "Yeah, Dancer? This is Rainbow Roberts. Curtis Godfrey in Saint Lou told me you could help me find somebody."

" . . . Possible," Dancer said.

"Small-time pool shark named Robinson. Calvin Orville Robinson."

"Aw, Jesus, I should of known." Murph carried the suitcase full of money to the door, held up a hand in a limp wave, "Lock it when you leave, would you?" and walked out.

"Very possible," Dancer said. "Why you want him found?"

"You know him?" Rainbow crossed his legs to quiet the twinge shooting through him. "He's here?"

"My business to know people, know what I mean, Roberts? Now I asked why you want Cal Robinson found."

Dancer knew him, all right. That's what they called the old bastard: Cal Robinson. *Lousy name.* Rainbow used his calmest tone, the one that made his lies seem matter-of-factly real. "Just a score to settle. Business."

"Let me get back to you." The squeaky voice sounded hurried. "What hotel?"

"The Congressional. Suite three twenty-five."

"Got it." The line clicked dead.

Rainbow set the phone on the table. What began as a tight smile drew into a sneer. Old Cal might be walking Broadway right now, less than a half-mile away. The .45 pinched his side, his hands were trembling. He picked up his briefcase and went into the hall, pulling the door shut, testing the knob to be sure it was locked. *Very possible, my ass. The bastard is here.* If he could have been certain that no one was watching, he would have jumped to tap the globe light hanging from the ceiling. He walked into 325 smiling.

All the lights were on, casting a sheen on white walls, gold-painted molding, dark wood chairs and couches. He locked the door and went between the main room and parlor into the bedroom. Light crept under the bathroom door. She was humming to herself and splashing water in the tub. She hadn't wanted to make love when he carried her to bed, she had thought only of herself, teasing him and pretending she had to freshen up first. She was making a career out of that bath. And probably waterlogged by now. Would she spend all her time in there—hiding? At least he had things to do and, if need be, he could use Murph's bathroom. It would work out, he'd see to it that she didn't get in the way too much.

He dropped his briefcase on the bed. His clean shirt was hanging in the closet. Who told her to do that? His suitcase stood against the wall. Had she put his underwear in the bureau, too? And why had she moved his panama to her trunk in the corner? The hat was fine where he had left it. He put it back on the chair. If he hurried, he would be gone before she finished that bath; he wouldn't have to deal with her. She would only want to know why he was so restless. And he might wind up telling her: "Finally got a line on the old bastard I spent my life looking for. He's my father. Only he ain't because he never was one. I'm gonna blow his brains out." But that would spoil it for good. She would leave before he finished talking. He hid the .45 under his hat and took the shirt from the closet.

The song she was humming sounded like the one the jazz band had played for her at Grand Central. She didn't do the melody justice.

There was a loud splash, a metallic *clunk*, then the gurgle of water down the drain. The bathroom door opened. She came out dripping wet, wrapped in a towel with a gold crest on it. She wasn't humming anymore. "I didn't hear you come in. You're so quiet."

He tossed the clean shirt on the bed and got out of his jacket. "Didn't want to bother you in the middle of a concert."

"Not very good, am I. Tone-deaf." She picked up his shirt and brought it to him. "You should leave it hanging until you're ready to put it on. It won't wrinkle that way."

He had been ready to put it on until she walked in. He nodded and hung up the shirt. "I'll be a few hours. Call room service if you get hungry."

"I couldn't eat a thing, I'm still tired from the train." She pulled back the bedspread, climbed under the sheets, rolled out of the towel, and folded it over the pillow. "Would you turn off the lights when you go?"

He laid his dirty shirt on the chair, grabbed his briefcase, went out to the other rooms, turned off all the lights, and came back to the doorway for one more look. She was alluring, so clean, lying there naked under fresh linen. He turned off the bedroom light, slid out of his pants and undershorts, and got in bed, leaving his case by his shoes.

"I thought you were going out?" She smelled like laundry just back from the cleaners. Or was that the sheets? "I really am tired."

"Me, too." He snuggled close, his chest to her back, his nose resting on the wetness of her hair. "Always was partial to short naps."

She didn't laugh or giggle. She sighed. "I'm *too* tired."

"And I couldn't if I wanted to." He tucked his hardening penis between his legs: it hurt. He closed his eyes, tried to convince himself that the soft breasts and hard nipples touching his arm couldn't lure him, that the cool beads of moisture on her skin, the curve of her back and the way she fit into him—like one spoon laid on top of another, bowls together, stems lined up flush—that none of that was going to matter: he was going to sleep. The Greek wouldn't disappear in an hour, the town would still be there. And it was working. He was convinced.

Then she rolled over, kissed his chest, slid a hand down his side and between his legs, feeling for him like a blind woman: "Stop hiding."

He laughed and stopped hiding.

22

The lobby was still packed and noisy. And that idiot bellhop was still grinning: "Everything all right in three nineteen, Mr. Roberts?"

Since their first encounter at the door an hour ago and all the way up in the elevator, Murph had tried to straighten him out. He tried again now. "I'm Murphy."

"Yessir, the gentleman in three twenty-five made it clear. Murphy Roberts."

"No, he's Roberts."

"Ahh, brothers!"

"We ain't brothers. He's Roberts, I'm Murphy."

"Robert Roberts and Murphy Roberts." The jerk was hopeless. "Not brothers? Cousins, then. Family vacation, is it?"

Maybe this was Rainbow's idea of a joke. Murph squeezed the suitcase handle, then sighed. "Everything's fine in three nineteen." He went to the side of the front desk, where a cashier made him fill out a card before handing him a long metal box to put valuables in. Transferring his money from the cardboard suitcase, Murph locked the box with the big key he found taped to the lid. He was still angry about being cheated out of $15,000. Some partnership. But that was typical of Rainbow: he always used money like a whip. When the cashier took the box behind the partition, Murph pocketed his key, left his case by the wall, and struggled through the crowd to the doors, wishing he had a sword to hack his way along, one with a fat blade that curved up at the end, the kind they used in jungle movies. Or was it in the pirate movies? Anyway, that kind of sword would have been nice.

Outside, the lawn rolled under night shadows toward the thick band of light from Broadway. Freshly oiled macadam carried a blue tinge and a foul smell, like unwashed feet. He walked north past Spring Street to the next corner, marked PHILA. *Must be an abbreviation for Philly.* Across the way, the porch of the Rip Van Dam Hotel was noisy with men, and a line of people waited to get into the street-level restaurant of the other hotel, the Adelphi: four stories of red brick, its face sliced vertically by white posts that formed arches just below a flat roof. He lit a cigarette, blew the smoke toward the big hotel on the corner. It was a fortress of brick and stone and Stavros the Greek and his bodyguard were coming down the steps off its wide porch. Their tuxedos shone under the streetlamps as they crossed Broadway. Murph hustled after them. But closing the distance to less than a half a block, he slowed to a walk, feeling more uncomfortable with each step. What could he say: "See, I got your card, Greek—I'm the college kid from the train—Rainbow'll be here soon, okay if I tag along?" *Tag along.* The Greek would only laugh. Murph stopped. The two men in tuxedos made their way over the torn-up pavement of Woodlawn Avenue, past the Knights of Columbus headquarters, a penny arcade, and a row of cheap stores, to an ugly brownstone building, the Chicago Club, which looked like a police station. They climbed the steps and disappeared inside. Murph kicked a chunk of blacktop across the street, drew a deep breath, then sidestepped chuckholes and walked to the brownstone and up the steps.

Bank-type cashier cages and a chalkboard labeled SCRATCHES & RESULTS took up the entire wall by the door. It was noisier in here than back at the hotel. This was a dingy barn, crammed with every sort of gaming device favorable to the house: chuckaluck, faro, roulette, and four rows of slot machines by the front windows echoing their metallic symphony: *kachink, lick-lick-lick, whirr, clink—clink—clank.* Men were in shirtsleeves, the few women in here walked around in loose-fitting dresses. The heat: a Turkish bath with cigar smoke instead of steam. The fans on the ceiling didn't help at all. Wilting straws stuck out of pop bottles, mustard dripped from hot dogs. This couldn't be Saratoga, the fabulous resort, the famed "Three Weeks in August" he had heard about on the train. This was a shoddy carnival, a county fair held indoors. He crushed out his cigarette and went to the base of the stairs that Stavros and Asses were climbing. The guard reattached a chain across the landing and shook his head: "Dinner jackets required upstairs."

It was probably swank up there. How much would a dinner jacket cost? With a shrug, Murph went to the cooler, where a woman was splashing water on her heated, floppy breasts. He took a drink and started for the main doors. He almost made it. They begged him to stop. *Kachink*, please, *lick-lick-lick*, try me, *whirr*, feels good, *clink—clink*, hold your breath, *clank*, better luck next time. Grabbing the handle of the machine at the head of the row, he dropped a penny in the slot, put a hand in his jacket, and rubbed Ellen's locket for good luck. He pulled the lever down. And laughed. There he was, standing with one hand in his pocket, playing a one-armed bandit. It was a natural. *Clink*, berry, *clink*, berry, *clank*—orange. He kicked the machine. Some of them told fortunes. That was worth another penny. But they were all rigged. He squeezed her locket and went through the doors, down the steps and up the narrow street.

The railroad station was only one block away. He took Church Street back to Broadway. To the north, replicas of Harlem hot spots dotted the way: the Cotton Club, Satchel Rags, THE Club. The music pouring out of each of them got mixed in the street. It sounded like war. He headed south, back toward the Congressional. Now was as good a time as any to check in on Iris. Maybe she knew a decent place to go in this town. He crossed the street and stopped to let a limousine glide up the drive to The Park Casino. Nestled in the trees, that looked like a good place. He followed the drive into the woods.

It was a box, three stories high and brown. Most of the people going in and out the door were dressed in silks. The light coming through the tall windows looked soft. Murph straightened his tie, brushed his bangs out of his eyes, and went inside. The air was cool. There were a lot of gamblers here and a lot of tables, but hardly any noise except for the roll of dice and the clatter of little balls falling into slots on the roulette wheels. Everything in here looked solid and refined. Real leather on the chairs. This place had class.

He found an empty chair at a roulette table in the corner and bought $200 worth of chips from the croupier. Yellow chips, worth $5 apiece. No one else had yellow chips: they must have been special. Murph bet 29 Black. He lost. 29 Black again. Lost. Again, again. The number kept losing. But the odds were with him, weren't they? 29 Black would hit soon and pay off thirty-five-to-one: $175 for a $5 bet. The more he bet, the more he would win. Some people were playing combinations of numbers, putting their chips on the lines between the numerals. Murph tried that, too. No luck. Then he tried betting the columns of numbers by putting his chips in the boxes below lines of numerals. Next he bet colors: red or black. He won once—even money. He went back to playing 29 Black. And losing.

The house changed croupiers every half-hour, but it didn't help. Murph went through his first $200 and bought $300 more of the special yellow chips. That didn't help either. But 29 Black had to hit soon. Another $300 worth of chips. 29 Black had to hit very soon now. It did and Murph let out a yell. Some of the other players thought it was funny. He raked in his winnings with a straight face and bet his number again. His streak didn't last. He went to betting the colors again. And 29 Black hit. He cursed himself and started playing the number again. And he ran out of chips. But he was going to show them. This was his last $200, yet that made it better because this money was important and it made sense that if he was going to win, he was going to win when he had to, not when he only wanted to, not when he had extra cash on him. This cash was going to do it for him. He bought more yellow chips.

And lost half of them in ten minutes. But that was all right, what he had left was really important money now, so it made even more sense that he was going to win with it. And when he got down to his last chip—money that was absolutely vital, if he was going to win at all, this was it, and it made so much sense to win with the last chip, to come back all the way on one bet, to get justice when it was now or never—he took a deep breath and bet 29 Black. And it lost.

It didn't make any sense at all. He had $36.15 in his pocket and the crumpled red band with $1,000 printed on it. He got up from the table. It was over. A tall man took his seat and asked the croupier if his credit was still good and the croupier said the tall man's credit was fine and how many chips did he want? The tall man got $1,000 worth of chips. Yellow ones.

"Who do I see about getting some credit here?" Murph asked the croupier.

"Cashier's window, sir. Ask for Mr. Tagliafera."

Murph started walking to the cashier cages. *Tagliafera?* Ellen's brother! Frank, wasn't it? Angelo's what—cousin? No, nephew. Getting credit here was going to be a snap. Murph was practically one of the family. "Like to see Mr. Frank Tagliafera," he told the cashier. While he waited, he rubbed Ellen's locket. It made a lot of sense to play on credit because he had all that money in the hotel safe and why spend it if he didn't have to? After all, he was going to win this time. He would never have to touch his bankroll. He spat on his hand and ran it through his hair.

The man who came to the window didn't look like a Frank and he didn't look anything like Ellen or her grandmother or that wart-nosed crone. He looked sick. The pouches under his eyes were dark, his fingernails were badly bitten. He coughed into a dirty handkerchief and said: "I'm Tag. Can I help you?"

Murph kept staring at the man's coal-black hair.

"Did you want to see me?" Frank Tagliafera said.

"I . . . I need to get some credit here. . . ."

Another hacking cough into the handkerchief. The man looked ready to die. "New account, then. How much?"

"Ah . . . a thousand . . . ?"

"And your reference?"

". . . What?"

"Your reference," Tagliafera said. "Who's standing behind your credit?"

"Oh . . ." Murph dug into his pants for the locket. But that was silly, no one was going to give him credit because he had her locket on him. This wasn't going to work. Ellen or no Ellen, member of the family—practically—or not. Murph swallowed and gave the man Stavros the Greek's business card.

Tagliafera studied it for a moment, then handed it back. "Yes sir. No problem." He started coughing again and didn't stop until he had asked a lot of questions and written the answers down on a file card. Then he gave Murph a piece of paper. "Show this at any table. You understand this is for twenty-four hours only. After that, it's six percent a day on the unpaid balance."

Murph nodded and folded the piece of paper. The man left the window and disappeared into an office, coughing all the way. Did Ellen know how sick he was? Probably had TB. Murph decided to call her in the morning so that arrangements could be made to ship the man to the desert. It was the right thing to do. And Ellen would appreciate it, she would see how much Murph cared.

He went back to the roulette table and took a seat on the opposite side, away from the tall man and the yellow chips. The croupier put the slip of paper into a slot and handed out $1,000 in chips. Blue ones: $5 each. Murph started betting 29 Black. Blue was a good color, a great one, he couldn't miss this time. And this was borrowed money, it belonged to the house. How could anyone lose with house money, blue chips, and 29 Black?

It took only fifteen minutes for the house to get its money back. And for Murph to find out why. The table was rigged. The croupier had a foot button and could make the wheel stop where he wanted it to. Rainbow had been right—the bastard was always right—this was a setup.

Murph pushed himself up from the table and moved toward the doors. But why take this lying down? Why let them make a pigeon out of him? Rainbow wouldn't. He'd draw his gun and shoot them for running a crooked game. Bristling with anger, Murph marched to the office by the cashier cages, knocked twice, and let himself in.

Seated behind a small desk, Frank Tagliafera was coughing and trying to drink a glass of water.

"I ain't paying off on that grand," Murph said.

Tagliafera squinted and muffled his cough with the handkerchief.

"You run a fixed wheel here," Murph told him. "I seen it and I can prove it. And if you think you're getting a dime out of me, you're out of your mind." He turned to walk out, then turned back and glared. "And don't come trying to scare me, neither. Or I'll come straight back here and blow you in two."

He marched out of the casino before Tagliafera could speak. It felt good. He had shown them. Rainbow couldn't have done better himself. He cut through the elms toward Broadway. In the clearing behind the casino, a fountain trickled. It was a statue of a lady standing over a small square pool. Nearby, a man in work clothes turned a spigot with a forked pole. The fountain went silent. Murph followed the path through a set of arches. The big sign above the trellis read, ITALIAN GARDENS. It was too dark to tell if they were really gardens or not. But there were a lot of plants and shrubs, each one staked with an identifying marker. Except the markers were made out in a foreign language, which was so stupid he felt like laughing. Only foreigners could read the things.

And Ellen was going to know everything. Not only how sick her brother Frank was, but how crooked he was, too. No wonder that little kid—Mascalzone—knew how to cheat. It ran in the family. But Ellen wasn't like that, she was honest. She would understand. And believe what Murph told her because he could show it to her if she didn't want to believe it at first. And she would see how much he cared about her. And maybe love him for it.

He had walked so fast and so hard up Broadway, that he was almost out of town when he stopped. He turned back toward the sound of music and went into Satchel Rags. They had just what he needed. A drink.

Rainbow couldn't move his arm: it was numb. Iris had been resting her head on his shoulder for the last half-hour, ever since he had finished making love to her. Or had she been the one who finished first? Her wetness was still on his crotch, seeping into twists of pubic hair, clinging to the folds of skin around his penis, which had flopped to one side and lay like a sticky finger against his leg. The top sheet was sticking to the hair on his thigh, but that was his own doing. He had told her when it was time and slipped out of her, pressing against her belly like a burrowing animal while she had held him close and moaned as though she were the one shivering from spasmodic eruptions of fluid. To thank her for holding on, he had used the top sheet to wipe her skin, even when she had told him, "You don't have to, I don't mind." But she had to mind, she couldn't possibly like having all that stuff on her. Maybe she had just been grateful that he pulled out of her when he did, before the first explosion. He reached down to pry the sheet free. He didn't want all that stuff over him either.

She nuzzled deeper into his shoulder, pinching flesh and bony joint. "It does matter to you, doesn't it."

He had known last night, even before he was inside her for the first time: he wasn't her first lover. She was too easy with the whole process, too experienced. And yes, it mattered. But he didn't tell her then and he wasn't going to tell her now. He half expected her to apologize. After all, it was her fault, letting herself be used like that. How many times? Did she keep count? Did she and The Jerk always do it in the same position or did they try it with her on top or sideways or in the bathtub? As much as she liked to soak, she would probably be crazy about that. The sink, too. But Rainbow couldn't ask. She would probably tell him. Then he would have to live with images of her and The Jerk tangled up every whichway, grunting and laughing, pushing against each other. He tried to lose the vision of her bent over a broken chest of drawers, The Jerk mounting her from the rear with his ball spikes still on, the brim of his cap turned up, and a fungo bat in his hand. Rainbow blinked twice, then yawned. "No, Iris. It's not important."

She hugged him, but gently, as if to get a feel for how thick he was around the middle and compare him to The Jerk. "And you? Have you been with a lot of women?"

She probably wanted to hear, "Yes," to be impressed by some large number like 412. There were no large numbers. Rainbow had stopped counting years ago. When the count was zero. Now it was one. All the rest didn't rate being counted, they were whores, starting with the big ball of flesh Curtis had fixed him up with in Memphis—*"Because it's time you got yourself laid, boy. Getting tired of going around with a damn virgin for a partner. It ain't healthy."*—straight through to

202

the dark-haired girl with the nice ass Curtis had fixed him up with in Saint Louis—*"How was she, sport?"* She was like all the others. Even the nice lady in Friendship, West Tennessee, between Jackson and Dyersburg, just south of the highway Old Cal must have taken all the time before he headed east. That light-haired lady whose husband had died and left her a house and some chickens—*"I swear, Curtis, I woke up with this fucking rooster standing on my chest, staring down like he aims to peck my eyes out!"*—that lady didn't make him pay for the privilege of having her, but she turned out to be a whore just the same, running to bed with any tramp who came along, even other women! Did Old Cal have her too? After that perverted lady, Rainbow had stopped counting. He blinked now and started another yawn. "I'm a virgin."

She growled into his chest and pushed with both arms as if to shove the silliness out of him. "I'm serious."

Me, too. "I don't keep a scorecard," he said.

"You know that's not what I meant. We don't have to talk about it if you don't want to."

To thank her, he moved her hair away from her cheek. "Still waiting on your answer. Lot of good land out in California."

"They have earthquakes."

"We could grow oranges or something."

"You'd be gone all the time."

His head shook without his telling it to. And the words came out all by themselves: "Not if we had kids."

This time, she growled in disgust and rolled away.

Staring into dim light, he flexed the fingers she had been lying on. A tingle walked up his arm. "With a house on a hill, you could see all of it. Maybe a hundred acres. Orange trees are real nice to look at, you know."

She drew her legs up. "Do you hate me? For Ernie?"

"I told you, it's not important how many—" He tore the sheet from his leg hairs and winced. "Don't see why we have to talk this thing to death."

"He was the only one." She said it as though some virtue should be associated with how she had limited herself. "Only Ernie. And now you."

He kept bending his arm to work out the stiffness. It felt strange, as if what he was really doing was pumping a well to get "I forgive you Iris" to rush out and splash all over her. Ridiculous. Why should he have to forgive her? For being unfaithful before they had even met? For not saving herself? His arm went limp. It was more than ridiculous and he knew it. She was here. His. Now. And maybe, someday soon . . .

"Part of me still loves him." She sniffed and dabbed her nose with the sheet. "Funny, I still look on the sports page to see how he does."

How could she bother with a jerk like Ernie Wobers who couldn't hit his way out of a crib? And what about that idiot in the white Packard? Did she check the stock market to find out how he was doing? Rainbow sat up, draped his feet over the edge of the bed, tucked the sheet between his legs to cover his groin. "Hungry yet?"

"Don't do that."

". . . What?"

"Change the subject all the time." She fluffed the pillow and put her head back down. "It's not a large part of me that loves him. Not anymore. Not since—you."

His pants, with undershorts filling the leg holes, were bunched on the floor. His dirty shirt was dangling off the chair by his hat. His tie curled around the armrest. Her things were out of sight: hanging in the closet, packed in that trunk, unpacked with care in bureau drawers. How could anyone be so neat? She would be impossible to live with. Out the window, light from the lobby crawled onto the lawn toward The Park Casino. The Greek was undoubtedly dealing stud, wondering why it was taking Rainbow so long to show up. Without turning around, he reached back to find her. "I'm sorry you still hurt over—him. Might be you'll have better luck with me."

She recoiled from his touch, pulling herself into a tighter ball. "You don't know anything about growing oranges!"

Now who was changing the subject? "Figure I could learn," he said.

"She's lived there a long time." Her sob was clipped. "Almost twenty years."

"Where? Who?"

"My mother. With some man who digs oil wells. Long Beach. I got a postcard from her once."

"Yeah, well . . ." Why had he picked California? There was plenty of good land in Kansas, or Texas or . . . Because California was as far as a body could go. As far as Sweet Dee Flagg had gone. But Dee wasn't Iris.

"Your mother wouldn't have to know we lived there," he said. "I mean, she'd probably never think of looking for you because your name'd be—" he swallowed and said it: "—changed."

She was crying again, the same as last night. "I almost believe you."

"I'm asking you to." Surprised by how easily the words came, he wanted them back, to weigh them, store them inside for a while and take them out to look at them later. Yet he was ready to repeat them in case she hadn't heard. "It'd be good for me," he said. "Give me some roots."

"You'd only leave me."

"Wrong."

"And Murph would be lost without you."

"I'd be doing him a favor." He rubbed the heel of his hand in tiny circles over the knob of her shoulder. "Force him to be a legitimate golf pro. It's what he wants. Besides, with what I taught him, he won't have a problem taking care of himself." The kid would get slit open the first time he tried to hustle alone. Did they have golf pros in California? "It'll work out fine," he said.

She got out of bed. From her purse, she took the cigarettes, tapped the pack to free one butt. The match flared, then narrowed before she blew out the flame and forced smoke through her nose. Her robe was within easy reach on the funny-looking chair, and her bath towel was at her feet, yet she didn't bother to cover herself. She didn't look like any other woman—or girl—he had ever seen. Love did that. It made something familiar look special. Arms folded across her breasts, she inhaled more smoke. Here and there, patches of filtered light bounced off her, shadowing the squareness of her hips, the slope of her buttocks, the narrow flat of her back. The rest of her nakedness was hidden in darkness so hard and black that she might as well have been chiseled out of stone. The glow of burning tobacco reflected in the open window. How many eyes were raping her from the lawn? How many seconds before some brute stormed up the stairs and broke down the door? All because she was standing there like an advertisement: Come and Get Me. Her whisper rode cigarette smoke out to the night. "Even if it didn't work out at all, I'd still like to go. With you."

Little bumps dotted his skin, stretching it, making him shiver. He stood, wondering if he had the strength to reach her. At the window, he fingered the loop on the shade cord. The lawn below was empty of eyes. The only thing moving out there was the fire escape. It was a rope—a brown rope—swaying and twisting from its anchorage above the sash and disappearing in coils inside a white laundry bag a few inches below. Some fire escape. Three stories down, hand over hand on a single strand of hemp. Or was there a rope ladder stuffed into that bag? She would never make it without a ladder, he'd have to carry her on his back. And now he couldn't get his face to obey: the smile died. "Well then, we'll just go. The two of us."

"You don't want me, you couldn't." She kept her eyes on her cigarette. "You don't know anything about me."

He squeezed her shoulders to wake her from her trance. "You live in Louisville, right? Your father owns a stable, Horace trains for him, your mother lives in Long Beach with some oil jockey and sends you postcards. You got green eyes," *Small tits but a real nice ass*, "and dark hair," *You moan a lot when we're doing it*, "and you smoke too much." He snatched her cigarette and tossed it out the window. "Anything else I ought to know?"

She studied him as though something were wrong with his face. "Yes."

She slipped through his grasp. He couldn't stop staring at the spot she had vacated. On the lawn, a man and a woman were looking up at him, pointing and grinning. He yanked the shade down.

"I don't really care." Facing the door, she was holding on to the post at the foot of the bed. "About oranges, I mean. I'd just like to leave." Her head sank. "I'm sorry, I know we just got here but—"

"I don't care about oranges neither." He glanced around the shade: those yokels were gone. "What I meant was the land. Don't want it all built up or already spoiled by crops. We could just leave it like we find it, let it do whatever it wanted to."

"My father wouldn't let me go." She hugged the post. "And I can't just walk away from him. Like my mother did. It would kill him."

His smile got lost in the dark. Was she feeling guilty about hopping into bed with him so soon after she met him? Her type didn't do that sort of thing. Unless they had already made up their minds they were in love. In love. With a jerk like Rainbow Roberts. No wonder she looked scared. He stepped to her, traced a finger over the groove of her spine. "No reason to be afraid of me."

"I'm not." She turned and looked at him with such force that he wanted to cover himself and hide. Her look didn't last long. Her face seemed to lengthen and take on weight. "I simply don't want anything to happen to you."

"Nothing's going to happen to me."

"You don't know this town. The people who come here are thieves."

"They're just people. I never have a problem with just people." He cupped a hand on her cheek. "Need to settle a couple of things here first. Then we can head anyplace you like. It doesn't have to be California. We'll live in Louisville if you want, so you can be close to your old man. Been thinking a lot about what I told you—buying into his ranch and getting it on its feet again? Be fine with me."

"He won't let you. Not that way."

He drew his hand back and made a fist beside the sticky hair around his crotch. "What's the matter, my money not good enough for him?"

"Your money is fine. Your money is—"

"Well all right then! I don't care, is what I'm saying. Anyplace'd be fine. Long as it's with you."

Said. It was right out there for her now. Or did she want him to get down on his knees and pray that she'd take what he was offering? He didn't kneel in church and he wasn't about to start kneeling in bedrooms. He opened his fist, rubbed his thigh. "Believe me, Iris. I mean it."

Her eyes were wet. She was staring at a spot just above his groin now as if she planned to stand there forever and never say another word. She found a wornout smile. "Weren't you supposed to meet some friends? It's late."

He sat on the edge of the mattress. He should have been on his way to see Stavros the Greek over an hour ago. It was an important association: The Big Time. But Rainbow wasn't going. And he wasn't going to worry about not going anymore. He was staying. Here. With her.

He reached up, put his hands on her waist, and guided her across his lap onto the bed. Leaning toward the headboard, he nuzzled her belly, the soft nipples which grew firm against his face, then he kissed her throat, that round chin of hers. He rested on an elbow, staring into her eyes, twin circles of forest green with black holes in the center, wishing he could crawl inside them and hide. "I know what I want, Iris."

She took his face between her hands, pulled him down beside her, and rocked him as though he were a newborn child. He didn't even try to come up for air.

23

Dance . . . ?

Murph rocked slowly from side to side and slid his feet without lifting them off the parquet floor of Satchel Rags. *Dancing?* More like shuffling. And getting shoved, bumped, stepped on. Sweat dotted the space between his lip and nose where his beard was heaviest. His forehead felt slick. He couldn't brush back his bangs, his hands were stuck to the little glass beads sewn into his partner's dress. A flapper's dress. And this woman had a flapper's bobbed hair, like Iris. But something was wrong with her eyes—the sockets seemed to push against her nose as if it were a pimple and could be squeezed off her face. Maybe she only looked that way when she smiled. She hadn't stopped smiling all night. Now she was clinging to him, both arms low around his middle, head sandwiched between his neck and shoulder— how did she breathe in there?—her thighs rubbing the inside of his, the warm bump between her legs pressing against the bulge in the front of his pants. She didn't want to dance. She wanted to go to bed. With him.

And there was a big man standing against the wall, staring hard. Was he the flapper's regular boyfriend?

The music stopped. Instead of applauding like the others around him, Murph let go of the flapper and put a hand in his pocket to disguise his erection. The gold-plated locket was warm and slippery, as though it were melting. He brushed his bangs across his face and wiped the sweat on his jacket.

"Thanks, Dave." The flapper kissed his cheek. "You're a good dancer."

Dancer? He had never danced before in his life. All that pink stuff she was making him buy her must have muddled her brain. "Well, there's no room to do nothing in a crowd like this." He tried a grin, but it wouldn't work. She wasn't really ugly, just strange-looking. And old. At least thirty. She was stroking his arm as though to warm her fingertips. Very strange. And was she really staring at his crotch or was that just how her eyes worked? The bulge in his pants wasn't as large as he thought it would be. He was proud of his self-control, yet a little disappointed at the same time. Those two whiskeys and sodas were taking their toll.

"Want another drink, Dave?"

"Ah, no." Three was enough. He might spoil his chances of getting her into bed if he got drunk. His collar was growing tight, the spotlights tacked up on the ceiling hurt his eyes, the throng of dancers seemed to sway back and forth in front of the green stripes on the walls. It was a smart thing he had done, limiting himself to four drinks.

"It's late." The flapper walked her fingers up his sleeve. "I don't think she's coming."

". . . Who?"

"Your girl friend. Ellen. I think she stood you up, Dave."

At first sight, the flapper had looked so ugly that Murph had invented a rendezvous with Ellen as an excuse for being in this place. And for being unavailable. But he should have known better. He didn't like hearing something as sacred as the name Ellen tumble off the flapper's lips. That was a sin. It would be different if Ellen were really here, in his arms, hugging him, pressing against him. He would burst right through his pants, five drinks or not. But he wouldn't take her to a dive like this. Ellen deserved class: a quiet place where the customers and waiters were refined, staying out of each other's way instead of jamming together in a sweaty clump.

The big man against the wall was still staring. He had a birthmark on his chin. A red blotch. He kept picking at it with his fingernails. He was definitely the flapper's regular boyfriend. He looked something like the man back home who used to make little kids sick to their stomachs by eating live tadpoles like candy.

A drum thumped, a cymbal cut in, a trumpet broke out crying, the whining flutter of a sax filled the gaps—and people became partners again, holding on to each other, banging backs, shuffling over the little squares of wood down there that some dizzy idiot had set in every whichway so that the grain didn't match. And the flapper's mouth was moving, her dark stare wandered over his shirtfront to his belt buckle. Then her lips went still, freezing a smile that dimpled her cheeks. She led him between dancers, past the big man with the birthmark on his chin, up steps to the hall. The stripes on the carpet and the walls were easier to look at than that floor. It was time: she was taking him to bed now. She probably wanted to do it at her place. Murph had to gulp down his laugh. If the big brute back there came after her and tried to make trouble, Murph could pretend that he was only escorting the flapper home and that he was glad—relieved!—the big man had come along to take over.

It would be better in her room, anyway. At the Congressional, Rainbow might barge in and give instructions on exactly how this flapper should be screwed. Like the first time, at the Shade Tree cathouse in Hot Springs—*"Don't go wasting your time taking off your socks, kid. If you can't stand looking at her, bury your head over her shoulder. And remember, roll off her. Roll."* Those instructions had come in handy then: the fat whore didn't care if Murph knew how to do it or not, she was going to lie there for five minutes and get paid two dollars anyway. But this was different. So were all the other times—fifteen—in all the other cities and towns along the highway when he had wanted to say, "I ain't no goddamn virgin no more, you don't have to keep telling me what I already know!" But he hadn't opened his mouth. With Rainbow, there was always one last thing before he let Murph go up the stairs or through the door—*"And don't grab her so hard you pinch her, whores hate being pinched"*—always said as though Rainbow had a personal stake in it and really cared. He did care. Rainbow cared about not being embarrassed. How Murph had to do all the right things in exactly the right order mattered more to Rainbow than how much Murph might enjoy himself. Just once, Murph wished he could come out of the whore's room and down the stairs and announce, "Hey, I pinched her real hard and she's crazy about it." But he never did that either. He never talked about what had happened up there because Rainbow never asked. Not even a "How was she, kid?" or one "Everything go all right?" Only silence, and now and then a smile, a hand on the shoulder. It wasn't enough.

He shook his head to clear the ringing in his ears. The sounds in that room—the different musical instruments, the clink of glasses, the shuffle of feet, of clothes, the voices—somehow all of them got stuck, stuck together like a crystal of noise, making it impossible to hear or remember hearing anything but that one consolidated blare. He couldn't shake it out.

"Dave, you all right?" The flapper had lost her smile. "Not tipsy, are you?"

"Of course not." He put a hand out to the green stripe on the wall, straining to reach it because it was farther away than it looked. "Only had six drinks."

"Two's more like it. The fresh air will do you some good." She guided him out the door, past a sign announcing the future arrival of Miss Bessie Smith, then around the corner and up a little cobblestone alley at the side of Satchel Rags. Dented garbage cans stood against dark brick walls. No windows. A small door at the far end.

"You live up there?" He pointed toward the door. No one could really live up there. "Looks real nice."

"Silly." She nudged him with an elbow and steered him through the V of light coming from a hatted lamp below the rain gutter. "This should be fine."

"Oh, sure—fine!" He raised an eyebrow and let out a burp of laughter. It was so dark here that he could barely make out how her head turned back and forth toward the street, as if she were waiting for an overdue bus. Or her boyfriend. And the ground was dirty. There were probably hundreds of rats back here. "Real fine, but see, this here's a new suit. Don't want it all messed up, so maybe we best—"

"You won't." She eased him back to the wall. For an instant, she was as pretty as Iris. Or Ellen—she even had the same features. Then she was two dark circles slipping in and out of one another. And then she disappeared. But she kept talking to him, a mumble that he couldn't hear right. It sounded like questions.

He tried to clear his head by snapping it down and to the side. The ringing didn't go away. On the opposite wall, bricks shimmered as if they meant to start moving. It got worse when he shut his eyes. And he couldn't hear her questions anymore. But something was crawling on him, digging through the front of his pants, grabbing at him—a rat?—pinching. His hand trembled. He reached down: fur, small ears. No, not fur. Hair. Hers. She had very small ears. Sudden warmth surrounded his penis: she was putting him in her mouth, licking him, pulling him out and toward her with her lips, squeezing him, sucking. He coughed and glanced down the alley, praying that no one, especially the big man with the birthmark on his chin, was watching. There was no nice way to explain this. And what if she bit him by accident? How was he going to explain that to Rainbow? He wanted to reach down and pull her off, but his arms wouldn't obey. His stomach churned. He swallowed salty saliva. Any second now he was going to vomit all over her. He jerked his hips to the side, yanking himself out of her mouth. He leaned on the wall and worked fast to button his fly.

"It'll be fine, Dave." She grabbed him again. "I'll make it hard."

He slapped her hands and faced into the wall.

"Well, you still have to pay," she said. "Fifty bucks."

Fifty! She was a whore! The big man inside had to be her pimp, then. Walking the flapper home was a ridiculous excuse now. Murph brushed past her and walked away, up the alley.

"You agreed to it inside." She caught his arm, spun him around, reached into his jacket. "Not my fault you can't get it up. But you have to pay."

He batted her arm and staggered along the wall, back through the light. The smell of garbage rushing up his nose and over his face stopped him. His skin was clammy. He couldn't hold the vomit down much longer.

"Hey, you little jerk. Fifty bucks."

He got out the only money he had left, a one-dollar bill, and hoping that in this poor light she wouldn't notice it wasn't a fifty, he handed it to her behind his back.

She noticed. "You little prick. Don't think you can cheat me."

"I'll owe it to you then." He didn't mean it: she ran a rigged game, too.

"I don't give credit, sonny."

She was probably going to tell her pimp now. The air was ripe with the stench of day-old fish. Murph's stomach was bubbling over. A wretched taste, like rancid licorice, swam up his throat. He swallowed and the thing went down: a bitter lump, stinging his insides, making him gasp. "I'm gonna be real sick here in a minute." Even his voice was going. "Better stand back. Or leave."

The flapper giggled. "What's the matter, jerk-off, did I scare you?" The giggle became a cackle. "You fucking little queer. . . ."

"Leave me alone." He barely got it out before he had to swallow again.

She stood there for a moment, muttering obscenities, making him feel like vomiting right down her dress. Then she grabbed his testicles and squeezed. "I ought to take these as fucking collateral, you lousy, diddling prick. *Queer!*" She yanked hard, doubling him over with pain. Another cackle and her shoes clopped up the alley and around the corner.

He peered toward the street to be sure he was alone. Teeth clenched to bite off the pain in his groin and the burning in his gut, he drew in air that whistled over his lips. Sweat rolled off his nose, trickled down his chin. He turned away from the garbage cans for a clean breath. And coughed. His stomach erupted all at once. Then over and over again. The vomit came up like a solid river, filled with chunks, splattering his new pants and shoes. But he couldn't move his legs out of the way. It was all he could do to brace stiff-arm against the wall and stand up. Between heaves, he cursed: himself, her, her pimp, the garbage, the whiskeys and sodas, the ground. Finally, he was done. He got out his handkerchief, blew his nose. His eyes were sweating. Even his ears. Each crease in his skin felt full of grit. He took three deep, satisfying breaths and turned toward the street.

The big man with the birthmark on his chin was standing a foot away. Smiling.

Something fuzzy and black shot straight at Murph's face. His jaw exploded, his head banged against the wall, his feet slipped out from under him, the base of his spine crashed on the ground. His eyes stayed open, but he couldn't see anything. Only heavy shadows. He tried to speak. His jaw wouldn't work anymore. It hurt to breathe. Little pats darted over his body. Hard tugs pulled his pockets inside out, then rolled him over, facedown in his own puke. He was drowning in the stuff.

"That's a little reminder from E.R., punk," the big man said. "Have the grand you owe him by noon tomorrow. Plus interest. Or I'll be back to collect it myself." A hard foot jabbed Murph's ribs. "Plus interest." A short laugh punched the air, then footsteps beat the cobblestones. The alley got quiet.

Murph tried to get up. Something hit him again, but from inside, at the back of his skull. His scalp began to pop as if it were prying free from the bone, the ringing in his ears became a scream, flooding his brain. And suddenly, all the fluid in his head was gushing someplace else. The screaming stopped. A smile was growing, not just on his face, or where his face used to be, but all over. His whole body was smiling. Then it was gone and blackness danced in to take its place.

The telephone rang.

Rainbow groped in the darkness for the table beside the bed, grabbed the slender stem of the phone, and picked the receiver off the hook. His voice cracked awake into the mouthpiece: "Hello?"

Through the pop of static in the earpiece came a grumble so sharp and low that it didn't sound human: "Roberts?"

He sat up. The thin sheet hugged the rhythm of Iris's breathing, her head lay in a well of the soft pillow. He whispered. "Who is this?"

"Dancer," the voice said. "I checked you out. We can do business."

The air was too warm to chill him, that shiver crawling over his back had to come from inside. "Where can I find him?"

"You find me first. Dan's Luncheonette. South Broadway. Eight A.M. And bring two hundred bucks."

Behind him, Iris stirred, the hand beside her face curled into a fist as if this part of her dream had made her angry. Or afraid. Rainbow got up and carried the phone to the window. The breeze pushing the shade off the sill mirrored the way she was breathing in her sleep. He steered his words to the farthest part of the room. "How do I know this ain't a setup, Dancer?"

"Look, I don't make no fucking promises. Eight A.M. sharp."

A *slap-click* and the line went dead.

Rainbow hung the receiver up. Holding the phone to his stomach, feeling the coolness of metal seep into his sticky flesh, he studied his panama, its wide brim hiding the .45 on the chair. Old Cal really was here. *Here.*

"That was Horace, wasn't it." Her head was raised off the pillow, half-closed eyes searched the dark for him.

"No one," he said. "Go back to sleep."

"Aren't you coming?"

"In a minute." He waited for her sigh to end, her body to lie still. *A minute.*

Out on the lawn, stars, a moon, electric lights, and distant music were slicing up the night, the same sights and sounds which would be washing over every angle along the streets, over everyone else in town: Murph, Horace, the Greek and his giant, E.R., Tom The Whip, little Angelo, Dancer. Even Old Cal, whose face was out there, not just as an unclear memory anymore—sky-blue eyes—but as a face. Alive. Every bit as real as the countless others from the train and those who lived here year-round. Though free to move about as their minds and hearts willed, all were trapped by something few of them would understand, and fewer still would stop to notice. Yet it was here. As clear to him now as Iris was with her body bathed in faint light and nestled under a plain white sheet.

An hour. Two. Six to wait till 8:00 A.M.

It was always there, constant, changing everyone and everything, whether living or dead: the townspeople and gamblers, those trees down there, the lampposts, the phone against his chest. By his doggedness, his longing—and hatred—he had forced it into this compact village, shaped it, colored it a certain way so that it would never be the same again. He had created this moment.

Time belonged to him.

A laugh crawled out the side of his mouth. He had done it alone, with no help from God, no little angels running around planting signs for him to follow or blowing trumpets to steer him on the right course, no saints materializing in flowing robes to guide him through doors, no martyrs to sacrifice themselves so that he could be saved. Just time. His.

And by this time tomorrow, Old Cal Robinson would be dead.

A life.

He set the phone down, climbed into bed, pulled the sheet to his waist. Iris snuggled close and mumbled dream-talk into his ribs. He put his arms around her, resting, not holding. The tightness of his smile made his face ache. Sleep would not come easily tonight, but it would come.

In time.

Book Three
OLD CAL

24

The sign was tin and blue lettering was pressured into it: DAN'S LUNCHEONETTE. The thumblatch on the handle didn't work, but the screen door opened smoothly. Rainbow stopped by the cash register. He felt naked without his briefcase. All that money, left in a hotel vault. What if the place burned down? He decided to make this a quick morning.

The booths running along the wall looked empty. A lone man sat on a stool about halfway down the long counter. He ate toast noisily, his stare not quite focused on the rack of pies and the bin of rolls behind the frail waitress with a pencil sticking out of her hair bun. On the phone, Dancer had sounded tall. The man at the counter was tall. Dancer had sounded brawny, or at least athletic, as if he had earned his nickname as a fighter or on the vaudeville stage. The man at the counter was old and gaunt; he was waiting for nothing and for no one in particular; he couldn't be Dancer. But he had blue eyes.

Rainbow swallowed and stepped toward the man. The .45 was almost out of his belt, the name Cal Robinson was almost off his tongue. Then he saw them, back by the restroom: thick fingers turning a coffee cup in nervous circles on a saucer that was sloppy with milky brown. He went by the man at the counter and stopped at the last booth. "Dancer?"

Big round eyes looked up at him. Over him. A triple chin sagged into the open collar of a short-sleeved shirt with red and yellow circles on it. A porkpie hat was pushed back high on a smooth forehead. "You Roberts?"

Rainbow nodded. "That's not him at the counter, is it?"

Dancer shook his head and slurped coffee. "I can take you." He was studying Rainbow's jacket as if trying to look through the fabric. "Like to see the two Cs first."

Rainbow got out two bills, spread them apart, then slid them back into his suit. "You ready?"

There was the shrug of heavy shoulders and "Some breakfast?" said as more of a hope than a test.

"Already had mine." Rainbow hadn't eaten since Dancer's phone call last night and he hadn't slept well either. He faced the door.

Dancer grinned. Two dimples which had probably been cute once now creased like wrinkled wax paper. "What's Cal to you?"

Rainbow didn't answer. He kept staring at the door.

"Well, I should really get a better line on you first," Dancer said.

"Ask the Greek then."

The stout man swallowed. "Didn't know it was like that, you with the Greek, I mean. Should of told me." Another slurp of coffee. "How long you known the big nigger?"

Rainbow leaned against the booth. "Curtis and me grew up together."

"Grew up together, that's rich." The laugh that came up past all those chins sounded like a growl. "I like that, yeah. You're all right. Christ, I ain't seen Curtis in—must be six years now. Tried calling him to check you out. Word is he left town."

Rainbow turned. "Left town? Curtis?"

Another dark laugh. "You know him all right. Must be in hiding's the way I figure. He'd never leave that city. Only guy I know who claims Saint Louie is paradise."

"He had a lot of trouble getting there," Rainbow said. Curtis did love that city, loved it like a dream, ever since he had been there for the Fair. The only way to get him out of town was to run him out. He must have lost more to that poker player than he could pay.

"You really should of told me you know the Greek." Dancer was out of the booth, drinking the last bit of coffee from the saucer. "I would of give you a discount, see. But I can't now, I mean, we already set up a bargain. . . ."

The clock over the restroom door read 8:02 A.M. "Look Dancer, I got an appointment later this morning to see E.R., so let's get a move-on."

A whine passed through wide lips. "Jesus, should of told me. Got a car? It ain't far, but if you want to ride—"

"We'll walk." Rainbow went up the aisle. Behind him, a coin

plunked on the table and the waitress said, "Bye, sugar." The old man at the counter was still staring at the space between the pies and the rolls.

Dancer led the way up Long Alley to the corner of Church Street. "It's right up there. Baldy's. You pay me now."

The alley continued paralleling Broadway, but there was no sign of a pool hall up there. "I'll pay you when I see him," Rainbow said.

"Yeah, but it ain't good for me to take you in." There was the slow turn of no neck at all. "Word might get out that I—you know. Only doing this as a favor. So pay me. Now."

"What if he's not in there?"

"You wait for him. He'll show."

Rainbow tugged his panama. "I'll keep waiting till I find him. And when I do see him, I'll give *him* the money and tell him to find *you* so you can get paid." With a grin, he stepped off the curb.

"Hold it." The stout man's heaving chest caused his arms to lift. The red and yellow circles on his shirt quivered. "What do you take me for?"

"Good point. Now let's both go in and find him so you can collect."

Dancer sighed and walked across the street, his shoulders dipping from side to side. He took a short breath between each step, and when he stopped at the door to the poolroom, he huffed as if he had just scaled a mountain.

Two feet down from the top of the window, a sun-streaked green curtain hung on large brass rings from a brass rod running the length of the glass. The tail of the Y in BALDY'S had been scraped away. Rainbow opened the door to the tinkle of a rusty bell and the smell of day-old cigars. An angry man carried a hat through the doorway. A shout followed him outside:

"Could win it back the next game!"

The man put on his hat and walked faster. Inside, an old man with a cue stick watched the door swing shut. His laugh was a snort. Gray stubble dotted his sharp chin, shadowed it. A string tie fell like crinkled ribbon over his shirt. His jacket and pants had been slept in. Often. He had sky-blue eyes. Laying his cue on the pool table, he stretched a bill between his fingers and showed it to the men standing around him. "C-note for Old Cal," he said. He put the cash away and moved around the table, taking billiard balls out of the pockets. "What you got there, Dancer?"

"Wants to play you, Cal. Says he heard of you."

"Lots of people heard of me." Old Cal rolled balls up the table.

There was a chorus of chuckles from the men around him. "Up yours, shitheads." He slipped a wood triangle over the balls. "He got a name?"

"Roberts," Dancer said. "Rainbow Roberts."

"Now what the hell kind of a name is that?" Old Cal laughed and shook his head. "Oops, I better watch it. This boy might sink me good." He laughed and shook his head some more.

"You pay me now," Dancer whispered.

Unable to take his eyes off Old Cal, Rainbow gave the stout man the $200. The bell jangled, the door closed. For a moment, Rainbow wanted to run outside, just to come in again and see the old man for the first time. It *was* the first time. This was not a face from the highway or the cities or the towns, this face had not passed by on a train or a car. But it was the face of the man who had run away from the cabin by the lake. Or was it? That was too long ago, too far away in space and time. Rainbow unbuttoned his jacket and stepped to the table.

"Game's twenty." Cal picked up his cue and chalked it.

"Make it fifty?" Rainbow said.

The old man turned to a short man in a lumpy yellow hat. "Okay, Mustard?" The short man nodded back and Old Cal grinned. "I can stand fifty just fine."

There were cue sticks resting against the wall. Chalk marks skidded over light green paint, or what was left of it. Rainbow sighted down a shaft. Warped. He picked another, put his fifty-dollar bill on the side of the table, set a chalk cube on it, and slipped out of his jacket.

The small room came alive with murmurs. The men had seen his .45.

"You gonna shoot pool?" Old Cal wiped a sleeve across the bottom of his nose. "Or jackrabbits?"

With a smile, Rainbow pulled the gun from his belt and emptied the cylinder chambers, catching the bullets in his hand. The short man with the yellow hat came over and put his face close to the white tape on the pistol grip:

"Wrap it so's they won't find no fingerprints, don't you. Done it myself."

"Don't listen to him," Old Cal said. "Mustard Mike ain't never even held a gun for Chrissake." He bent to the table and lined up the cue ball. "Eight ball."

"Don't we lag for break?" Rainbow asked.

"My table, my break." The old man took aim. "And we call

everything." He drove his cue into the white ball, sending it up the table into the rack. A loud *crack*, that hollow, rolling scatter. The number-six ball slid into the corner pocket. Old Cal grinned and chalked his cue. "Everything, that is, except the break." When the snickering of his friends died down, he went to the short side of the table. "I'm solids, you're stripes. Where you from, boy?"

"East Tennessee."

"Done some gambling there myself." Old Cal's stare swung out to the balls, then back on line with his cue stick. "Done some gambling just about everywhere."

Rainbow stood by the chair near the window. He spoke softly, not sure he wanted to hear the words himself. "You're a hard man to find—Cal."

"Three ball. Side." A faint *click*, the soft *plop* of wood falling into a leather hole: the bright red ball dropped out of sight.

Rainbow kept watching, but he saw no colors, no angles—no game. Only a bent old man, wrinkled like untanned hide. A skeleton. He sat in the chair, and while everyone else looked over the next shot, he began loading his .45 and waiting for his turn.

Iris dropped her bathing suit into the carry bag. The black tunic, with coal-dark stockings, had been out of style for years, but she wasn't ready for the newer fashions. They made her look like a Mack Sennett bathing queen. Not ladylike. She put her rubber bathing cap in on top of the suit, drew the canvas bag closed, and walked out of the bedroom. The lake nearby would still be cold with morning. But that doctor—the man who claimed to be a doctor—advertised heated mineral baths in his private spa on Regent Street, among the mansions the rich called "summer cottages." It was only a short walk, as was everything in this village, and it made sense to occupy the morning with a healthy bath in natural springwater. There wasn't much else to do. Rainbow had left hours ago, stealing off to someplace that Iris didn't even want to try to picture. But it was probably a casino. Or a private game of poker.

She left the fan on, tucked her purse under her arm, and went into the hall. Something putrid hung in the air.

Murph was fumbling with his key, trying to open the door to his room. His clothes were rumpled. Big yellow stains discolored his jacket and pants. Clumps of something were stuck in his hair. He smelled like garbage. Worse.

"Good morning, Dave," she said, moving toward him and the stairs at the end of the hall. He spun around, dropped his key. One side of his face was red and puffy. He grabbed the key and turned his back on her, mumbling under his breath. Iris stepped closer. "What happened to you?"

"Nothing." Murph kept trying the lock and hiding his face.

She braved the smell and turned him by the shoulders. His jaw was badly swollen. She touched it and he jerked away. "We should have that looked at right away, it might be broken."

"It's fine. Don't hurt or nothing." His stare wandered over the carpet. "He still in there?" His words were muffled by the swelling.

"I don't know where he is." She took his sleeve and pulled him toward the suite. "I want you to lie in here until the doctor comes up."

"No, honest, I don't need no doctoring." Murph leaned away from her. "What if he comes back now? And sees me like this?"

She unlocked her door and steered him inside. "He said he'd be most of the morning. Out finding someone. Besides, he'll want to know how this happened to you." She helped him off with his jacket. The stains were from vomit. So were the chunks in his hair. "You'd better get out of those clothes."

"Yeah, well . . ."

"Go into the bathroom and give me your key. I'll get you a fresh set to wear."

He wasn't able to raise his gaze from the key in his hand. "Don't want to mess up your morning. I can take care of this."

She took his key. "Draw yourself a bath. I'll phone the doctor when I get back with your clothes."

"No, hey, wait—no doctor. I'll have the bath and everything, but . . . Maybe you could have them send up some ice?"

She pointed to the bathroom and waited for him to lumber through the doorway. Then she went out and into his room, found a change of clothes, and brought them back. She called the front desk. And asked for an ice pack. It came five minutes later. Murph was out of the bathroom before the bellboy was out of the suite. The red hair was dripping wet, but Murph was still in his soiled clothes. He reached for the ice pack.

"Put these on first," she said, handing him the fresh clothes. "And change everything."

He sighed and went back into the bathroom. The ice was already beginning to melt by the time he came out. Iris made him lie on the couch in the sitting room while she applied the ice pack.

"Thanks," he said. He winced and held back tears.

"How badly does it hurt?"

"It's okay. I meant that about the doctor. Didn't call him, did you?"
She shook her head. "How did it happen?"
". . . I fell."
"Who hit you, Dave?"
". . . In an alley, I tripped. . . ."
"You know Rainbow will never believe that."
Murph closed his eyes to the pain. "He won't even notice. You got
to promise not to tell him."
"Dave, he'll notice."
"Nah, he don't even look at me half the time he's talking. What
time's it, anyways? He say when he was coming back?"
She moved the ice pack higher on his jaw. "I think he'll want you to
see a doctor."
"Told you, he won't notice nothing. I got to get the clubs over the
course and chart it or else he'll blow up at me."
She nudged him back down on the couch. "You're going to lie here
and rest."
"You don't understand, he's gonna be in a bad mood. It'll be
terrible."
"He has no reason to be angry at you. You're hurt."
"No, not me. If he's out looking for Old Cal, he's gonna be steaming
when he comes back and ain't found him."
". . . Who?"
Murph's eyes got wide. "Jesus, ain't he told you?"
"What?"
"He said he told you everything. That he was a gambler and . . .
You mean he ain't said nothing about him and Old Cal Robinson?"
She shook her head.
"Well, that's who he's looking for," Murph said. "Only he ain't
gonna find him 'cause he's dead. Yeah, that's right. Don't ask me why
he's still looking. Shouldn't of opened my mouth."
"You can tell me, Dave." Iris stroked his forehead. He felt warm. "I
won't say anything to him."
"Tell you what I know. Don't make no sense to me neither. But
that's why we come up here in the first place. That's why we go
everywhere, hunting Old Cal like he was a bear or something."
It sounded important. Why hadn't Rainbow ever mentioned it? Not
even a hint.
"And be ready to duck if you ever say 'Old Cal' in front of him,"
Murph said. "Makes him knot all up and take it out on you. I got to get
them charts done on the golf course or—"

She pushed him back on the couch this time. "I'm going to order you something to eat. Can you chew?"

"Of course I can, I tell you it don't hurt."

She phoned room service and ordered farina.

"I hate that stuff," Murph said.

"It will be up in a minute. Now try to relax."

"I ain't no baby, you know. Look, you have them send that back and I'll order myself steak and eggs. In *my* room." He stood. His knees buckled. He fell back onto the couch.

Iris reached for the phone again. "Dave, you have to see a doctor, you're—"

"No doctor. Just got a little dizzy, is all. Didn't sleep real good." He held the ice pack to his face and took deep breaths. "But don't let me keep you from the track. I'll be fine here. Might even eat some of that farina before I leave."

"I'm not going anywhere until I'm sure you're all right."

The hint of a smile came onto his lips. Then he winced. "But won't your horse get antsy unless you bring him them oats?"

He meant the canvas carry bag. Three years ago, she had it made up out of an oat holder, a feeder. For Horace to use as a duffel. He hated it. It reminded him of his work—of feeding horses every day, and never riding them. Iris put the bag beside the arm of the couch. "I was going to Dr. Talbert's."

"You sick?" Murph said. "Doctors can kill you, you know. Rainbow won't go near one."

"He runs a spa here. It's not really medicine."

"And you was bringing him—oats?"

She laughed. "The stable takes care of feeding the horses."

Murph nodded. "Just thought you had him on some special feed, you know, on account of the race and all."

"My—trainer will take care of that when the time comes."

"Yeah, well, we got a lot riding on it, so I just hope he's as good as Rainbow thinks he is."

Iris lost her smile. Her hands stopped short of her purse on the table. Horace was up to something after all. She cursed him. Then herself for not knowing better. "Yes, well, Horace is very good." She cleared her throat. "How much are you betting?"

"Don't ask me, I don't got nothing to say about it. But I bet you it's everything. The whole bankroll."

All that money in the briefcase. On one race.

With Horace.

". . . And how much would that be, Dave?"

"About a hundred and fifty." He frowned and closed one eye. "Plus another fifteen which is rightfully mine."

"One hundred and fifty—thousand?"

Murph nodded. "Plus my fifteen. He stole it from me, you know. On account of what happened with Angelo."

No wonder Horace was in such a hurry to get Old Smoke to the track. But he was out of his league. None of his schemes would work against Rainbow: none was convincing enough for that kind of money. She started another smile. The old fool wasn't going to get to first base this time.

"But I got me an ace in the hole," Murph was saying. "When Rainbow picks up four-to-one on my fifteen, he's sure to give me back some of it. See, he ain't a welsher or nothing. And this fix is real important to him, so he's just holding on to my cash and using it as what you call leverage, you know?"

The smile was gone. Horace was back to running fixed races. And he was very good at them. The best. If he could stay sober long enough to avoid getting caught by the track stewards. Again. The last time, they put him in jail for a year, as an "incorrigible." That was four years ago, and Iris had been on the road, selling fake yearlings, ever since. Just to keep Horace free. And to convince him that he didn't need to fix races to survive. And now this.

The strain of all those wasted years must have shown in her face because Murph was moaning:

"Aw, Jesus, I should of known. He didn't tell you about the fix neither, did he. Christ, he's gonna kill me."

She forced a smile and put the ice pack back on his jaw. "I won't say anything to him—if you won't."

"You mean it?" He looked ready to kiss her. "That's, I mean, you're really, well—" Tears were building in his eyes. He rolled over to hide. "Guess it'd be okay if you called the doctor."

This smile came through on its own. She patted his head and went to the phone. The hotel doctor said that he would be up as soon as he could. How long would it take? And how long would it take her to find Horace and force him to change his plans? If she could.

A waiter brought in the farina on a room-service cart. Iris sent him back to the kitchen with another order: bacon and eggs, orange juice, toast, sweet rolls, and coffee. For her. The diet had to be broken. Today, she was going to need all her strength.

25

The black ball hit the top of the cushion and angled back down the length of the pool table. Rainbow watched it pass the tip of his cue and roll quietly by his elbow and drop into the corner pocket. It was the fifth game in a row he had won. He laid the cue down on the felt. "Another one?"

Old Cal let his stick fall against the wall and pulled out the hundred-dollar bill. He studied it with a pained look, then tossed it on the table and faced the window. "You cleaned me."

Rainbow had not expected to win. Pool wasn't his game—and it had been Cal's life. Somehow, it was sweeter this way. A surprise. He grinned and put on his jacket. "Heard you were pretty good, old man. Heard wrong."

"Ain't used to the table," Cal told the window. "Take your dough and get out of here."

"And they said Old Cal Robinson was the man to beat. A real shooter."

"Bad day is all."

"I could of beat you blindfolded, that's how bad it was." Rainbow watched the old man's eyes: faded blue circles drifting sideways. "Don't see how you could beat anybody. Wouldn't be fair to take your last dollar. So pick it up, old-timer. Your money's no good."

Cal fingered the brass rings on the curtain rod. "You won it, damn you. Now head back to where you come from and leave us." He nodded at the men around the table. "Rack them up, Mustard. Play you for lunch."

"Still my table." Rainbow pulled out his .45 and the short man in the lumpy yellow hat stopped moving. "Nobody plays till the old goat picks up the money."

The room went still. There was only the sound of troubled breathing. Rainbow snickered. "See, I was brought up to be charitable to my elders."

Cal spun around. Veins stood out in his neck. He picked up his cue stick, then rolled it sharply into the side cushion. "Cal Robinson don't take charity from nobody."

Rainbow cocked the pistol hammer and trained the barrel on Cal. "Pick up the money, old man."

The other men backed up in a nervous shuffle. Cal's bony fingers searched the table for a spot to hold, both elbows rattled inside his dingy suit. He stared at the bullets in the cylinder, then studied the hundred-dollar bill. "You won it fair and square." His words were firm, but when he looked up, his eyes were pleading. "Take it, sonny."

Silence. A slow smile crept onto Rainbow's lips. "I waited a long time to hear you call me that." And the smile was gone. He moved along the side of the table toward that pale mass of wrinkles, the gray hair that wouldn't lie flat, that stupid string tie. He stopped and jabbed the point of his .45 against Old Cal's temple. Then he picked up the crumpled bill and stuffed it into the old man's mouth. "Big C-note for Old Cal."

Cal was trembling, those sky-blue eyes were wide with fear. Sweat beaded his skin, saliva trickled past the money in his mouth, down his chin. A little grunt escaped through his nose. He seemed afraid to die. It was perfect.

And Rainbow couldn't pull the trigger.

The man at the end of the gun barrel was a stranger. A nobody. Worthless.

After a few seconds, he uncocked the pistol, drew it back from the old man's skull, and walked to the door. The knob almost slipped out of his fingers. The dull *ping* from the rusty bell, then a warm sidewalk, a noisy street. His feet felt heavy. And for some reason, he turned around. From under a corner of the curtain, near the scraped-out y in BALDY'S, Old Cal was peering out at him. Rainbow tried to spit. No saliva. He stepped into the street and at the other curb, he turned again, just as a car passed the front of the billiard hall. He wanted to yell "Stop! Park right there!" But he didn't because the man behind the wheel would have kept on driving anyway. The car rumbled by. That face was still there in the window: hollow, searching. Rainbow couldn't look away.

Two more cars drove past. At last the curtain fell limp and the pool hall window was solid green once more. Rainbow raked the brim of his panama to keep bright sun off his eyes, and turned the corner onto Church Street.

All the confetti had been swept away. The train platform was empty. Behind the bars of the ticket window, a man with a green visor pulled down over his forehead was pounding a handstamp as though he had a vendetta against the papers he was sorting. "Next train ain't due in for five hours," he said and set the handstamp to work again.

Rainbow sat on the bench. Down the track, great rusted bolts jutted out from splintered holes. He let his gaze swing down the line until the rails became thin gray strands, sinking into the distance. Lost. The years, the miles . . . a waste of time, all of it. He hated himself for every second, every step. Was it him, the one, the only, Old Cal Robinson? His sigh came out like a cough. The man in the string tie was everything Rainbow had thought he would be. Feared he would be. If only it could have been someone else. Someone worth killing.

He started walking. Short, aimless steps took him toward town center, past columns, pediments, large mansard roofs. And everywhere: that face, those dead eyes, like faded sky. How much time had he spent trying to remember that face, to shape it into a smile, to hear it speak, to touch it? *A life.* Now, when he wanted to, he couldn't forget the emptiness in those eyes. There had been too many wrong turns, a broken line through nameless towns. To here. Dead end.

He kicked a rock into Broadway and followed it to the far curb.

The hole-in-the-wall haberdashery had just what Rainbow wanted, but the haberdasher didn't want to sell it. "Why buy off the rack," he said, big eyes screwing up into a small and knobby skull, "when you can have custom?" Because the price was right: $25.50 per suit. Rainbow bought two. For an extra dollar, he got the pants altered while he waited and walked out wearing everything new: suit, shirt, tie, underwear, socks, and shoes. If they had stocked the right style, he would have bought a new hat, too.

The cardboard suitcase he lugged back to the Congressional was crammed with clothes, new and old. It was heavy. And this jacket felt stiff. But he didn't mind. He was celebrating his pool hall victory. Or trying to. He wasn't his father's son, carried none of the old man in his blood: winding up wasted and broke couldn't run in the family. *Family?*

By the steps of the United States Hotel, he stopped when someone called his name. He turned slowly, fearful that it might be Old Cal come to haunt him in the flesh.

At the end of the wide porch, Stavros the Greek waved from a high-back wicker chair. Surrounded by five men, he seemed to be holding court, with his giant, Aziz, blind to the ceremony. "Come up and meet some people."

Rainbow went up the steps and met the Greek's people. They were bookmakers, the Old Guard of Saratoga, each with his own territory: Leo The Hat from the United States Hotel, Fingers from the Grand Union, two others from the Rip Van Dam and the Adelphi, and Dancer from the Congressional.

"Welcome to Millionaire's Piazza." Stavros pointed out the railroad tycoons and stock-market types seated nearby, then made a half-swing with an imaginary golf club. "I feel like a game this afternoon. Six strokes you give me, right?"

Rainbow didn't answer. On the train they had agreed on four strokes. But it didn't matter: golf, cards, The Big Time. Old Cal had been found. And now there was no way to lose him. He wasn't out there anymore. He was inside.

The Greek slapped his knee. His bookmakers started to chuckle before he opened his mouth. "This guy," Stavros said, "he almost drops thirty grand on the Special. Jesus, it's something. The little wop from *The Century*, Batori, E.R.'s new cook?" Five heads nodded as one. "He gets him to . . ." Tears filled the dark eyes, the plump body shook with laughter. "You tell them."

The bookies looked at Rainbow as if expecting to hear one of the Ten Commandments. He told them about the spelling bet. They listened, but their grins faded with each word, their faces went blank. When he finished, there was the silence of open mouths. Then Stavros laughed and his bookies joined in immediately.

"Sorry about not getting over last night," Rainbow said. "I got tied up."

"Sure, I figured it." Stavros winked. "Real shy type, ain't she. Like them that way myself. New suit? Looks just like your other one. Get yourself a stickpin like this here." He fingered the emerald in his tie. "Over at Tiffany's. They got a branch in the Grand Union. Class all the way. Only get maybe a ruby or a diamond." Another wink. "The emerald's my trademark."

There was more. The Greek would have been happy to take Rainbow to Tiffany's and help him pick out a tie stud, but he had to work on tomorrow's odds: he always laid down the law before opening day, to keep his books in line. Rainbow listened, but he didn't care about listening anymore. The conversation was boring him. When the Greek stopped talking, he smiled at what he hoped was the right time and said, "What time you want to tee off?"

"About one-thirty." Stavros wiped a tear with his finger. Whatever he had said, he must have thought it was funny. "Tell them you're with me. They'll give you a nice locker."

Touching the brim of his hat, Rainbow turned for the steps. But Dancer's voice stopped him:

"How'd it go with Cal?"

". . . Fine." The new shoes felt stuck to the white boards.

"What's this?" Stavros said.

"Just some guy he was looking for," Dancer told him. "I set it up. A two-bit stickman name of Cal Robinson."

Stavros was leaning forward, shaking his head. "Never heard of him."

"Hardly anybody has." Dancer lit the Greek's cigar. "Strictly bottom-rung."

A few puffs of smoke, a strained look, and Stavros said, "I don't get it."

Rainbow tested those jet-black eyes, then forced a grin. "See you on the tee, Greek."

"Five strokes, right?"

"I'd be happy if you only gave me two," Rainbow said. The Greek's mouth dropped open, a clipped gasp started the laugh. Rainbow held up four fingers, nodded, glanced at Dancer, and hauled the suitcase off the porch. The sound of Stavros's laughter followed him to the street.

The Grand Union was close by. A diamond stickpin might help break this mood. Rainbow went across to the big stone and timber hotel and through the lobby to a row of store windows. The Tiffany's script lettering was easy to spot. The door was open. At the counter, he looked down through the glass at trays of blue-black velvet, the shine of polished metal, the sparkle of trapped light. But he felt forced here, as if someone or something else were steering him around. If the Greek had said, "Nice suit but you should wear it for a swim in the lake first," would he have bought that, too?

The salesclerk was over in the corner, showing a mound of jewels to that gray-haired lady from the Congressional, the one with all the rings in the safety-deposit box. She couldn't possibly wear what she already owned. What would she do with more? Maybe she didn't know what to do with her money. Rich people were like that. She might be related to Taylor North after all. The clerk left her gawking over the gems—several thousand dollars' worth of stuff which the old lady could have stashed in her purse and run out with—and stepped to the counter. "Yessir, something I might help you with?"

"I need a diamond," Rainbow said.

"Yessir. An engagement ring?"

The clerk looked so full of anticipation that Rainbow didn't have the heart to disappoint him. Besides, he could always have the stone reset in a stickpin. And if he accidentally let the ring fall out of his pocket so that Iris had to pick it up, he could pretend that he had won it in a card game. That way she couldn't laugh at him. Then he could ask her if she liked it and if she said she did, he could give it to her, and if she said she didn't, he could sell it or keep the diamond for his tie. It would work out fine. He put down the suitcase. "An engagement ring."

The clerk's mouth stayed open as he unlocked the back of the counter and pulled out a tray. He pointed a long finger at the small diamond set in plain yellow gold. "One of our most popular styles, sir. Simple, yet elegant."

The gem was too small for a bow tie. Or a string tie. Rainbow scanned the others in the tray before he moved down the counter and pointed to the middle shelf. "Like this."

The clerk strained for a look. Three quick steps and the small tray came out of the counter in a hurry, but the clerk took his time setting it down. Rainbow pulled the ring he wanted out of the velvet slot and held the stone up to the light.

"You don't have to do that, sir. The light stays inside because of the facets and—"

"Real?"

"Of course!" The clerk took the ring and turned it in his fingers. "Two carats." He read from the tiny circular tag attached to the band. "Two-point-oh-four carats, to be precise. A very clear white. And perfect."

"And you guarantee it's real?"

"We stand behind each of our sales, sir." There was an angry whistle in the clerk's voice now. He rotated the ring again. "The brilliant cut gives it a style all its own, so uncluttered, so—"

"How much?"

The clerk sighed and studied the tag. "Nine hundred and twenty-five dollars. This is an exceptionally fine stone and the setting is—"

"Can you put it in one of those little boxes with your name on it?"

The clerk's eyebrows tilted. He cleared his throat. "You would like to have it sized first, I presume?" He grabbed a long cone-shaped cylinder from a hook behind him, then removed the tag and slid the band over the cone until it would go no farther. "This is a six. What size is your fiancée?"

Rainbow stood up straight, glanced at the clock over the rear door, tapped the glass countertop. What size was she?

"Is she a large woman?" the clerk said. "Petite?"

"No, she's real small." When Rainbow leaned toward him, the clerk inched backward. "Look, if it don't fit, I can bring it in and you'll fix it, right?"

"Of course, sir. But wouldn't you like to have her in before you buy? She might prefer a different style. . . ."

They were probably told to say that—to say anything that would get the woman into the store so that she could ask for the biggest rock they had and maybe walk out with two rings instead of one. That was undoubtedly how gray-haired Mrs. North over there got started on her collection, by being brought in to look over a pea-sized diamond back when she was young and had some man on a love string. But that wasn't going to happen to Rainbow. He let his jacket fall open and watched the clerk's eyes find the taped handle of his .45. "Just put it in one of your boxes and let me pay you."

The clerk smoothed down his shirtfront and began copying the numbers off the tag onto a sales slip. His eyes darted to the pistol, back to the paper. Tiffany's had probably never taught him what to do when a customer wanted to buy before the sales pitch ended. This was a good experience for the little man. He put the ring in a satin holder, the holder in a black velvet box. His finger traced the lettering over the inside of the lid. "You see? That says Tiffany's." He snapped the lid shut.

Rainbow grinned at him, "You read real good," and peeled off ten bills from his wad of folding money.

"It will only be a minute while I have this wrapped for you," the clerk said. "Any color you prefer for the ribbon?"

"I'll take it as is." Rainbow tossed his money down.

There was a little silence. Then the cash register chimed twice and the clerk handed Rainbow his change. He picked up his pencil again. "Could we have your name and address, please?"

Rainbow held out his hand. "The ring."

"It's for your own protection, sir." The clerk was hugging the tiny box. "In case of a problem and you bring it back, you'll need a complete sales slip and—"

"R. Roberts."

The clerk smiled and scribbled the name. "And the address, Mr. Roberts?"

"Jefferson Hotel."

"And that would be where . . . ?"

"Saint Louie," Rainbow said. "That would be in Missouri."

The clerk squinted out of one eye. He filled in the last line, dotting the *i*'s by jabbing his pencil to the page. "We get quite a few customers from the Midwest. For the races, you know." He separated the copies of the sales slip. "And thank you so much, Mr. Roberts. On behalf of Tiffany's, may I be among the first to congratulate you and your lady on—"

Rainbow stuffed his copy of the slip into his pocket with the ring box, picked up the suitcase, and walked out the door. In another second they would have thrown him a party in there and that Mrs. North would have wanted to kiss him. He threaded his way through the lobby. Each time he passed someone, he patted the bulge in his jacket: still there. He stopped short of the front door. The Greek would still be on the big porch across the street. With Dancer. More questions? How was he going to explain buying a ring when he went in for a stickpin? He found a side door out to Broadway.

Traffic was jammed for two blocks. Police cars and an ambulance sped up the drive to E.R.'s Park Casino. Villagers, tourists, even the Greek and his entourage hurried to see what was happening. The air was noisy with sirens and the thunder of a stampede. Rainbow squeezed through the cars to the other curb, and using the cardboard case as a persuader, fought his way past the crowd on the sidewalk to the bushes and onto the grass. Alone, he held the ring up to sunlight, imagining her face, her excitement. It was real. Old Cal was behind him, Iris in front of him. No more wasted time.

The box went back together with a snap. Under any circumstances, this ring was not going back to Tiffany's. He tossed the sales slip away. Long eager strides took him up the lane to the Congressional. He decided that it had been a good morning after all.

26

There was no answer inside room 319. The kid had probably left for the golf course. Rainbow rapped on the door one last time. And a man carrying a black bag came out of the suite down the hall. Suite 325. The man walked past the bench and down the stairs. He looked like a doctor. Was Iris sick? Maybe she was pregnant. Rainbow swallowed air and went to the door of his suite. It was unlocked. "Iris? You sick or—"

Murph was sitting on the couch, Iris on a chair. They were eating off the room-service cart between them. There was no ice bucket, but the bubbling liquid in their glasses had to be champagne.

Rainbow locked the door. "Is somebody sick?"

Iris shook her head and finished a crisp slice of bacon. Murph turned sideways as if looking for something and licked creamed cereal from the back of his spoon. "Find him?"

"That champagne?" Rainbow put down the suitcase and tossed his hat on the chair in the corner. "At this hour?"

"Mineral water." Murph offered him the glass. "She ordered it. Has what they call purgative powers. And it don't taste nothing like it smells. You find who you was looking for?"

Rainbow put the glass back on the cart and sat on the couch. "You were right, kid. Word is he's dead. I'm through looking."

"About time." Murph spooned more cereal and took another drink of water. "Never thought you'd give up on him till—"

"I said I'm through looking." Rainbow unbuttoned his new jacket, but kept the flap over his pistol. "And what are you still doing here? You chart that course already?"

"Ah, no, not yet," Murph said. "I, ah, overslept. That suit new or just cleaned up?"

"I set us a game with the Greek for one-thirty. What do you mean you overslept? Didn't I tell you to—"

"It was my fault." Iris swallowed her food in a hurry. "He was on his way out when I asked him to join me for breakfast. I hate to eat alone."

Rainbow stopped his fingers from curling into a fist. "You could of waited for me to get back. Said I probably wouldn't be all that long."

"I'm sorry," she said. "But it was my fault."

"Look, Iris, you don't have to do this." Murph put down his spoon. "It's like I said. I overslept."

"Now, Dave, you're confusing him." Iris tried another piece of bacon. She really did like food after all. "You may have overslept a bit, but it was my fault that you came in for breakfast and haven't left yet."

Rainbow studied both of them. She was smiling. The kid was hiding. And no one had explained that doctor yet. Rainbow got up and moved Iris to the chair by the phone. "Sit right here and don't say a word."

"What about my breakfast?" she said.

He rolled the cart to her, then sat across from Murph. "Now what's going on here?"

"We've already told you." Iris plunked her fork on her plate. "He was on his way out and I—"

"Iris." Rainbow got up again and went to her. "I understand what you told me. I understand what he told me. I don't believe I'm being told the whole truth here and I don't know why and that's what's bothering me, so why don't you just *sit* there and try to be quiet while I ask him to tell it to me again, all right? Fine." He touched her cheek and sat in the chair opposite Murph. "Now start all over."

"Those *are* new duds," Murph said. "Looks real nice don't he, Iris?"

"Start from when you overslept and needed a doctor to wake you up," Rainbow said.

"Oh . . . him." Murph's stare fell to his lap. There was a long silence. "I didn't feel so good when I got up."

"It was my fault," Iris said. "He told me he didn't feel well and I had the house doctor come up and—"

"Iris? *Please?*" Rainbow glared at her, then tried a smile. "I'm asking *him*, okay?"

She pouted. "Can't I say anything?"

"No." He grinned at her, frowned at Murph. "Well?"

The telephone rang. Then again.

Rainbow turned to Iris. "Could you answer that?"

She glanced at the phone by her elbow. "Would I be allowed to say anything into it? Besides hello?"

Murph was snickering. The phone kept ringing.

"Yeah," Rainbow said. "You can tell whoever it is that I'm busy, take a message, and say I'll get back to them."

On the sixth ring, Iris picked up the phone. She smiled and pointed to herself, then carried the phone into the bedroom, taking the final slice of bacon with her.

Rainbow let out a long sigh: "Women."

"Really something, ain't she?" Murph said. He was grinning. Something was wrong with his face. Very wrong. One cheek was puffed up and dark, the crease around his eye was swollen. And his jaw was spotted with tiny black circles: broken blood vessels.

Rainbow reached for the kid's face. "What the hell hit you?"

Murph pulled away. "Nothing. I, ah, tripped. Last night."

"Like hell you did." He grabbed Murph by the shirt and yanked him forward, studied the bruises, felt their heat. "Didn't that quack give you some ice?"

The ice pack came out from behind the pillow. Murph put it to his face. "It was her idea to call him. I said the ice'd be fine, but she—"

"She did right. You sure it ain't broke?"

Murph nodded. "Looks worse than it is. See, there was these garbage cans and it was dark and when I fell—"

"Quit lying to me. You been in a fight. Any fool can see that. Can't leave you alone for a single night without you getting all busted up. You know who did this?"

"Never seen him before. Big guy, though."

"Strong as a mule, too." Rainbow touched the bruise again; the ice had made it feel strange, like cold soup. "What did you do to make him crack you?"

Silence. Murph muttered something under his breath.

"Well," Rainbow said. "Tell me for Chrissake."

Murph opened his mouth, but the words never came. Iris called from the hall to the bedroom:

"Excuse me." She was holding up the phone. "It's Horace. He says he has to talk to you."

Rainbow stood and pointed a finger at Murph. "Don't move a muscle till I get back." He got his suitcase, took the phone from Iris, and shut the bedroom door. "Horace, you just about settled in?"

"Been so for half a day." Horace's voice sounded scratchy. Maybe that was just the phone connection. "Got us in a field for tomorrow. You got the cash ready?"

Rainbow sat on the bed. "Tomorrow? Why so soon, I mean, you sure about this field?"

"It's perfect. Six horses. Bunch of nags. Nobody'd think twice about Old Smoke winning in this class. One standout, and we can get to him easy. Morning Cup. Him and the Smoke'll make the odds, should see us at three-, maybe four-to-one. See, I'm only gonna breeze Old Smoke today. Workout time'll look real bad. Now you got the cash?"

"I got it." Instinctively, Rainbow felt for the key to the safety-deposit box. He found the ring box instead. "We better get together before you go any further with it. I need to know what it looks like."

"Looks like a goddamn fix for Chrissakes." The bald man sighed and moaned. "Look, this is the best field I could find for the first week and a half up here. No guarantee we'll get one better even if we was to wait."

"Yeah, but—tomorrow? Opening day?"

Another moan. "That's what's best about it. Nobody'd expect to see a boat race on opening day. Roze and the rest of them hoodlums ain't had time to get full control yet. Hell, they'll be all over the track by the end of the first week. Won't be able to slip nothing past them then. What this is, son, is an opportunity."

Son.

Rainbow cleared his throat. "When can we meet?"

"Anytime you like. I'm down here waiting on track time now. If I ain't at Oklahoma, I'm at the main course."

"Oklahoma?"

"Yeah, that's the training track across from the main oval. Thought you knew about things up here."

"No problem," Rainbow said. "But I can't get down until late this afternoon."

More moans. "Look, there ain't nothing to seeing a horse breeze three furlongs anyways. No point in you coming. So why don't I just meet you for an early dinner at your hotel. That way, whatever I set in motion down here, you can okay or nix before you're out any money."

"Sounds good. Say about six?"

"Yeah, fine. But you got to have a few Gs loose for me tonight. I'll have to put something in the jocks' hands if we're gonna get them to run our race. They won't go for getting paid after. Not in full, at least. I never did. . . ."

"Sure," Rainbow said. "If I like the setup, that is. I warn you, Horace, I'm gonna have some tough questions for you tonight."

This moan sounded far away. "See you at six."

The phone went dead. Rainbow hung up the receiver and walked into the main room.

"What was that all about?" Iris said, finishing her toast.

"Ah, Horace just had some news about the Sales." He went behind the couch and glanced out the window onto the lawn. There was still a big crowd around the casino. The ambulance was pulling down the drive. No sirens. "Murph, you better get the clubs to the course. And pick up a melon."

"Sure you don't want me to do a quick chart?"

Rainbow shook his head. "We'll use the bingle-bangle-bungle. And the melon. Now get going."

The kid got up and stopped by the door. "About last night. See, I was—"

"Not now, kid. I got a lot on my mind. See you around one. And tell them in the clubhouse I'm a guest of the Greek. They'll give you a locker."

"You want the melon put in there?"

"No, in the bag."

"What if I can't find one in time?"

Rainbow glared at him. "Find one."

Murph lowered his head and opened the door. "Bye, Iris. Thanks. For everything."

She brought the ice pack to him and kissed his cheek. "I'll be walking toward the golf course myself in a few minutes. Could you wait for me downstairs?"

The kid blushed and nodded and went out the door.

Iris grabbed her canvas bag by the tie string. "I have some errands to do. And I'm going to the spa while you're on the course. Unless you'd like me to come watch."

"Women on golf courses make me nervous," Rainbow said, smiling. "Take my mind off my game."

She didn't smile back. "In that case, I'll see you before dinner."

"Ah, yeah, listen, maybe you and Murph could have dinner together. Just for tonight. I got an appointment, and, well, it's the only time this'll happen, I swear it, so—"

"I'm sure Murph will be delighted to take me to dinner." She walked to the door. "Incidentally, the clothes in the bathroom are his."

"What's that supposed to mean?"

She turned the knob and grinned. "It means he changed his clothes in there."

Rainbow couldn't stop his hands from making fists now. "And what's *that* supposed to mean?"

"You're so hard on him you don't see anything. He's hurt. And all you do is yell at him."

"I wasn't yelling. I was being direct."

"You were yelling. But then, he said you would. Because he knew you weren't going to find that man."

Rainbow moved toward her. "He told you? What? Tell me."

She opened the door as if to give herself an escape hatch. "That you were looking for someone you'd never find and that you'd be angry when you got back. He was right, wasn't he?"

"Yeah, I guess." He stopped by the couch. "Sorry about dinner tonight."

"We'll manage." She put on her gloves. "What time do you expect to be through with your—appointment?"

"Don't know." He found the ring box in his pocket, felt the bristle of velvet being rubbed the wrong way. "I really am sorry, Iris. Last time. I promise."

There was a long silence. She stepped away from the door and hugged him. "I don't want to be angry at you. I'm sorry."

He held her tight. "No, I shouldn't of snapped at you like that. I'll work on it, okay?"

She nodded against his chest, then kissed him lightly and pulled away "I wish you had let me help choose your new suit." From a corner table, she got her hat and went back to the door. "If you finish early on the golf course—I'll be here." She blew him a kiss and walked out.

He hurried to the door, opened it a crack. The canvas bag draped over her shoulder swayed to the rhythm of her hips. She could make anything look good. Maybe he should have asked her to help pick out his new wardrobe. But with her along, it would have cost a fortune. Past the bench by the staircase, she disappeared. He locked the door and took the velvet box from his pocket. The lid popped open, star-bright rays exploded into the air. It was all there, everything he felt and wanted to feel, staring out at him from just beneath the shine, compressed like a handful of packed earth—warm and alive. He set the box on the cart. Clean white light bounced off the satin liner, playing games with each letter in the Tiffany name. Easing back against the soft pillows of the couch, he touched the bottom edge of the water glass to the diamond, then sipped a silent toast. To himself. To her. To them. Together. The bitter smell made him cough. A mouthful of mineral water splattered the gold carpet, and instantly, the stain began to seep into the wool.

Iris wasn't going toward the golf course at all, she was going in the opposite direction, and Murph wouldn't let her go out of her way. Both shoulders laden with golf bags, he insisted on taking her carryall so that she could walk unburdened. Claiming he didn't want to fight the crowds milling around the sidewalk of The Park Casino and the United States Hotel, he walked her south on Broadway to Circular Street, adding at least a mile to his trip to the golf course. Just short of Park Place, where the roadway curved north, he brought out a small gold locket and said something about a girl giving it to him, an American girl named Ellen. Just the way he say it made that locket seem alive in his hand—soft. The swollen jaw made his wide face look even wider, and when he smiled, only part of his mouth curved up, the rest of it lay there inside the puffiness, paralyzed by tender flesh. She pretended not to notice.

"She's real pretty," he said, staring at the locket. "And kind. You'd like her. . . ."

"I'm sure I would, Dave. After all, we both have something in common. We both care about you."

He stole a glance at her. That half-smile again. The locket went back into his pants. "See you about five for dinner, okay?"

"I'll be ready."

He left her at the corner of Union Avenue and trudged up Circular toward Church Street. There was something in his walk, the way he handed back her canvas bag, something in the way he couldn't smile now. It was as if in saying this good-bye, he really meant it. Iris stood at the corner until he was out of sight, hidden by shady elms—gone. She had the feeling that she might never see him again. It didn't make any sense: she would be seeing him for dinner in a few short hours. She wrapped the bag's tie string around her hand and started walking.

Union Avenue was lined with broad lawns and big houses with high windows. The rich who lived here lived here only for three weeks in August. The rest of the year, these "cottage" mansions stood vacant. This part of the village didn't exist then, there was no reason for anyone to come here. With the track closed, this street—Race Track Row—was deserted. It seemed a terrible waste of geography, a blind mistake—even now, with the lawns neatly manicured, hedges neatly trimmed, flowers planted in neat bunches according to color schemes so tame they appeared painted on rather than grown naturally. In spite of all this controlled beauty, Iris found nothing worth looking at. She kept her eyes straight ahead down the long, straight street until she passed the last house, a brick monstrosity with a great porch on which the fat man from the train sat dressed in a lime-green suit, drinking with his friend, the movie-star cowboy. She hurried through the gate in the racetrack fence, then walked down the Paddock Trail, through the wavy shadows of towering elms, following the curve of the track past the clubhouse and to the stables on the back-stretch.

Long clotheslines sagged under the weight of dripping blankets, bright silks, gray underwear. Boys walked tethered horses in small circles. Jockeys in dungarees and ball caps brought their mounts to and from the track. There was the smell of soggy hay. A soft, surreal quiet. The sun was still cold, the morning air brittle. For the first time since leaving the hotel, Iris felt relaxed. She had just walked home.

One of the exercise boys said that he couldn't be sure, but that he thought he had heard about Horace Wells putting a horse up in a back stable somewhere. He wanted to know if it was the same Horace Wells who had once been a jockey. After a long breath, she told him she wasn't really sure, then she thanked the boy and sidestepped manure to the back stables. She felt strong. Horace wasn't going to win this time.

The back stables needed a coat of whitewash. There was a MAJESTIC FARMS plaque on the half-door of an end stall. Before she reached it, a large chestnut head peered over the door. Old Smoke was restless. And big. Fifteen and one-half hands high, measured from the ground to his withers: five feet three and one-half inches, as tall as Iris. She stroked the flat bone that ran down between wet eyes. "Hello, boy. Miss me?" She dug into her purse for the sugar cubes she had taken from her breakfast tray and fed them to the horse.

"Hey, ho! What you giving him there?" Horace came around the stable corner with a bridle in his hand. "I got to run him in a second."

She let the horse lick her gloved palm. "Only sugar, Horace. That won't affect his workout."

"You're a fine one to tell me my business." He nudged her aside and slipped the bridle onto the horse. "Used to feed them apples whenever you felt like. Took me years to figure out why they was always letting their bowels loose on the track." He checked the horse's tongue on the bit. "Didn't know you'd be down today."

"I came to see how you were."

"Feel good." Horace opened the stall door and led the golden chestnut out. "Can't help but feel good at Saratoga. Something about the air up here." He filled his lungs and yanked on the rein. "Big oaf couldn't run speed for the Ruler. Want to see him breeze? Got him entered tomorrow. The sixth race. Nice field."

Iris walked beside him down the trail to the track. "That was fast work."

"Yeah, well, see, no sense in paying for feed if we can't get some of it back out there, now is there? Real nice field. Should do fine. Of course, it depends on the ride we get. Bobby Monroe's gonna take him. I'm, ah, making the arrangements right now."

Bobby Monroe was a fine jockey. When he wasn't suspended by the stewards for unfair rides. Or taking part in a fixed race.

"I hope we can afford him," Iris said. "What's the distance?"

"Mile and an eighth. His sire loved that run." Horace steered the horse around the stable row. "Chalk eaters will make our main competition the favorite. Morning Cup. But I seen him eat today and he don't eat ready. If I had the cash to spare, I'd bet on our chances, I would. Got this good feeling."

Iris kept silent. He was in his glory now, throwing track jargon around, calling those who bet only on favorites "chalk eaters," talking about his racing intuition. She wanted the balloon to swell some more before she burst it.

He gave the horse over to an exercise boy with instructions to ease the mount around three furlongs. At the railing, he drew a mug of coffee from a standing pot and escorted Iris to a spot near the far turn where he could get a better view of how the horse leaned into the bend against a loose rein. Down the railing, a string of five men studied their stopwatches as a horse drove down the backstretch. In unison, the men's thumbs pressed the stop buttons of their watches and their eyes dropped from the horse to their hands in a single, flowing motion. They were clockers, employed by the likes of Efrem Roze and Stavros the Greek, selling information that would help bookmakers determine the best odds.

"We're in luck," Horace said, nodding to the horse on the backstretch. "That was Morning Cup." He shouted toward the clockers: "Birdseye! What'd you get?"

The first man in the row turned his back to the others and held a hand close to his chest. Three fingers shot up straight, then two fingers flashed horizontally. Then a closed fist. Finally, three fingers thrust out parallel to the ground and the man called Birdseye turned back to the railing.

Horace grinned at Iris. "Did you get it?"

She nodded. "Thirty-seven even. For three furlongs."

The grin got wider. "Good girl. Learned something after all." He chuckled. "Only it was really thirty-six flat. At least it would of been over Oklahoma. Full second faster over there than here, leastways till they get a few days into the meet. The idiots always water this here main track too much, expecting to make it faster. Just dries it out quicker, is all. Horses can tell. They won't give you a full run on hardpan." He nodded to himself and sipped coffee. "Full second faster."

In a moment he would be telling her why the clockers used hand signals: to keep their information confidential. It didn't matter that she already knew. What mattered was that Horace knew. He had never really taught her anything, not in all those years. He had only told her things, over and over. He liked to have the answers.

And it was time. She draped her bag over the railing. "Thirty-six flat. Not bad at all." She mustered all her strength and stared at him. "I wouldn't bet a dime on Morning Cup."

Horace shivered and tapped the side of his coffee mug. "Well, I wouldn't say we had it cinched."

"But you have this . . . good feeling. . . ."

More taps against the mug. He shrugged. "Been wrong before, you know."

"I know." She was proud of how long she was able to stare at him without flinching. "But you've seen to that, too, haven't you."

Silence. Horace seemed to grow shorter, as if shrinking from the cool air. Another sip of coffee, a long sigh. "Should of known better than to trust a plowboy to keep his mouth shut."

"They won't ever let you near a track again."

"Only if they catch me." His eyes narrowed. "You wouldn't be thinking of turning your old man in, now would you?"

It was a joke to him, a game. Going to jail was probably some sort of victory for him, a badge. Like alcohol, it was a way of fighting back. And losing. She hated him for being so weak. But her stare failed her, she couldn't look at him anymore. And no, she wasn't going to turn him in to the stewards. "I wish I could," she said.

"Now what kind of talk is that?" He turned his back to the railing and leaned heavily on it, staring at the sky. "I swear, I wonder if you're rightly my daughter sometimes, don't seem possible that my blood's running through you."

Iris felt the same way. She had for most of her life.

"We got us a gold-plated opportunity here," he was saying, "and there ain't no way it can go sour. And you come down here making me feel like slime. Christ, it ain't fair. Doing it for you, ain't I?"

She was biting down so hard, her teeth felt sore. "Why can't you just run him and see what he can do? With all your training, he—"

"And let go of this kind of advantage?" Horace spat to the side.

"Crazy. Tried that, didn't we? It don't work, no matter how much I work with him, he ain't got it in him. Neither did his sire." He took a long slug of coffee. "We ain't set up for that, Iris. Takes more cash than we ever had. But after tomorrow, we'll have it, see? We can buy us a string of champions, right here—at the Sales! Be on top again."

"Or in jail," she said, still not able to look at him. "For the last time."

He sighed and let out one of his angry moans, which meant he was both angry and bored. "Don't want to talk about it, it don't concern you. I'm doing it. You'll thank me, too, once you see how much comes in. *If* that plowboy of yours has the cash."

"He has it."

"Well, he just better, I'm going through a lot of trouble as it is, and—" He ran a hand over his scalp. "Can't bring myself to trust him. Something about him sets me on edge. Maybe it's that dumb grin of his."

It was Rainbow's height. Horace couldn't trust anyone tall. It was the same with Ernie. Tall athletes had something God had cheated Horace out of. With power and range, with height, Horace believed he could have done anything. And he detested seeing those gifted with six-foot frames letting their talents go to waste. Like Ernie, who played baseball because someone once asked him to. Like Rainbow, who played golf and God only knew what else because he could cheat at it. Iris drew in a short breath. "He's six-one."

Another angry moan. "What I could of done with that. Christ, I'd of been another Christy Mathewson, be in the Hall of Fame . . . Giving speeches . . ."

"You're Horace Wells," she said, staring at the canvas bag as if something secret lay inside it. "That would be enough for most men."

"Well, I ain't most men." He wasn't moaning anymore, he was whining. "Now just tell me if you're gonna get in my way with this thing or not. I got enough on my mind without hearing nothing out of you."

The canvas bag kept turning on its string. He had beaten the fight out of her. Again. She shook her head softly.

"All right then." He slurped his coffee. "What'd you come down here for then, just to rile me? Christ, I ought to take you over my knee for that. Never should of listened to your mother about not hitting you. What'd she know, brung up like a queen. Spoiled you rotten and I'm living to regret it."

He never had hit her: he had hugged her. And tried to protect her. To love her. Even when her mother ran away, he had not let anyone raise Iris, he had done it himself. Because he had wanted her close by, to be close to her. And he had cried when he sent her away to school for the first time. She couldn't forget that. Or his letters. His visits. The holidays he planned so carefully. Even later, when his drinking put things wrong, he had made her feel that she was everything in his life. He cried the first time she had to bail him out of jail for fixing a race. And the second time. The third time, he started using his moan and never cried again. And she started to help him. He resented it: he didn't want anyone's help, especially hers. But that was only because she hadn't helped him enough, wasn't it? She stopped the canvas bag from turning in the breeze:

"I'm sorry, Daddy."

He stood there for a moment. Then he hugged her. "Wasn't easy for you, with no woman around, I mean. Did the best I could. You got cheated, is all."

She was crying. But she couldn't feel the tears, she could only see them dropping into the dust. He wiped her face with his handkerchief, then leaned on the rail to watch Old Smoke round the bend. The big horse galloped by with the boy standing high in the saddle.

"Leans like a champion, don't he?" Horace said. "Christ, I don't know why he can't stride like one." He finished his coffee. "You say you seen Rainbow's bankroll? How much?"

"One hundred and fifty thousand." Her voice sounded lame, as if someone else were talking.

"Christ, are we in it this time." He slapped his forehead. "He must of robbed a goddamn bank. A whole slew of them!"

"It's all he has in the world." That voice again. "He has plans. . . ."

"Fuck his plans." Horace smacked the railing with the mug. "This puts a different color on it. I asked for fifty on the spread, but that's taking a big risk. I mean, even in a boat race I don't want my money riding on a nag like Old Smoke. We got to arrange it, Iris."

Her face hardened, her fingers tightened on the rail. "No."

"Hell, it was your idea," he said, leaning in close. "We could of pulled it off in Lexington if that bastard hadn't of got cold feet!"

"It's all he has, Horace."

"Sight more than we got, ain't it?" He was rubbing her shoulder. "Look, he'll never know, you'll get out clean, maybe even stay behind with him awhile. Sure, that'd be okay, you don't have to come with me right off."

She wanted to cry now, but couldn't. "I can't."

Horace walked in a little circle, then came back to the rail and took her hand. "I ain't saying you got to. We can go with this thing like it is and maybe clear a hundred-fifty anyways. If Rainbow pays off clean. But damn, you was so smart to come up with this in Lexington, I don't see why we got to risk running a race when we could have the whole hundred-fifty in our pocket before post time!" He squeezed her fingers. "Just you think on it, you'll see I'm right. Don't want you to do nothing you're against, that ain't how I raised you, now is it? I'm having dinner with him tonight, so you let me know by then, 'cause I got jocks to pay or not pay, depending on how we run it."

She didn't answer and she didn't look at him. She watched dust settle out on the track. Another horse was taking its run, hugging the rail in the turn, the jockey low in the saddle, pushing for speed.

"Benecia Boy," Horace said. "In our field tomorrow. Hell, you call that a blowout? Seen better on dairy farms."

The horse looked tired. The jockey was trying to blow him out over three furlongs, sharpening the horse on its final drill before the race. That horse would never run sharp. It was a loser.

"Got work to do." Horace kissed her on the cheek and gave her a little hug. "Glad you came by. Need all the moral support I can get these days. I tell you, it ain't easy being on the wagon, no sir. Feel tired all the time." He started toward the stables, then stopped and turned. "Wouldn't want to curry him for me, would you?"

Iris hadn't put a currycomb to a horse in years. And Horace did look tired. The drive up from the city must have taken a lot out of him. Then getting a stall on short notice, arranging for feed, workouts, entering a race—it was a wonder that he had the energy. And no whiskey. A half-hour curry job on gentle Old Smoke was a small favor. Then she could go to Dr. Talbert's spa. And soak. She slung the canvas bag over her shoulder and, wrapping her arm in his, she walked Horace back to the stables.

27

The golf course lay in a series of valleys off Church Street, about a mile from village center. Alongside the green and white caddy shack, a group of men, some old, some just boys, played cards in the shade, using cigarettes as money. Behind them, black caddies slouched around a bench. In the front doorway of the shed, with a newspaper over his face, a cigarette burning toward the yellow stains on his fingers, a thin man who had to be the caddymaster leaned his chair back against the wall as if he were sitting on a balance board.

Rainbow finished swinging the spade mashie and started off the practice field with Murph in trail. "Because you can't, so quit asking."

"But you could play with the lefty clubs," Murph said. "C'mon, it ain't every day I get to play with Stavros the Greek. I don't want him to think I'm just a caddy. I'm a pro, just like you."

Rainbow forced himself to look away from the shed. "Saw in the paper they favor Jurgy to take the PGA. Still think Hagen'll whip him."

A breeze beat against the leaves of the tall trees. Murph took the club out of Rainbow's hand and shoved it in the bag. "It's 'cause I'd beat you, ain't it? You don't want the Greek to know I'm better than you."

Rainbow stopped just past the caddymaster's chair. "I mean to make him pay to find that out, kid. And I can't be playing left-handed right off. That'd give away our secret weapon. The Greek's got lots of rich friends. We could clean up."

The kid tugged at his shirtsleeves, which he had rolled up to his elbows. "Well then, why can't you use one of them caddies. I got—things to do."

"Like to get in another fight? No sir, you're staying close by." He led the way up to the first tee. Stavros came out of the clubhouse dressed in light blue knickers. Aziz lumbered after him, carrying a golf bag as if it were a purse. "See that," Rainbow said. "Those two stay together. All the time."

"Yeah, well he's the Greek's bodyguard for Chrissake."

Rainbow gave Murph the .45. "Don't let anybody kill me. Unless I'm losing bad, that is." He chuckled and shook hands with Stavros.

"Four strokes you give me," the Greek said. "How about a thousand a Nassau and automatic presses?"

"Sounds a little rich for my blood," Rainbow told him. "Thought you might like to try a round of bingle-bangle-bungle."

Stavros passed a wood tee between his fingers. "Never heard of it."

"It's custom-made for guys like you—busy guys who don't get to play much. It's got nothing to do with how you score. Just a fun sort of thing."

"What, no betting?" The Greek looked disappointed.

"Sure, we could bet a little on it. Put some excitement into the game." Rainbow stepped onto the tee. "Guarantee you'll like it. If you don't, we'll play any way you want."

Stavros nodded and teed up. He half-topped his drive and sent the ball bounding along the ground.

"Right up the middle," Rainbow said. "Base hit."

Jet-black eyes narrowed. "Yeah, well, I'm still shook after this morning. Where'd you go to, anyway? Should of come with us to E.R.'s club. His manager shot himself through the brains. Christ, I never seen so many people trying to get a peek at a dead man. Blood all over the place."

Rainbow waited for Murph to finish building the sand tee. The kid seemed to be having trouble keeping his hands still.

"Nice enough guy, too," Stavros was saying. "E.R. must of nailed him skimming off the top and rewriting the books, but, hell, you got to expect that with your people when you handle so much cash, right? Well, this guy's a guinea Catholic and he can't take the heat of being held up as a cheat, so what's he do? Suicide! Ain't that a kicker?"

Murph bobbled the ball. "Wasn't—Frank Tagliafera, was it?"

"Yeah, Tag, right!" Stavros took a light from Aziz and rolled the thin cigar in his teeth. "Know him, kid?"

Murph stuck the ball on top of the sand mound and walked to the bag at the side of the tee. Rainbow watched him for a moment, then glanced at Stavros, shrugged, stood over his ball, and knocked a drive down the narrow fairway, into the short rough.

Stavros marched off the tee. "Good hit. So how's it work, this bingle-bangle shit?"

"The bingle is whoever hits the green *first*," Rainbow said, matching the short man's stride. "No matter if it's your second or tenth stroke. As long as you're on the green *first*, you get the bingle. Say, a hundred bucks a hole."

With a *cleek*, Stavros hit a ground skipper up the fairway. "Sonofabitch killed every bug in its path."

Rainbow laughed with him. "And the bangle is whoever winds up closest to the pin after *all* of us get on the green. Again, no matter how many shots it takes."

Stavros nodded and smoothed down his hair. "How much for this bangle?"

"Say, one-fifty a hole." Rainbow waited for the Greek to hit another low line drive toward the green, then headed for his ball. "And three hundred for the bungle. That's whoever holes out *first*, regardless of the score you take on the hole. That's all there is to it. We make it even fairer by putting in strict *rotation*. The last guy on the green putts *first*, the first guy on putts *last*. Rotation." He drew a mashie from the bag and tore through the heavy grass, knocking his ball between the bunkers guarding the green. Using the club as a cane, he started walking. "So if we each put up five-fifty a hole, that's all we can lose."

Stavros climbed down into the bunker. A shovelful of sand sprayed over the lip of the trap, his ball skidded across the green, stopping a yard off the back edge. "That counts as a bingle, right? I hit the green."

Rainbow shook his head. "You're still off. Looks like I got the bingle if I can chip it on."

"But I still get a crack at the bangle." Stavros grabbed Aziz's hand and walked out of the bunker. "And the bungle, too."

"We each get a fair chance at something every hole," Rainbow said. "Even if you shoot a fifteen! That's why it's fun. You're never out of the match." He closed the face of his spade mashie. A short, chopping stroke: the ball hugged the top of the short grass and stopped one foot below the cup. "The bingle's mine."

"Yeah, yeah, pick it up." Stavros started for his ball. "That's a gimme."

"Wouldn't be fair," Rainbow told him. "You still got a chance for the bangle and the bungle, and we putt in rotation, remember? I'm on the green first, I putt last."

Stavros was grinning. "Right. And I could get this close. Might even hole it out." He squatted to gauge the roll of the green, then knocked his ball through the frog hair, leaving himself a twenty-foot putt to the hole. "Okay, I'm on. So it's still my turn." He shook his head disgustedly. "But you're closest, so you get the bangle, right?"

Rainbow nodded and fought the smile. Murph pulled the flag stick out of the hole.

"Hey, College!" Stavros put his hands on his hips. "I didn't tell you to pull the pin, did I? Tend it for me."

Murph jammed the flag stick back into the cup and held it there until the Greek's putt ran three feet by the hole.

"My turn now." Rainbow signaled Murph to yank the pin, then tapped the ball into the hole with the back of his putter.

"So you get the bangle for being closest and the bungle for being the first one in the hole." Stavros looked pleased that he had figured it out.

"That's the game." Rainbow picked his ball out of the cup. "But without my lucky chip shot, you would of taken the bungle. Maybe the bangle, too."

"Yeah, I muffed my chip." Stavros knocked his ball off the green with a swipe of his putter. "The Greek don't miss many of them. You was lucky this hole."

"Got to be sometimes, Greek."

But Stavros wasn't laughing, he was striding toward the next tee. Rainbow waited for Murph to come off the green. "What the hell's wrong with you? You know better than to pull the pin before someone asks you to."

The kid kept his stare on the grass. "It was her brother."

". . . Who?"

"Frank Tagliafera. Ellen's gonna be real sad. Them people is close."

Rainbow didn't know what to say. On the tee, Stavros lunged at the ball, his body turning like a tree trunk, his flesh shaking under his clothes. The sole of his driver scuffed the top of the ball and dribbled it off the tee. He slammed the club into the ground. Rainbow muttered, "Nice bunt," but the Greek didn't hear him. It was just as well. He put an arm on Murph. "If you want to go back to the hotel, it'd be all right. I can get the giant to carry the clubs."

Murph shook his head. "I got to talk to you, Rainbow."

"Yeah, we can talk about it. But not now. This match won't take long."

"I don't want to go back to the hotel," Murph said. "Not now."

"Hey!" Stavros called. "You playing or talking?"

Rainbow got a wood tee from his pocket. "I'll tee myself up from here on, kid." He patted Murph's shoulder and walked to the tee. His drive cut through the heavy air like a rocket.

It wasn't fun. It was boring. Stavros was a terrible golfer. Murph walked around as if in a daze. Aziz never said a word, never looked at anything. And the course was short, only a few holes were challenging. Rainbow was ready to quit. At the lunch stand on the ninth hole, he bought a bottle of ginger ale for himself and brought a sweet roll back to the tee for Murph. The kid bit through the drizzled icing, but chewed slowly. The Greek hadn't noticed the swollen jaw. It was probably one more thing that was making Murph unhappy.

"I'm gonna tell him," Rainbow said.

Murph looked up as though he had just swallowed an ice cube. "I don't believe it. He'll jump all over you."

"Doing him a favor, he'll see that."

"You—giving up your rightful edge? *You?*"

Rainbow took the bag away from him. "Why don't you go back to the hotel and call her. Might be nice if she was to hear from you."

"Don't have her number. Don't even know if they got a phone."

"Well, ask Angelo, he'd know."

"Yeah . . ." Murph tore the sweet roll in two. "But he lives with E.R. and, well . . ."

"You just tell E.R. you're a friend of mine. He'll roll out the red carpet."

"No, it ain't that, Rainbow. See, last night, well . . ."

"Hey! You got it figured yet?" Stavros was coming out of the men's room by the lunch stand, buttoning his fly. He took a hot dog sloppy with mustard and sauerkraut from Aziz, tore off a hunk, and walked onto the tee. "Four bingles I got."

Rainbow took out his scorecard. It was like reading a weather report: dull. "And two bangles. Look like I got the rest."

Stavros studied the card. "So what's it come to?"

"Seven-hundred for you, three thousand one-fifty for me." Rainbow gave him the card and pushed back his panama. "Think we ought to forget it, Greek."

"I'm just getting my feel back," Stavros said. "Wait'll you see what I do to you this nine."

There was a little silence. Murph was pawing at the grass. Rainbow shook his head. "I can't lose. You're trying so hard for the bingle, you're letting me walk off with the bungle—every hole."

Stavros wiped mustard from his lip. "I got two bangles, didn't I?"

"Out of seven holes. Lucky we don't count par threes."

"So you beat me this side. But I'm gonna come back strong."

Another silence. Rainbow pressed his lips together. And said it. "It's a hustle, Greek."

Those jet-black eyes got wide. "You better hope to Christ you're joking."

Rainbow sighed. "Put the bingle and the bangle together, they still don't equal the bungle. So why try to win something that don't pay off? You're forcing me to win. It's a sucker bet." He put a hand on the Greek's shoulder. "Let's call it off, you don't owe me a cent. We'll play the last nine straight. For the fun of it." He started onto the tee, but Stavros spun him around.

"Nobody takes the Greek for a sucker." His eyes were black specks now. "Last time some punk tried to hustle me . . ."

Murph stepped in between them. "He don't mean nothing by it, Greek. He's trying to tell you so you *won't* lose."

Stavros glared for a moment, then bit into his hot dog. "Fucking second-rate hustle." He spat out the mouthful and threw the half-eaten food on the ground. "This ain't no pickup game where you rub their noses in your shit for Chrissake." He yanked a club out of his bag, then threw it down and kicked the shaft. "Bingle-bangle-bungle . . . shit." A brooding sneer cracked his lips. Then he grunted. And started to laugh. "How come I never hear of this one before?"

Rainbow tried to smile, but he couldn't. "A Rainbow Roberts original."

The Greek's laugh began as a sputter and evened out into a steady roar. He picked up his club. "Not bad. I'll use it sometime." He took deep breaths to calm his amusement, then teed up and hit a low line drive down the middle of the tenth fairway. "Come on—hit. If we ain't gambling, I don't want to spend the whole day out here."

Rainbow sent a towering drive down the right side. He gave the club to Murph. "Okay if he plays along with us, Greek?"

Stavros lit another cigar. "Won't slow us down, will he? I mean, he ever played before?"

"A little," Rainbow said, grinning at Murph, who was pulling a ball past the .45 in the bag pouch.

"Yeah, okay, I guess," Stavros said. "Come on, College. Hustle it up."

Murph teed up in a hurry and smacked his drive well down the fairway. The Greek followed the flight of the ball with a long stream of cigar smoke: "Jesus." He squinted at Murph. "Rainbow gives me four strokes. If I play you, kid, how many I get?"

The kid looked up: a reflex. Rainbow nodded to him. Murph grinned: "Six."

Stavros let his driver slip through his fingers, then aimed a throaty laugh at Rainbow. "I knew it. Can't fool the Oddsmaker."

"Guess not, Greek." Rainbow hoisted the bag onto his shoulder and winked at Murph. "We'll alternate carrying. Each hole." Then he started down the fairway.

Hello, Ellen? This is Dave—Mr. Murphy, remember? I got some bad news. . . .

Bad. Maybe a letter would be better:

> Dear Ellen,
>   By the time you get this you'll already know your brother Frank is dead. I'm really sorry he had to go shoot himself in the head. . . .

Worse.

The only way to do it was to go see her in person. By the time the train got into the city, by the time the cab got all the way out to the Bronx, Ellen would have found out about Frank Tagliafera, and Murph could just show up on her front porch and offer to ride with her back to Saratoga if she wanted to go to the funeral.

He missed an easy niblick shot on the short par 3.

Ellen would be grateful for his thoughtfulness. And probably worried about his swollen jaw. And touched that he still had her locket on him. Deeply touched when he told her that he wore it even when he took a bath, which was a lie because the chain was still broken. But by the next time he took a bath, he would have fixed the chain and he'd wear the locket and it wouldn't be a lie anymore.

He hooked his drive on the eighteenth hole, then took three miserable shots to the green. He couldn't hit anything straight.

And Rainbow was actually carrying a golf bag! That had never happened before, not in all the years since they had teamed up in Hot Springs. It was like a real partnership now. At last. This was the wrong time to talk about the big man with the birthmark on his chin who had come to collect the gambling debt. Murph was going to take care of that himself. And spare his partner any worry. After all, it was only a thousand dollars. Even if Rainbow didn't give back the fifteen thousand he was holding, Murph could pay off the debt easily. No one would know. But damn it, that table was rigged. He wasn't going to pay thieves for stealing. No matter what. He could leave town and see Ellen and when he got back, E.R. and his henchmen might have forgotten all about the debt. Or take $2,000 to The Park Casino, pay off his debt, and use the extra money to win back his losses. Playing poker, of course. There was no way to rig a poker table. He smiled, and while he waited for Stavros to play out of the bunker on the final green, he asked Rainbow about the $15,000. The answer: "I'll think about it." Something had come over Rainbow: he wasn't barking orders and he wasn't playing to win. All this and he had given up looking for Old Cal, too. It was unbelievable. The reason had to be Iris.

A blast of white shot high into the air and showered the green like a thousand drops of winter rain. From the bunker came a loud "Damn it," then a new spray of sand sent a ball racing over the short grass. Rainbow stuck his foot out, stopped the ball, kicked it into the hole, and waited for Stavros to climb out of the trap. "Don't believe it, Greek!" Rainbow yanked the flag stick. The ball jumped out of the cup. He booted it back across the green. "Luckiest damn shot I ever saw."

"What luck?" Stavros said, out of breath. "Hagen couldn't of done better."

Even Aziz was shaking his head. He had seen it all from beside the bunker. Was that really a smile on his face?

Murph missed his putt. Rainbow made his and led the way to the clubhouse. Stavros was still wheezing: "Hell of a match. Great shot I hit back there, right?"

"It was in all the way." Rainbow leaned the bag on the rail near the porch. "Soon as I saw it come over the lip, I knew it."

The Greek wanted to hang around the clubhouse for a while and see who dropped by. Rainbow decided to stay with him. Though asked to stay, Murph thought it best to buy his train ticket, then work on what he was going to say to Ellen. Before he left for town, he reminded Rainbow about the .45 and the watermelon in the ball pouch of the golf bag. But his partner didn't seem interested. For Rainbow to neglect his pistol and to pass up a chance to pull the watermelon con, he would have to be on his deathbed. Not even then. It had to be love. Murph grinned all the way to the train station.

The man who sold tickets said that the next train in was at 5:00 P.M. and that it left for the city at 5:45. Then he asked Murph for a name.

"Dave Murphy."

The man checked a list on the wall just inside the window bars. He grunted and his finger stopped on a line near the bottom. The line read: *David Murphy, Room 319, Congressional, The Park Casino— $1,000.* "Can't," he said. "Your name's on the list. You'll have to settle up your debts and get an okay from the sheriff before I can sell you a ticket anywhere."

Murph started to protest, but he didn't get very far. It was the law. In Saratoga, no one could leave town still owing money to a village merchant. The man behind the ticket window said city hall was one and one-half blocks east, just across Broadway. Then he went back to stamping a bunch of papers.

And Murph started walking. There were lions around the big clock on the tower of city hall. 3:00 P.M. E.R.'s people would be out looking for him by now. Murph took Broadway north, past Satchel Rags, and turned east on York Street, working his way back to the Congressional Hotel, hoping to bypass The Park Casino. He took his time and tried to sort this thing out.

What would Rainbow do?

The flask was empty again. Aziz left the clubhouse for a refill.

"Invitation still stands," Stavros said.

Rainbow dug into the paper sack of peanuts he had bought inside and cracked a shell. "Can't, Greek. Business, you know how it is. No point in trying to beat the casinos anyway."

"So just come for dinner. E.R. lays out a nice spread. And bring that Winslow dame along." Stavros leaned close. "She any good?"

"A gen'leman does not discush his women." Sloppy diction. But he didn't feel drunk. Just good. He tossed a peanut. It bounced off the brim of his panama.

Stavros put his feet on the chair opposite the bench. "Dancer tells me you paid two hundred to find that small-timer—what's his name?"

Rainbow's arm stopped in midtoss. "Drop it, Greek. It was a personal score."

"Yeah, sure. But how come you don't come to me to find this guy?"

Rainbow didn't answer. He fed a peanut into his frown.

"Well, anybody else you want a line on," Stavros said, "just tell the Greek. But stay clear of them punks. You got a reputation to think of." He lit a cigar, fondled it with his lips. "How's it look for a friend of mine to hustle some two-bit piece of shit?" He aimed his smoke at his shoes. "Never holed one out from the sand before. Felt real good when I hit, though. Sometimes you can tell, right? So, I figured it was gonna be close, but . . ."

The words kept coming, but Rainbow wasn't listening. The trees were shiny with light, the sky was getting dull. And by this time tomorrow, he would be rich. And free. No more pigeons to coax, no more payoffs to force. He held in the laugh. Maybe just one last hustle. On the Greek. He tossed the peanut high and slammed the back of his head into the clubhouse wall. The nut trickled to the deck.

"Quit doing that," Stavros said. "What are you—a juggler?"

Rainbow reached for the shell and tipped over the sack. Nuts the shape of lumpy figure-eights rolled on the wood. "Used to be able to throw one of these clear over a three-story building."

"Got to learn to hold on to them first." Stavros was laughing.

"Clear over, I tell you. Bet I still can."

The throaty laugh ended in a smirk. "Loaded peanut, right?"

Rainbow grinned. He tolerated the Greek's playful shove, but that laugh, that nagging sputter, made him want to spit toward the railing. He walked off the porch for a look at the roof. It was at least thirty feet high, and arched. It would do fine. "Make it a watermelon, then. Throw a watermelon. Clear over." He held out his hand. "Bet I can. Thirty grand. All or part."

Stavros kept laughing. He looked like a stuffed bird. He took the flask from Aziz and mumbled something to the big man, who trudged into the clubhouse. The Greek came off the porch grinning: "All."

A firm handshake. Rainbow draped his jacket over the rail, pushed back his hat. He was laughing. Maybe he was drunk after all. He opened the ball pouch on his golf bag, found cool, smooth skin inside. He pulled out the watermelon and gave it a hefting toss. Murph had found a good one.

Jet-black eyes went dead, hypnotized by the up-down motion of a sphere the size of a softball. "No fair," Stavros said. "It's got to be—"

"We said a watermelon, Greek." Still that laughter, there was no stopping it. Rainbow cranked into a baseball windup and let go a Walter Johnson fastball that shot over the roof. He sat next to his bag, slapped the dirt, and held his stomach to keep the laugh from ripping him apart.

Stavros was glaring at him. He snapped at Aziz when the big man brought a large green watermelon out of the clubhouse door. Then the

Greek marched around the corner toward the parking lot and his giant plodded after him.

Rainbow grabbed his golf bag and hurried to catch up. "Hey, c'mon Greek. Where's your sense of humor?"

There were four cars left in the parking lot. Stavros stopped short of his black limousine. From the back, he looked about to come unglued: thick wrists flapped, his wide body hinged off-center as he bent over with a laugh. He pointed to the edge of the lot where a gray sedan stood alone in the sun. The black chauffeur, uniform starched, stood with cap in hand, staring at the slimy chunks of red and green that slid down the hood of the car. "Perfect," Stavros said, his roar growing dark. "That's one of E.R.'s limos, the ones he uses to shuttle people to his club. That'll teach the Jew." He slid into his car, his gaze fixed on the chauffeur. "Poor nigger don't know whether to wipe it off or eat it."

Rainbow stood there, watching bits of shattered melon plop off the fenders.

"Hey, get in," Stavros said. "You wanna leave your clubs in the shack?"

With a nod, Rainbow got his .45 from the pouch and handed the bag to Aziz, who took it down to the caddy shack.

Stavros kept staring at the pistol in Rainbow's belt. "What's that on the handle there?"

"Tape."

"You any good with that thing?"

"Decent." Rainbow got in the car and closed the door. "But this ain't exactly Dodge City neither, now is it."

Stavros let out another laugh. "Hey, bring College with you tonight if you come. I'll fix it with E.R. He'll get a kick out of the kid." He slapped his knee. "I know a guy who's a *cinch* for fifty grand on this watermelon thing. Christ, we'll clean up."

Rainbow took the flask when it was offered. The Scotch burned his throat, but he kept drinking. With any luck, he would pass out and not have to listen to the Greek's stories or that coughing laugh. He let his head fall back against the seat, and stared at the smoke-stained ceiling. Somewhere along the line, Aziz must have come back because the engine was humming, the clouds were moving by, the tires were gliding over gravel. Rainbow shut his eyes and drained the flask.

28 ─────────────────────────────

With a soapy brush, Iris scrubbed her swimsuit. But that musty smell remained. She had soaked in Dr. Talbert's mineral baths too long. Would the bitter odor ever wash out of the wool?

Would Rainbow ever forgive her for stealing his money?

Never.

"It ain't stealing," Horace had reminded her at the stables this morning. "Not the way you figured it. Damn if you ain't got my brains after all."

He was right, it wasn't stealing. Not back in Lexington, where she dreamed up the scheme to separate a lewd man from part of his inheritance. She couldn't go through with it then because she had been afraid. Of getting caught. In spite of Horace's protests—"Not a flaw in it anywheres, it's foolproof!"—she resisted. And lied to make it look like the lewd man's fault. Yet it wasn't stealing, it was simple banking. With Rainbow, it was different. It might look like simple banking, but it felt like stealing.

And he would never forgive her. He would hate her.

She could live without him, without any man. Rainbow promised her fences and desert winds that would bury her in dust. She yearned for miles of windswept shore on an island strong with trees, deserted but for the solitude of shells. She felt sorry for him, the way he looked at her, his touch. And she hated herself for the secrets she had let his hands discover. In some other city—on the dance floor downstairs—she could drift away and lose him in the music of the street. There would always be someone else. She would think of him now and then, and that would be his reward. Pack and leave, she told herself. There will always be—

Daddy . . .

A dark smile took her lips. Horace was such a little boy at heart, so vulnerable to his dreams, those simple longings of cowboy-pirate-kings. She would have to be the one to save him. No one else could.

And Rainbow would hate her forever.

Her hands trembled, her legs locked together. She dropped the scrub brush, left her suit in the tub, and went into the bedroom for her cigarettes. The light knocking at the door to the suite startled her. Had Rainbow forgotten his key? Or was it Horace, come to find out her decision? She walked out to the sitting room and opened the door a crack.

The old man in the hall looked ill. One hand ran back over slicked-down hair, the other played with a crumpled string tie. He stared at the room number and cleared his throat. "Rainbow here?"

There was the smell of liquor on his words, dried sweat on his clothes. Iris started to close the door. The man put his palm flat against the wood:

"You be his wife?"

She was held by the softness of his eyes, bleached blue like sky after rain. "You can leave a message for him at the front desk."

His smile was thin. He wouldn't let her shut the door. "Prefer to leave it with you, ma'am. Probably told you all about me, didn't he. Cal Robinson." His bow seemed more like a lean. Nodding to himself, he peered into the suite. "Got any kids yet?"

Her hands lost the feel of the door, and when she got the words out, her voice sounded hollow. "I'll tell him you came by."

The old man drew back his hand. "You tell him Old Cal needs to see him. He knows where he can find me." Another nod and he stepped away. That thin smile again. "I thank you, ma'am." He got halfway to the bench in the hall before he stopped. Feet were thumping up the stairs.

Rainbow?

Murph. He walked past the old man and came to the door. "He back yet?"

Iris shook her head. The old man was watching; he sat on the bench.

"I got to see him," Murph said. "They won't let me out of town and I don't know what to do." He looked ready to explode. She opened the door but he turned away. "I got to pack and get ready. Could you

have him come over soon as he gets back? Tell him it's real urgent."
And before she could ask what was wrong, Murph marched down the
hall and into his room.

The old man just sat there, rubbing his hand back and forth over
the wooden armrest. Staring at her. Was this the dead man Rainbow
was searching for? Iris fought his gaze and shut the door, throwing
closed the dead bolt. In the bathroom, she began scrubbing her swimsuit again. It was cold and sticky. The brush felt hard, like the iron
currycomb she had used on Old Smoke this morning. Something about
that old man in the hall—his eyes?—made her hope she would never
have to face him again.

Got any kids yet?

She turned on the hot-water tap, and while soapy bubbles snarled
down the bathtub drain, she held her swimsuit and scrubbed and
scrubbed.

Someone had been in 319. Clothes were strewn on the floor, suitcases
were lying open on the bed. All the dresser drawers were out and
turned upside down by the bathroom door. A dull ache began
pounding in Murph's jaw. He locked and bolted the door to the hall.
His kidneys hurt. If he didn't get into that bathroom in a hurry, he
was going to piss in his pants. He unbuttoned his fly and stepped over
his clothes.

The big man with the birthmark on his chin was standing next to
the toilet. Smiling.

Murph ran for the room door, but before he could get his key into
the lock or his hand on the bolt, he was being lifted off the floor and
flung backward. He landed on the dresser drawers. The wood cracked
under his weight, sharp edges dug into his side. He rolled into the
bed. And wet his pants.

"Four o'clock, Murphy," the big man said. "You're a little late with
your payment, ain't you." Picking at his birthmark, he moved closer,
planting his feet on all those new clothes. "And I don't find nothing
worth taking here, kid. So what do we plan to do about settling up?"

Murph couldn't speak. Urine was soaking his crotch, running down
his legs.

"You got the cash—I hope." The big man leaned against the wall
and when Murph nodded, he smiled back. "Good. Let's get it."

There was no way past the man to the door, no way to get out,
nothing to hit him with. He probably had a gun on him anyway. Or a
knife. And he'd use it. Murph nodded again and tried to get to his
feet. He was going downstairs, get his bankroll out of the hotel safe,

pay the man, and come back and take a bath. One thousand dollars—plus interest. On a rigged table. It wasn't fair. On his walk he had decided to tell Rainbow and find out what to do. Rainbow would know. He might even be able to fix it with the Greek or E.R. But now Murph had to pay first and try to get his money back later. He gritted his teeth and pushed against the bed to stand.

Then he saw the open window and the rope fire escape hanging off the sash. A way out. If the big man did have a knife, Murph could still get to the ground before the rope was cut. But it was only $1,000 plus $60 interest. He had it. Why not pay?

Why pay a thief and thank him for robbing you?

"That's real smart, Murphy," the big man was saying. "Sorry about your jaw. Don't look so bad, though. You was lucky. Tag told me to make sure you got the message, understand? Lot of guys heard you tell him off last night. Bad for business. So it ain't the grand, kid. E.R.'d like it if you was to apologize and pay off nice. In front of his patrons, to give them the right idea, see?" When he smiled, the birthmark stretched across his chin. "And that's what we're gonna do now. You and me."

Murph wasn't about to let anyone, not even Efrem Roze, use him as an example. Not with money that was as good as stolen from him. Not with piss all over his pants. He was going out that window, down three short stories, and back to the golf course to find Rainbow and the .45 Colt. "Okay," he said. He took a step, grabbed the Shakespeare book from the dresser, hurled it at the big man, then spun toward the window. And ran.

One leg over the sill, he untied the string on the laundry bag. The bag fell away, the rope inside uncoiled toward the ground.

And the big man had a handful of Murph's jacket. "Little shit-ass, teach you to—"

Murph batted the arm. His new jacket ripped. He fought his way out the window. But couldn't reach the rope. The big man still had hold of enough sleeve to swing Murph sideways. He kicked for it with his feet. That only made things worse: he was hanging there, too far from the rope to grab it, held above the ground by the torn sleeve. He clawed for the sill. And slipped out of the sleeve like a greased rod.

Falling.

No screams. No way to get enough air to scream. Red bricks blurring pink, sky deepening gray, the flash of sunlight off a passing window, then another. The long, thin branch of a tree, like a waving arm. Then ground. Hip-first. *Burning.* Bounce. *Turning . . .*

Snap.

Something exploded inside his ears: the *clap* of a thousand doors all slammed at once. Then the softest sound he had ever heard, like hail against a snowy roof: *pop—pop—pop*. And somewhere, far away, a woman's wail rode the same gentle wind that sucked him into deep blue silence.

Rainbow hurried up the stairs, taking two steps at a time, burping whiskey-breath and slapping his thigh with the envelope of money. The Greek's money: $30,000. First stop—319. Murph was going to get half this time, not his usual twenty percent. The kid had earned it. That watermelon was perfect. This $15,000 would square things. No more talk about who owed what to whom.

And Old Cal was sitting on the bench, twirling that string tie around his finger.

Rainbow lost his grin and tried to stop before he got through the doorway to the hall. But he was moving too fast. He kept going, almost running now, reaching for his room key. The old man was up, something was about to come out of his mouth: *Junior?*

The door to 319 opened and a big man with broad shoulders and a fedora pulled down tight on his head rushed out to the hall, slamming the door and moving toward the back stairs.

Rainbow skidded to a stop in front of 325, spun toward the big man, and reached for his .45. "Hey, what're you doing in there?"

The big man drove his fist into the pit of Rainbow's stomach, then ran to the hall door and down the back stairs. Doubling over with pain, Rainbow clutched his gut. His panama fell at his feet, the envelope tumbled to the carpet, spinning a trail of green paper. His .45 banged the floor. And he was on his knees, gasping for air.

"Jesus!" Old Cal said, picking up the money. "Must be twenty grand here!"

Rainbow grabbed his pistol and staggered to Murph's door, yanking it open, leveling the .45 at the open window. The room was littered with clothes, broken bureau drawers, and the big book was lying open on the floor, its thin pages fluttering in the breeze. But there was no one inside.

"Maybe twenty-five!" Old Cal had most of the money off the rug and cradled against his chest. "Say, that wife of yours is a real looker."

Shutting the door with his foot, Rainbow walked back and picked up his hat, then took his cash from the old man. "Go down and get the room clerk up here. See that he locks this room."

"What about that young fellah?"

"He has his own key," Rainbow said. The old bastard must have been sitting out here for most of the day, watching Murph and Iris go in and out. "And hurry it up."

"Yeah, but—"

"Damn you. *Move!*" Rainbow shoved him. Old Cal shuffled to the stairs, shaking his head, rubbing a hand against his side. The big man who had been in 319 must have wanted something in particular: he didn't look like a plain thief. A nightclub bouncer? And there was something peculiar about his face—something red around the mouth. Rainbow pushed down the back steps, out the rear door.

Sunlight hid behind trees. Several sets of footprints led away from the walk. Three paths snaked through the park like the graceful cuts of an ice skater. He felt the dirt for warmth. Pearlie could have tracked the scent. For a moment, he thought to slap his thigh and call the memory to his side.

But a siren spoiled the air. A red and blue ambulance was speeding up the drive. Drawn by the sound and motion, he walked to the front of the hotel, then around to the other side where a ring of weaving heads had gathered. He peered over the hats. A flaccid arm was lying still on a mane of red hair.

He squeezed through the crowd and knelt beside the body. Turned sideways, the swollen jaw looked too large. The small nose and smooth cheek were reddish brown. Those bangs seemed pointed and sharp, but the hair was soft to the touch. And fine, like thread. Only the bottoms of the irises were showing: the eyes were almost solid white. Blood trickled out an ear into a pool that had formed near an arm which wore only half a sleeve. The pants were soaked with urine. Murph wasn't breathing.

Small wheels squeaked over the grass. Two men in white moved Rainbow back, then felt the kid's wrist for a pulse. Murph's neck turned side to side in one of the men's hands. They lifted him. His arms kept sliding off the stretcher.

"Anybody know this fellow?" A policeman took out a pad and pencil and stared up at the hotel. "Guess he thought he could fly."

The nervous laughter in the crowd died like a wood fire in drizzling rain. Rainbow breathed in the silence:

"David Murphy."

A gray blanket slid over Murph's face. The stretcher rolled away, wheels crying under the strain.

"Did you see it, sir?" The policeman readied his pencil.

Red and blue doors closed. The engine fired. The ambulance moved down the drive. Not even a siren now, just a slow crawl out to traffic.

"I didn't see it." Rainbow rubbed his stomach, stuffed his money in his jacket. The ambulance got lost behind the giant elms on Broadway.

"They do crazy things up here, playing games of every sort." The policeman cleared his throat and put his pad away. "Probably fancied himself a regular Douglas Fairbanks, swinging on ropes. It's the same every racing season."

The rope outside the open third-floor window was turning in the breeze. Rainbow swallowed a rancid taste. "How do I claim his body?"

That pad came out again. "Any relation to the deceased, are you?"

". . . Yes . . ."

The policeman asked for a name and Rainbow gave him one. Then came an official-sounding monotone about the coroner's office and filling out forms. There was no sign of Old Cal in the maze of unfamiliar faces. No surprise. The old bastard probably ran down the steps and back into his bottle. Rainbow stared at the blood on the grass while the policeman strode into the hotel and the crowd dispersed in whispers. A janitor threw a bucket of water down, then swept the stains with a long-handled broom. Where the grass met the cement walk, a small lake formed: slivers of flesh and strands of hair floated on the surface. A final swish of the broom—rain on the lake— then the janitor carried his bucket back behind the bushes.

Rainbow went through the lobby, up the stairs. A few people hovered around the desk clerk by the door to 319. Near the window inside, the policeman was scribbling on his pad: "It'll all be written down in a proper inventory, Mr. Roberts." He held up the pad as a guarantee. "Quite a mess, though."

Everything was in full view. Nothing private.

Rainbow grabbed a new dark suit from the floor, a pair of new shoes from the closet, underwear and a white shirt and tie from the broken bureau drawers. "Write down I took these to bury him in." He glared at the policeman, then brushed past the clerk into the hall. Inside his suite, he set the clothes on the chair nearest the door.

"Rainbow?" Her voice seemed far away. "There was someone here to see you. A Cal Robinson." Iris came out of the bedroom and stopped by the phone. "And Murph. He said it was urgent. He looked upset. . . ."

She kept talking, but he didn't hear. He walked by her into the bathroom and shut the door. A black swimsuit lay flat in the tub. A wet scrub brush and her canvas bag stood beside the washbasin. He locked the door, put his hat on the sink, raised the toilet seat. And stood there, waiting. When the vomit was about to come up, he turned the bath taps on full blast and got on his knees and put his head to the mouth of the bowl.

The dull echo of tumbling water leaked through the walls. Iris took one last drag, then crushed out her cigarette. The nerve of him, making her feel as though she didn't exist, as if what she had to say didn't matter! Down below, the early glow from the lobby leaned toward a stand of quickening trees, and over Broadway a sheet of light struggled to remain aloft under the brown weight of dusk. Turning her back to the window, she rubbed the shiver from her arms. Her mind ran cold with shouts, each step became a test of balance. She sat on the couch, opened her compact, steadying the little mirror and forcing herself to concentrate on hair, eyebrows, rouge—any item she could list, then draw a line through. A tightness spread across her head, as if those inner screams had settled into her skin. The compact snapped together in a sandwich of mother of pearl. She was going to leave him. Now. Without packing or saying good-bye. *Escape.*

The doorknob seemed to stare back, frozen in place, and she couldn't rise to challenge it. Rainbow didn't care about her. About anything. His navy blue suit, which he had probably won gambling, was in a heap on the chair: shoes overturned on the floor, tie and shirt draped over the armrest. He treated all objects the same way. Even people.

She put her compact in her purse and carried it to the door. The knob was easy to turn. She walked out.

The bellman who was terrible with names was standing near the staircase. When he saw Iris, he lowered his head and started down to the lobby. The desk clerk and a policeman came out of 319, locked the door, and went toward the stairs. Iris didn't want to know what they had been doing in Murph's room. She was afraid to ask.

She asked.

The policeman told her. Then the desk clerk told her. Then both men told her again. And each time, it was the same: the young man had fallen to his death, the victim of his own recklessness. Murph was dead.

The desk clerk said, "Very sorry about your cousin, ma'am," and led the policeman down the stairs. The hall was empty. And too quiet.

She sat on the bench, wanting to cry, but unable to feel the least bit of sadness. Rainbow must have felt the same way. No wonder he hadn't been able to hear what she had to say: he had needed to be alone with his grief. Just as she had so many years ago when Horace told her that her mother had gone away and would never be back. Iris walked back inside the suite and locked the door. The water in the bathroom had stopped running, the walls were silent. Was he still here?

The toilet flushed. Several times. The sound reassured her. She sat on the couch, its soft cushions swelling around her like a sea of sponge. A glance at her watch: long minutes. She took the navy blue suit into the bedroom, hung it in the closet. On her way back for the rest of the clothes, the bathroom door opened. Rainbow came out, his face drawn and as pale as his white jacket, his eyes reddened and wet. He started for the phone in the main room. Cutting him off at the doorway, she slid into his arms, hugging him, and breaking into tears.

29

Head still, hand quiet on the arm of the chair, Rainbow kept his gaze low, wondering why he had bothered to talk to her about Murph. Words trickled out, punctuated by long silences, and when he had finished, he remembered only thoughts unsaid, the things he could never teach Murph, the spaces never filled.

She was silent for a long moment, then: "He said they wouldn't let him leave town. That it was urgent he talk to you. I can't believe he would do something so foolish as hanging on a rope when he was so upset."

He wasn't going to tell her about the big man with the red spot on his face.

"It doesn't have anything to do with that man," she said. ". . . Does it?"

His stomach muscles stiffened against the ache of wounded flesh. "What man?"

"The man who was here this afternoon. Cal Robinson."

Wrong man. His body sagged, he wanted to sit, to lie down and pull her close, consume her; himself. Instead, he shook his head and stared at the rug.

She walked to the couch, looked at the bedroom doorway, and turned. "I hung your suit in the hall closet. . . ."

". . . His suit. For burying in." Rainbow picked the tie and the shirt off the floor. "Never even got to wear it once. . . ."

She came back to him and squeezed his head to her breast. The scent of her clothes lay secret on her skin. She was crying again, but softly. "He was so much like you."

The molding around the ceiling was painted gold to mask the natural color of the wood. "Not anything like me," he said and he stood and went to the phone. "I got to make a call, so . . ."

"Why don't you let me call Horace. You rest."

"Not Horace." He carried the phone through the bedroom doorway. Then he stopped and turned. He didn't have to ask. The way she was standing, her eyes hidden, a cape of guilt about her shoulders—that was enough. She knew. The little bastard must have told her when he phoned this morning. She had known all that time. "What sort of a game is this?"

She didn't answer, she stared out the window.

"All right," he said, "don't tell me. But you can bet Horace will."

Still no answer. She was probably angry at him, disgusted with him, wondering how she could go to bed with anyone who would stoop low enough to fix a horse race. But she didn't look angry. She looked sad.

He toyed with the telephone cord. "It's what's best, Iris. For all of us. Including your father."

"I don't want to talk about it. Not now." She was definitely angry, yet trying to hide it.

"If it suits you," he said, "believe that I'm doing it just for the money. Only—don't ask me to apologize."

He watched as a tear started down her cheek. He had lost her. The ring box in his jacket pocket was no more than a lump now. He pulled the phone cord back behind him and began closing the bedroom door.

"I want you to call off the fix," she said. "For me."

He felt like laughing, but nothing came out.

"Then I'm going to be part of it," she said. "To make sure no one cheats you."

He found the laugh. "I don't want you involved."

"I'm already involved." It was almost a shout. But her eyes softened and filled with night. "I only want to help. Please . . ." A whisper: ". . . don't shut me out."

It felt all wrong, yet he couldn't say no. So he lied. "Might be I'll call it off. Don't know if I got it in me after what happened with Murph."

She shook her head as if she didn't know she was doing it. "You won't call it off. Not for anyone."

He couldn't meet her stare. She had made him feel small and heartless. There was no point to arguing with her: she saw him too clearly. He gripped the phone like a club. "I can't change."

More silence. He didn't have the energy to close the door or turn away. He stood there, waiting for her to chip more pieces off him and scatter them at his feet.

She glanced at the lights out the window. "Will you bury him here?"

"Not on your life." A flood of details took him by surprise: stacks of forms, each one with an X at the bottom; dingy rooms where stone-skinned faces lay flat on slabs of steel; a coffin shiny with wax; a slow train to a small station, a car up a road to a country graveyard. "Hot Springs," he said. "Leave as soon as we can. Right after the race."

"If you did want to call it off," she was rubbing her arms as though trying to get warm, "I'm sure Horace would agree."

"Horace will do exactly what I tell him to," he said.

"I just meant that . . ." She glanced at him, but her gaze fell to the carpet. "Don't you have enough money already?"

It had been a mistake to let her see the bankroll. He touched the $30,000 in his breast pocket and made a note to get Murph's cash out of the vault first thing in the morning after seeing the coroner and signing for personal effects, which had to include the safety-deposit-box key. "I got money," he said, reaching for the doorknob. "Since he already told you about everything, you might as well join us for dinner."

"Are you sure you want me to?"

"Got to eat, don't you?" He shut the door. Taking the phone to the bed, he called the United States Hotel and waited for Stavros the Greek to come on the line.

"Hey, I was just thinking about you," Stavros said. "I know *three* guys we can pull that watermelon thing on. Christ, we'll clear a couple hundred grand! You about ready to go to E.R.'s? I can pick you up."

"Can't, Greek . . ."

"Okay, so join us at The Park later. Upstairs. In the private rooms."

"Greek, I need a favor."

"Sure," Stavros said. "You got it."

Rainbow's head felt heavy, his feet sore. He laid his .45 on the bedspread and ran a finger over the long barrel. "Murph's dead. Shoved out his window at the hotel here." He tried to swallow. "I want the bastard who did it. For myself."

"Jesus . . . You see it?"

"I saw it." Rainbow picked up the gun and sighted out the window. "Big guy. Looked like a thug. A bouncer maybe. Something wrong with his chin, it looked red, like a scab."

"Anybody else see it?" Stavros said. "The cops?"

"Just me. And I want it kept private. I'll pay what I have to, but I want this guy found. And believe me—I'll know him when I see him."

There was nothing from the other end. Stavros was probably smoking his cigar and giving himself a manicure. The longer the silence continued, the more Rainbow thought that he had made another mistake by asking the Greek to help.

"It's good you came to me," Stavros said, his voice laced with a sigh. "If there's anything, I'll have it by tomorrow. My word on that."

". . . Thanks, Greek, I—"

"Yeah, hey—sure. Look, if I don't see you tonight, I'm at the track around six-thirty in the morning. We can meet for breakfast."

"Breakfast, at the track?"

"Right. And look, I'm sorry about College. Real nice kid. . . ."

A quick good-bye and the line filled with static. Rainbow left the phone on the floor, got out of his clothes, and went into the bathroom for a shower. No hot water. He had used it up earlier, covering the sound of his heaving. In the mirror, he studied the red welt in the center of his stomach. The stickiness in the creases in his skin didn't leave when he splashed himself with water from the washbasin and toweled dry. At the dresser in the bedroom, he took a clean pair of shorts from the top dresser. With that first step into clothing, he felt taller, and his nakedness disappeared piece by piece until he recognized the jigsaw puzzle in the mirror. He wasn't sure he liked what he saw. He was going to kill a man in Saratoga after all. And this time, he knew he could pull the trigger. Fitting the .45 into his belt, he buttoned his jacket and went out to take Iris down to dinner.

It was a stalemate. The maître d' kept his back to the line of people that was bunched up from the middle of the lobby to the fat velvet rope across the dining-room doorway. Angry whispers stirred in the line, but the maître d' refused to turn around.

Rainbow stepped over the rope.

The maître d' faced around quickly. "Sir, you'll have to wait in line like everyone else."

"Don't mind us." Rainbow unhooked the gold rope and let Iris through, then led her past the outer row of tables. Near the dance floor, he glanced back at the entrance: the maître d' struggled to reattach the rope against the press of outraged faces.

Iris stopped by a busboy's cart. "Why didn't you simply tell him we were meeting someone who was already inside?"

"I don't owe him an explanation for what I do," Rainbow said. The room was enormous. Suspended by a dusty cable, a massive chandelier tossed facets of crystal white over smoky noise and, as if spawned by this giant, miniature chandeliers patterned the rafters in geometric precision. Candles on each table, breezy shadows on every face, waiters stretching and sidestepping each other while balancing heavy trays. Near the windows on the far side, Horace was standing on a chair, waving a napkin like a flag of surrender. Rainbow waved back. Once past the throng of dancers, he could use the big chandelier as a landmark to prevent getting lost. "Hang on to my jacket," he said and when she gripped his coattails, he started the busboy's cart moving, opening a swath on the dance floor.

Between the bobbing heads and dipping shoulders flashed the movement of a slide trombone. A drumstick seemed to hammer down on dancers' heads, releasing a cymbal chime with every stroke. The melody was of another era, one of those songs that had become a standard in spite of itself and was destined to stay around forever. But tonight, it didn't have a chance against all the room noise.

He negotiated the aisles past a man in a blue jacket who announced that he wasn't going to pay $10.50 for the wrong dinner. The music stopped, applause scattered. A procession of dancers tramping across a major intersection momentarily forced Rainbow to wait, but before the woman in pink could finish asking him why her dinner was so late, he had the cart up to full speed again, challenging the spangled gowns and silk suits with his arsenal of asparagus stems in white sauce, cups of unfinished coffee, the sticky crumble of chocolate cake. Waiters jumped aside, captains glanced in every direction but his, diners slid their chairs in close to their tables. He fought the urge to pound a serving spoon on the metal plate covers, and parked the cart near the table.

"What kept you?" Horace dropped his napkin and stepped down from the chair. "Been waiting half an hour." He sent the cart rolling up the aisle. "Damn trains just brought in the rest of these tourists. No room to breathe no more." Behind him came a muffled crash. The cart was lying on its side amid a cluster of tables, leaking brown fluid and half-eaten food. "Nothing's wrong is it?" His bald head was a mass of wrinkles. "You said six, right?"

Iris sat and took off her gloves. Still standing, Rainbow watched a busboy right the cart and scoop up the debris. "Why did you tell her about our business, Horace?"

Weathered lines stretched cold across the little man's face. "Me? I thought—"

"It doesn't matter," Iris said. "Now both of you stop this. And sit down. Like gentlemen."

Horace threw his squint like a punch, but his hands were trembling, weak hands suddenly, spotted yellow-brown and afraid to show anger. He sat. "It's just as well, I guess. Never could keep her from finding out what she wanted to know, anyways."

A raucous drum roll launched the band into another song. Rainbow took the chair beside Iris. From the envelope in his pocket, he counted out $5,000 and slapped the money down. "This should take care of the jocks."

Horace studied the cash. "Did she say anything to you about how we might—"

"I want you to call it off," she said.

Rainbow draped an arm over the back of her chair. "Thought we settled all this, Iris."

She glared at Horace. "I don't want any part of your kind of fix."

"Only kind of fix there is." Horace covered the money with his napkin and grinned at Rainbow. "Don't know what gets into her sometimes."

Her lips drew tight. "His partner, a young boy—you never met him. He killed himself this afternoon."

The taste in Rainbow's mouth was flat and bitter; he couldn't spit it out. When it was time, when he had taken care of things, she would know the truth about how the kid had died.

"Too bad," Horace said. "But if Rainbow here still wants to go through with the race, I don't see how we got a right to—"

"Damn you both!" She smacked the table with her purse. "Don't you care about anything except your silly games? He was only nineteen."

"Eighteen," Rainbow said, unable to look away from the steady flame of the candle before him. Everything was wrong: the crowd, the music—her. He gripped the ring box in his pocket; it felt cold and square, the curve of the lid no longer fit his palm. He wanted to leave both of them sitting here. But there was noplace to go, not even Saint Louis anymore if Curtis had left. From behind, someone called out his name. The little box slid down into his pocket well, his hand came out empty. He stood.

"Saw you push that cart." Taylor North made it a firm handshake, grinning and nodding toward the dance floor. "The wife and I are right over there. Plenty of room. And hello there, young lady. Didn't know you two were acquainted."

Iris kept her stare on the table. "Go away."

Rainbow cleared his throat. "We're right in the middle of something, Mr. North. Maybe we could drop by later on."

The banker's smile was tentative, his gaze drifted to the center of the table. "Fine. And please—bring your guests." He walked back down the aisle.

"Why'd you have to act like that for?" Rainbow said, bending to his seat.

She rummaged through her purse, then dropped it on the table. "I would like a cigarette."

Rainbow put a hand on hers. "Stop being this way."

"It's the way I am." She pulled free, folded her arms, and glared at him. "How should I act? The way *you* want me to?"

Horace peeked around the candle. "Settle down here, Iris."

"Don't you tell me what to do." She stepped to the next table. The man in the white dinner jacket was surprised, but he gave her a cigarette and a light. She came back to her chair and aimed her smoke at Horace. The candle flame blew out.

The bald head shook solemnly. "Real ladylike. . . ."

"There's nothing wrong with it." A little smoke cloud hung above her like a cartoon caption. "Stop showing your age."

Horace glanced about the room, hunting for stares of disapproval. He found a lot of them. "She gets into one of her moods and . . ." More headshakes.

"Maybe she'll feel better after something to eat." Rainbow grabbed the arm of a passing waiter and stuffed a fifty-dollar bill into his hand: "I want three dinners. Whatever's ready. And keep the change."

Pocketing the cash, the waiter scurried away. Iris kept taking deep drags off the cigarette. Rainbow tried to ignore her. He fired questions at Horace. The old jockey had the right answers—all he needed was money to pay the riders, and he was jamming that inside his suit.

"Better get on my horse," he said. "Can't be walking around with so much on me. This town gets mean when it wants to."

"Have some dinner anyway," Rainbow said.

"Nah, this place is a madhouse. I'll stash this so we got it handy. The jocks'll want their share before the race."

"I'll be at the track early," Rainbow told him. "For a total look around. Have those jocks ready to talk to me."

"No need for that. Might draw too much attention." Horace managed a grin. "Whatever you say, Rainbow." He reached for Iris's hand, but she pulled it away. "If you want to talk to me about anything," he said, "I'll be having coffee at Ford's most of the night." She didn't look at him. He shook hands with Rainbow and walked toward the entrance, squeezing out of sight among tall bodies.

The waiter brought a tray to the table. Three platters of chicken.

Not once did he look up from the gold-rimmed dishes. Finished, he hurried off as if he didn't want to witness the first bite.

The band stopped playing. The room noises grew louder, closing in all around. Iris put her cigarette out in her mashed potatoes. "Don't you have enough money for your—orange groves?"

Only a whisper, yet so devoid of hope that it split the air above Rainbow's head like a thunderclap. He felt ashamed of that simple dream. And vulnerable. He cut into the chicken.

With her fork, she pushed peas across her plate. "It seems like such a risk. What if something went wrong and you—lost?"

"I can always build a new bankroll," he said. "Money's the easiest thing in the world to replace." The chicken tasted dry. At least it was hot. He guided his knife with secret anger: would she ever understand—he was doing this for her and that father of hers as much as for himself. "Besides, you can trust Horace. Now stop worrying over something you don't know anything about."

"I'm worried about *you*," she said.

On the downbeat, he began a tight box-pattern, hoping the shuffle would pass for a fox-trot. "We'll only stay a few minutes with them,"—*dip*—"I want to get to bed early."—*two, three, four*.

She pressed against him like an extra layer of skin. The anger had gone out of her, but a tension remained. He didn't blame her for being angry or worried. The fix could backfire: they could get caught.

And no matter how well he explained it, she wouldn't understand that Horace was their rightful edge. That kind of logic wasn't in her makeup. He started to say "Don't worry," but what came out was "I don't hate people."

Her head popped back. ". . . What?"

"Nothing." He hid behind her hair and offered silent thanks to the band: *Keep it loud. Loud is better.* Rising within him like a wellspring was the sudden shock of contradiction: tomorrow he would walk away from the world of gambling—the noise, the elbows, the bustle—and he was never coming back. He wasn't sure he could do it. Even with Iris at his side, it would be lonely: Curtis had vanished, Murph was dead. And if she packed up and left one day, he would have nothing. Again. Such a risk. A true gamble. No way to hedge the odds. And he still had a man to kill. . . .

"Rainbow!" Iris wriggled free and covered her embarrassment with applause. The band had stopped playing.

His hands went together, but there was no strength to his clap. He led her across the floor to a table down front.

Taylor North was on his feet and smiling. "We were just remarking what a fine couple you two make." He introduced the gray-haired woman at his side as his wife. The jewel lady. He must have married her for her money. "Grace and Iris are old friends," he said. Grace didn't act like anyone's friend. She nodded carefully, afraid of sudden movements: on her head was a diamond tiara and in the center of it sat an emerald the size of a nickel, glittering like a third eye among the weeds of hair. She must have emptied her vault box for tonight. She could barely sit up straight for all those jewels.

"Iris, why didn't you tell me you were coming to Saratoga," Grace said. Her pout was lopsided. "I feel absolutely crushed not knowing."

Iris whispered in her ear, then sat beside her. "It was a secret."

"Oh, I see, yes, of course!" Grace's smile was lopsided, too. "And does your clan come here every season, Mr. Roberts?"

Iris was grinning. Rainbow adjusted his tie. "Just the summers, ma'am."

Grace touched Iris's hand. "How charming. No, I meant—the race season!"

"He knows what you meant, Grace." North took a flask from his hip. "It was a joke. *He* has a sense of humor. . . . Drink?"

"No, thanks," Rainbow told him. "We can't stay but a minute."

North swigged whiskey. "Will Broder's still furious you aced him out of all that money."

Rainbow grinned. "Old Will never did like losing anything."

"But he's afraid to ask me for it." North laughed, took another swig, then put his flask away. "Now, the arrangement I have in mind for our partnership would guarantee you the autonomy you've been looking for. Murph, too."

Rainbow's chair felt like a brace. Unsettled stares fed the silence. He pushed back from the table. "Thought this was gonna be a social visit."

"Now don't misunderstand, my boy." North's eyes flattened into slits, as if he meant to reduce what he saw to a more acceptable size. "I've given this a great deal of thought. Perhaps we could meet later and talk it out by ourselves."

"No point to it." Rainbow got up and took Iris by the hand. "It's just a game to you, a little sport to pick up some extra pocket money. But for me, it's how I live. And I'm long through being told how to do it."

North began to protest, but his wife cut him off. "Taylor," she said. "Mr. Roberts appears to have his mind made up. It's so nice these days to meet a man with *definite* plans." The emerald eye swung toward Iris. "Is he always this forceful, my dear?" The answer Grace got was a thin smile. She offered her hand. "I'm sure you'll succeed, Mr. Roberts. Don't let my husband's greed stand in your way."

The rings on her fingers felt cold. Rainbow mumbled "Good night," and led Iris along the edge of the dance floor to the near wall, then past the maître d', who frowned as he unhooked the velvet rope.

In the lobby, a man was slamming his fist on the front desk. "I tell you they have a *dog* in their room! I can hear it!"

"No dogs," the clerk said. "We don't allow them in the hotel."

"How on earth do you expect me to get any sleep with that stupid yapping going on all night?"

"Why don't you shoot him," Rainbow said, throwing a quick salute to the man at the desk and moving toward the staircase. He swallowed his laugh. "It's a madhouse, all right. Think you could be all packed by noon? I want to leave as soon after the race as we can."

Iris let out a sigh and nodded.

"And maybe you'll have to go on ahead without me for a couple of days," he said. "Only so I can be sure about making arrangements for Murph."

She stopped at the stairs and held her purse to her chest.

"Something wrong?" he said.

"Just tired."

He put his arm around her. "What was all that nonsense back there about my clan?"

"I told Grace you brought me here to meet your family."

He laughed to cover the shiver running up his spine. "I get real worried about that brain of yours sometimes."

". . . Me, too," she said.

He squeezed her waist and followed the mitered corners of the banister up to the third floor.

Where someone was sitting on the bench in the hall. A man. Body speckled in shadows. No face. Something shiny in his hands. Waiting . . .

30

Rainbow stopped short. Guiding Iris behind him, he reached for his .45.

The man rose from the bench. He was small. And thin. Lots of hair. Two fast steps, a little bow, and the wall lamp lit his face. Olive skin. Haunted eyes. The shiny thing in his hand was a trumpet. "We talk!" The urgency in Angelo Batori's voice made his request sound like an order.

Rainbow let go of his pistol and led Iris to the suite. "It's late."

"Not late." The little cook inched into shadows again. "We talk!"

"I'll be right in." Rainbow closed the door behind her. "Look, Angelo, I'm tired. Can't this thing wait till—"

"No wait!" A glance over the shoulder, another guarded step. "We talk—inside."

Rainbow sighed and opened the door. With a last look down the hall, Angelo hobbled into the suite. "You lock," he said. Another order, now laced with fear.

Turning the key and throwing the dead bolt, Rainbow walked to the bedroom and spoke to the crack in the doorjamb. "I'll be out here for a couple of minutes, Iris." No answer. He opened the door. She was sitting on the bed, head bowed. "Just a few minutes," he said, "that's all." Her nod was shallow. He shut the door.

Angelo kept running his hand over the bell of the trumpet. "Murph, he no home. I knock. Is true what they say?"

The chair slat pressed into Rainbow's back: "Murph's dead." How many times had he said that today, how often had he whispered it secretly—stupidly? He was an old hand at it by now, able to walk down the street and announce it to strangers: *Murph's dead.* Back home—back there in East Tennessee, someone's home perhaps, but not his—they said "passed." *Old man Tandy passed a year ago Tuesday.* "Dead" was simpler. Dark in the box. Graceless. Without feeling. His style. And it worked. He didn't believe it for a second.

The little man's sigh was more like a growl, yet full of grief. He sat on the couch, his trumpet and cane at his side. "I know who does this."

Rainbow gripped the armrest. The welt on his stomach burned.

"Same ones shoot Tag," Angelo said. "My nephew. Runs the casino for this big-shot Roze. They say suicide, send flowers. Pay the grave." His head shook slowly. "But they kill."

It was the worst kind of silence: milky, in need of sorting out. Rainbow moved to the window. The Broadway sky hung like a band of gold over the trees, the glow from The Park Casino sliced through the woods. "I'm sorry about your nephew. The kid—Murph said you were close. Your whole family. . . ."

"How much it cost—you gun?" Angelo tossed a stack of bills on the table. The red band was still in place, but most of the $1,000 Rainbow had given him on the train was missing. He set his trumpet on top of the cash. "All this. You sell me you gun. Special, eh? No miss."

"Ever shoot one before?"

"You teach. Good shoot. Murph, he tell me."

"What do you need with my gun?" Rainbow said.

"For l'uccisore." Angelo's hands turned over in space as he groped for his meaning. "The man who kills." A long pause, then: "And for this Roze, too."

More silence. Dark hands stroked the trumpet. "I'm outside to hear. Tag they call the traitor. They shoot. Same man, when later he say Murphy dead out the window," his thumb jabbed his temple, "it make the sense, I remember. He sees you, too, this one. Use you name like he knows. Says to come find, take the money. But Roze, he no want."

Rainbow liked the idea of being hunted. It simplified things. "You saw this man?"

"Big like this." Angelo patted his shoulders, then touched his chin. "Spot here. The birth."

Right spot, right man. Rainbow rubbed his stomach. "And Murph owed him money?"

"To Roze, sì. One thousand. He sends this man to get." The little cook's voice cracked. "Church no bury the suicide." He nudged the money and his trumpet. "Take for you gun."

A measly $1,000. The kid had the cash, why hadn't he just paid it?

Why hadn't Rainbow taken the time to hear what was troubling Murph? The kid had tried to tell him about it. Too many *important* things to consider, too many selfish plans to make. Too busy to spare five minutes. A life. Wasted. Rainbow leaned against the windowsill. "You'd never get past his guards."

"They no look on me, they trust." No smile, yet the hint of pleasure lay behind those hollow eyes. "I shoot in the sleep."

"They'll kill you, Angelo. You know that."

"I do for Tag. And you Murph." The little man crossed himself and stared at his shoes. "How I tell his mother? Little Gina?"

Rainbow stuffed the cash into Angelo's breast pocket and handed him the trumpet. "It's suicide for you, too. No sale."

"I come because you, the boy like this." Two fingers went close together. "You no care! So I get the gun. Someplace. You see." Neck veins swollen with anger, Angelo turned to leave.

Rainbow spun him around. "Stop acting like an idiot. You can't—"

Angelo tore free. His trumpet banged into the wall. His face went suddenly sad. He picked up the horn, wiped it with his jacket.

The bedroom door swung open. Iris stepped out. "Rainbow . . . ?"

"What?" A verbal slap.

"I heard a noise like . . . I just wanted to see if you were all right."

"Of course I am. Now go back to bed."

The door closed softly. Angelo started past the couch. "I go now."

"I'm not through." Rainbow blocked the exit. "It won't work your way. Go back to Roze's house and do *nothing*. Leave this to me."

"You shoot?"

Rainbow opened the door. "I'll take care of it."

Angelo looked up and down the hall, then pulled his head back inside. "They kill you, too, no?"

"No." Rainbow put a hand on the small shoulder. "I'll find a way to square this. For both of us. You trust me, right?"

"Tonight, I listen," Angelo said. "When they dead, I trust." He glanced at the bulge on Rainbow's hip, then limped to the rear stairs, his feet hard on the carpet—not a servant's gait, not easy on the ears. Tucking his trumpet under his arm, he pushed through the door, leaving it to flap on spring hinges, each swing growing shorter until the wood fell silent once more.

Rainbow locked and bolted his door. The air was stale with unspent anger. *Too busy to spare five lousy minutes.* He felt like vomiting again. He walked into the bedroom wearing a tired face and sighing: "Long day." Iris was under the covers, reading. But her eyes followed him to the chair. He slipped out of his jacket, put it on the chair, hiding the .45 under the flap. "Good book?"

"You didn't have to snap at me," she said.

There was a knot in one of his shoelaces. "Sorry."

"In front of a—a *cook!*"

"It was business." He kicked off his other shoe. "You interrupted."

"I don't like being treated that way."

He unbuckled his belt. "And I don't like being interrupted. Now I said I'm sorry. About tomorrow. I want your bags at the station before we go to the track."

She smacked her book. "Why do you carry that stupid gun?"

He checked his surprise, stepped out of his pants, and draped them over the chair back.

"You don't have to hide it from me," she said.

He reached for the light switch on the wall.

"I'm not through yet." Leafing through the pages to find her place, she came up with a pencil. "Leave it on."

"It's late, Iris."

"Crossword puzzles relax me."

"Use the other room if you have to." He turned off the light and climbed into bed.

She turned on the lamp on the nightstand. "*This* shouldn't bother you."

"Iris . . ." He waited, but the light stayed on. ". . . *Off!*"

Sheets rustled, the mattress sagged, she huffed again. With a metallic *click*, the room went dark. And she snuggled next to him. "Talk to me."

"In the morning."

"For a few minutes. Please." She tugged his shoulder. "I get excited when you come to bed. Hold me a little."

He rolled onto his back. She rested her head on his chest, wrapped a leg around his, and let out one of her satisfied little groans. He pushed her hair out of his face and moved his arm out from under the pinch of her body.

"There's still time," she said.

"Not tonight."

"I mean—time to call off the fix."

"Don't start in on that again." But for some reason, he found himself stroking her hair. The sound of her breathing lulled his eyelids shut. Sleep no longer seemed so far away. "It's gonna be fine."

The telephone rang three times before he got to the receiver in the hall. It was Horace:

"We got problems, Rainbow. E.R.'s boys is all over the place. Checking with stewards, snooping around. They smell something."

"You didn't pay the jocks yet, did you?" Rainbow said.

"Of course not, I ain't no fool. It's like I told you. This is Saratoga! Roze don't let nobody get in his way."

"Leave E.R. to me." No curse could have tasted sweeter.

"Yeah, sure." In the background, plates knocked together: an all-night diner? "We're in the clear so far. But that'll all change when you lay down the cash. The books here is tapped straight to E.R. It's like tipping our hand. . . . Has Iris said anything to you about making the bets?"

Rainbow sat on the arm of the chair by the bedroom door. "Leave the bets to me, too."

"Listen to me, now," Horace told him. "We got to find a clean way of putting the money down, else they're gonna know for sure we got us a boat race here. This chance won't come around again. You know what it means to me."

"I know," Rainbow said, but he was thinking of himself.

Horace's voice quavered: "The books ain't gonna pass no heavy bets. Word's got to travel. And you being a friend of the Greek only makes it worse. While Saratoga runs, he belongs to E.R. You know that."

Rainbow hadn't known that. But it made sense. Everything in this village belonged to Efrem Roze. And Efrem Roze now belonged to Rainbow Roberts.

"Now, I ain't telling you how to do nothing," Horace was saying. "So don't blow up at me. But I figure we got to use somebody else to lay down the cash. Somebody we can trust. And who the bookies won't blink at. Otherwise, we might as well line up against the wall and let them shoot us."

Iris was sitting up in bed, making faces. Rainbow shook his head at her and turned away. "It's you or me, Horace. Either way, we got the same problem."

"That's how I seen it, too." The old jockey's whisper swelled excitedly. "Till I figured—Iris could do it! They'd never give her no trouble and—"

Rainbow lowered the phone, turned to study Iris for a moment, then put the receiver back to his ear.

Horace hadn't stopped for breath. "—and Jesus Christ, who'd suspect her? It's a natural."

"She don't know the first thing about it," Rainbow said.

"So teach her!" It was almost a yell. "She's got brains, you'd be surprised. And you can watch over things, make sure she does it right. Long as they see her and not you, we got us a clear ride."

Iris was on the edge of the bed, squinting as if she knew she was being discussed.

"I don't like it." Rainbow reached in and pulled the bedroom door shut.

"Hell, neither do I," Horace said. "But what choice we got?" His voice lost its strength. "If word gets out I been in on this, no track worth a damn'll ever touch me. I ain't ready to head south and train swaybacks at no damn gator ranch like Hialeah. And that's the *best* what could happen to me!"

"Nobody's gonna finger you, Horace. No matter what happens."

"You ain't seen what E.R. does when somebody crosses him."

The little silence hurt. Rainbow dug his toes into the rug.

"I got no way to make a quick bundle like you can," Horace said. "Takes me fourteen hours a day just to clear rent and board. And if I ain't allowed on the big tracks, I'm better off shining shoes with niggers."

Rainbow wound the phone cord around his hand. "Want to call it off?"

Horace breathed into the phone. "You know better than that. I'm telling you what it's like around here, so you know what we're up against. Talk to her, that's all I'm asking."

"I'll be by at dawn. Have the jocks ready." Rainbow hung up and went back into the bedroom.

The nightstand lamp was on. Iris had her book open. "Anything the matter?"

"Your trainer's got cold feet."

She put the pencil down. "Are you—calling it off?"

He slid under the covers. "He trains a bunch of nags for a stable that's gone bust, and he's worried about wrecking his career for Chrissake. Excuse the goddamn French."

The book slapped shut. "You don't have to belittle him."

He got out of bed and grabbed his pants. "I'm gonna take a little walk."

"I thought you were tired."

The belt buckle gave him trouble. "What I am is tired of being talked out of what I know is right. By a pack of amateurs!" He jammed his feet into his shoes, pulled on his shirt.

"Horace is no amateur," she said.

"Well he thinks like one." He flung the tie around his neck and slid the .45 into his belt. "No wonder he's on the outs. Afraid of his own shadow."

"He's been through a lot, Rainbow."

He grabbed his jacket and started for the door. "Tell him to join the club."

"You don't understand. He *is* afraid . . . of everything."

He walked back for his hat. "If I had a reputation like Horace Wells, I'd take my pick of stables."

She was shaking her head. "He's a good trainer. But . . . when he got too old to ride, he . . . No one wants a—drunk."

The panama slipped out of his hand, but he caught it. First Old Cal, now Horace: both drunken has-beens. He felt like laughing. "Jesus Christ, maybe I should open a charity ward."

"Stop it!" She threw the book on the floor. But the rage ran out of her before the sound could fade. She got out of bed and walked toward him. Nude. Delicate. "He's ruined things before. I don't want you to have to pay for his mistakes." Pressing against him, she put her arms under his jacket. "Can't we just go away? Tonight? We don't need any of this."

Her skin was smooth, like the velvet ring box. "You should have told me," he said.

She nodded against his chest. "I was only trying to protect him. I want to protect you now. No one will get hurt if you call off the fix."

"What about your father? He's already hurting."

Her arms tightened around his middle. In another second she would be crying. "Would you help me make the bets?" he said. "If I showed you how?"

She slipped out of his arms. "Horace put you up to this, didn't he."

"He was only trying to help me cover the angles."

Her fists opened slowly. "You'd better take your walk now. Before it gets too late."

"Look, it's the only snag in this whole thing." He tossed his hat on the bed. "And it'll make Horace calm down a little, so he can concentrate. Now think on it. It makes good sense. Nobody'd figure you to dirty your hands in a boat race. They'd just smile and think they cornered another rich lady."

She was standing near the bureau mirror, not looking at her reflection. But he was. Every part of her was visible, front and back. In full light. Nothing hidden.

"You said before you wanted to help," he told her.

"That was before." She rubbed her arm as if to erase a blemish. "Can't you get your friend Stavros to do it?"

"He's part of the reason why I'm asking you." Rainbow grinned and turned her by the shoulders. She wouldn't look at him. He kissed her forehead. "I'd be right there with you, in case you ran into something you didn't understand. No cause to worry. It's as simple as buying a new pair of shoes."

Her body trembled. "I don't think I can. . . ."

He drew her close to warm her. "Sure you can. And just think of what it'll mean. To me. Horace. Your father. . . ."

She tried to pull away again, but he held her fast and stroked her back until she stopped shivering and relaxed. Then he kissed her hair and carried her to bed.

Iris still tingled from his sweaty power, the caress of his hands. His snore was soft, yet she couldn't sleep. She slid out of bed and went into the sitting room and closed the bedroom door. The black phone felt heavy, like a weapon. On the couch, she lit a cigarette, blew smoke into the darkness.

It was too easy. Rainbow had volunteered to play into the scheme she had designed in Lexington: he wanted to bet the money through the casinos. The Park Casino. "The perfect way to pay E.R. back," he had said. "Make him pay where it hurts the most. Break the sonofabitch."

What had Efrem Roze ever done to him? She knew better than to ask. Rainbow would never tell. Not if it were important to him. And so it was settled. She would do this and then do that, following his instructions to the letter, and then it would be over. He guaranteed it. There would be nothing left to do.

"Just add the zeros," she whispered. "But not this time. I won't do it. Not to him."

She took the earpiece off the hook. Dull static turned into the desk clerk's voice. She drew a breath. "Ford's on Broadway."

More noisy air. Finally, a grunt broke the pattern of rings: "Ford's. Bobby speaking."

She swallowed the taste of smoke and tightened her grip on the slender stem of the phone. "Horace Wells, please."

Not with Rainbow. Please, Daddy.

"Hang on, lady." The bang of metal on wood echoed like gunshot. Then:

"Wells here."

It was his four-drink voice.

She shut her eyes. "You bastard. . . ."

A series of *clicks* filled her ear. "Iris? That you?"

Her mouth opened, but nothing came out.

"Iris?"—*click*—"You there?"—*click, click*—"What's the matter?"

Five drinks. Perhaps six.

The hot cigarette ash fell on her naked thigh. She let it singe her skin. The words came out all by themselves: "He went for it."

"Now, that's my girl!" Horace said, talking fast. "I knew you'd do it, yes sir, I knew you wouldn't let me down, not my girl, no sir, why—"

She hung up. A final drag and she crushed the cigarette out. There was no room inside her for tears. Not anymore. Taking the phone off the hook so that Horace couldn't call back, she stretched out on the couch, eyes open, waiting for dawn to break, wishing—praying—that she didn't have to see it.

31

Iris was gone. . . .

The bed was empty, but her big trunk still stood against the wall, her clothes filled the closet. She might have gone out for a walk. In the middle of the night? On the chair, his clothes were gray with filtered light. His $25,000 and the keys to his safety-deposit boxes were still in his pockets. At least she hadn't robbed him. She had just run off. And left him. When he needed her the most.

The light over the bathroom mirror hurt his eyes. Finished shaving, he came out and emptied his pockets in a hurry, leaving the wrinkled clothes on the chair, taking his other new white suit from the closet. The new tie was stiff, and when he cinched it, it squeaked.

She might have been hungry, she hadn't eaten any dinner last night. But the hotel dining room wouldn't open this early. An all-night restaurant? If he hurried, he could get to Ford's on Broadway before she had her second cup of coffee.

He stuffed Murph's burying clothes into the canvas bag Iris had carried to the spa yesterday. No socks. From a bureau drawer, he took a pair of his own and put them in the bag. With the kid's new shoes under his arm, Rainbow put on his panama and got his .45 from the chair. Only five paces to the door, yet each step made him feel like a thief—gun in one hand, someone else's clothes in the other.

That same gray tinge hung over the main room, as if everything had been frosted with night. Cold air came in the open window. Along the curb at the end of the hotel driveway, a pair of headlamps burned weakly. The whole village seemed forgotten.

And Iris was lying naked on the couch.

Head turned toward the window, a wrist bent under her chin, fingers slightly curled, the curves of her body were swathed in gray. Even her hair. For a moment, she looked like someone else. Someone old. Dying.

He went back into the bedroom and pulled the sheet off the bed. She was breathing softly, as if whispering to herself. He tucked the sheet around her. It felt good. Not like winning. Not even close. This was full and deep, it made his shoulders broad, his smile real. He moved the phone from the floor to the table. Who could she have been calling at this hour? Horace? Old Grace North? Her father back in Louisville? How much was *that* going to cost? Taking careful steps, he carried her bag and the shoes out to the hall. A last look inside, then he slid his pistol into his belt and closed and locked the door.

Stuffed with newspapers, a pair of shiny shoes sat outside a room three doors down. Small lamps painted each landing of the main staircase. In the lobby, Dancer was sitting on a couch, drinking coffee he must have got from a friend in the kitchen. Little slips of paper cluttered the table before him. Balancing his cup on the saucer, he waddled over before Rainbow could reach the front doors.

"Heard what you done at Baldy's." The fat man's chuckle made all those chins shake. "Scared Old Cal right out of his pants. Listen, I give you something free. He's looking for you. Said he was coming here to find you." He slurped coffee. His eyes started to rise. "Says you're his kid."

Rainbow clenched the drawstring on the bag. "My father died a long time ago. Whatever Cal Robinson says, he's no kin of mine."

Dancer raised a hand. "Only saying what I heard. Why you figure he'd go around blabbing that if it ain't true?"

"You tell that old bastard to keep his mouth shut," Rainbow said. "He comes near me again—" He was ready to say "and I'll blow his head clean off his shoulders." He didn't say anything. He pushed out the door.

Heels twisting on gravel, he crunched his way down the drive, through the still grip of morning. Who'd believe a drunken has-been? People would laugh at Old Cal. Wouldn't they? And Rainbow wouldn't be around long enough to be bothered by the rumor, he would be far out of town before dark. At least, everyone would be convinced that he had left. That was part of his plan.

Not a soul on Broadway. The black sedan at the curb was a Packard and a man in a tuxedo was sleeping behind the wheel with a woman in an evening gown dozing on his shoulder. It was a beautiful car, exactly the kind Murph would have loved to drive. Or own. Rainbow reached in and switched off the headlamps. The couple inside didn't wake up.

Blind houses stood stiff on the quiet lawns of Circular Street. But Union Avenue was busy with lights, party music, and couples petting near the hedges in the last few minutes before dawn. Silhouettes of dancers moved against a window shade like cardboard cutouts. Like targets in a shooting gallery. In the middle of the block, three big men lounged on the portico of a white house across the street. Two of them had escorted Efrem Roze to and from the poker game at the Shelton Hotel. The front rooms were dark, drapes drawn. In the tiny upstairs window, a light burned yellow. Rainbow kept walking. This revenge was going to be sweet: Roze would be fleeced for over a million dollars. And everyone would know exactly how Rainbow had done it. E.R. would be the laughingstock of The Big Time. It was a good plan. After that, in a hidden alley or a deserted parking lot, the time would come. Time to shoot the man with the red mark on his chin.

Set back from the street, the next house looked like a storybook manor: Queen Anne tall, high windows. The sign on the lawn had a horse carved in the center, framed by S. D. RIDDLE'S MAN O' WAR. Across from the big brick house at the end of the block, the racetrack fence was shrouded in fog. Past the grandstand, noises flapped over the ground. Horses. He could smell them. Where twin elms grew from a plot in the middle of the road, the sounds got stronger, surrounding him. A big gray form slid out of the mist. The boy in the saddle pulled the reins and Rainbow jumped out of the way. As if irked by the delay, the bay snorted, then beat a slow *clop* across the street. More horses followed, browns and blacks, easier to see. Others came from the opposite direction, heading into the main oval. Here, along the backstretch amid trails of dung, was the focal point of the track, the Times Square of Saratoga. He went through the wood gate, making sure of his footing.

Hooves thundered down the straight. Like a specter, a coal-black horse burst through the mist under a stiff-legged rider. Along the rail, stopwatches went *click* and a row of men scribbled on their note pads. A few feet away, black waiters in starched jackets were setting up tables for breakfast. The stable trail was spotted with dew and urine. And everywhere, that smell. The air was royal sweet with it. The groom rubbing down a colt pointed the way to Old Smoke's stall. Rainbow reached over the lower half of the divided door and tried to coax the horse forward.

"Careful what you're doing there." A small man in a New York Yankees cap emptied a slop bucket on the dirt. "Took away his oats this morning and he don't like it one bit."

"Is Horace Wells around?" Rainbow asked.

The man pointed down the row of stables. "Commissary. Nursing his head with java." His small eyes got smaller. "Seen you before, ain't I? You an owner?"

"Jockey . . ." Rainbow threw him a mock salute and walked away. Wet hay stuck to his shoes. Around the stable corner, in a pool of hard light, he left Murph's shoes with an old shineman. Inside the commissary, the aroma of bacon, eggs, and coffee hovered over the men in the serving line. The short ones in dungarees and ball caps looked like sleepy children. Rainbow drew coffee from the standing urn and walked to a table near the silverware bin, where Horace was reading a paper.

Eyeing the canvas bag, Horace finished his coffee and pushed the mug to the side. "What'd you do, bring down some special feed?"

Rainbow set the bag on the extra chair. "Where are the jocks?"

"Won't be ready till after breakfast."

Rainbow slid his mug across the table. "How's your head?"

"My head's smart as ever." But the old jockey's hands were trembling around the mug. "Told you, didn't she."

"No secret, is it?" Rainbow said. "A guy by Old Smoke's stall told me, too."

Horace held the mug with both hands as if to absorb its warmth. "That'd be fucking Georgy Morris. The asshole never could make it as a jock."

"Had any nips today?"

"Of course not. Biggest goddamn day of my life, you don't think I'd risk it on whiskey, do you?" Horace gulped coffee. "Did you and her get things settled on the wagers?"

How beautiful she had looked lying on that couch. Rainbow nodded. "She call you last night?"

"Me? Nah. Smart thing you done bringing her in on it. I knew you was no piker. Nothing can go wrong now. Unless you still want to make a big show of meeting the jocks in front of E.R.'s goons." His bald head swiveled toward the table by the door, where two men in brown fedoras held newspapers they weren't reading. "Things is already strung tight, it being opening day and all. Leave this part to me, I got it handled on the quiet."

The men in the fedoras kept glancing about the room. Rainbow put his hat on top of the bag. "I still want to talk to the riders."

"Be smarter if you was seen talking to just our jock," Horace said. "Them goons'd think you was only a friend. An owner maybe." He passed an envelope under the table. "Three grand in here. I ain't paid but two jocks. Rest of the field couldn't catch us if we run backwards. Ask Birdseye or any of the clockers."

"I told you to take care of all the jocks, damn it."

Horace shoved the envelope into Rainbow's knee. "Be like buying a car with five fucking motors when all you need is one."

"Pay them all." Rainbow pushed the envelope away and peered at the door. The two thugs were looking at him. "Got the run laid out?"

Horace rubbed the top of his head. His words came out like wax. "We pinch the front and take a box into the stretch. Benecia Boy'll set the pace on the rail without anybody telling him to. I'm putting Morning Cup outside and us in between. We get room when Morning Cup goes wide off the turn. Just drive on through. Make it two lengths at the line and looks like a tough ride. Lots of whip." His grin was full of savvy. "Not a raised eyebrow in the house. Just like you wanted."

"I wanted all the jocks paid by now," Rainbow said.

Horace gulped more coffee. "We lay anything on them, we're asking for it. They got no chance to win and nothing to lose by squealing. No sense taking that kind of risk. Just pay for what you need and not a goddamn thing more. Am I right?"

He was right. Rainbow rapped his fingers on the table, wishing he had fixed a race before. But Horace knew the ropes. And looked sober enough. Rainbow wiped sweat from his forehead. "When can I talk to our jock?"

Horace glanced at the rear of the big room. "He's almost finished now, I'll catch him before he leaves. Bobby Monroe, real good boy. Stole him from the guy who owns Man o' War."

"S. D. Riddle?"

"Dr. Sam himself," Horace said. "Lucky bastard bought Big Red right here at the Sales for only five grand. Now this was back in 1917 when five big ones meant something. Christ, they talk now of shelling out sixty thou. For a fucking yearling!" He batted the table with his paper, then flicked the body of a fly to the floor. "Be best if you was to stay clear of me till we hit the paddock just before post time."

Rainbow glared at him. "That depends on what your jock has to say. And how clear you stay of the bottle. I catch one whiff and—"

"Told you I'm free of that stuff. No matter what nobody says."

Horace offered the envelope under the table again. "It's rightfully yours. Wouldn't have a clean conscience carrying all this around."

While the men in the brown fedoras were glancing in another direction, Rainbow slipped the cash into his jacket. "I'll see if I can lay this down for you with the rest of the wager."

"Real fine of you to do that," Horace said, smacking his lips. "Liked you right off. Sounds like we got us an easy walk now that she's helping out. I'd trust Iris with my life. . . ."

Before Rainbow's grin was fully formed, Horace jumped up and waved at the small man heading up the aisle. Jockey Bobby Monroe had dark pouches beneath his boyish eyes and a strong handshake. He agreed with everything Horace had said. The race was set: Old Smoke would win by two lengths or more, under a hard ride. Satisfied, Rainbow shook hands around the table, then bought a paper from the boy hawking the early edition and walked outside. Murph's shoes looked freshly painted. The shineman asked for a nickel. Rainbow gave him a dollar. He squinted back into the light: the brown fedoras were looking the other way. He smiled and started walking toward the orange sun now inching above the stables.

Along the backstretch, the breakfast tables were crowded with men. With Aziz at his side, Stavros the Greek sat near the rail. Rainbow took the empty chair:

"Got anything for me, Greek?"

Stavros aimed cigar smoke at the horse rounding the far turn. "Could be you're a dead man. . . ."

Yellow petals in the vase on the center of the table fluttered when the horse galloped by. A waiter set down two bowls of lumpy oatmeal and a plate of fresh fruit. Stavros pushed his bowl in front of Aziz and sighed. "Breakfast with the horses. A Saratoga tradition."

"Eggs over easy," Rainbow said. "With ham."

The waiter shrugged and walked away.

"I tried calling you last night," Stavros said. "But your line was tied up. What you asked me—forget it."

Rainbow leaned back in the chair. "Because it involves E.R.? Your boss?"

The thin cigar drooped between angry lips. "The Greek's got no boss! What are you, a moron for Chrissake? They'll put you and your fucking bingle-bangle-bungle in a wood box if you try to muscle Roze." Stavros fingered his tie stud and shook his head. "You're way over your head. Believe it."

The waiter came back with more oatmeal and fruit and a small white pot. "I ordered eggs." Rainbow took the lid off the pot. "And this is tea, which I *didn't* order. Don't you hear?"

"All I'm allowed to serve," the waiter said. "Tell him, Mr. Greek. Can't give the gentleman something we ain't got." He left scratching his neck.

"Oatmeal's all you get, Big Time." Stavros rolled the cigar in his fingers. "Oatmeal, fruit, and tea. The tradition stinks, don't it."

Lumps rolled off the spoon like the gruel at Fairway House. Rainbow pushed the bowl into the center of the table and stood.

"About College," Stavros said. "I hear it was an accident. The kid made a big stink at The Park about not paying. E.R. was only trying to scare him a little. He's even willing to forget about what College still owes."

"I'm not." Rainbow peeled $1,000 from his wad and threw it down before the Greek. "Pay the sonofabitch."

Stavros ignored the cash. "I already offered to take care of it. E.R. don't feel right about it." Those black eyes looked cold. "I'm on your side, friend. Stay on mine."

Rainbow grabbed his bag and the shoes. "You buy that accident shit?"

More cigar smoke, blown like a cloud at the new horse heading down the backstretch. "I accept it," Stavros said.

"I don't." Rainbow hurried between tables, bumping into one man, brushing past another. The dirt track felt mushy. A water truck was spilling a fine spray around the turn for the finish line. Horses kept filing through the gate by the street. Cars puttered over Union Avenue, shadows stretched, the sidewalk was warming up. Murph would never give anyone a hard time. He didn't have it in him. Rainbow wrapped his paper around the kid's shoes to protect the shine. He yanked the MAN O' WAR sign out and threw it onto Dr. S. D. Riddle's lawn. Across the way, the Roze portico looked smaller, the new guards seemed less threatening than before. The front curtains were still drawn, but that upstairs light was out. The .45 pinched Rainbow's hip. He tried to beat the sun back to Broadway.

The white straw skimmer should have been a homburg. And the chin should have been angular, the frame gangly, like the Skeleton, Mr. Drumlin. Instead, the coroner had a weightlifter's build and a round face. He pulled the long drawer out of the wall and lifted the sheet.

Murph lay stiff and naked on the steel slab.

Rainbow turned away, put the shoes on the little table, and pulled the clothes out of the canvas bag. "I'd like these pressed before you put them on him."

"This *is* your cousin then?" The coroner read from the tag on Murph's toe. "David Murphy?"

Rainbow nodded and stacked the clothes in neat piles.

"Some funds will be required," the coroner said. "Before I can call in a mortuary to complete the arrangements for railroad passage to . . . ?"

"Hot Springs."

A well-practiced smile spread over the coroner's lips. "If you like, you may leave the payment with me."

Rainbow gave him $1,000. "I don't want any mistakes."

Thick fingers counted the cash, then scribbled on a small piece of paper. "We'll have it all in order. You'll need this receipt to get the baggage ticket." That smile again. "We wouldn't want an unclaimed coffin in Arkansas, now would we."

The paper was warm, unlike the cold air of the morgue. Rainbow peeled off another hundred-dollar bill and held it out. "For your trouble. Just to make sure."

The coroner closed the drawer and Murph disappeared into the wall. "Unnecessary, sir."

Unnecessary?

Rainbow pocketed the money and the receipt. "Need me for anything else?"

"You'll want his personal effects, I presume." The coroner gave him a small sack with MURPHY, DAVID printed on it. Then he picked up the blue jacket on the table and ripped the center seam. "The death certificate will accompany the coffin." He tore the shirt, too. "Sorry about your cousin, sir." He took a knife from his back pocket and started slitting the back crease of Murph's new pants.

Before the coroner could get to the kid's shoes, Rainbow walked out. The hall was painted pea-green. At the stairs, he stopped to look inside the sack: a key to a box in the hotel vault, a key to room 319, the gold locket, $2.56 in cash, and today's scorecard from the golf course, annotated with arrows and initials. The kid had not been ready to die, he had been preparing for another round of golf. The coroner's receipt looked like shorthand, too. Under the official letterhead: a scrawled name, some initials, and "deceased" scribbled as casually as the other words on the note. Not much of a testimonial. Not much of anything. Rainbow stuffed it back into his jacket.

No ring box.

He checked his other pockets. Wrong suit. But Iris wouldn't be up yet. She wouldn't bother with his clothes anyway. Would she?

He ran up the steps.

Luggage carts were being wheeled down Broadway. More tourists from the morning train, come to drink and gamble, to whore and crowd nightclubs in a town already brimming with bodies. He felt sorry for all of them. Hurrying through the trees guarding The Park Casino, he took a shortcut back to his hotel.

Except for a few early bettors around Dancer, the lobby was quiet. So were the stairs. But in the third-floor hall, a young boy was falling headlong into the wall, his newspapers flying away from him.

And Iris was falling sideways. She banged into the bench, tumbled onto the carpet.

Rainbow bent to help her up. "You okay?"

"In there . . ." Her voice trembled, her hand twitched when she pointed to the open door of the suite. "A man. A big—"

"It's all right." Rainbow sat her on the bench and smoothed out her dress. Leaving her canvas bag on the floor, he drew his .45, cocked the hammer, took up the slack on the trigger, and walked toward the room. For the kill.

32

A large black head peered around the doorjamb. Curtis doffed his blue hat and smiled into the gun barrel. "Spoil the whole reunion if you blow my head off, sport."

"Jesus." Choking on a laugh, Rainbow uncocked the .45 and put it back on his hip. "What are you doing here?"

Curtis slapped him on the shoulders. "Damn, I don't believe it! You shelled out for a new suit. Must of made a million bucks overnight." He grabbed the panama. "Nope. Still the same old hat. Must only of been a half-million."

Rainbow snatched the hat back, then turned to reassure Iris with a wave. Taking tentative steps, she carried her canvas bag to the doorway while the paper boy cursed under his breath and gathered the early edition off the floor.

"Hello, Saratoga." Curtis was beaming at her. "You could always pick them, sport. This one's a little flighty, though. Likes to run."

"What's she supposed to do when you come barging in on her." Rainbow pushed him aside and led Iris into the suite.

Huge hands rose defensively. "Now you knows us folks ain't got no manners." His grin got wider. He kicked the door shut, then bowed and stayed hunched over. "Where's you sense of etiquette? Announce me!"

"Curtis Godfrey, from Saint Louis." Rainbow tossed his hat on the couch. The bedsheet was bundled near the armrest. "This is Miss Winslow."

"*Miss* Winslow!" Curtis straightened up, touched his hat brim.

"A definite pleasure, *Miss* Winslow." He leaned close to Rainbow. "Got a first name, don't she, sport? Or ain't you got that far yet?"

"He's your—friend?" Iris said.

Rainbow stared at the floor.

"When you get to know him better, *Miss* Winslow," Curtis said, "you'll see when he don't say nothing, that means—yes."

Eyes low, she hurried into the bedroom and closed the door.

"Yes sir, real flighty." Curtis helped himself to a sweet roll from the room-service cart by the couch. "Took that fool at stud two nights running. Twenty-five grand all to myself." He looked over the room. A big red handkerchief spilled out of the breast pocket of his powder-blue suit. "Thought me and my bankroll'd have a look at The Big Time." His gaze swung to the bedroom door. "Think we're gonna like it just fine."

The sound of running water came through the walls. She was all dressed, yet taking another bath? Rainbow marched into the bedroom. She had hung up his clothes, but the ring box was still in his suit jacket. Relieved, he came out to the main room and shut the door, then tossed the box to Curtis. "Before you say another thing about her . . ."

Curtis stared at the velvet square. "Don't think I want to open this." Finally, he popped the lid. His eyes narrowed. ". . . Real?"

"And so's she," Rainbow said. "A true lady."

Light bounced off the black's face when he tilted the ring. "Well, if she ain't, this'll go a long way toward making her one."

"Stop talking about her like she was a whore, damn it!" He recalled the first time he had seen her, outside Saint Louis, and the sting of her slap. "I'm leaving today."

"Shit." Curtis finished the pastry. "Not goddamn oranges again."

". . . Oranges."

"Your *Miss* Winslow don't look like no orange grower's wife to me."

"Got class written all over her, don't she," Rainbow said. "Society-bred. Been to the best schools. . . ."

"She ought to be real happy spending the rest of her life picking fruit with you." The box snapped shut. Curtis left it on the cart, beside an egg-stained plate, pieces of toast, and a teapot. "Real nice, sport."

"You're supposed to congratulate me."

"Congratulations." Curtis poured a cup of tea and put his feet on the low table. "Scored big in Chicago, didn't you."

"I'm through with all that."

"Way I see it, sport, you got no choice."

"What are you talking about?"

Curtis slapped a newspaper clipping on the table. "Went and made yourself real visible, fool. Tell me, Mr. Celebrity, just how many pigeons gonna be dumb enough to take on the Great Rainbow Roberts now?"

The clipping was two days old. Dateline Chicago. Byline, Bob Jurgenson, golf pro, Tam Lin. Story about hustling. And two hustlers, one named Roberts, the other a kid known only as Murph. It was all there. Rainbow crumpled the paper and hurled it toward the wall. "That sonofabitch."

"Part of the reason I come after you, sport. You need a new angle."

"I got one. Retirement."

Curtis sipped tea. "Something's eating you. And it ain't retirement."

"I can retire if I want to."

The black's stare deepened. "What's wrong. You and Murph go bust?"

"Nothing's wrong. For Chrissake, can't a guy retire around here?"

Curtis took an envelope from his jacket. "Here, I can stake you if—"

"I don't need your money."

The envelope went back into the suit. "Then I'll just sit here till you tell me what it is you do need. Else I'll find out from the kid."

"Should of called me," Rainbow said. "I'd of told you to stay in Saint Lou."

"Take your time, sport. You'll get to what's bothering you. Sooner or later."

The bath tap went silent. Rainbow put the ring box in his pocket. "It's a different crowd up here. They won't mess with—outsiders. You being . . . colored, well, it's best if you stayed clear of me for a while."

Curtis was shaking his head. "I don't buy that, sport. Not from you."

There was a little silence. Curtis would never leave once he found out about Murph and the plan for revenge. Rainbow worked up an angry face. "You want the truth?"

"Uh-oh," Curtis said. "Here *comes* the truth!"

Yesterday, it would have made Rainbow laugh. Today, it fed the rage he was trying to muster. "Yeah, the truth, damn it! I'm into something for more cash than a two-bit piece of shit like you'd ever see in ten lifetimes. I don't want you here. Don't need you, either. You're in my way. For Chrissake you're a colored!"

Curtis exhaled deeply and set the cup on the cart. "So—that's the truth, is it?" He stretched out on the couch, using the bundled bedsheet as a pillow. "If I thought it'd do any good, I'd beat it out of you. But you always was a stubborn mother. Just don't expect me to believe this nigger shit. Or that you went and conned yourself into believing all them dreams you got. *Miss* Winslow—*Oranges!* Day you see fucking oranges, sport, is the day this nigger turns white."

Rainbow couldn't find any more anger. He faced the wall. "Believe what you like. Just catch the next train out."

Light knocks on the door to the hall broke the silence. Curtis stood. "That'd be my bags. Had them sent over from the station. Didn't figure they'd give a *Negro* a room in this town."

"Send them back." Rainbow tried to hold his frown flat, but when he spied the cart, he couldn't stop the smile. "Ten bucks says it's room service."

"Boy, you are so pitiful. . . ." Curtis let out a disgusted sigh and opened the door.

He never had a chance.

Thwack.

Head snapped back, hat falling off, Curtis reeled like a square dancer caught in midturn by a phantom partner. His knees buckled. He crashed onto the cart face-first.

Before the plates hit the floor, Rainbow dived into the alley between the wall and couch, yanking his pistol free, somersaulting into a firing position, whirling toward the door, and—

And *thwack.*

The thing that hit him felt too hard for a fist. It must have been a club. Or a bat. No taste of blood yet, but there had to be blood. *Can't get hit with a bat and not bleed. All right, so the bastard's got a bat. And he's quicker than me. But I'm smarter.* He lay perfectly still, finger tensed on the trigger, eyes cracked open. *Come on, you mother. Come get the possum.*

The mother got him by the wrist and tore the .45 free. Rainbow stopped playing possum. He cocked a left cross, his best punch, one that would stun any man when thrown to the groin. He didn't get the chance to throw it. He was flying. Then bouncing—off the couch, onto the coffee table. Wood splintered, a table leg broke off and rolled away. The perfect weapon—a bat—out of reach. There was nothing left to do but run. He sprang to his feet.

And stared straight into a gray vest.

Aziz shoved him down.

The door closed. Stavros the Greek walked to Curtis. "Who's the nigger? Bodyguard?"

Rainbow wanted to laugh, but his face hurt too much. He felt for blood. "Some sharper. Never saw him before."

Stavros had the envelope Curtis was carrying. "Only twenty-five grand here. You took more than that off me yesterday. Now who is he?"

"Didn't say I agreed to borrow from him, did I?" No blood. Amazing. Rainbow leapt over the couch to find his gun. No gun. The giant was holding it, his eyes glazed like hunks of petrified wood. "Keep him away from me, Greek," Rainbow said. "Or I swear I'll—" It was one of those sentences he wished he had never started.

Jet-black eyes seemed amused. "Okay, the nigger wants to lend you money when you don't need none and you say no thanks." Stavros flicked a cigar ash to the floor. "Now get your hat. We're gonna see E.R. and you'll tell him you understand what happened to College was an accident. And all's forgiven."

The East Tennessee Mauler was out cold, ground tea leaves slithering down his lapel, pats of butter in his hair. "Maybe we could get him some water first," Rainbow said.

"The nigger'll be all right." Stavros stepped over the broken plates and picked up the panama. "Let's go."

Rainbow took the hat and turned it in his hands. "I was on my way to tell you, Greek. You're right. Makes no sense to try anything against E.R. Especially when you say it was an accident. I accept it. Gonna catch a few races, then leave town. Today."

Sitting down in the chair, Stavros shook his head. "You're a real fucking treat, you know that? And full of shit."

"It's the truth, Greek. You got my word on it."

With a shrug, Stavros puffed on his cigar. "Under different circumstances, I wouldn't give a shit what you do. Makes no matter, E.R.'d have your ass anyway. But things is bad enough between me and him without you fucking me over." He got up and walked to the door. "Okay, Big Time. But if I find your word's no good, I see you on that train—personally." He frowned at the mess on the floor. "Smart guy like you knows better than to deal with niggers. You need cash, the Greek can fix you up." He managed a small smile and walked out. Aziz left the .45 on the chair and plodded into the hall.

Suddenly, the room felt large. Rainbow stuffed the gun into his belt, closed the door, threw the bolt. It was over.

"Are you all right?" A voice from behind. Her voice.

It was just beginning.

"No . . ." He turned to see Iris come into his arms.

"I thought they were going to kill you." She was hugging the air out of him. "Isn't Stavros your—friend?"

Rainbow stared at Curtis. "Let's throw some water on that." He shooed her toward the bathroom and knelt beside the cart, pulling butter from kinks of black hair. The red handkerchief did a poor job of wiping up the ground-in tea. He tapped Curtis on the cheek. Not even a groan. "I tried to get rid of you, damn it." Another tap. "You and your goddamn china chin."

Iris came back with a glass of water.

"You do it," he said. "When he comes to, I want both hands free to knock him out again."

She drew a breath and dumped the water out.

Still nothing.

She put the glass down. "Should I call a doctor?"

"Get packed, we got things to do." He pulled Curtis from the debris and leaned him against the couch. Like the yawn of a hibernating bear, a murmur crept past swollen lips. Dark eyelids began to flutter. And Iris was still standing there. "Hurry up," Rainbow said. When she went into the bedroom and closed the door, he slapped Curtis. The big head bobbed like a marionette on a loose string. More slaps. The bobbing stopped. Brown eyes searched for focus. The groan grew louder, transforming itself into speech:

"Ra—ru—Rainbow . . . ?

"Welcome back, slugger."

"Sonofabitch hit me with a gun or something." Curtis winced as if he were trying to remember not to move his jaw when he spoke. "What the hell kind of trouble you in, anyways?"

"You're not gonna believe this," Rainbow said. "But they're on our side."

"In that case, we can't lose." Curtis rubbed the tea on his lapel. "Shit, it's ruined." He touched the welt on his chin. "Bleeding?"

"For Chrissake quit thinking of yourself. You slept through the whole thing." Rainbow helped him up, but couldn't support the weight. He eased him onto the couch. "I'm the one who got us out of it. As usual."

"As usual my ass." The laugh was there, but it was buried in pent-up anger, anger that must have been stored for a long time. "I'll have to think of a way to thank you, sport."

Rainbow kicked pieces of china out of his way. "You want a doctor?"

Working his jaw from side to side, Curtis spat on the floor. "You gonna tell me what's going on with you now?"

"All I'm gonna do is put you on a train out of here."

"Only way I'm leaving is with you." Curtis arched his head over the back of the couch. "Preferably in one piece."

"Here's your bankroll." Rainbow tossed the envelope on the couch and offered the tablecloth. "And wipe your head. You have butter in your hair."

"Butter . . . ?" Curtis touched his scalp as if afraid of what else he might find there. "In my hair?"

"Yeah, they got a strange sense of humor."

Ignoring the tablecloth, Curtis toweled his hair with the bundled sheet. "By the way, sport. It wasn't room service. You owe me ten bucks."

Rainbow kept watching the sheet move. He swilled cold tea in his mouth and spat it into the cup. "I'll deduct it from what I owe for the cart you broke. And the plates. And the table. And—"

"And don't forget my suit." Curtis peeked out from under the sheet.

Rainbow matched his grin. His laugh came out like a sigh. It felt good to have a friend here. Better than good. Like old times. But it changed everything. And somehow, he would have to find a way to get rid of Curtis before the roof caved in.

33 ————————————————————————

Iris sat on the lid of her trunk, but it wouldn't close. A good test of character for the bellman, she thought, and she checked the bureau drawers again. Nothing missed: packed. She wanted to throw all her clothes on the floor and start over—anything to postpone what was coming. But she couldn't. Running another bath hadn't helped either. Before the tub was half filled, she had turned off the tap, opened the drain, and changed into her green dress. The game would be over soon, she was powerless to stop it. And she would be alone. Again.

In the closet: two suits, both white. Rainbow could be packed in three minutes. Blindfolded. It had taken her all morning to cram her things into suitcases. When she had stopped to hang up his wrinkled clothes, a little black box had fallen at her feet. Velvet. Inside, a diamond. Cold white. But just a ring, not meant for her. It wasn't her size: she had not been able to keep it from slipping off her finger. Rainbow must have won it in some card game, or on the golf course. No sales slip in any of his pockets. Tiffany's would have insisted on a sales slip if he had really bought it there. For her. It was simply part of Rainbow's bankroll, something he would sell so that he would have more to bet on the race.

But it was so beautiful. Standing before the bureau mirror like a child posing in old clothes from an attic trunk, she had been fascinated by the new person she had become. Without lipstick or rouge, dressed only in her robe, the effect of the diamond on her hand had been stunning. Her grin didn't go away until she had looked for an inscription on the band. There was none. By noon, the diamond would be translated into ready cash—gone. Putting the box back into his jacket, she had busied herself with packing and breakfast. But now, she wanted one last look.

The ring was gone. She went through all his pockets. Had it been a dream? No, it had been much too real. Every bit as real as that black, Curtis. Answering what she had believed to be the knock of a waiter come to pick up the room-service cart, she had opened the door to the biggest black she had ever seen. His dark eyes tracking over her, his smile growing by the second, he had stepped inside before she could shut the door in his face. Then he had started calling out a bunch of numbers: "Twenty-five! Single! Nine!" She didn't wait to find out who he was or why he was here, or what those silly numbers meant. She ran. And hit the paper boy dead-on. The rest was just as jumbled as her crossword puzzles. The black was Rainbow's *friend?* Stavros the Greek was not? There were no answers, only more questions. Rainbow wasn't going to tell her anything. He was no different from Ernie. Or Taylor North. Women had their place and it was a very real place: shut out.

She got her cigarettes from her purse and sat on the edge of the bed. Perhaps if she asked, if she insisted on knowing . . . But Rainbow would only see that as nagging. She lit a match, then waved it out. Rainbow would just have to get used to her nagging. It was the only way to stop this nightmare. To stop Daddy. She was going to ask until she found out everything. Smoothing out her dress, she drew a breath and walked to the bedroom door. Another breath, the turn of the knob, and she yanked the door open and marched into the sitting room.

And Rainbow was gone.

The wreckage of the brawl made the room look like her apartment after Horace had "cleaned up." She found herself sitting on the couch, holding the sheet. How thoughtful Rainbow had been to cover her with it last night. Now it was greasy with butter and messy with curly black hairs. She dropped it on the floor. Gone, too, was the sweet roll she had ordered, the one she had been trying to find the courage to eat. Perhaps it was lying among the debris. Ruined. She leaned back against the cushions and shut her eyes, hoping for sleep: time out.

The phone rang. She stepped over the broken table and took the receiver off the hook, all her questions ready to come out:

". . . Rainbow?"

"Just called to see how you are," Horace said. "Can you talk?"

"... Yes, Daddy...."

"We're all set on my end. He give you the money yet?"

"... I'm—fine, Daddy."

"That's good. Now don't get fancy, just follow it through like you planned, and we're on easy street...."

She kept listening to his drone, sinking farther and farther into herself, until all the distant noises coming through the open window went away and there was only her father's voice, and her own whisper:

"... I love you, Daddy...."

She hung up and went into the bedroom to get ready.

Rainbow opened his briefcase on the front desk and waited for the clerk to bring the boxes out of the vault. "How'd you find me so fast? The train couldn't of been in more than twenty minutes."

Curtis was rubbing the tea stain on his lapel. "You real easy to find these days, sport. Real easy."

By the couches, a small crowd stood around Dancer, who was doing a vaudeville shuffle, note pad held high in one hand, a tambourine shaking in the other:

"Don't wait for the odds to shoot. Take Dancer's line and count your loot!"

The chant worked. Fists jammed with money, the crowd battled for the fat man's attention. He pushed the porkpie hat back on his head and started handing out pencils and slips of paper.

"Puts on a nice little show, don't he," Curtis said.

Hurrying so that Dancer wouldn't get the chance to see Curtis and start talking about Murph and Old Cal, Rainbow took three safety-deposit boxes from the clerk, unlocked them, and left the keys on the desk. "Won't be needing these anymore. Check me out of three twenty-five, too." He opened the boxes. It was all there, including the $16,000 that belonged to Murph.

"Holy Jesus." Curtis glanced at the clerk who was busy with forms. "They know what you got in there?"

"Of course not, wouldn't be safe." Rainbow stationed Curtis like a shield against eyes in the lobby, then transferred the money to his briefcase.

"If it was mine, sport, I'd never let it out of my sight."

"Then don't get careless." Rainbow thrust the case into Curtis's arms and took the hotel bill from the clerk. "What's this one here for?"

The clerk studied the last item. "Room service, this morning. Your wife—"

"Three bucks for breakfast?" Rainbow peeled a hundred-dollar bill from his folding money. "We got some damages up there. A room-service cart. And a table." He nodded at Curtis. "He sat on them. By mistake."

"Thought they was chairs," Curtis said. "I ain't housebroke yet."

The clerk stopped scribbling long enough to gaze into the black's grin, then cleared his throat and stared at the pad. "If that's all there is, it comes to twenty dollars."

Rainbow tossed down his money. "Use what's left for tips. Have my bags to the station by noon. And send for my golf bags at the country club. Two of them."

"No problem, sir." The clerk gave him a copy of the bill. "Anything else we might do for you?"

Rainbow crumpled the hotel bill and dropped it on the desk. "Have this framed." He led Curtis to the stairs. "Twenty-seven bucks a day. Without meals! Highway robbery for Chrissake."

"Hey, Midget!" Dancer came through the crowd and spun Curtis around. "Damn if you didn't grow another inch."

Curtis handed the briefcase to Rainbow. "And you put on another twenty pounds."

"More to jiggle." Dancer patted his stomach. "Better show, bigger bets." He shook hands and laughed. "How long you staying?"

"Ask him." Curtis jabbed a thumb over his shoulder.

"Oh, hi, Rainbow." Dancer's enthusiasm suddenly waned. "Saw the Greek come through here. Said you took the news about your friend real good. Sorry, you know." The porkpie hat came off. "And I ain't had the chance to see Cal on account of business here. But I'll get to it soon as I can." He put on his hat and elbowed Curtis. "If you can't find a place to put up, come see me at the Adelphi and I'll sneak you in." With a wink and a grin, he whirled about, rattled his tambourine, and strutted back to the swarm of bettors, his chant rising to the high ceiling: "Graveyard of favorites they call this track. But winners and losers, they always come back."

Head low, Rainbow traced a finger over the stitching on the briefcase. "I was gonna tell you. . . ."

"You still are." Curtis grabbed him by the collar and pulled him up the stairs.

The suite was quiet. For the last few minutes, Curtis had stood motionless in front of the window, looking down on the lawn. Now he nudged the shade cord and watched it swing back and forth. "I'm real sorry, Rainbow. Never met Murph, but I know I would of liked him.

Christ, I'm sorry. . . . You need any help with the funeral arrangements?"

Rainbow shook his head. *Murph's dead* had not come out easily this time, nor had the details about how the kid had died. Maybe it was because Iris was sitting next to him on the couch, holding his hand. Or because he had just seen Murph laid out. Or because most of what he had told Curtis was a lie. He glanced at Iris's wristwatch: 10:45 A.M. "They run an early post up here. We better get started."

"Don't think you ought to go through with the fix, sport." Curtis stepped around the broken cart. "The state you're in, you might of overlooked something. And I ain't never heard of no Majestic Farms."

"Heard of Horace Wells, ain't you?" Rainbow squeezed her hand and smiled, but she wasn't looking at him. "He works for Majestic. And he's taking care of all the details. It's all set."

"I don't like it, sport. None of it."

"You don't have to." Putting her canvas bag between his legs, Rainbow opened his briefcase and began transferring his cash.

"Forgetting something," Curtis said. "It's got to be an *oral* wager in New York State. Bookie can't write the slip. No money changing hands, either. So ain't nobody gonna take a heavy bet from a nonregular customer like you."

"She's making the bet."

"Oh, that's perfect. Bookies like Dancer gonna *love* that."

"She's not betting with the bookie," Rainbow said. "We're using The Park."

"They still won't touch it." Curtis was pacing the floor. "Not unless they know her."

"I got it figured perfect." Rainbow packed the last of his money and put her swimsuit and bathing cap on top. "She makes the bet separate from depositing the money with the house. That way it's still an oral wager and E.R.'s happy because the bet's backed up with cash."

There was a little silence. Curtis stopped and stared at Iris. "How much of this was *her* idea, sport?"

She kept looking at the floor as if none of this concerned her, as if she were in another room, far away.

Rainbow cinched the drawstring. "We worked it out together. Why?"

Curtis opened his mouth, then grinned. "Nothing."

"Tell me. You see something wrong with it?"

"No, sport, you got it all figured out, you don't want to hear anything from me. Even if—nah, forget it."

308

"Not a hole in it anywhere," Rainbow said. "It's foolproof."

"Right." Curtis was still grinning. "It's real smart. And it don't sound nothing like how you'd do it if *you* was making the bets."

"That's because I ain't making the bets."

"Yeah, I figured that out when you told me." The black chuckled to himself and shook his head. "Considered every angle, huh?"

Rainbow balanced the bag on the table, which slanted toward the missing leg. "This don't concern you. It's my bankroll. Now you got something to say or don't you?"

"What could I possibly have to say?" More chuckling. "Nope, you got it set all right."

A long silence. Rainbow loosened the drawstring, rearranged the cap and swimsuit, cleared his throat. "I'd be willing to listen to any holes you found in it."

"That's real hospitable of you, sport. Think you better get a move-on, though. Don't want to miss your boat race."

Rainbow kicked the table. "What do you see?"

"Who, me?" Curtis yawned. "I been wrong so many times, it's got to be nothing."

Maybe it was nothing. Or a big act just to create fear. Rainbow smiled and picked up the bag. But his legs wouldn't move. Curtis was rarely wrong. And now he was beaming.

"No games," Rainbow said. "Tell me."

"If you insist." Curtis coughed a laugh into his fist. "What if E.R., nice fellah I heard him to be, what if he decides he don't want to pay off?"

Rainbow grinned. "It's a legal wager, you idiot. He's got to pay off."

"That's right, I am an idiot. It's a legal wager. Even when E.R. finds out you threw a boat race on him."

Silence. Rainbow put down the bag. Iris was trying to keep her fingers still.

"Of course, E.R. don't have any contacts in this town," Curtis said, "so you're real safe. He don't get mad, either. Safe again. And him holding your precious bankroll, why, that don't mean a thing."

"She's my edge." Rainbow put on his hat. "Society, like all of E.R.'s clients up here. He welches on her, he's through." At the door, he threw the dead bolt open. "Come on, Iris. It's time."

She got up slowly and took the canvas bag by the string.

"Yeah, she's a good edge," Curtis said. He meant it. "How much?"

"One eighty-five. At four-to-one." Rainbow opened the door. His smile felt weak. "Not quite a million, but it'll have to do."

"Just how sure a sure thing is this, sport?"

"I don't have time to explain it to you." Rainbow took Iris by the hand. "You bring me the wager slip and the deposit receipt. Make sure Roze signs both of them."

Her nod was soft. The little green hat made her head seem perfectly round. "Is—he coming with us?"

"He's gonna wait here till his bags arrive," Rainbow said. "Then he's gonna haul them back to the station and catch the next train out."

Curtis put on his hat and walked toward him. "He's coming with you."

"I told you how it is up here." Rainbow tugged his hat brim. "Stay put."

"Didn't come all this way to stay put, sport." The envelope came out of the powder-blue suit. "Twenty-five grand. I'm putting in with you."

"I don't want your money."

"Didn't *ask* you to want it." Curtis took the bag and stuffed his money inside, then crumpled the envelope and threw it on the floor. He held the bag out to Iris. "Makes two hundred and ten thousand. You can remember that, now can't you?"

She gripped the bag by the neck and when he let go, she drew the drawstring tight. Her stare found the crumpled envelope. She reached into her purse and pulled out the newspaper clipping. "I found this on the floor. Did you want it?"

Rainbow shook his head. She put the clipping back in her purse. With a hard glance at Curtis, he led the way down the hall to the stairs.

The crowd in the lobby had grown. Dancer couldn't hand out slips of paper fast enough. Rainbow dropped his key on the desk and followed a trampled path over the lawn. Stopping in a grove of elms near Broadway, he put his hands on her shoulders. "Can't let them see we're together, otherwise—" The snarl of traffic finished the apology for him. He wanted to kiss her for good luck, but it was awkward in front of Curtis, so he touched her cheek. "I'll be close by if you get worried or . . . if you need me."

"*We'll* be close by," Curtis said. "Very close by, *Miss* Winslow."

Iris stared at the bag for a moment, then leaned on Rainbow and kissed him. He squeezed her shoulders. She tried a smile, but it wasn't her smile. Stepping through the grass as if afraid of snakes, she had to duck branches to reach the sidewalk. But she didn't look back.

"Best hawk your lady so nothing goes wrong with *our* money, sport."

Rainbow grabbed him by the arm. "Your payoff's only two-to-one."

Curtis turned slowly. ". . . What?"

"Two-to-one. I set it up. You want in—you take my odds."

"You want your skull in one piece—you'll short some other sucker's odds, not mine."

Rainbow shrugged. "Might go as high as five-to-two."

Curtis glared at him. Then he saw the smile. And started laughing. He put an arm on Rainbow's shoulder and walked him out of the trees.

The street ran quick with flesh and painted steel. Horns and voices blared over the grumble of engines. On the corner near the trolley station, drumsticks beat the sidewalk, a clarinet played counterpoint to a strong and jazzy trumpet, and the young dancer was up to his old tricks, thrusting his stovepipe hat out to strangers, grinning like a straw boy in a field of hungry crows. There was a sadness to all this energy. This was not a place anymore, it was something to wear. Peering over the hats and parasols, Rainbow spotted Iris a short distance ahead, turning up the casino drive. He winked at Curtis and began to knife his way through the crowds.

The gaming rooms were almost empty. Past the cashier's cage, the door to the manager's office stood open. The furniture had been rearranged, or was about to be replaced. Light squares patterned the walls where once pictures had hung. No chair behind the desk, no curtains on the windows. No manager. The paint on the back wall had been scrubbed down, but the shine of something thick and red remained. Iris went down the hall and knocked on the door of the office marked PRIVATE. No answer. She knocked again.

"Looking for me?" A man's voice: he sounded short.

The canvas bag began to shake, its string made her hand hot. She turned. He was tall and thin and badly strung together. He wore a black suit and a strange smile, almost a sneer. Two big men in brown fedoras stood behind him. She swallowed to find her voice. "Are you the manager?"

"I just own the place." His eyes were too large. He looked like a fish. "Efrem Roze, at your service."

Another swallow. "I'd like to discuss a wager with you, Mr. Roze. . . . Privately."

"Of course." He unlocked the door and gestured her inside. "Horses, baseball, tennis . . . ?"

"Horses," she said. One of the big men reached in from the hall and pulled the door shut. Alone with Efrem Roze, Iris let him help her to a wicker chair with chintz pillows. "Actually—*a* horse."

He sat behind his desk. Spotless, not a paper anywhere, not even a pen or a blotter. "I take it this involves a serious sum of money?"

Her face felt heavy and hard. When she spoke, she couldn't feel her jaw move. "I plan to leave this afternoon, and if I should lose, I don't want the delay of stopping back to pay the wager. They still have that law, don't they, about not leaving the village without paying your debts? Couldn't I just leave a deposit on account with you to cover what I might lose?"

Fish eyes lit with concern. "I'll see to it myself." From a desk drawer, he got a pad and pencil. "The law does say you have to write your own wager."

Iris put the pad in her lap and crossed her legs. "Thank you, I have my own pen." And with it she wrote: *Old Smoke, Sixth Race, Saratoga.* "Do I get odds on Old Smoke?"

The chalkboard on the far wall carried a neat list of race numbers, names of horses, and odds at major tracks on the East Coast. "Five-to-one," Roze said, flashing his sneer. "Not quite the favorite."

She wrote down the odds, the amount of money she was betting, and her name, then handed him the pad.

He looked disappointed. "Two hundred and ten?"

She drew in a little breath and let it out. ". . . Yes."

There, it was done.

"But miss, why not round it off to two hundred or, say—two-fifty?"

Eyes low, Iris watched the string of the canvas bag twist around itself. ". . . Superstition."

Roze chuckled while he tore off the top page and scribbled on the pad. "Your wager slip, Miss Winslow. And a voucher for your deposit."

Her whole body was numb now. From her purse, she got out $210 and laid it on the desk. "Could you sign them please?"

More chuckling. Roze signed both slips. They would do fine. She put them in her purse. ". . . Thank you."

"My pleasure." He came around the desk and escorted her to the door, his fingers fondling her elbow. "And when you win, come back and I'll make good on your wager. Personally."

Any second now he was going to wink. When he didn't, part of her felt cheated. She walked past the big men at the door and took the stairs up to the ladies' room on the second floor. The stalls were empty. She locked the door. The window was easy to open. A laundry-bag fire escape dangled in the breeze. No lady would ever think of using *that*. Iris couldn't picture herself going down a rope either. Not with all those men looking up her skirts, having a grand time. It would be better to fight the crowd down the stairs. Or die in flames.

On the grass below, a dog stopped sniffing at garbage cans long enough to watch her open the laundry bag. She laid the stacks of money on top of the coiled rope, then tied off the bag and set it outside the window again. As soon as she let go, the bag began a downward slide. She grabbed it before it spilled open, but the weight was pulling her out. Braced against the ledge to keep from falling, she watched the bag play back and forth over the ground. Her stomach turned. The dog began to yap. Sweat beaded her forehead, her skin grew clammy. She wanted to let go, let the money tumble out. And a secret part of her wanted to follow the cash to the ground. She struggled to pull herself back inside and haul in the rope.

Her hands kept shaking as she wound the hemp around the neck of the bag and tied a double knot. She couldn't catch her breath. When she set the bag outside again, it didn't slip anymore. It just hung there. Lumpy.

She shut the window. The dog's bark sounded far away. Putting her bathing clothes back into her canvas bag, she went to a stall and sat on the toilet. For a long moment, she didn't move. But the tears never came. Nothing got through the numbness. Finally, she opened her purse and took out the slips of paper and her pen.

All she had to do was add the zeros.

34 ————————————————————————————

The hood of the black limousine was too hot to lean on. Rainbow scuffed a heel in gravel. Any minute now, they might bring her out at gunpoint. He should have gone inside to protect her. He kicked the tire and walked toward the casino doors.

Iris came out as if in a daze, sunlight brightening the dark green of her hat and dress, her eyes.

He turned, pretending he hadn't seen her, and started down the drive. At the giant elm, he ducked into cover. Her footsteps got louder. If he hadn't called her name, she would have passed right by.

"Something wrong, sweetheart?" He had been meaning to call her that for a long time. It felt good. She shook her head and gave him two slips of paper. When he saw the five-to-one odds and E.R.'s signature, he picked her up and whirled her around. The canvas bag swung wide into the tree. "You're incredible."

She didn't say anything. Fitting her hair back under the tiny hat, she turned to the sound of tramping feet.

Curtis saw them instantly. With a glance up the drive, he stepped into the bushes. "They wouldn't let me upstairs. Couldn't see what she was doing."

"I used the powder room," she said.

Dark eyes narrowed. "What for?"

"Do you have to ask?"

Curtis reached into the canvas bag. His hand came up empty. "Ought to check her purse. And her clothes."

"Sure, it's all in here." Rainbow tapped the tiny clutch purse.

"Every cent. She's a magician." He waved the betting slips. "Signed by E.R. himself. And we got five-to-one! She's helping you get rich, so quit hounding her. I told you it would work."

Studying the notes, Curtis frowned, his lips got tight. "Ain't worked yet." He gave back the slips, glared at Iris, and walked out of the trees and down the drive.

"I thought he was going to the track with us," she said.

"Just walking off some steam." Rainbow kissed her. "Worried about his cash, is all. Besides, he always was an ass." She blushed. He kissed her again, then led her out to Broadway and into the crowd.

With her on his arm, the sidewalk seemed friendlier, less boisterous. He followed Spring Street into Circular and kept to the north side of Union Avenue. "Sam Riddle lives there," he said, pointing to the house with the hole in the lawn a half-block ahead. "Owns Man o' War. Bought him right here at the Sales. For five thousand!"

"You've been talking to Horace." Her face was drawn and glazed by sadness, as if someone had just told her that she had flunked out of one of those fancy schools her father had sent her to. "Did he tell you he had the chance to buy that horse himself?"

Rainbow laughed. "Never mentioned that. Of course, I don't go around telling people I missed a bet on the Black Sox Series, either."

Instead of smiling, she looked over her shoulder at Curtis, a hulking figure in pale blue, fifty feet down the street. "Why doesn't he walk with us?"

"Maybe he knows his place." Rainbow went off the curb to pass a group of soldiers. A klaxon blew him back onto the sidewalk. Beside the portico of E.R.'s house across the street, three guards played mumbletypeg with a pocketknife. The drapes were pulled back, the front door stood open. But there was nothing to see.

"Did you serve?" she said.

"Serve what?"

"In the war . . . ?"

He glanced back at the soldiers in tan uniforms with brightly colored ribbons sewn above their breast pockets. She probably liked those outfits. He laughed and drew her close. "Yes ma'am. And if them Germans had ever got to East Tennessee, I'd of been ready for them." A smile broke through her frown. He rubbed her arm. "Besides, I didn't have to join the army to learn how to shoot."

Past the row of bookmakers by the fence around the track, the sign over the gate read: FIELD STAND—$1.00, GRANDSTAND—$1.50, CLUB HOUSE—$2.50. Rainbow bought three clubhouse tickets and waited for Curtis to come through the crowd. "Better stay close in case they make trouble for you inside. We'll tell them you're my bodyguard."

"Don't worry, sport. I ain't letting you out of my sight." Curtis grinned at Iris. "Either of you."

Pressing her to his side, Rainbow got on line and followed the throng through the gates. Near the edge of the path to the saddling area, he found an empty spot beneath high branches which drooped and overlapped to form a natural dome.

"Don't you want to see any races?" Iris said. "The clubhouse will be filled soon."

"At two-fifty a head?" Rainbow held up the torn ticket stubs. "Shouldn't be more than a handful of people up there. We'll leave here after I see Old Smoke and talk with Horace. Don't want to chance losing a place at ringside."

She stared at the ground. "But it's at least two hours until the sixth race. That's a long time to stand—isn't it?"

"Two hours to wait," Rainbow said, "and it only takes them two minutes to run from line to line. Something to think about, all right."

Curtis tapped him on the shoulder. "I think your Miss Winslow wants to sit down, sport. Why don't you spread your jacket on the grass and make like a gentleman."

Holding back his anger, Rainbow dug into her canvas bag and spread the swimsuit on the ground. "This'll be fine. Won't stain if you don't sit on it too hard."

Iris looked at the suit for a long moment, then sat softly, pulling her dress to cover her legs.

Rainbow grinned at Curtis. "See? No problem here."

"No problem," Curtis said, folding his arms across his chest. "And right after we collect our money, you can tell me all about that other problem you don't got—Old Cal." His smile hardened. "Didn't shoot him, did you?"

Rainbow stared at his shoes. Finally, he shook his head.

"Might just be hope for you yet, sport." Curtis put an arm on his shoulder. "But I ain't giving no odds on it."

Streaks of sun coming through the branches played on the paddock buildings. Rainbow sat on the grass beside Iris. Two hours seemed like a long time to wait. He busied himself with killing ants.

The string of horses for the sixth race minced up the paddock trail. A saddle stuck under his arm, reins lashed to his hand, Georgy Morris tugged at his baseball cap and led Old Smoke onto the grass.

Alongside, Horace studied the white bands wrapped around all four shanks. He helped turn the golden chestnut between elms, then pushed Georgy away and began the work of saddling.

Curtis stepped closer, putting Iris in shadow. "You see what I see, sport?"

She leaned on Rainbow's arm. "He always saddles them himself."

"He means the front wraps," Rainbow said. "We never bet a horse with front wraps on."

". . . Superstition?" she said.

Rainbow shook his head. "Forelegs are the most sensitive. If they're sore enough to need wraps, we don't bet the horse." He waved, but the bald man was too busy with the girth to see.

"Better run her right back to The Park and get our money out, sport."

Iris kept her stare on the ground. Her voice sounded small, as if she had swallowed most of it. ". . . Maybe he plans to take them off before the race."

People near the clubhouse began to clap. Up the trail came jockeys in circus-colored caps and shirts. The final three tucked fresh silks into their riding pants and wiped the dirt of the last race from their cheeks. Bobby Monroe swaggered by, slapping a short whip against his palm.

"That's our boy there," Rainbow said.

Curtis nodded at the bright yellow silks emblazoned with a blue M inside a blue circle. "Awful loud colors."

Her voice came back strong: "My father had them designed in Paris."

Shaking his head, Curtis let out a sigh. "Didn't know they had niggers over there."

Iris huffed and threw a *tsk* into Rainbow's chuckle, then raised a gloved hand to cover her own grin.

After he had walked the ring and glanced at each horse, the paddock judge announced, "Riders—*up!*" Horace built a seat of hands for the small brown boot and gave his jockey a leg up into the saddle. Each rein was given separately to form the rider's cross. Stirrups were adjusted to suit the habit of the seat. Two nods of the yellow cap, a tug at the bit, one tap on the rump, and Old Smoke moved out in a lazy walk. The front wraps were still on.

This time, the wave worked. Rainbow waited for Horace to scamper across the grass. "Why are his forelegs wrapped?"

"For protection." Horace winked. "Meet you in the winner's circle."

"I want the front wraps off."

"Why? I just told you—"

"He thinks the forelegs are sore," Iris said.

"Sore?" Horace scratched his neck. "I'd never run a horse with hurt legs. Old Smoke's sound as a dollar."

"Bad sign if you ask me, sport," Curtis said.

The old jockey glared at the black, then glanced from Iris to Rainbow. "You handle your end all right?"

Rainbow nodded. "You sure his forelegs are okay?"

"What's got into you? Ain't nothing to worry about. What odds you get?"

"Five-to-one." Rainbow looked at Curtis, then rubbed his chin. "We—I don't like betting a horse with front wraps on. Lost a bundle once."

"Well, you stand to make a killing here," Horace said. "Relax. Them wraps gives us an edge in case we get clipped—if, say, there was a three-horse box?" Another wink. "I seen to everything." He squinted at Iris. "Gonna do your old man proud today. Kiss for good luck?"

She bent down and kissed the top of his head.

"Only wish we had you in the saddle," Rainbow said.

Fingers strong from years of racing leather squeezed Rainbow's shoulder. "Winner's circle," Horace said and off he went down the trail and into the trees.

With military bursts, a bugle called the colors to the track.

"Don't like this one bit," Curtis said.

"Relax. He took care of things just like I told him." Rainbow led Iris toward the clubhouse. The jingle of a tambourine was rolling off the leaves. Outside the gates, Dancer romped along the iron fence, imprisoned there by law and besieged by men who hungered for his scraps of paper hope. Rainbow tucked the wager slips deep into his pocket and worked up the crowded stairs. Down front, Taylor North read a magazine while his wife peered through jeweled opera glasses. A box five rows over was vacant except for the large head of Aziz and a billow of smoke.

"We sit on the finish line today." With a smile, Rainbow led her down the aisle. "Mind if we join you, Greek?"

Stavros lowered his field glasses, bit on his cigar. "Help yourself."

Behind him, Aziz got up to seat Iris at the rail. Rainbow slid in next to her. Taking the aisle chair in the second row, Curtis made a sour face:

"Ain't this the goon that slugged me?"

"Forget it." Rainbow could sense the strain of eyes in back of him, the clenched fists. He forced himself to concentrate on the horses now breaking parade ranks and trotting up the stretch.

"Got any hunches?" Stavros said.

Iris lowered her gaze, shook her head.

"Favorite color then." The cigar swung to the other side of his mouth. "Everybody's got a favorite color, right?"

Her voice sounded broken again. "Green."

Stavros scanned the field. "No greens." The glasses fell limp on the strap about his neck. ". . . Rainbow?"

"Haven't looked yet, Greek. We just came to watch them run. Before we leave."

Flicking an ash over the rail, Stavros nodded sideways. "How about the—the colored? He a horse player?"

"Old Smoke," Curtis said. "It's a sure thing."

Rainbow squeezed the wood slat on the back of her chair, then turned and chided dark and smiling eyes. "Listen to him and we'll all go broke."

"No, not a bad bet," Stavros said. "I made Morning Cup the favorite, but your colored's right. Old Smoke figures. Coming off a slow workout, though, so I made him five-to-one. Decent bet." He nodded to himself and raised the glasses for another look.

One by one, the field of seven came off the backstretch to line up abreast the black and white pole. Reins tight to still their pawing mounts, jockeys eyed the wooden scaffold where a man in a red jacket poised a small red flag.

"Mile and an eighth." Stavros took a stopwatch from his vest. "Track record's safe with these dogs."

One minute and fifty seconds. For $1,050,000. Rainbow kissed Iris on the cheek: "For luck."

The flag cut the air, the stopwatch button clicked. A few horses backed up flat-footed before they dumped their heads and bolted down the stretch. Roars filled the stands, everyone stood. Everyone but Aziz. And Iris.

With jockeys posted high, the pack charged across the finish line and leaned into the clubhouse turn. A rain of dirt followed them into the backstretch. The yellow and blue silks ran fourth.

"Look at this bum I got," Stavros said. "Five lengths off the pace." Teeth chomping his cigar, he muttered, "Close it up," over and over again as if the horse could hear.

"I'll raise you up if you want to see," Rainbow told Iris.

She didn't look at him. "I don't have to see."

He fought off a twinge of laughter, then sat and took her hand. "You're right."

Below, where the clubhouse met the grandstands, the patio fence turned back on itself at right angles to cut a square of emptiness out of the swarm of arms and hats. Inside the square: a white chalk circle only large enough to hold one horse.

"What you said to Horace—about his riding again." She was looking straight ahead. Her eyes were wet. "I love you for that."

By the time Rainbow had shaped "I love you, Iris," the words were already lost to a deafening crescendo that set the crowd on tiptoe. Fists shook, newspapers flagged. Caged baboons could not have done a better job of cheering. Any horse worth a saltlick would have kept on running, if only to escape the tourists.

"Men from the boys," Stavros said, his glasses trained on the top of the stretch.

Rainbow savored a smile and cluttered his head with long division to determine how much money he was making per second. But suddenly, his armpits ached, his body left the seat, feet dangled to the ground.

Curtis tightened his grip. "Look!"

Yellow silks, now golden in the sun, led the race for home. But not for long. Old Smoke lugged out from the rail in a broken gait, legs striding up instead of out—climbing—fading in the stretch. Dying.

The rest of the field closed fast, yet it took a long time to end. Each inch of ground became a wound. The big chestnut was running sideways. No rein, no whip could save it.

Wild screams tore the air apart. Then silence, a pantomime of twisted forms: colors streaming by, jockeys popping tall in the saddle, horses running out to the turn.

Old Smoke hung on for third.

Curtis let go. Rainbow stumbled on rag-doll legs and slid onto the seat. The sound came back. Confetti floated down in swirls.

"The white and blue, Taylor!" Grace North kept bouncing, her diamonds lighting the shadows. "The white and blue!"

"Morning Cup," Stavros said. "One fifty-three flat. Seen better workout times." He pocketed his watch and tossed a laugh at Curtis. "Some sure thing you had. Almost keeled over."

Rainbow chewed the taste of bile. He grabbed Iris by the wrist, pulling her from her chair.

"Stick around," Stavros said. "Got a nice thing for you in the eighth."

But Rainbow had her moving up the row.

"Hey!" Stavros called. "No hard feelings about this morning, am I right?"

Rainbow shoved past the men at the head of the stairs and hurried down the steps to the paddock, away from the crowd and toward the stable path.

Iris wrenched free. "You don't have to drag me."

"I'll kick his little butt back to Kentucky!"

She rubbed her wrist. "It wasn't his fault."

At a run, Curtis came over the lawn and spun her around. "Set us up, didn't you, Miss Winslow."

"Take your hands off her," Rainbow said.

"Don't you go telling me nothing, sport." Curtis shook her by the shoulders. Her hat fell off. "She'll tell me. Everything."

The .45 seemed to come off Rainbow's hip automatically, the hammer cocked. And he heard himself talking: "Still no law against shooting niggers."

Black skin stretched tight. Curtis let her go. "Just can't see, can you."

She ran to Rainbow, buried a whisper in his chest. "I'm sorry."

"No way in hell to lose a boat race, sport. We was set *up*. Don't ask me how. For all I know she *is* a goddamn magician."

"She only did what I told her." Rainbow winced. His head began to throb. His stomach turned, skin flushed hot, and something sharp like splintered bone curled inside him. He put the pistol away, wrapped his arms around her to cradle her tears as if they were his own. "It wasn't her fault."

"Shit!" Curtis kicked her hat along the path. "Gonna bust that runt wide open."

"Don't let him hurt Horace," she said.

"We're just gonna go see him, sweetheart."

"The sucker done run us into the ground, sport. Ain't no time to pay him no *social* visit."

"I'm warning you," Rainbow said. "Lay off!"

"You warn me shit!" The light-blue suit bulged with muscle. "I just dropped twenty-five grand here. On account of that bald mother. And her."

"What about my bankroll?" Rainbow yelled. "Christ can't you think of nobody but yourself?"

"You *ass!*" Curtis brandished his fist. "I ought to pole you flat. After I get done with the great Mr. Wells."

Iris spoke quickly, but her voice flattened out against the leaves. "He's so—old. Rainbow . . . please?"

Hooves beat on distant clay. Fresh horses were heading toward the paddock, there was no way to stop them. Time kept moving to its own rhythm: a new race was about to be run.

"Nobody's gonna hurt him," Rainbow said. "We better get to the stables."

She didn't move. "I can't face him. Not now."

He pushed back his panama and stared at Curtis. "Got any money left?"

"Don't go pretending to worry about me, sport. I'll make out just fine."

"I want you to take her back to the hotel. Buy her lunch or something, let her get fixed up."

The big black hand came out of the suit pocket with a crumpled bill, a few small coins. "Can't do it."

"I have a hundred dollars," she said. "And I don't need *his* company."

Rainbow turned her gently. "It'll be all right. Won't it, Curtis. You even look at her wrong and I'll—"

"Yeah, I remember all about that law they don't got." The laugh came out like a growl. "Where you think you is, boy—East Tennessee? Point that gun at me again, I'll see you eat it." Curtis dusted the little green hat against his leg as if beating a rug. "Wouldn't soil my hands on Miss Society."

Rainbow snatched the hat from him and set it on her head. Her cheek tasted of salt. "Meet you in the lobby. I won't be long."

Metal jangled, leather slapped. New horses came onto the trail in a slow, steady plod, the cadence of a dirge. He walked between the elms and told himself that he didn't need to look back—Curtis wouldn't touch her, she would be safe.

He looked back. She was gone.

Past the shadow of the grandstand, the path was caked and yellow, as if a narrow strip of desert had been bent to the curve of the track. Flies swirled at his shoes, then flew back to feast on mounds of dung. Around the corner, tethered to a post at the last stall, Old Smoke stood blanketed, hobbling in pain on three legs. Seated beside the post, Horace swigged from a tiny bottle and stared into a handful of bloodstained gauze. Rainbow positioned himself directly over the little man, tucked his jacket flap behind the .45, stroked the taped handle.

"Blown. . . ." The old jockey didn't try to stand. His breath was soaked with rye. He pulled a second bottle from his pocket. Both labels were written in French and carried the same word: PARFUM. Taking another drink, he crawled next to the unwrapped foreleg. From a gash above the swollen fetlock, blood trickled over shiny hair. Jutting out of the wound like an arrow's broken shaft—a slender bone. Tenderly, he dabbed the cut with the gauze. The horse shied.

"Got clipped," Horace said. "Even went through my wraps. Jock says it was from Benecia Boy, top of the stretch. Hardpan likely did the rest. Bastards always water it too much, dries it out." He drained the second bottle. "You seen his heart, though. Ran lugging out to the linc. Nobody could of held him straight. Not even me."

Rainbow couldn't get the pistol off his belt, couldn't make a fist. Couldn't take his stare from the wound.

Horace stood and stroked the withers. "Kind as they come. Paid his way, too. Could of retired him this year, let him run free and punch the slickest mares in bluegrass. Now—" He tossed the bottle down. Old Smoke whinnied and snorted, then let out a horrible sound, weak like the cry of a lost child. Horace winced. "Reckon he knows what's got to be done."

At the stall box, he began breaking down a bridle, crownpiece first. "It ain't so much the plans I had for that money. I just wanted to show them Horace Wells can still bring them home. Matter of time now before they'll be calling me the guy what can't even take a fucking boat race." Angry fingers worked over a leather knot. "Suppose you'll be wanting to talk with our jock. Told him to stop by after his next ride."

Rainbow scuffed a shoe in the dirt. "No need. I saw what happened." He hadn't seen any of it. But it didn't matter. Old Smoke struggled to maintain balance. And failed. The big horse collapsed, rolling on its back, three legs kicking, one bent and motionless. He freed the tether from the post ring and stroked the horse's head. "Buy you a drink, Horace?"

As if both insulted and surprised, the bald man squinted, then shook his head and mocked himself with a laugh. "Splinters a shank and still takes show. . . . We're due a couple of hundred from the purse."

Blood kept flowing over that bone, dripping into the dust. "Keep the purse," Rainbow said. "For seeing to him."

Horace nodded with the gratitude of beggars in the street. "Like to see Iris get some of it, though."

"I'll take care of her." Rainbow stepped away from the horse. "I could have a word with the Greek, maybe find you another stable to work. Right here."

"Got to get them yearlings ready to sell, no twenty-a-week job can save them now." Horace used his shirtsleeve to wipe his nose. "Something fine in you to think of me like that. Especially now."

"Never did like losing," Rainbow said, but when he reached deep for words, he found instead the silken image of her face. So beautiful. And fragile. "At least it's only money."

"Style, son. What I liked about you from the first." The strength went out of the old man's handshake. "Won't let on about Old Smoke, will you? Likely she's upset enough, knowing how this'll affect her old man." He sighed and leaned against the stall. The bridle strips came loose in his hand. "Better leave now. Vet'll be here in a minute. It ain't gonna be pretty."

Rainbow stood there for a long moment, trying to think of something to say. Nothing fit. Across the track, a bugle sounded: another parade. He stepped around the fallen horse and turned the corner.

Down by the well, little Georgy Morris hauled a pail so heavy that his shoulders slanted from the weight of it. A few steps behind him walked a man with a large black bag. " 'Stay away, don't come near me,' he says, 'you don't know what you're talking about,' " Georgy was saying. He didn't stop to pick up his ball cap when it fell off. The bucket carried him around the corner. "Well, I heard him myself, doc. He ain't right in the head to do a thing like that."

The sun burned white. Rainbow crept back to the edge of the stable.

"Told you to stay clear of me." Horace cracked the strips of leather like a whip. "Give it to me, doc."

The black bag clinked when it hit the ground. "Morris has some serious allegations concerning you."

"He's full of shit," Horace said. "Got clipped in a box. Racing luck."

"Liar!" Georgy set the bucket down. "You told Monroe to run him up their heels." He pointed toward the commissary. "I was standing right there."

Rainbow ducked back behind the wood. A loud smack was followed by a crash. He peered out again. Georgy lay next to the overturned pail, among chunks of ice that sweated in the dust.

"Talk to me like that, will you, you little never-was-been?" Horace cuffed him with the straps. "Think I'd run a horse right into a pack? For a lousy couple of bucks?" He picked up a piece of ice from the dirt and put it on the wounded shank. Old Smoke lay quiet. "Now get! Both of you. Just leave me the gun. I'll do it myself."

"A lousy couple of bucks," Rainbow said, his voice soft like a church whisper, his fingers tight on his .45. That bald head made such an easy target. Too easy. The bastard deserved to be castrated. Then drawn and quartered. Then . . .

"It's my job," the vet said. "And when I'm finished, we'll see the stewards."

Shouting curses, Horace dug into the black bag, tossing shiny instruments out in search of the pistol. "Said I'd do it myself. And quick. My daughter'll be here any second. She never did have the stomach for putting them out of their misery. Where the fuck is that gun, doc?"

Leaning heavily against the siding, Rainbow pulled out the wager slips. No wind came to blow them away, they lay flat in his palm, the ink blurring, numbers and words—her handwriting—becoming a broad black band. He blinked to clear his vision and jammed the worthless notes in his pocket, down beside the ring box. His daughter? *Iris?* His mouth stiffened over clenched teeth: "The little bitch." He yanked his .45 out and started to step around the corner, then stopped. And smiled. *Let them think they pulled it off. Slow them down.* More time to catch her. And get his money back. He slid the pistol into his belt. A roar blew out of the grandstand. He ran.

Once through the stables to the path paralleling the backstretch, the rumble came straight at him, the ground began to shake. His legs pumped, arms swung, his mouth got dry—*Stupid cunt!*—but he couldn't outrace the thunder. The horses drove past in a momentary stripe of blues and reds, greens and golds. Then hooves pounded into the distance, the colors bent around the turn. He pressed for more speed, as if the crowd's cheers were meant for him. The screams exploded, then died on a wind of sighs.

And from behind, far away, a single gunshot split the air.

He ran faster. Gasping for breath, he vaulted the white rail fence and pulled up near the curb. The sidewalk was dappled gray with shade. Down by the gates, tourists milled around bookmakers. How far could she get in all those people? She might not have reached the hotel yet. He broke into a trot.

All at once, his legs locked.

On the fringe of the crowd, hollow blue eyes stopped searching the gutter for stray coins long enough to focus up the street. Lips moved, an arm raised high. Old Cal began to jog.

Rainbow jumped behind the twin elms in the middle of the road. But it was no use: Cal kept coming. Farther down, Stavros was getting into the black limousine straddling the sidewalk and the road. Exhaust kicked up, tires rolled, the horn blew tourists out of the way. And Old Cal was moving through traffic, jacket flapping, his mouth open to yell.

"Greek!" Rainbow's shout had no power. Sprinting to break the collision course with the old man, he lunged at the car, banged on the trunk. The limousine stopped, a rear door popped open. "Greek! Give me a ride to—"

He never saw the hand that grabbed his tie and pulled him inside and down to the floor. He saw only a red birthmark on a big chin. A dusty foot of leather slapped against his ear, pinning him to the carpet. A hand yanked the .45 from his belt. The door slammed. Then knuckles rapped on glass. And the engine built up speed.

35

A car with the dented fender slowed to a crawl. Out of the passenger window leaned a milk-chocolate face: "Do she have a sister?"

Iris turned her back to the street. But another dark voice came at her:

"If he ain't sweet enough, lady, I *am* the man for you!"

Curtis stepped off the curb and kicked the rear bumper. "Get on out of here, you little bastards."

Laughter mixed with the racket of pistons. The car sped off and squealed around the corner onto Lincoln Avenue.

"Some folks got no sense of what they see." Curtis smoothed the wrinkles in his jacket. "You want to walk ahead of me, it'd be all right."

Iris took three brisk steps, then stopped. "Thank you for making them leave."

"Wanted to see them go just as bad as you. Little bas—beggars."

"Bastards," she said and turned to let him see her smile. He let out a laugh and matched her stride. Far down the block, where Regent Street fed into Lincoln, two boys threw rocks at the GREENRIDGE CEMETERY sign hanging on a fence of iron spears. Wood splintered. The boys jumped and went into their windups again. Iris stared at the grass sprouting from sidewalk cracks: "What will happen to him now?"

"Don't you worry," Curtis said. "You'll be right here to find out."

"I can't . . ." She couldn't raise her eyes. "He won't want me."

"He'll want you all right. Rainbow always did want what was bad for him." His grin lasted a few paces. "Man like him does the wrong thing all the time. Still busted up inside about his old man, no matter what he says. I can see it in his eyes. That thing he carries for Old Cal ain't left him yet. Expect it never will. It'll be the same with him and you. The sucker's hopeless."

His father? That grimy, worthless imbecile? No wonder Rainbow told Murph that the man was dead: Cal Robinson was a disgrace. Iris knew the feeling. "His name is . . . Robinson?"

Curtis stared into the distance. "Calvin Orville Robinson, Jr."

"Why—why did he change it to Roberts, then?"

The black's laugh came from deep in his stomach. "Only reason according to him was—it went better with Rainbow."

Rainbow Robinson, Rainbow Roberts. She didn't see a difference. Not like the difference between Wells and Winslow. One was common, the other almost regal. Perhaps Rainbow hadn't given names as much thought as she had.

"Tried every combination under the sun," Curtis said. "Finally landed on Roberts when we was in Memphis. Just signed the hotel register that way and kept looking at it till it sunk in. Dumbest thing you ever seen." Another laugh. "Might be a good idea you had. About leaving him. Right after we all sit down with that bald runt and find out *exactly* what happened, why, I'll help you on a train myself."

She walked a few steps in silence. "It's kind of you to let me go to the spa to freshen up."

"I ought to thank you. For making it easier on me." Curtis was beaming. "Like our man says: sometimes, you got to let folks have their own way."

Something in his laugh sent a shiver up her back. She turned onto the walkway to the spa, tracking hollow steps over white tiles which had been scrubbed so often they bore a patina, like antique silver. Set back deep on the lawn, the old house looked warm and inviting. Its Victorian gables were painted gray, its siding white. Over the door, a large sign: DR. TALBERT'S EARTH AND MINERAL BATHS—THE NATURAL CURE. Inside, lace curtains and velvet seat cushions. The parlor had been converted to a waiting room, with offices to one side. She went to the woman sitting behind the window of the last office and asked for the mineral bath.

"Ladies' Day for another two hours." The woman put down her newspaper and rattled a small key on the counter. "Locker number sixteen, through the door on your left, past the pool, be two dollars."

Curtis covered the key with his hand. "She don't need a locker."

The woman stared at the black skin for a moment, then cleared her throat. "He'll have to wait outside. The two dollars, miss?"

Iris opened her purse. Curtis took it from her, found a five-dollar bill, and gave it to the woman behind the window. Counting his change, he smiled and snapped the purse shut. "This'll be a lot safer with me than in any tin locker. So will your clothes." A big grin. "See what I mean about my thanking you?"

"As soon as I've changed into my suit," Iris said, glaring at him, "I'll have my things sent out to you."

He grabbed the canvas bag, pulled out the suit, tucked it under his arm. "Won't need this either. Be just like skinny-dipping in a lake." Another grin. He handed back the bag. "Don't you run away now."

She spun around and marched down the hall. Curtis followed, despite the protests of the woman behind the window.

"And just so we understand each other, *Miss* Winslow . . ." He stepped past her to block the forward progress of a small black woman who trudged by with a bundle of towels. "Keep an eye on this lady for me," he said, laying a dollar on the towels. "Let me know if she tries to rent a suit. Or sneak out."

"You ain't allowed back here." Even when the small woman straightened up, she looked stooped over. "Water ain't for darkies." And pressing her chin down on the dollar, she shuffled toward the heavy door at the end of the hall.

Curtis was beaming again. "Have that pretty green dress and whatever else it is you got under it out to me in five minutes. And yourself back out here in thirty. Else I might have to come in and get you. Wouldn't want to give me no thrill like that, now would you . . . ?"

Iris fought the big brown eyes that worked over her with contempt. "Will you have my clothes sent in when I ask for them?"

"We aim to please, miss." He doffed his hat. "Excuse me now while I make a phone call to the hotel so Rainbow don't think we ran off to elope." Whistling through his teeth, he sauntered back into the parlor.

Iris clenched her fists, then stormed through the locker-room door. Past the sign, SHOWER BEFORE USING BATHS, she found benches below a row of high windows. Undressing quickly, she folded her clothes and stacked them in the canvas bag, underwear first. But it wouldn't matter where she tried to hide them, Curtis would go through everything and take inventory. At least he had left her the bath cap. She took a towel from the black attendant and gave her the bag of clothes to take out to the parlor. Only three minutes had passed. She left her wristwatch on the bench and stepped into the last shower stall. The nozzle spray felt hard on her skin. She turned off the tap, wrapped the towel around her body, and walked across the room and out to the pool.

A metal rail guarded the steps at the shallow end. Overhead lights put a sparkle on the rippling sheet of water. The hint of steam rose about jeweled flesh: some of the women were naked, breasts swaying in the currents, hides shimmering as if coated with oil; others wore wool suits which sagged and billowed. Around the pool, a few ladies lounged in white body wraps, arms limp over the slats of wooden chairs. Iris left her towel on the bench against the wall and hurried into the cresting waves, hoping to cover her nakedness with water before anyone noticed. But this was how they bathed in Europe, wasn't it? Even if she had ever really been to London or Paris or Bonn, she would have worn her bathing suit to the baths.

The glare from diamonds and emeralds made her squint. She swam past the other women to the far side. Arms crossed on the edge of the pool, she nestled her head, closed her eyes. From out of the poolside, jets of water pulsed against her and lulled her into a floating daze. She spread her legs wide to the wind of fingers. Hips rigid to the surge, she pushed against the current, rocking and swelling with warmth until the tingles between her legs jelled into one fast knot and she felt slippery, like blood-soaked meat. Her mouth stretched wide, breath passed between her lips like a sweaty prayer. She drew cool air off the concrete.

"Ask me, you'd be better off with one of your own kind." The voice sounded far away. Iris opened her eyes to white shoes and socks that wrinkled over bulging ankles. Foreshortened by the angle, the black attendant's head appeared to grow out of her legs. "Just 'cause I took his money," the small woman said, "don't mean I got to do what he says. Ain't right for a man to look through a lady's clothes like that. Don't you ask me to do nothing else for you." Her shoes scuffed the cement and she sat on the bench by the locker-room door.

Now the water tumbled hard like a runnel of pellets. Iris swung her legs up and out to avoid it. Around her, gossip swirled over the tide, bubbles burst against her skin. She felt porous, dangling off the side like a sheet of lace. Shutting her eyes, she let go of the wall. Water rushed past her ears, over her bathing cap. She sank in what seemed like a fathomless well. The spring of muffled concussion blew her away from poolside and pushed her down. Fingers locked about her knees, legs pulled in close, she crouched in a ball on the bottom. And though she pressed her eyelids tight, some tears still escaped. She was never going to see him again, never be with him: Rainbow would be only a memory now. A beautiful one, but forever stained by what she had done to him. *No future, only a past.* To haunt her.

She tried to concentrate on pieces of memorized crossword puzzles, praying that she could forget she was underwater, take a breath, and drown. Her lungs grew hard, neck cords strained. Slowly, and with no effort on her part, a natural buoyancy she never knew she had lifted and carried her toward the surface.

The chair was too small. Rainbow crossed his legs; the rub of material broke the long silence. Laid out on the table in front of the fireplace: a crumpled wad of paper slips, the ring box, his .45, the coroner's receipts, the gold locket, and thirty-six cents.

"How much longer?" Stavros leaned on the couch cushions to take a light from Aziz. At some point during the last half-hour, the sun through the windows had lost its power to highlight specks of dust, which now turned and rolled as a pall of crumbling haze. "I'm missing opening day here."

"E.R.'ll get here when he can." The big man with the birthmark on his chin stood by the bookcases and flashed a wry grin. "You're not in any hurry, Greek."

The library door swung open. Roze walked in, shut the door, nodded politely. "Gentlemen."

"Whatever this is," Stavros said, "I got no part of it."

"Like to believe that, Greek." Roze moved behind the table, rubbed the taped handle of the .45, cocked an eyebrow, then shook it off. "But I can't. Not until I know how much. And how."

Stavros aimed cigar smoke at Rainbow. "This another of your two-bit hustles?"

"I'm just as confused as you are, Greek." Rainbow dodged the smoke. "But let's find out so I can catch the early train. Got business in the city."

Roze chuckled. "Which race?"

The chair pressed against Rainbow's spine, a squint ruined his deadpan mask. The bastard knew.

"We can do it any way you like," Roze said. "But since I got to get back to my club, I'll tell you I got a phone call saying it was Old Smoke in the sixth. At five-to-one." He picked up the ring box. "Now you tell me how you and the Greek placed the bets. And how much you're gonna give me out of the winnings." The velvet lid sprang open, a glitter reflected onto his black silk jacket. "Very nice," he said, turning the box for all to see. "For your lady? Must be love. Bring her by so I can meet her."

The diamond stared back. Rainbow studied heelmarks on the plank floor. "Won it in a poker game. Off . . . Taylor North." He let out a defeated sigh. "Your books wouldn't handle more than five grand a shot. I never got the money down."

A little moan came from Stavros. Then: "You stupid sonofabitch. . . ."

"The Greek had nothing to do with it," Rainbow said. "It was my idea."

Roze set the ring box on the table. "You fix a race—and don't make the bets?"

"I couldn't figure a way to place it without you finding out, E.R. Even if I did, my horse lost."

Cod eyes got milky with suspicion. ". . . Greek?"

"Morning Cup by three lengths over Benecia Boy," Stavros said. "Old Smoke takes show on three legs." He held up an open palm. "First I hear of this, right now. I swear."

"What odds you give on Morning Cup?" Roze said.

"Five-to-two."

Roze's pale eyelids closed halfway. "Still a nice payoff. So this thing with Old Smoke is just a game. You have somebody call me to throw me off. And all the time you got it fixed the other way." Thin lips parted as if to savor a delicate taste. "Very nice."

"It wasn't like that," Rainbow said. "I told you. I never made the bets."

Roze examined the coroner's receipts, glanced at the big man by the bookcase, then put the stiff pieces of paper next to the pile of coins. "Sorry about your friend, Murphy. You understand, it was an accident."

Rainbow kept his gaze low. "I understand. . . ."

"Regrettable. . . ." With his palm, Roze rolled the ball of wager slips back and forth over the tabletop. "So how'd you get the money down without it showing heavy in my books?"

That paper wad looked like the fulcrum of a juggler's balance board. Rainbow rubbed the shoeprint on his collar. "I bet it by phone. Saint Louie. Got the same odds as here. On twenty grand." He shrugged, but backed the lie with truth. "Won't cost you a dime. And the Greek's telling the truth, he didn't know. I had it planned a long time.

So just let me have my stuff and I'm on the next train out."

The paper ball went still. "Who in Saint Louis?"

"Sam the Bootblack King," Rainbow said. "From the East Side. Know him?"

Roze turned to the fireplace and traced a finger over the mortar between gray stones. "I'll take fifty percent."

Rainbow tried a laugh. "Already got a partner, E.R."

"You throw a boat race up here, you pay me." Roze leaned on the table. His hand flattened the paper wad. "And I want it before you catch that train."

Rainbow swallowed hard. "The cash is in Saint Louis. And I got people to pay off. Be lucky to clear fifty percent myself."

"Your problem, not mine." Roze started to unravel the slips. "Should have told me. I might have helped it along."

"Next time." Rainbow's voice strained higher than normal. "I'll come straight to you, E.R., and we'll—"

Too late. Roze had one of the slips free. His eyes narrowed.

"Maybe I can raise fifteen grand today." Rainbow got up and grabbed for the slips. Instantly, cold fingers wrapped around his throat and dragged him back down into the chair. The fingers relaxed, but the big man with the birthmark on his chin stayed within arm's reach.

"Sam the Bootblack King?" Roze held both slips and shook his head. His laugh came sharp and hard. "Greek, I'm sorry. I thought—"

"Those are phony," Rainbow said.

"No, they're real." E.R. brandished the slips. "I signed them. You really give her this much cash. We ought to have these framed." Another laugh. "Greek, this dame, Winslow, she comes into my office at the club." He handed the slips to Stavros. "And you know how much she puts down? Two hundred and ten bucks. Get it?"

Stavros kept reading the notes as if they were a puzzle.

"The zeros!" Roze jabbed at the slips. "She adds the zeros!"

Stavros glanced at Rainbow, then shook his head sadly.

"Where the hell's your sense of humor?" Roze grabbed the notes, wadded them up, and tossed them to Rainbow. "So much talk I hear about how smart you are? All the time you're a sucker for a pair of tits."

Rainbow stuffed the wad into his jacket. "I bet with the Bootblack King. Call him, he'll tell you."

"This for her, too?" Roze laughed and dropped the ring box into Rainbow's lap. "Greek—think my guests tonight will get a kick out of the reputation your boy's earned? Of course, I'll have to say who his oddsmaker was. Christ, they ought to put you guys on the radio."

Stavros snuffed out his cigar. His face was stern, but tired, as if he had given up and now hated himself for it. "Maybe we should call off the game, E.R."

"What, and break tradition?" Roze stepped back to the table. "Guests are already invited. We start at eight. Five-card stud, head to head. Like always. Maybe you can persuade your boy here to stick around. Sure, bring him along. We can always use a good laugh."

The Greek's black eyes fired at Rainbow. "Get out of here."

Sliding the ring box into his pocket, Rainbow got up. "I'll take my things now, E.R. Don't try to stop me."

Roze laughed, then nodded to the big man, who came to the table and unloaded the .45.

"Sure you want him to have this, E.R.?" the big man said.

"Yeah, maybe he's gonna shoot her." Roze's chuckle ended as a nasal sigh. "Christ, I wonder where."

With a grin that stretched the birthmark, the big man held the pistol out in one hand, bullets and coins in the other. "Here you go— loser."

Rainbow put the gun on his hip, the loose metal in his pockets, and swept his things from the table. "Greek, I'm sorry. . . ."

Stavros didn't look up. "Get the fuck out of here."

Turning down the brim of his panama, Rainbow opened the library door and stepped into the hall.

"One thing," Roze said. "And this I tell you as a favor. Whoever it was called and tipped me off, this guy almost gets you killed. Remember that next time you see him." And the door banged shut.

The caller had to be Horace. Rainbow was going to remember that. And pay the little bastard back. Once he had taken care of the drunk's daughter.

"We do now?" Angelo Batori limped out of the shadow of the staircase, one hand wringing his cook's apron, the other gripping his cane. "I help to shoot, yes?"

Rainbow turned on his heels and walked out the front door, past the guards and off the porch. Halfway across the lawn, he started to run.

36

The man who had been kept awake by the barking dog last night was now the only person in the hotel lobby. He sat on the couch, eyes closed, an unopened newspaper in his lap. Rainbow tried the door to the dining room. Locked. He cursed under his breath and meandered through the arcade, glancing into shops and around corners until he found himself back in the lobby. The couch was empty. Iris and Curtis were nowhere to be found.

"On the board, Mr. Roberts," the desk clerk said without looking up from the cards he was sorting.

"What board?"

A garter above the elbow tugged at a white sleeve when the clerk's arm stretched out. Near the front windows, a tall bulletin board stood on an easel. Across the top, MESSAGES, and tacked to the cork face, a hundred little slips of paper. And one napkin with *Jon, I'm at Dan's— Ray* scribbled in black ink which had dried in blotches. Rainbow stared at the notes, but couldn't focus. The board blurred white and gray.

"Your friend called again a few minutes ago," the desk clerk said. "I didn't think to put that one up since he already left a message the first time."

"What the hell are you talking about?"

The clerk patted his file cards into a stack, then came out from behind the desk. He snatched a paper from the center of the board and gave it to Rainbow. "He made it sound important, sir. Incidentally, we moved your cousin's things out of three-nineteen. What do you want us to do with them?"

The note felt crisp: *For Rainbow Roberts—31 at Dr. Talbert's Regent St. Spa.*

"Where's Regent Street?" Rainbow said.

"Straight down Broadway to Lincoln, sir. It's two blocks east. Now about your cousin's things . . ."

Rainbow ran out the doors, down the drive, and south on Broadway. Somewhere before Lincoln Avenue, the paper slipped out of his hand. He let it blow away. Curtis had probably told her about 31— their code for "join up": the sum of 25 and 6. And now she even knew that.

Loose coins and bullets jingled, the .45 rode high on his belt. He passed the boys by the cemetery and cut north onto Regent Street.

Curtis was waiting on the lawn outside the spa. "Took your damn sweet time, didn't you."

Rainbow didn't slow down. He slipped on the tile walk and landed on his hip. "Where is she?"

"In the baths." Curtis helped him up. "Should be ready to come out any minute now."

Up the porch steps and into the parlor, Rainbow stopped by the couch against the wall. "There a back way out of here?"

"Already seen to things, sport." The canvas bag swung back and forth on the string Curtis held. "She tries to leave, she does it in the buff."

Inside the bag: the black swimsuit, the green dress and hat, shoes, stockings, her underwear. The clothes smelled of her.

"I told you you'd have to wait outside," said the woman behind the office window.

"C'mon, sport. I got her purse, too."

Rainbow dropped the bag on the couch and started down the hall toward the pool.

"Sir, you can't!" The woman in the office got off her chair. "It's Ladies' Day!"

Curtis grabbed Rainbow's arm. "You crazy? She can't get out, I got that iced. You go in there, they'll jail us for sure."

"Stay here, then." Rainbow tore free and marched to the heavy door, yanking it open. With his first step toward the steamy pool, his jaw dropped, his eyes got wide. All that naked flesh. But he doffed his hat and said, "Afternoon, ladies," as if he had come to tea. It felt good.

Screams exploded all at once. They got louder when Curtis walked in. Bathing caps ducked underwater, breasts flapped, chairs toppled, feet skidded through puddles, towels flew, and the locker-room door opened and shut as if it led to a busy kitchen.

Rainbow took his time and eyed the ripples. Two heads shot up for air, then stole beneath the surface. Iris wasn't down there.

"Get!" A little black woman dressed all in white shuffled toward him, a yardstick cocked above her head. "You get right now!"

He dodged the blow. Wood struck cement. He kicked the stick out of her hand, into the pool. "Wait here, Curtis," he said, then pushed through the swing door and strode toward the showers.

More screams. Half-dressed women pulled on skirts, robes—anything close by—and hid their faces in the walls. One blonde fought her way inside a tall locker, but when her breasts got stuck, she covered her nipples with her hand and whispered a prayer to the top shelf.

Rainbow grinned. He was going to find Iris naked, drag her out to the pool, fetch the yardstick, and spank her until her fine ass bled. He searched the locker rows, eyes peering at him around tin corners. The screaming stopped. And so did he.

A rubber bathing cap lay in a puddle on a bench by the back wall. Another bench leaned upright, like a ladder, and directly above the top flat of wood, a casement window stood open wide. Sunlight flickered down, a cooling breeze blew in. She was gone.

"Get!"

A life preserver slammed into his neck, knocked him into the wall and onto the bench. He booted the white rubber circle out of the black woman's reach. Hands on hips, she looked like Mother Goose stooped over a flower. From a locker, she pulled out a coat hanger, raised it high. "I'll call the police if you don't get! Right now!"

Rainbow stood. His neck throbbed, the seat of his pants felt soggy. The wet bathing cap fell to the floor. He inched along the wall until he regained his footing, then raced up the shower lane and out the door.

Curtis was studying the water. "She ain't down here, sport."

"Seen to everything, did you? Had it iced, huh?" Rainbow measured the distance to that black chin. "She's escaped, you fucking ass." His right cross landed full on the button.

Curtis staggered back, teetering on the edge of the pool. His jaw snapped sideways, his legs wobbled, and his eyes started to close, but he didn't go down.

"Got out the goddamn window." Rainbow rubbed his knuckles and readied another punch. "She bilked us out of my bankroll—and you let her waltz off with it! Can't trust you to take a shit by yourself."

"Last time you're ever gonna slug me, goddamn it." Curtis worked his jaw around, tugged his hat, clenched his fists. "I'm the one who told you what she done long before you ever seen through this love shit you been pretending at. She's every bit as phony as that Majestic Farms. Say your prayers, sucker." He set his stance and cocked a fist. Then his eyes widened in alarm. "Look out!"

A piece of metal ripped Rainbow's jacket from collar to elbow. The little black woman drew her coat hanger back for another strike. "Right now, I says!"

Rainbow ran out the door, up the hall. The woman behind the office window held a phone to her mouth, but she stopped talking and smiled at him. Through the parlor, down the porch stairs, he raced over the tiles. At the sidewalk, he called to the boys hurling stones at the cemetery sign:

"Seen a lady come out of here? Real pretty, dark hair, wearing . . . naked. A towel around her maybe."

The boys giggled and went back into their windups. Two stones hit the sign. And the wail of sirens pierced the distant air.

Rainbow pushed back his hat. The street was empty. How far could she have gone in an hour? And practically naked?

"Little bitch cut me with that hanger." Curtis came out to the curb, holding his handkerchief to his cheek. "Still owe you a shot, damn it."

"I ought to shoot your ass off, you goddamn imbecile." Rainbow leaned toward the racetrack. The sirens were getting closer. He started running. "Letting her slip out on us like that. And with my goddamn money!"

"Our money," Curtis said, pulling alongside.

The sirens kept coming. Rainbow kept running, turning the corner onto Lincoln Avenue. The two young boys dropped their rocks in the middle of the street and hustled over the cemetery fence. The roar from the racetrack got louder with every passing street. With luck, there would still be time. To catch her. And make her pay. . . .

The dark colors of nightfall bleared the windscreen. Trees filed by—*vit-buzz, vit-vit-buzz.* Suddenly, a clearing stretched low to the horizon. Furrows ran together toward a white frame house two miles back off the highway. Then the flat field became a forest once more and the road got loud with the hum of passing tree trunks. Iris stared at the dashboard. Stacks of money littered the floor and seat. Rainbow's money. She turned a big black knob: the headlamps came on.

"Careful what you touch there," Horace said, his hands full of steering wheel. "She gets real sensitive if you throw the wrong switch. Liable to break down on us and we'd be sitting ducks out here in the pitch of night."

"No one's following us, Horace."

"Yeah, well, so far so good, I say." He studied the road, then turned and glanced in back of him. "Can't see a damn thing with that trailer."

The horse trailer he was dead set on returning to Belmont so no one would accuse him of stealing it—that trailer was empty. Iris forced herself to keep her eyes straight ahead. "He was the most beautiful horse we've ever owned."

"Now don't go to feeling so bad. Got us enough here for some serious horseflesh." He rippled bills against the wheel. "Out of his misery now, I done it myself. Gonna bury him there, ain't they? If I was a horse, I'd want to be put under at Saratoga myself. Nothing better. Except maybe Louisville. Besides, Old Smoke's being—gone, well, it sort of frees us up, don't it. Easier to travel without a horse, we'll make better time."

She nudged the money on the floor to make more room for her feet. The tan dress felt tight, her undergarments pinched: she had dressed too quickly after leaving the spa in a body wrap, and there hadn't been time to fix her clothes until the car was well out of town. And by then, she hadn't felt like fixing anything.

"And I'll tell you," Horace was saying, "I was wrong about him. Ran his heart out for us, he did. Told that boy to hold a tight rein and keep him back in the box. But damn if Old Smoke didn't want to make a run for it. Takes show on a busted leg. In all my years I ain't never heard of anything like it." The engine whine mimicked the sound of his sigh. He patted her knee. "And you done me proud, too. Handled Rainbow to a tee. He bought it five yards deep and more. Ain't no way he'll see it. We got us a free ride."

"You may be wrong."

"Nah, he didn't smell nothing." But Horace glanced over his shoulder again and wiped sweat from his forehead. "Odds are he accepts the loss, so he won't check."

"I meant about his coming after us," she said. "Someday soon. He won't want to find us."

"Can't count on that kind of luck. Rainbow's a smart one. Had me worried, I don't mind saying—you with that big act about wanting to call off the fix. I see now you was just laying it out there like bait, but—"

A bitter taste hit her stomach all at once. "Stop, Horace."

"All right, I'll keep quiet, but it's just I was confused by what you was doing till I caught on."

"The car," she said. "Stop. Now!"

Horace frowned. "What's wrong? Ain't mad at me, are you?"

Iris yanked the wheel toward the shoulder. The car braked to a stop. She shot out the door and bent over the weeds, hands on knees. And waited.

"Losing time, Iris. Stick your finger down if you got to, but let's get a move-on."

Her eyes felt sweaty. A stream of yellow came up her throat and through her nose. It hurt. Weeds staggered under the weight of warm fluid. She coughed until her mouth went dry.

Horace gunned the accelerator. "Feeling better now?"

She straightened up and walked back to the car. Strapped to the roof: her Saratoga trunk, hatboxes, suitcases, and a rolled duffel bag. The road was empty, only trees, dense walls of them, and telephone poles standing hard against the deepening sky. From her pocket, she got her handkerchief. The embroidered initials, *I.W.*, made the lace feel hard. She wiped her mouth, blew her nose. Her sinuses burned with the tang of vomit.

"C'mon, Iris. Do that inside, can't you?"

She blew her nose again, but this time, at him. "You don't have to worry, he's not coming after me." All that money, just lying on the floor. "I'm not that lucky. . . ."

"I ain't worried about him," he said. "I seen to that. Want to beat the train into the city. Then maybe sail for Europe, you and me. Find you a lord or an earl." He waved a stack of bills. "Be willing to brace a dowry if need be, set you up fine. Always did like it over there. Got real style, them limeys." The way he was smiling said that he was about to tell her about Epsom Downs again. "Treated me like royalty when I took the Manor Run at Epsom. Probably still remember me for that ride. Got letters long afterwards, too. Some of them was— personal, I guess you'd say. Always wanted to go back." He looked at her as if she belonged somewhere else. "You wasn't even born yet."

She tossed the handkerchief into the weeds. "They don't remember, Horace. No one does."

He looked back up the road. "Might. . . ." Then he cleared his throat. "C'mon, get in. Making bad enough time as it is with all the damn bags of yours I got to haul."

"I need them."

"I need them," he said, mocking her voice. "Spent a fortune on them. All I get is a duffel. Well, it's time I got me something for once, instead of shelling out for more goddamn dresses. Now get in."

She slammed the door and stepped away from the car.

"Now don't start, Iris. Christ, she was the same way, hauling bags to kingdom come. Even when they was empty she still had to have them. What is it with you women, anyways? Can't you understand a man for not wanting to haul a goddamn haberdashery around all the time?"

She turned her back to him and kept silent. Finally, he sighed and smacked his lips:

"All right, I'm sorry. Just nervous about having all this money and being stuck out in the middle of nowhere with it. Look, we got everything we want now. Have a heart, Iris. Let's get to driving."

He was hopeless. And she was stuck with him. She lowered her head and opened the passenger's door.

And it hit her like cold wind: *I seen to that.*

She squeezed the door handle. "Just what do you mean, you saw to Rainbow so he wouldn't follow us?"

The bald head wrinkled up, hazel eyes got small with guilt. "Never said such a thing."

"You did!"

"Noooo, I don't know what I say or don't say. But you always do. Ain't that right?"

"You said it, damn it. Now what did you mean?"

"Quit using that language in front of me."

She glared at him. "What did you do, Horace."

"Me? I shot my horse for Chrissake. Then I came and got you. That's all."

She stepped back and slammed the door. "Tell me."

Horace smacked his head with an open palm. "What's going on here. . . . I just did tell you. I done nothing. Now get in and we'll talk about it on the way home."

Her face came alive with a smile: she was going to make him tell. "He fucked me, Horace."

"Aw, now, Iris, don't be saying—"

"Every night. Twice. In the afternoons, too."

". . . You know I can't listen to this. You're my daughter, don't you understand?"

"And I loved every second of it," she said.

He drove a fist into the seat. "Shut up, damn it!"

" 'Fuck me!' I begged him. And he did—*Daddy.*"

Hard fingers gripped the steering wheel. "One more word like that and I swear to Christ I'll drive off and leave you here. Now you get inside this car or I'll come haul you in."

"Not until you tell me."

He exhaled deeply, ran a hand over his scalp. "Makes no difference now. I let the word slip about the boat race, figured Rainbow knowing Roze, well, it wouldn't be so bad, they could just talk it out, you know."

She felt her hands tremble and couldn't stop them. "Oh . . . Daddy . . ."

"Carries a gun the size of a cannon, don't he?" Horace slapped the dashboard. "Probably shoot E.R. if it came to that. Rainbow's no slouch, he can take care of himself. Just bought us a little insurance time, is all. Smart thing I done if you ask me."

She braced herself against the car. "You might have killed him. . . ."

"Ain't none of our affair no more. Can't be worrying over him. We got places to be, a whole future of living high." He waved another stack of bills at her. "I done what was best—for *us*."

Iris stepped on the running board, pulled the duffel bag from the roof, opened one end and dumped the contents onto the ground.

"Hey! That's mine, goddamn it!"

Two of her little perfume bottles broke on the rocks. Liquor stained the dirt. She gnashed her teeth: "You bastard."

"Put that stuff back and for Chrissake let's get out of here."

She opened the door and began stuffing cash into the bag.

"Hey, hold on," he said, reaching down to stop her. "That ain't for you to be fooling with."

She batted his arm away and kept packing the bag with money. "I ought to kick your balls in, you—you . . ." But nothing was vile enough. "Keep the suitcases for yourself. I'll take this." She held up the loaded duffel bag and slammed the door in his face.

"Where the hell you think you're going? And with my money?"

"Back," she said and started up the road toward Saratoga.

"It's the goddamn night, Iris. You can't be walking with all that cash on you. Somebody might rob you. And hurt you bad."

She kept walking and yelled over her shoulder. "Someone already has."

Horace was out of the car, honking the horn. "I ain't waiting much longer, goddamn it! You get back here. Right now!"

Pushing her hat down on her head, she walked faster. There

couldn't be more than $60,000 in the bag, but it felt heavier than a full suitcase of clothes.

"Right now, Iris. You hear me?"

More honks of the horn, more shouts. The road rolled toward a valley where the frame house stood. A light glowed in what looked like the living room. Perhaps the farmer had a car. Or a horse. She could be back in Saratoga before midnight.

"He'll just laugh in your face! Then beat you!"

Let him be alive to beat me. But Rainbow wouldn't strike her, he didn't have that in him. *Please, God, let him be alive.*

"I'm counting to fifty, then goddamn it I'm leaving!"

She marched down the little hill, squinting into night to find the farmhouse driveway.

"You can't run off and leave me!" A series of horn blasts punctuated his shouts: "That's my money! Iris! Iris? I need you! I done it all for you! *Iris!* I'm your own father!"

Biting her anger, she swallowed so hard that she barely had enough strength to force the whisper past her lips:

" . . . Just drive, Daddy. . . ."

And up the lane she went, building a smile with each step.

Book Four ————————
RAINBOW

37

Her fountain went silent.

The caretaker dropped a forked sprinkler pole beside the rectangular flat of water that stretched out in front of the statue to catch her spray and her reflection. "You lost, fellah?"

Rainbow sat on the edge of the retaining wall. "Just waiting."

"Call her *Spirit of Life*." The caretaker studied the statue, then shook his head. "Paid a lot of money for her, too. Real shame. Hardly anybody comes by to look at her."

Motion flowed in the sculptured gown. One arm trailed in the wind, the other was bent at the elbow as if she were trying to raise the cup in her hand to pour its contents into the urns on either end of the curved wall behind her. She seemed to be running.

"Lots of money." The caretaker turned off the spotlight at the base of the wall. "Kids spoon here, see them all the time. Wouldn't let my young girl near this place. Or those gardens." He glanced up the path toward Broadway, peeled off his gloves, slapped them together. "Be glad to show you the way out if you're lost."

"I know where I am." Rainbow ran a hand through the water. A firefly blinked low across the ripples and hid in the elms that blocked the lights from Broadway. Only the glow of The Park Casino filtered through to patch the star-filled sky. "Roze owns this, too, don't he. . . ."

The caretaker was gone.

But the quiet didn't last long. Leaves rustled, leather scuffed the dirt. Up the path came Angelo Batori, a black hat pulled down on his head, his cane thumping the ground. He peered over his shoulder and limped to the water's edge. "I stay only ten minute. Big party tonight, Roze he wants the cake. Why you leave his house to come back later?"

"I had to get this." Rainbow pulled the .45 from his belt. "Can you hide this someplace in the room they're playing poker in?"

Angelo grabbed the pistol, shoved it into a front pocket, and tried to cover the bulge with his jacket. "I keep in the pants. Under the apron. Nobody see."

"I want it hid someplace. So I can get to it. What room are they using?"

"His library." The little cook patted the gun, then his palm went flat above his head. "I'm with the cart, high from the cake. Nobody see anyplace."

A smile was carved in her face of shadowed stone. Rainbow matched it. "What kind of cart?"

"Big, like a wagon." Again, small hands drew a picture in the air. "All the time, I keep behind."

"Can you put a tablecloth over it?"

"Nice white one, I fix. Keep in the pants, yes?"

"Give me it," Rainbow said.

Slowly, the .45 came out of the little man's pocket. He gave it back with the reluctance of a child forced to share dessert with a friend.

"Drive a nail underneath the top of the cart," Rainbow said, "and bend it so the gun fits like this." He put his finger through the trigger guard: the .45 hung upside down. "Can you do that?"

Angelo inched closer. Finally, he nodded. "Use big nail. No fall off."

"And put a tablecloth over it. I'll take care of the rest."

"Who you shoot first?"

Rainbow twirled the gun like a movie cowboy, then snapped it into firing position. ". . . Nobody."

The olive face wrinkled. "No shoot?"

"Get blown apart if we tried anything in that house, Angelo. I'll force the big guy outside, like I'm taking him in to the police. When he goes for his gun—I'll shoot him. Dead center of his red chin." He pushed back his hat. "Self-defense."

"What if he no try for the gun?"

The smile was still there. "I'll shoot him."

Angelo leaned on his cane and stared at the statue. "Then you come back, kill Roze?"

"No way to get him, it'd be suicide." He put a hand on the small man's shoulder. "We'll have to settle for your cousin's killer. And Murph's."

348

"But Roze, he—" Angelo bit his lip, ran his gaze over the ground. He let out a sigh and shrugged. "I nail like you want."

"Good. Nail it close to the edge, understand? So it's easy to reach."

The little cook stood motionless. "No worry. Batori, he makes perfect."

Rainbow gave him the pistol. "I'll be there around ten."

"I wait." Angelo put the gun in his pants and started down the path, then turned on his cane and took a letter-size envelope from his jacket. "You money. You need, yes? They make the joke, say you lose everything."

"Don't listen to E.R.'s talk." He smoothed out his jacket: it felt lopsided from the bulk of the ring box. "I got money."

"Keep right here. No forget." Angelo stuffed the envelope back into his suit, turned and limped away.

It got quiet again. Rainbow reached for the diamond, but found the wager slips first. Even her handwriting was beautiful. He wadded the notes, threw them, trying to clear the curved wall. He didn't make it: direct hit to the upper body of the statue. Paper bounced off stone, into water. He raked the brim of his panama and walked up the path.

Two pillars held an arch of boughs. White latticework ran around the sides. The plaque read, ITALIAN GARDENS. Past the entry, the smell of moist night earth lay cool over a jungle of shrubs and flowers, gnarled trees. Ahead, the amber glare of Broadway crept through branches like an electric dawn. The sound of crunching leaves made him freeze in midstride. The trail behind him was dark. Empty? He stepped off the path, onto grass. Something wooden cracked under his foot, but he forced his body still. And listened. Across the way, the bushes were alive with soft grunts and pants, whispered moans: Lovers. He picked up the broken stake. A flat plate was attached to it, engraved with SWEET FLAG and something else in Latin. Sweet Dee Flagg, sweet Iris. Lovers. Liars. Cunts. He stuck the splintered end back into the soil beside sword-shaped leaves that drooped away from large white flowers now half closed against the evening chill. The petals felt like velvet. And they smelled—he bent close to be sure— they smelled sweet and clean, yet thick like the taste of molasses. And he was sure. His Aunt Ruth always kept a little bag of it, it had a French name, in her underwear drawer. Only one pair of underwear and she only wore those with her red dress. Drawing the scent deep into his lungs, he strode out to the lights.

Across Broadway, a line of men stretched from Dan's Luncheonette to the lamppost a block down. A car drove by, its headlamps sweeping over faces dark with sorrow, filling in the shadows, then putting them back as if they had only been borrowed for a moment. None of those faces looked familiar: Old Cal was not on the line. Rainbow pushed past branches and stepped into the street.

The screen door of the luncheonette groaned. Dancer came out, his pudgy fist loose around a wad of folded money. He wore a big smile, but his gait was no longer lively, it was more like the waddle of a bloated ox whose rolling flesh had suddenly congealed in fast night air and yoked him to a sense of his own enormity. He stopped at the head of the line: "Dusty! A ten-buck guy!"

The man called Dusty spoke to the sidewalk. "Pay you soon as I get back from the city."

"I should live so long." Dancer jammed a bill into the man's shirt pocket and stepped to the next man. "Randy? Didn't I give you yours inside?"

"No, not me, Dancer."

"Yeah, you, goddamn it." The porkpie hat sat on the fat man's head like a warped pancake. "What do you take me for—a stupe?"

"You got it wrong, I been out here since dinner. You ain't got to me but just now."

"I ain't no stupe." Dancer dug into his pants and dropped coins on the walk. "Here's all you get this time."

The man named Randy chased clinking metal into the gutter.

"Got a sure thing tomorrow," said the third man on line. "Make it twenty, could you?"

"Master Charlie, you always got a sure thing." Dancer slapped a bill into the outstretched hand and kept walking the line.

Rainbow yanked the screen door open. The aroma of ham steaks frying to a crisp and the dank odor of smoldering tobacco settled together over the men at the counter. He walked to the booth in back.

Curtis didn't get up. "How much you get for it?"

"Still negotiating." Rainbow slid onto the bench. "Everything set?"

"The bill of lading's already taped on it," Curtis said. "Have to change trains at least three times between here and Hot Springs. What you mean, still negotiating? Thought North said he'd buy the rock."

"Wants me to hustle for him. Else he won't buy no matter how much his wife likes it."

"Then unload it right here, sport. Dancer's out front. He'll give us a fair price."

"Taking it from him's like taking a handout. I ain't like the rest of them small-timers on his charity line."

"Not charity, sport. Those are his clients. He gives them enough to catch the Dig it Up Special to New York. They scrounge up a new bankroll and come right back to bet it with him the next day." Curtis grinned. "Dancer always did understand the true meaning of goodwill." He nudged the empty coffee cup. "Order me another, will you? That bitch behind the counter won't serve me."

Rainbow took the cup to the counter and came back with two cups. Staring into the dark face, he wanted to thank Curtis for all the years of friendship, all the times shared. But he couldn't. The black would know something was wrong. And Rainbow would have to tell him: there was little chance that he would leave E.R.'s poker game alive. He sat and slid one cup across the table. "So you'll let me know when you get Murph in the ground . . . ?"

Curtis nodded. "They got his coffin laying out on a steel cart. Porter told me they just slide it in with the rest of the bags." He nursed his coffee and shook his head. "Be a whole lot easier if you was to bury him here. Cheaper, too. First-class ticket for a dead man. Real stupid law."

"Least I can do is see he gets back to where he came from." Rainbow took off his hat and fingered the smudges on the wide brim. "Got to buy me a new panama."

"With what? We barely scraped up enough for my ticket. Don't see why I'm the one riding with that coffin. He was your partner."

"I'd do it for you," Rainbow said.

Curtis leaned back and tossed a claim check across the tabletop. "Left your stuff with the stationmaster. Feel like a damn fool doing this."

"I got to get back to Mr. North." Rainbow pocketed the baggage receipt. "Been asked to dinner."

"This late? Christ, it's after nine!"

"How they do it in Europe. Real civilized."

Curtis grabbed his arm. "Got three hundred off Dancer. You always talking about them easy pickings down the Arlington Hotel in Hot Springs. I'll stake you."

"Need more than three hundred. Besides, with North setting up the matches, I can clear fifty grand by fall." Rainbow forced a grin. "Be able to take those pigeons in style then."

"I seen your idea of style, sport. Just sell that goddamn diamond."

Rainbow put on his hat. "I told you how I'm gonna do it."

"What about me? What do I do while you get rich up here?"

"Still remember how to caddy, don't you?" But he had to look away as he said it.

"Shit. You the perfect fool, boy. Don't you hear what Roze is spreading around about you? Can't stick in this town now."

"Can always use it to my advantage. Let them think they can take me, only make them want to try harder." He winked. "I got it all figured out."

But the dark stare didn't change. "Ain't nothing you got figured out except you is a dead bust. With everybody laughing at how you got that way." Curtis held up a clutch purse, then set it on the table. "And they gonna keep laughing till we set it straight."

Her purse looked like a black mole growing out of the wood. Rainbow couldn't reach out to push it away. "Told you to get rid of that."

"Told me you was in *love*, too," Curtis said. "Don't see now you even care she cleaned us out. We could track her real easy."

Rainbow held a sugar cube to the surface of his coffee. As if hungry for a different color, the block of white drew eagerly and turned solid tan. He dropped it into the cup. "Last thing I want to do is find *her*."

Silence. Curtis pulled away like a slow-moving freight, all boxed up with cargo that needed to be someplace else. "Busted up past fixing, ain't you."

"Well, well, if it ain't the tit-sucker himself." Dancer braced against the side of the booth. "How are the girlies treating you tonight?"

"Leave him be," Curtis said.

"What's the matter, can't he take it?"

Rainbow stirred his coffee. "Why don't you take your fat ass outside and spread a little—goodwill."

"Still got his sense of humor, don't he." Dancer patted his stomach. "Gonna need it, too. Why, I hear even your old man's laughing in his piss over how you got took to the cleaners. By a dame."

Rainbow grabbed the fat man by the neck and pulled him down. The big skull bonked on wood, the porkpie hat flipped over. Coffee streamed against the purse.

"You ass!" Curtis pried Dancer free and shoved Rainbow into the corner of the booth. "Ain't you done enough?"

Rubbing all of his chins as if to make sure he still had them, Dancer snatched his hat out of the coffee. "Fix you good for this, tit-sucker." He stormed off. The screen door flapped in the wake of his footsteps.

Curtis stood. "Now I got to square *this* with him, too."

"Don't do me any favors," Rainbow said.

"All right, goddamn it. Suits me just fine. Don't want no pitiful slob for a partner anyways. Feel good and sorry for yourself, sport. But just see you hustle up my twenty grand. And don't think I won't track you to get it, I ain't afraid to go after *my* money." Curtis threw down a dollar. "Pay the lady, sucker. And keep the change." He marched up the aisle and pushed through the screen door so hard that it bent back on its hinges and stuck open.

The narrow room seemed to take a breath: a hush became a whisper, webbing the air like silk, then breaking into a dozen murmurs, each building up and toning down until the old balance had restored itself. Rainbow pushed her purse out of the lake of coffee. He left the dollar on the table and kicked the screen door shut on his way across Broadway.

Up the main staircase, one flight short of the familiar third-floor landing, Rainbow went down the hall to suite 225 and knocked on the door. No answer. He straightened his tie and knocked again. "Mr. North?"

Nothing.

He walked down to the dining room. The maître d' remembered him and blocked the entryway like a goalie: "Back of the line."

Beyond the shiny black tuxedo, the dance band's milk-sweet song fought the stir of plates and silverware, a muddle of voices that never stopped to swallow. "Show me to Taylor North's table," Rainbow said.

"Mr. and Mrs. North left hours ago." The maître d' raised his chin and enjoyed his smile. "Back of the line."

Rubbing the velvet box in his pocket, Rainbow faced into the lobby.

And a plump woman in gray ran into him head-on. Her armful of blanket unraveled down the front of her dress. The silver French poodle that had been wrapped inside pounced on the carpet.

"Oh no!" She bent to pick up the dog. "Walter's not hurt, is he?" But Walter shot out of reach and under the blue velvet rope, hot on the scent of food.

The maître d' led the chase. Shouts came from every corner: some of the diners wanted the poodle left alone, others wanted him shot. The woman in gray dropped her blanket and fainted. And the band kept playing.

Rainbow couldn't find the laugh anyplace. He tried to get outside before they caught the dog. With his first step onto the hotel drive, cheers filled the dining room. He kept walking. It was going to be easy, he told himself. As easy as shooting targets in a penny arcade. And opening and closing his fingers to keep them from trembling, he cut through the trees and started the short walk to the house of Efrem Roze.

38

House numbers on Union Avenue seemed to pop onto doorjambs as if someone were running ahead, nailing them up and taking them down just for him. The street was busy with parties again tonight, but even the music sounded fake: a dozen Victrola needles scratching, the slowing rhythm of tin-sharp tones, cranks turning, and one by one, the bands came back up to speed. Man o' War had been returned to the Riddle lawn, a pile of stones holding the signpost straight. And in front of Roze's house, four big men in brown fedoras wandered about as if looking for something lost in the grass, something so trivial that they wouldn't stoop to pick it up if they found it. They stopped when Rainbow stopped, waited while he waited. But they didn't smile when he did, they came toward him and searched him.

"I was invited," he said. "By E.R. himself."

The guards were studying his suit, his old suit, which he had changed into in back of the train station. This jacket wasn't ripped, these pants weren't wrinkled, but the suit looked dingy, as if left out all night in gray drizzle. With a wave, one of the guards led him up porch steps, down the entry hall to the library.

Tuxedoed guests clustered around a small poker table where Efrem Roze sat across from Stavros the Greek. On the couch under the window, Aziz stared at the bookcases as if hypnotized by multicolored leather bindings. Seated next to the fat Russian, Tom "The Whip" Edwards adjusted his celluloid collar:

"Drove all the way up from the city just for this. What say you two start betting for blood now."

"You took the Special up like everybody else," Roze said.

"Quit trying to make a movie out of your life."

The game was five-card stud. Roze was winning, but not by much. And there was no cake, no cart, no Angelo. Rainbow cleared his throat and walked in.

The big man with the birthmark on his chin rushed over and patted down Rainbow's chest and legs.

"We done that on the lawn," the other guard said. "He's clean tonight. Says you invited him, Mr. Roze."

"Yeah . . . sure," Roze said, but he didn't believe what he saw.

The big man's hands kept searching. "What did you do with the .45?"

"Sold it." Rainbow handed him his panama. "Careful, it may be loaded."

Roze cackled. "May be loaded—that's rich. Sure, come on in." He nodded at his guests. "Coming here like this, you show me some class after all."

Rainbow scratched his lapel. "Didn't know it was formal. Had to sell my tux, too."

"Not important," Roze said. "In fact, we were just talking about you. You and the Greek here."

Stavros made a sour face into his cards. "Your Jack bets."

"Five hundred." Roze tossed out a blue chip. "Still can't understand how the Oddsmaker knows nothing about your fix, Rainbow. Must be getting lazy, right? Or maybe he's planning to retire. You planning to retire, Greek?"

Stavros put down his cards and leaned away from the table. "Your pot."

With a thin smile, Roze raked in his winnings. "Glad you stopped by, Rainbow. Brought me some luck."

Rainbow sat next to Aziz and stared at the clock on the mantel. A few minutes later, a cart rolled through the library doorway. Centered on white linen that hung almost to the floor stood a five-tier cake, swathed in white icing, topped by a little wooden horse under a lace arch. So tall that it hid the man who steered the cart, the cake seemed to enter under its own power.

Tom The Whip led the applause. "Ought to have a bride to go with that."

"I tried," Roze said, "but Woolworth's doesn't rent them out anymore."

Amid the laughter, Angelo pushed the cart against the wall of bookcases. He glanced at Rainbow, then smoothed out the tablecloth, tidied up plates and silverware, tested the coffee urn to make sure it was still hot. The little cook was wearing an apron and a butler's serving coat four sizes too big for him. He looked like a circus clown without makeup.

"Thought I told you not to serve in that apron." Roze started another deal. "And go change into something that fits you."

"I cut first, yes?" Angelo held up the knife, smiled, and turned to the cake.

"Help yourself, boys," Roze said. "What we don't eat, I'll take to The Park and treat the tourists."

Tom The Whip laughed. "How much you gonna charge a slice?"

"Funny." Roze slapped the deck down on the table. "Your next movie, you should jump off the rocks and land in horseshit. Sell a lot of tickets."

The room filled with laughter. Rainbow walked to the cart. Angelo gave him a slice of cake and an anxious stare: "When you do?"

"Looks great." Rainbow took the plate. Then he dropped the fork, nudged it under the cart, ducked beneath the tablecloth. From a bent nail, his .45 hung upside down by its trigger guard. He wiped the fork on his pants, stood, tried the cake, and winked. "Couldn't be better."

Angelo didn't get a chance to return the smile. The big man with the red chin came over and scraped the knife with his finger, tasted the icing. He took a piece of cake to Roze.

"You're right, Whip, it does look like a wedding cake." E.R. slid the plate to the edge of the poker table and threw a smirk at Rainbow. "You ever catch that dame?"

Satin-smooth frosting went down Rainbow's throat like a lump of cold wax. He set his plate on the cart.

"Didn't think so," Roze said.

"This the same one I met?" Tom The Whip had turned in his chair. "Iris?"

"That's her, Iris Winslow." Roze watched Stavros bet and tossed in his chips. "What some guys won't do for a piece of ass."

More laughter. The Whip swiveled back to the table. "Hell of a looker. Reminded me a little of Clara."

"Clara Bow?" said one of the guests.

The Whip nodded. "Same eyes, don't you think, E.R.? Anyways, I was considering giving her a screen test. For my next movie."

Roze cocked an eyebrow, then grinned at the fat Russian. "What some guys won't do for a piece of ass." He cackled and tried the cake. "Too bad she ran off, Rainbow. We could have held the ceremony right here." He turned to his guests. "He had the goddamn ring and everything. Incredible. Hey—you hock that diamond yet?"

"Truth is," Rainbow said, "I thought one of your guests here might be interested in buying it." Moving past the chairs, he took the ring box from his jacket, popped the lid. "Two carats, direct from Tiffany's. Why, this'd make any lady friend think twice about saying no. Could be a few of you got wives who—"

"Put it away," Roze said. "What the hell do you think this is, a flea market? Hawk that rock someplace else."

"Only brought it out because you mentioned it, E.R."

"And I'm telling you now," Roze shoved his bet into the pot, "put it away."

"How much you want for it?" Stavros was aiming his grin squarely at Roze.

"Worth at least a thousand," Rainbow said.

Stavros waved him closer, eyed the ring. "Very nice."

"Bet's five hundred, Greek." Roze clawed at a mound of chips. "You see me or what?"

"Give him five hundred." Stavros snapped his fingers and Aziz got off the couch, pulled a big money roll from his pants, peeled off five bills.

"Thanks, Greek." Rainbow pocketed the cash. "Give me a start anyways."

"What you do is your business." The Greek worked the diamond in the light. "Just save enough for a ticket back where you came from. One-way." He grinned and set the ring box down in the middle of the pot. "I bet a grand."

"Funny." Roze snapped the velvet lid shut and tossed the box to Stavros. "You're a riot, both of you. My bet's five hundred. See me or fold."

Stavros took his time lighting a cigar. Smoke leaked out the corners of his mouth. Finally, he gave a blue chip a lazy toss. "Call."

Another round of cards came out stiff against the green felt. Rainbow walked back to the cart and picked up his plate. Angelo was drawing the knife out of the cake as if dragging a bridal train through sludge. He let go of the handle, eyes quiet and sad and afraid to look anywhere but down:

". . . We do—now?"

Rainbow swallowed the sugary dough. ". . . now."

Trembling fingers tugged at the long black coat as if to button it. Angelo stacked two coffee cups and carried them toward the poker table. With each step, he became more like Chaplin's little tramp: coattails flapping at his heels, his hand struggling to balance a cargo already doomed, the cane swinging out in front of him.

Rainbow turned, grabbed the edge of the tablecloth, lifted it. And almost dropped his plate. The big man with the birthmark on his chin was coming straight at him.

There was nothing left to do but laugh.

"Something you see amuses you?" the big man said.

"Just about everything." But Rainbow's grin was gone. The handful of tablecloth grew heavy.

"You guys are all alike. Losers." The big man dished himself a fat slice of cake, licked icing off his thumb. His tongue went dead in the middle of a thick white spiral and he squinted toward the window as though trying to make out a distant form.

Like a giant elm about to fall, Aziz had leaned sideways on the couch, eyes no longer blank but focused hard on what was under the cart.

Rainbow squeezed the fistful of linen. The fork began to rattle on his plate. "Never did catch your name . . ."

". . . Ralph." The big man stared at the wrinkles in the tablecloth. He started to lower his plate. "What the hell you got there?"

Rainbow swallowed air. Everything stopped as if sealed in a pocket of time. But someone else owned the pocket, so nothing stopped, not even for a second. The big man had the plate almost on the table, his free hand moved across his chest toward the bulge at his shoulder—the holster. His body coiled as if, somewhere deep inside, the first step had already started and now there was no way to stop its execution or that of succeeding steps which would come so fast as to be one fluid motion, a glide. And by then, it would be too late for anything, the bastard would spot the gun on the nail and the room would explode like balloons on fire.

"Nice to meet you, Ralph." Rainbow thrust his plate up and out. The big man walked right into it. The piece of cake went *splat!*—soft like frozen custard. Globs shot out the sides of the plate, the fork fell, the dish slithered off skin, over the birthmark. Lumps of crumbling dough and frosting stuck to flesh like a horrible white cancer growing out of the eyes and forehead, down to lips which parted now as if to breathe, yell, and vomit at the same time.

The plate hit the floor.

Rainbow dropped to one knee, reached under the cart and—and the nail curved up naked. The gun was gone.

The big man was clearing his eyes, jerking black iron from his holster. The guests were turning in their chairs. Stavros dropped his cards, Roze knocked over a stack of chips.

And out of Angelo's long black coat came the .45. Small hands choked the stock. He shoved the barrel into the back of E.R.'s head.

Rainbow sprang to his feet. *"No!"*

"I do!" Angelo pulled the trigger. The gun went off like a muted cannon.

Efrem Roze lurched forward, chips jumped out of his fingers, a spike of red gushed from his nose: chunks of brain and bone showered the men in the chairs.

"I do!" Angelo recocked the big gun and aimed over the heads of the guests, who had already started to dive, fall, and scatter. He pulled the trigger. The sound filled the room. The bullet tore off the top of the big man's shoulder just as he leveled his own gun at Rainbow. That ruptured arm seemed to leap toward the wall, spinning him into the cart, his gun cutting the air. Somewhere in the middle of its travel, the barrel spat fire and lead. The window shattered. Glass rained over the giant on the couch.

And Angelo kept coming, his bad leg dragging, eyes bright with hate. *"I do!"* He squeezed off three more rounds, each one jolting his arm and kicking the pistol up and back as if on a string.

Blood spurted through the clumps of white on the big man's face. He toppled headfirst into the cake. The cart groaned, one end popped up like a seesaw. Plates jumped, clattered, and skidded over the tablecloth in a landslide. Arms spread wide as though to regain balance, the large body only pulled the sheet of linen down faster. Hair and ears buried in five layers of cake, the big man crashed to the floor. Rainbow leapt out of the way. Frosting squirted onto the wall. The cart flipped over, its small wheels spun.

The door burst open. Pistols drawn, two guards from the front lawn peered around the jamb. Angelo turned toward them, the .45 held out like a divining rod in trembling hands. "I do. . . ." But now his words were weak and tired.

One of the guards must have thought the little cook was going to keep shooting. He opened fire. The other guard began to shoot. Angelo cringed, twitched with each incoming slug, gnarled up, and the gun slipped out of his hands. His legs gave way, the long coat billowed as if to smother him. He fell against the table by the fireplace.

In the doorway, steel hammers snapped down on empty steel: *click-click.* The guards didn't bother to reload. They stepped inside.

A rustle of silk broke the silence. And Tom The Whip started shouting:

"Get it off me!"

He lay rigid, legs soaked in blood, his dress spurs caught in the bullet-torn caverns of Roze's face. The fat Russian tugged the body loose. The Whip drew his knees to his chest, shivered, tried to stand. He kept falling.

Aziz picked slivers of glass from his cheek and helped Stavros into a chair in the corner. The other men were still crawling on the floor. A few whimpered as though wounded, but the gutty strands and quivering lumps that clung to their clothes and skin like raw giblets belonged to Efrem Roze.

Rainbow swallowed to unclog his ears. His knees were shaking. His pants were speckled red and at his feet, more red flowed into curls of rich vanilla icing that glistened and deepened pink. The little wooden horse slid through its lace arch and over the nape of the big man's neck. The tablecloth drank blood and coffee both. But neither fast enough.

It was over.

Propped against the bookcase, Rainbow loosened his tie, unbuttoned his collar. The night was spilling in, not cool or fresh, but warm and sticky, as if lacerated by the jagged shards in the window: even the night was bleeding.

The wheels of the cart stopped spinning. Now pointed toward the riddled corpse in front of the fireplace, the flat head of the nail looked like a hat, and its silver shaft, bent low and wrinkled at the crease, seemed to be bowing. Rainbow found a chair and sat and waited for the sound of sirens.

39

They had a car and a horse. But neither was in very good condition. Iris offered the farmer and his wife a week's vacation in Saratoga if they would drive her back there. The farmer said that he couldn't afford a week in Saratoga even if someone else paid for it. His wife said that the farmer would drive Iris to town.

The horse would have been more reliable than the old Model T. The farmer kept pulling onto the shoulder, getting out, looking under the hood, then getting back behind the wheel and driving another fifteen miles before stopping again. He never said what was wrong. Iris didn't ask. During the stops, she counted the money in the duffel bag. By the time the tin lizzie passed the city hall clock tower on Broadway, she had counted over $80,000. It didn't seem possible. How had she packed so much so fast?

Saratoga looked deserted. A few bums strolled by the nightclubs, but the street was otherwise empty. On the night of opening day? At only 12:45 A.M.? Where had everyone gone?

The farmer dropped her off in front of Dan's Luncheonette. Reluctantly, he accepted a hundred dollars for his trouble before driving away. Even the diner was empty. At the counter, the waitress was doing a crossword puzzle. Iris knocked on the frame of the screen door:

"Are you open?"

"Till two, sugar."

Slinging the duffel bag over her shoulder, Iris walked in. "Where are your restrooms?"

"Back of the last booth. You want coffee?"

Iris shook her head and started toward the door marked LASSIES.

"Be smart to get it now," the waitress said. "Gonna be a run on coffee when they all get back."

Stopping by the last stool, Iris turned slowly. "Where is everyone?"

"Been a shooting. Couple of hours ago now." The waitress erased a word she had written in the puzzle. "Yes sir, be a run on coffee for sure."

"Who was shot?"

"Don't ask me, sugar. I only make twenty cents an hour." The waitress slapped her pencil against the page. "Damn things—excuse the French—why can't they just use English words? Who ever heard of a sundog?"

"Parhelion," Iris said. Her legs felt weak.

The waitress started writing, then stopped. "Nope. Too long. I thought it was collie, on account of their color, you know? Seven letters, starts with *r*. What kind of *dog* starts with *r*?"

Iris sat on the stool and set the duffel bag on the counter. "Try . . . rainbow . . ."

"Yeah, that fits!" The waitress was beaming. "You're good, sugar. Sit right there, coffee's on the house." She stepped to the pot by the sweet rolls. Lying next to the bin: a black clutch purse.

"That handbag," Iris said. "It's mine."

The waitress put a full cup on the counter. "No you don't, sugar. I found it. Besides, I never seen you in here before."

"Inside, there's a newspaper clipping. From Chicago."

The waitress made a sour face and stuck the pencil in the bun of hair at the back of her head. She opened the purse, pulled out the clipping, put it back, and dropped the bag on the counter. "Too small for my use anyways."

The purse was wet and sticky. Iris got out the clipping, tucked it in her pocket. What if Rainbow had only been wounded? She should be there, to help him. What if he had limped off into night—escaped? She left the purse and hurried out the door.

"What about your coffee, it's on the house," the waitress called.

The only other place open on Broadway was Ford's Restaurant, two blocks down. The Congressional Hotel was just as close. Maybe he'd gone back there. She ran across the street. Where the hotel drive wound around the elms, Grace and Taylor North walked arm in arm, like lovers. Iris didn't stop to say hello.

"Iris?" Grace said. "Iris, stop! We've just been to the most marvelous place. Dancing!"

The gravel was loose and hard to walk on. Iris rushed into the lobby. Empty.

"Oh, miss—good." The night clerk waved to her. "We have your cousin's things out of three-nineteen. Will you be taking them with you or—"

"There's been a shooting." She dropped the duffel bag by the desk. "Do you know who?"

Before the clerk could speak, the bellman who was terrible with names marched down the passageway smiling: "Owe me five bucks, Whitey. It was Roze."

"Efrem Roze?" Iris said.

"Oh, hello, ma'am." The bellman touched his cap. "E.R. himself, I was just over there. They still got the street blocked off. Five bucks, Whitey."

The clerk paid the bellman. And Iris found the courage to ask:

"Was there anyone else—shot?"

"Couple of others." The bellman grinned at the five-dollar bill and shoved it in his pocket. "Nobodies though. Was a .45, Whitey. Heard these cops talking. Said it was a special. Handle was all taped up. For fingerprints, don't you see."

Iris staggered to the couches.

"You all right, miss?" The clerk put the duffel bag beside her. "About your cousin's things, we have them all packed and—"

"Go away." She couldn't stop the tears. Reaching into her pocket for a handkerchief, she came out instead with the newspaper clipping. More tears.

"Iris, dear, what's wrong?" Grace North sat next to her. "Tell me."

"He's—dead."

"Oh, how horrible. Who, dear?"

Crying too hard to speak, Iris waved the clipping. Grace took it, gave it a quick glance, and handed it over her shoulder to Taylor North.

"Yes, I saw this," North said. "Just before dinner. Jurgenson must be trying for Man of the Year himself." He shook his head and handed back the clipping. "She's right, Grace. After this, Rainbow *is* dead."

"I mean *dead!*" Iris drove her fist into the couch. "Shot!"

Grace took her by the shoulders. "Oh you poor dear. Come right along to our room and lie down. Taylor, bring her bag." She led Iris up the stairs. "I just knew something terrible was going to happen. It was such a marvelous night, too good to last. Such a droll little place, too. Satchel Rags. But Taylor hasn't taken me dancing in ages." She unlocked the door to 225 and turned on the light. "He was such a forceful young man. So much like Taylor when—"

Iris ran into the bathroom and locked the door.

"That's right, dear," Grace said. "Have a good cry. I'll turn down the bed for you myself. You're staying with us tonight."

It felt like a bad cry. The sobs came in waves, shaking her body. And as if thrown in for good measure by a punishing God, her bladder was ready to explode. The jostling she had received in the farmer's Model T, her own nervousness about getting back to town, and now these uncontrollable tremors and tears—they had all joined forces against her. She slid her panties down, raised her dress, and sat on the toilet. Urine ran out of her in a steady stream, then began spurting in time to her sobs. She had caused Rainbow's death. She reached for the roll of toilet paper and looked around for Taylor North's razor. It wouldn't hurt that much, her skin was thin. And it had to be done.

She cleaned herself and dropped the paper in the bowl, then stood and flushed the toilet. Swirling like an eddy, pink water gurgled down the drain. Somewhere deep inside her, blood was beginning to seep: her period was six days early. And Rainbow was dead. The children he had wanted would never come from her—children she had never wanted. Until now. The porcelain bowl washed white. She had stopped crying. Folding toilet paper into a wad, she filled the crotch of her panties and pulled them up. At the washbasin, she splashed water on her face. Perhaps Grace had some lipstick and rouge. Iris was determined that when she saw Rainbow for the last time, she was going to look her best. She opened the bathroom door and stepped out.

Grace and Taylor stood together by the bed. Smiling.

"Oh it's wonderful!" Grace rushed over and hugged her. "I just knew it. Winning at the races, then dancing. Now this!" She turned Iris. "Tell her, darling."

"He's not shot," North said.

Iris sat in the chair and started to cry.

"Didn't you hear me?" North said. "Rainbow's alive."

"She heard you, Taylor. Now leave her alone."

"No!" Iris couldn't stop laughing through the tears. "Tell me, are you sure?"

North nodded. "Bellboy saw him, in the house on Union Avenue. Recognized him by his panama. Is Rainbow's real name—Robert Roberts?"

More laughs. It was a wonderful cry. "It's Calvin!" Iris slapped the armrest, held her stomach. "Calvin—Orville—Robinson—Junior!" She almost fell out of the chair.

North mouthed the name and raised an eyebrow. "No wonder he changed it."

"Now Taylor," Grace said, "that's enough. Can't you see she's in love? Like we are?" She hugged Iris again. "I think it was that marvelous mineral water, dear."

Iris wiped her cheeks and gasped for air. "I have to go. Union Avenue, you said? Do I look all right?"

"Can't get near the place, Iris." North pushed the duffel bag aside and sat on the bed. "The police have it sealed off. I understand there's a big crowd outside, too. Been there for hours. Waiting. You'd never be able to find him."

"If I have to break through the police barriers, I'll find him." Iris smoothed out her dress before the bureau mirror. There wasn't time to patch her appearance. Rainbow wouldn't take her back anyway. But at least she could return his money. She grabbed the duffel bag, slung it over her shoulder. ". . . If I have to fight my way inside . . ."

"Taylor will go with you, dear. It isn't safe for a lady at this hour."

Iris swallowed the laugh and grinned. "I'm no lady."

"Now, dear, you must control yourself," Grace said. "Taylor, take her over there. And pay those silly policemen to get her inside. Use your influence."

"It's after one o'clock, Grace." But seeing his wife's wrinkled frown, he sighed and took Iris by the elbow. ". . . Yes, dear."

"And I'll have some food sent up." Grace clapped her hands. "We'll have a party. A homecoming. Like we did for my brother—after the war."

Iris rushed back and hugged the old woman, then kissed the old man and led him out to the hall and down the stairs. If there was even the slightest chance that Rainbow might still want her, she was going to try. She kissed the bellman in the lobby, the clerk behind the desk. Outside, she sailed her hat toward the stars and didn't wait for it to land.

It had taken the police and their sirens fifteen minutes to get to the Roze house. By then, the porch had been jammed with onlookers who arrived just moments after the last shot was fired. These were mostly men in five-and-dime-store ties, but others soon wandered over from the big homes up and down the avenue: ladies in flowing silk, gentlemen in tails, all of them packed together for the last two hours like presents in a grab bag.

For some reason, perhaps it had been the lateness of the hour or out of a sense of his own importance, the coroner had come last. Setting his white straw skimmer on the mantel, he had gone straight to work. Methodically. Brutally. Handling the bodies like slaughtered livestock, he had rolled them over, shoved fingers into black ringed holes where lead had gouged out portions of necks, faces, backs, and he had picked up the big man's head as though it were a bowling ball. He hadn't bothered to put a handkerchief to his nose: the beastly poison of the air didn't affect him. He was a man who enjoyed his work.

Rainbow had joined the other guests and answered police questions after two men in white uniforms loaded Tom The Whip onto a stretcher and carried him out the door. The ten-gallon hat and the cowboy boots with their bloodcaked spurs still lay in a pile beside the fallen poker table. But for the last forty minutes, there had been no questions. Only silence. Rainbow moved to Stavros in the corner:

"Can you give me a lift to the train station when this is over, Greek?"

"Poor sonofabitch." Stavros was staring at Angelo's body near the fireplace. "Still be alive if it wasn't for you. How's that make you feel, Big Time? Dumb little wop. Probably made him feel like you was doing him a favor, didn't you?"

"I didn't plan none of this to happen," Rainbow said.

Stavros flicked a cigar ash to the floor. "It happened."

The coroner broke his huddle with two policemen: "All right, gentlemen. Thank you very much. You can go."

The guests milled around the door. Not one of them looked back.

Stavros got out of the chair. "Get the car, Aziz."

On his way to the door, the giant stopped to pick the velvet ring box out of the chips on the floor. He handed it to his boss and lumbered off.

Stavros held it out to Rainbow. "Take this thing. And get your ass out of my sight."

Hands in his pockets, Rainbow faced the broken window. The lawn and most of the block was filled with people. "You paid for it."

"I only took it off you to rile E.R. for Chrissake," Stavros said. "You didn't see that? You think my head's weak, I need a goddamn rhinestone to carry around?" He stuffed the box into Rainbow's breast pocket. "What the hell do I need with a worthless piece of shit like this?"

"It's real, Greek. Worth twice what you paid me."

"I don't care if it's a goddamn crown jewel." Another ash hit the floor. "And don't call me Greek no more. To you, it's Mr. Karamonopolis. Better yet, you don't talk to me at all." He bit down on his cigar. "You got a fucking disease, you know that? Got to make pigeons out of everybody." He spat smoke and bits of tobacco at the couch. "Even me."

"I tried to straighten out the thing with the fix, Greek. For Chrissake what the hell more could I do? I'm sorry, all right?"

"Not all right," Stavros said. "I seen assholes before, but you're perfect. What you can do is have a nice trip. And make it a long one. Like forever."

Rainbow got the $500 from his pants. "So take it. . . . Could I keep a hundred? For trainfare?"

"Keep it all. A gift. Sometime when you grow up, come by and thank me." Stavros got as far as the overturned cart, where the big man's shoes stuck out of the sheet covering his body. Jet-black eyes were slow to smile. "Incidentally, Big Time, I think I like how you got took by that dame. While you bingle-bangled—she bungled." He laughed. "A Rainbow Roberts original, huh?" But his grin didn't last and his stare got weak, as if he had something to add and was apologizing for not being able to say it. He stepped over the debris and out the door.

"Mr. Roberts!" The coroner was toweling his hands by the fireplace. "A few questions if you don't mind. Actually, just one. Nothing official. The .45 is yours, isn't it."

Rainbow raked his hat brim. "Don't know anything about it."

"I saw it in your belt when you came to my office." The bloodstained towel landed on a chair. "That white tape on the stock . . ."

"Lots of guys tape their handles."

"I don't care whose gun it is. At least, not for the purposes of my report." The coroner took out a tiny square brush and began scrubbing his fingernails. "Mr. Batori left a note. Quite explicit. Revenge for his nephew. A Mr. Tagliafera."

"I got a train to catch," Rainbow said.

But the coroner was able to stop him with a smile. "It appears your friend, Angelo, had his heart set on this. He even arranged for a cemetery plot and left funds to pay for his funeral."

Rainbow leaned against cool gray stones. His throat closed up and the words that struggled through it and out his mouth sounded as though they had lost the battle: "What makes you think he was my friend?"

"He bequeathed any excess funds to you, Mr. Roberts. And all of his possessions. Which by the look of his room here, include some clothes . . . and a trumpet."

The panama felt wrong. Rainbow took it off. "Can you see it all goes to his family. In the Bronx, New York." He got the gold locket from his pants. "And this, too. And I want him buried in church ground. It was real important to him."

"That's stipulated in his note." The coroner tucked the locket and the little brush in his coat, then got his hat from the mantel. "It *was* your pistol. Not that it matters. A man like Efrem Roze shapes his own death sooner or later, if not here, then someplace else. But . . ." He glanced at Angelo's body: a small lump under a sheet, as chillingly still as a truck-smashed dog lying at the side of the road. ". . . Did you know what he planned to do with your pistol when you gave it to him?"

The mantel clock read 1:25 A.M. First Murph, now Angelo, both dead because of a fool, the same idiot who had done everything imaginable to force Iris to rob him. No way to refit the pieces of time. Unable to look at the coroner, Rainbow put his hat back on. ". . . Lots of guys tape their handles. . . ." Rubbing sweat from his palms, he went past the cart, giving one wheel a little spin, then walked out and down the hall to the porch. He had to squeeze through the crowd. And the voices:

"You see it?"—"Who shot who?"—"How'd it happen, buddy?"

Buddy. The perfect fool.

The lawn was soft. Dew shot off the tips of his shoes. The Greek's limousine pulled away from the curb, through the police barricade. Rainbow crossed the street, taking deep breaths and quickening his pace. But from behind came a voice that made him freeze up, yet want to run at the same time, a voice that snapped the starlit air in two:

"Junior! Wait up!"

40

He didn't want to turn around. He wanted to stand there like a tree and hope: *pass by*. His mouth felt swollen. He turned around.

Old Cal was running. Hair flapping like strands of milkweed silk, he coughed as if to spit up years of pool hall smoke and gain sympathy for his wornout legs. He stepped onto the curb. The hollow circles of pale blue that were his eyes, and that even the night failed to darken, struggled with the bloodstained white pants before him. The corners of his mouth lifted in a smile, but the eyes kept searching. "So you was in there, huh? Damn, I'd of give anything to of seen it. Might be they'll even put your name in the newspapers."

Rainbow started walking. "Don't plan to stick around long enough to find out."

"Yeah, I heard you went bust. Dancer said she cleaned you out of two hundred grand. That right? I mean, you really have that kind of cash to lose?"

"I had it."

"Damn if I didn't know you did. I could tell. You got that look." Old Cal was beaming. "And when I seen all that green you come back to the hotel with, well, I says to myself, 'He done all right for himself, just like I know'd he would.' Felt real good." He coughed, then patted his pockets. "Ain't got a spare smoke on you, do you? Must of left mine back at Baldy's."

"I don't smoke."

In one of the pockets, Cal found a butt that was bent three different ways down its short stalk. "This'll do for now." Scraping his thumbnail on the head of a match, he cupped his hands around the flame. There was a liver spot on his cheek. "Reason I come up there yesterday was, them fellahs around the pool table thought you meant to kill me. But I told them it was just your way of, you know, paying me back." Smoke streamed through his nose. He took another drag. "Ain't still mad, are you?"

Rainbow tried to lengthen his strides, but his legs wouldn't obey. He didn't know what to say to shut the old man up. He was thinking of Iris, how it might have been if she were here now. To hold him.

A final puff of smoke and the cigarette landed in the gutter. "I mean, you throwed a real scare into me. But I seen that's all you meant to do. By now, smart as you are, you most likely figured out how things truly was back home."

Rainbow's wrists felt loose, they dangled at his sides. "She meant to blow your head off."

And I couldn't do that for her either.

"Yeah, well, your Aunt Ruth didn't mean that," Old Cal said. "It was just her way of hating me 'cause I run off with her sister." He chuckled. "Had a crush on me herself, Ruth Huggins did. You know how they get, especially them what get past twenty without letting a man into their underdrawers. When it happens, why—they think it's magic!" He shook his head. "Anyways, she never did forgive me for running off with Rosland."

"Ain't that the sweetest name you ever heard, Junior?"

Old Cal sighed as though he meant it. "Always was sickly. Ever since she had you. What was you when she passed? About three I guess it was."

"I was five."

"Always was sickly. Must of had ten colds a year. Even got them in summer. Anyways, that's how it was with me and your Aunt Ruth, and you can see now, I was only following my heart."

"And she loved you, boy. Loved you more than anything in God's world."

Where Union Avenue funneled into Circular Street, Rainbow turned right. Behind him: the police barricades, the mob of sight-seers. It felt good to be rid of them.

"Say, you remember that time I took you out in the boat?" Cal ran a hand through his hair. "Went clear around the lake."

Not possible.

"Sure, you couldn't forget a day like that." The old man slapped his thigh. "Hell, you almost drowned trying to grab one of them little sunfishes. Leaning over the side like you was, I swear you thought you could do it. Well, you was only three or so and didn't know no better." He stooped over a hedge to blow out a spasm of coughs mixed with laughter.

Rainbow started to reach for the old man's shoulders, but his arms were heavy, his hands felt slimy, as if the fish had just wriggled through his fingers.

Cal straightened up, still hacking. "And when you fell in! I never will forget that look on your face." He coughed into his hand, looked at the phlegm, wiped it on the hedge. "Lucky thing I was there to pull you out."

"Are you all right?" Rainbow said.

"Of course I am." Shoulders thrown back, Old Cal started walking. "Where we headed?"

". . . Train."

"Gonna dig you up a fresh bankroll, are you? That's real fine. What I wanted to talk to you about anyways." With a grin, Cal made the turn onto Spring Street. "Now, if you and *me* was partners, she'd of never got five feet with that money, boy. No sir, I'd of seen to that." He put a finger to his temple. "Got a lot stored up here, Junior. Be just what you need."

Rainbow was watching his blood-spattered shoes kick out in front of him. She could have had all the money, he had only wanted it for her, to buy her things, to carve out the kind of life that made sense—for both of them. After the shock had worn off, it wasn't his money that he missed. It was Iris.

"Of course, you'd be doing me some good, too," Old Cal was saying. "That's how it's supposed to be with partners, am I right? Of course I am. I'd leave the true gambling to you. My eyes ain't what they was, you seen that when I missed that goddamn six ball straight in. Time was I'd of made that shot half asleep." Dead eyes narrowed and for a moment, came alive. "You'd of never beat me then." He cleared his throat. It took a long time. "Just don't see the table like I used to. But I'm still sharp with the setup. Dancer says your game's golf."

"Dancer talks too much." Over Rainbow's shoulder, buried in trees, stood a big building of wood and slate. The sign out front read HAWTHORN SPRING, DEPTH 900 FT. Ahead, lights painted Broadway a yellow that shimmered like candle fire. The glow would have danced in her green eyes.

"Which is fine with me," Cal said. "Be just like setting up any other sort of match, am I right? You pick the pigeons, I line them up. Hell, it'd be a cinch." He stepped off the curb. "C'mon now. That Special leaves right at two. Don't want to be late."

Rainbow followed him across and through the weave of streets to the train station. The platform was empty. Near the steps, the jazz band played blues for black porters who had gathered around while the young dancer slept on the bench, his tall hat squashed under his head, a coat draped over his body.

Old Cal stopped at the window with the light shining through the bars. "We need a ticket on this train." But before he had finished the sentence, he turned to Rainbow, eyes soft, voice quiet, then added: "Ain't got but a few bucks on me. You can pay for it, can't you?"

Inside, leaning back on a chair against a wall of crates and boxes, the stationmaster peered over the top of his newspaper. "Don't sell tickets this time of night. See the conductor on board."

"I need my stuff." Rainbow pointed at his suitcase and golf bags in the far corner and shoved his receipt under the bars.

The newspaper rustled. The stationmaster came up to the window, read the claim check. Muttering under his breath, he stuffed the receipt in his shirt, put the bags outside the side door and rebolted it before he went back to his chair and paper.

Rainbow rapped on the counter and called to the porters: "One of you. Got some bags here."

The blacks gave him a casual glance, then turned back to the sad clarinet, the mournful horn, the dull scrape of drumsticks on hardwood.

"Everybody on The Dig it Up Special's always broke," Cal said. "Them niggers know they won't get no tips. Got to carry your own."

With his money out and held high, Rainbow started to call to the porters again, but the look in Old Cal's eyes stopped him.

"I knew it!" The old man slapped his thigh. "Even when a big-timer like you is bust, he's still got cash." His chuckle faded into a sigh. "Thing is, I'm a little short right now. . . ."

Rainbow put his money away and walked to his bags. Cal stepped in front of him, took the suitcase by the handle, hoisted a golf bag onto his shoulder, and, staggering under its weight, bent for the other.

"Since you'll be raising some real cash in the city," he said, "might be you could let me have a couple of hundred. Just till you get back. Wouldn't spend but maybe twenty of it. And if it takes you a few days to dig up a new roll, well, I'd have something to fall back on." He got the other bag halfway up before it pulled him sideways into the wall.

Rainbow grabbed it and ducked under the shoulder strap. He reached for his suitcase.

But Old Cal wouldn't let go. "Be like an investment, see? What you give me now, you can take out of my share of what we made later on. Ain't like you was giving me nothing. Just putting some on account."

Rainbow slid the golf bag off the old man's shoulder and walked toward the train. Three cars down, a big steel door was closing. Inside, a coffin was stacked like an oversized trunk among the luggage. The door banged. A man in a railroad uniform cranked down the lever, attached a lock, and sauntered off to the back of the train.

"Now don't get the idea I'm trying to hitchhike on your coattails." Cal set the suitcase down near the tracks. "Truth is, it's only right we get together after . . . I ain't apologizing for how it was when you was little. If that's what you're waiting to hear, well—hell." The knot in his string tie had pulled his collar into a snarl of wrinkles. "I did come back, you know. House was empty. Sheriff sent me to that place in Knoxville where they had you." He blinked and brought his gaze up to the middle of Rainbow's chest. "Only you was gone. Skinny fellah what ran the show down there said you run off on account of some trouble. You and some nigger."

The procession of coach cars stood shadowed by trees and night. Rainbow felt a hand rub his jacket sleeve.

"I know'd that weren't true," Cal said. "Seeing how you was brung up and all. Still, it had me worried. But now—*well!*—I can see you turned out just fine." The old hand moved up and down the jacket sleeve. "Makes me real proud—son."

Down at the end of the train, a signal lamp was swinging slowly back and forth. A loud voice rang out from one of the cars. *"Board!"*

Rainbow slung the other golf bag over his shoulder. The strap pinched. He tried to move it to a more comfortable place, but couldn't find one. He yanked the ring box out of his breast pocket. The pinching stopped. He gave the box to Cal.

The old man shook it close to his ear, then sprang the lid open. And squinted at the diamond. ". . . Real?"

Rainbow picked up his suitcase. "Take it back to that store. They'll give you the best price."

"Thanks, son. We'll split what I get for it, fair enough? Straight down the middle."

Rainbow climbed the steps of the second coach.

"You come direct to Baldy's when you get back, son! That's where I'll be waiting for you! Okay, partner? Don't forget to—"

A blast of steam from the locomotive drowned out the rest. *Don't forget.* Rainbow edged through the doorway, swinging the bags past the posts one at a time. The train was almost empty: most men—even small-timers—managed to get through opening day without going broke. He felt like laughing.

The conductor coming down the aisle said, "Ticket!"

Rainbow leaned one bag on a seat by the window. Old Cal was still at the edge of the platform, staring at the flash of white in the little box he cradled in his hands, a piece of glitter that meant nothing now. Turning away, Rainbow gave the conductor a hundred-dollar bill:

"Ticket me all the way to Hot Springs."

"Only sell them to New York, sir. Buy a fare to anywhere once we get in." The conductor punched the ticket, handed it back with a fistful of crumpled bills, and brushed by, through the hatch door into the next car.

Forcing the wad of cash into his pocket, Rainbow shouldered the bag.

Through the dim light of Church Street, a woman was running. Dark hair, no hat. A long bag riding up her back. Beautiful legs.

Not possible.

She disappeared in shadows short of the station house. The train shuddered, then lurched into a heavy glide over the rails.

Rainbow grinned. That woman couldn't be Iris. Not here. Not now. But maybe someday soon. Because he would be seeing her on every street, in every train station that could take her farther away from him, in every town that could hide her. She would be everywhere, haunting him. Until he found her. Majestic Farms wasn't real. What Iris knew of Kentucky she had probably learned in the back seat of a white Packard. But Horace Wells was real. And with or without money, he'd never be far from a racetrack. Or Iris. If it took every bit of strength Rainbow could muster—the rest of his life—he would find her.

Because he loved her.

He loved her as he had never loved any other woman, not Sweet Dee, not his dead mother, not even his Aunt Ruth.

And now the woman back there was scurrying under the darkened overhang of the station. With luck, and those strong legs, she was going to catch the train.

Then the platform was gone, blending into tall trees that held the glow of Saratoga and slowly lost it.

The laugh he let out felt big and full. Like fate. His and hers. *Love.* Iris must have taken the money for her father, to help Horace out of hard times. Rainbow knew the feeling. He wasn't going to search for the money, she could have it all. He only wanted her. If she would have him.

Someday soon.

Clubheads jangling, bags swaying into seat backs, he walked down the aisle. There was no one in the next car. In the middle of the last coach, a Pullman blanket had been strung from wall to wall as a divider. On the other side, a few blacks were trying to sleep, their heads nestled against windows, walls, cushions, each other. Those still awake shot angry looks at the white invader. Now air rushing through the car held the sweetness of country night. The train shook, it rattled, it built up speed. Rainbow stopped. Putting his golf bags and suitcase on an empty seat, he tossed his panama into the corner.

"Wake up, friend," he said. "We got plans to make."

And he sat down next to Curtis.